I0636724

They Came in Twos

The 1st novel from the *Who Guards the Angels?* Series
Copyrighted and published 2014, 2022 by Guillermo Machado

Please address comments or inquiries to:
Guillermo Machado
gmachado@barriosmachado.com
323-384-8289

A note to the reader from the author: I extend my deepest gratitude to all who take the journey through *They Came in Twos* and, through it, hope you may find the voyage worthwhile. Thank you.

All rights reserved © 2014
TX 8-047-937
ISBN: 978-0-9907904-0-2
Printed in the United States of America

They Came in Twos

Guillermo Machado

To my darling Ursula: my ode to you.

- TRAVEL GUIDE TO GOOD LEAF METRO -

The Fix: Capital of the State of Great Leaf. Northeast Coast. U.S.A.
AKA's: Leaf. Oven.
Head Count: Heavy.
Law of the Land: Prohibition.
Lowdown: Cement prairies, crops of steel, brick and mortar. Skies clear as cataracts. Every alley is nicknamed "murder." Bridges, canals, a cacophony of lights, cars and cuss words. Rats to people: two to one. Rats in people: play the odds. The Twig Bridge divides North and South. South Leaf, including Sunks District, is plagued by tenements, human shells on utility vines, loan sharks, push carts, rotten produce stands, bakers, butchers, bum barns, smoke shops. All serve as cover for liquor stores except the smoke shops and sharks. The "finger" is considered "Good Leaf polite." Leaftons cut lines for a bowl of salt. Many a brawl for broth. A blind tiger growls on every block. The Low East, and its Thread District, offers mazes of industry. Downtown is marked by giants, mud and milked by day, freckled fake by night, always jagged and rough, and that says nothing of the tenants; rooftops cut clouds like knives through marble. East Leaf, and its Emporio District, is flanked by Hub Park to the west and the River Gorda to the east. It's where dirty money gets cleaned in a bath of booze, clubs and mansions. To the north, Matanza Heights is an offshoot of hell; people stay indoors to avoid street burn. Ghettoes and drug grottoes: Here, they're the same thing. To the west of Hub Park, the nascent town of Bigup, where landlubbers flee. To the southeast of Good Leaf: Breaks. Northeast sprouts Jester: two rural boroughs, but the commercial hand of man keeps stretching to the sea. Mills, both born and dead cover an archipelago, including Twenties Slip with its Factory Island and Harper to the northeast. And finally, Strobile Island. If Good Leaf is the brain, Strobile is the tonsil, and tonsils should often be removed.

"Quack, quack, ducky."

- Prologue -

No such thing as a bad miracle, so they say. May 29, 1931. The sticks. Jester's Bosom. One breath from calling it quits. The dock's rotted planks were drenched in a small-hour sweat. A quarter mile from the riverbank, a traumatized truck engine rumbled in low gear. As it closed in on the dock ramp, a pair of headlamps peeled back the mist. Cow bones littered the truck's path. The engine took five, followed by the lights. Coasting on three good shoes and a hobbled rim, it came to a stop yards from the quay. A string of hollow-points strafed across the words Dunfer's Linens Co. on the truck's trailer. Sheets of cool brume assaulted the sweltering shoreline and swallowed up the truck and anyone who came along for the ride.

Seconds later, two doors creaked open in spitfire succession. Seconds after that, the piercing moan of the trailer door being forced ajar. Two human breaths strained to heft something. A horse-count of heavy heels tapped onto the smoky landing. Their grunts were whispered; their exhales leashed. Moonlight poked through the clouds and revealed a slender figure, shaped like a woman, standing at the base of the finger pier. She was on the lookout. Close by were two men: one in a fedora, a thin beard and dark overcoat, the other in a paperboy, dungarees and arm sling. Their hands forklifted a wooden crate draped in burlap, but the one-armed character was struggling with his grip. A second woman, not as slender as the first but tenured in life, emerged to help. She wore a long, red slicker and black, rubber hat. All three crab-stepped forward like clumsy pallbearers. Squinty eyes reimagined the dirt road in search of the hounds that had been tracking their scent since the Benson Building.

The gangplank. If they could just make the gangplank. It was ten tremulous yards out, and the dock bobbed like it wanted them off. The ever-present notion that a vagrant bullet would check in for a permanent stay loomed large. The fedora head threw eyes to a lonesome farm house. It was gift-wrapped in mold, crumbling and vacant, but this man was a master of that illusion. He turned his faculties from the farm to avoid summoning any more bad luck. They reached the gangplank. No lead flies buzzed past them. The rabbit chase seemed over. It was easier than it was supposed to be. A sailor in green rubber boots and suspended pants greeted them with dissension before lending a hand and a grant of passage to his Eco Cruison shrimp trawler. Under their feet, the Plumber River shifted like a pool of calf blood.

It was time to sally forth, time to leave everything in the dust. The water cradled the trawler with contempt. They set the crate to rest in the hull. All around them, the walls appeared gauzed with collision mats. There were creaking and cracking sounds, a whining customary of whales, but they were all coming from the hull's walls. The fedora head returned topside for the slender lookout. When she was safely aboard, he shoved the gangplank from the boat. It cracked the dock. The sailor made quick moves to cast off. The boat's engine gargled and spit. Soon the Dunfer's truck was just another fleck of black in the dark. It was 4:57 am only because they were five hours late. That meant at most another thirty minutes before the sun decided to crash the party. And what a party it was. But the old days of keeping the bulls on their heels, of C notes trickling from sleeve cuffs, they were gone. And that wasn't even the worst part of it. The grave was calling to them all by first name because they had put innocent blood in the crosshairs. What awaited along those waterways of fate had become worth every risk. After all, what did a man have left to lose when he'd already given up his life?

Down in the hull, the man with his fedora low over a frosting of sweat lit a nico and let his eyes adjust to the darkness. The smoke autographed the air with ashen wisps. The tenured woman in the oilskin clung onto his hand, hoping that the touch of her palm would keep him going or at least keep him from going. He stood before the crate like it was an altar. The heartache that ravaged his body leaked from his eyes and channeled down his cheeks to a sponge of hair cloaking his upper lip, but he wasn't crying. He was done crying.

PART I

- 1 -

Last week of November, 1930. Eastern shore of Breaks Borough. The rear lot of the Crystal Plats Zoo was surrounded by cold steel, ten feet high and barbed. Hidden from tourists, a lone Rushman Freight Line Federal parked with its fanny to the wind. It was a biting and blurry eight at night. A rawbone in dusty brown denim and a gray coat appeared from the bowels of the boxcar with a manual pallet truck. He balanced his steps off the ramp and snuck back through the zoo's rear entrance and into a warehouse. It was connected to a building with the words "Reptile & Amphibian" on its signage.

A few tics later, the same man appeared with his pallet truck. The load: seven wooden crates of liquid gold. The lip of his skully was soaked. Beads of sweat crawled into the man's eyes and singed them shut. He wiped his coat sleeve past his bulbs and pushed the pallet truck back up the ramp and into the trailer. He positioned the pallet next to six others, each with the same cargo, and padlocked the trailer doors on his way out. The man approached the driver, another gee with a lather of hair on a porky face, and exchanged a quick glance with his passenger, some double-dipped bird. Both were strangers to him except for that he knew they would be there at that exact time. The driver passed the loader a zip-up cash bag from Good Leaf Central Bank. He unzipped the bag and flipped through the contents.

Stacks of face cards for a total of twenty large. He zipped up the bag and handed the man two slips of paper. The first read: "Six Bengali Tigers. Delivered. Ticket Closed." The driver marked an X on the middle of the page and returned it to the loader. The second page read: "Five Llamas. Relocation to Penntreal Menagerie." This was for the driver. He drove off with his cargo. The man watched the truck lights fizzle around the bend. He checked the cash once more to make sure. It was all there. He then fished a jazz from his coat pocket. It was half cooked. He lit it and sucked another dose. It was time to close the books on another day of fruit for Met the "Beast Warden." Age: 36. 5'11". 165 lbs. Brown eyes that never stopped wandering. Patchwork beard. A dying lawn of gray hair. Leather for cheeks. Nose grew to the left from one too many rights. Twitchy upper lip. Ran into a bath once a week. Wore the same brown denim and wool coat. Booze, jazz smokes, meals of choice. Charged: hooch mule, grand theft, racketeering, conspiracy, murder. Still at large. Occupation: zookeeper, fence. AKA Egg Meat.

Met barricaded himself inside the warehouse. From wall to wall, nothing but crates on pallets. A walkway was cut through the middle where he could lose himself if he wanted. He wanted.

"That's it," Met said with a noticeable smile. He passed the cash bag to a large bloke in a dead gray suit and open-collar silk that bore the mark of sweat even under the bitter cold. He rested his wide bottom in a torn swivel chair and was in the middle of cleaning his Super .45 automatic when he paused to sample the cash. His name was Mank "Rib" Mill. Age 42. 6'5". 240 lbs. Muscle. Moon pale. Smashed proboscis. Small forehead folded over his brow. Eyes in a steady squint. Two fists plastered downwind from his temples made ears. Gunshot scar cratered his left cheek. Crowned with cactus quills. Charged: train robbery, multiple counts of broken backs and deadened skulls, including a wife and her police captain lover. Convicted on the hits. Sentenced to the hotsquat. Appealed and reversed (Technical: "fruit of the poison tree." Actual: buying off the jury and a judge bent on sustaining every defense objection). No time in the can. Occupation: robber turned hitman. AKA Rub.

"What's with the grin? You T'd up?"

"A fella smiles nowadays, he's gotta be high?"

"You feed the tenants?" Mank asked.

"I'll get to it," Met responded like he was addressing a big balloon with no brain.

"Snap it up, and wipe that stupid mouth off your face."

Met went half on his nod. His smile eroded into a gray square. He appeared to be waiting for something like a dog at its master's empty table. Getting a dollar out of Mank Mill required an autopsy.

"Don't look all balled up, Egg. It's payday." Mank stood, reached into his pants and pulled out a green fold. He separated two sawbucks and stuffed them in Met's palm. Then he started for the exit. This wasn't Mank's flop of choice, but business was business. "And hose down the cages. Smells like someone died ten times." Mank vanished through the door.

Met looked to the sweaty bills in his hand. A stale grimace infected his mouth. "Watch you don't get struck by lightening ten times, you fuckin' asshole." Met's confidence abounded when no one was around. He sank deeper into the warehouse till he found his own version of pay dirt. Hidden behind a crate, a nice bottle of rye gave him the eye. He uncorked it with his molars and hosed down his cheeks, then returned to the swivel chair and took a load off his feet. The animals could wait.

- **2** -

The apartment living room was silent as an empty church. A bone-white carpet was padded thick to muffle footsteps, namely the resident's. The walls were bare, and there was scarcely a place to sit that wasn't on the floor. Hints of snowy fuzz blended in splendidly. A large window with shutters was cracked open to let in winter's whistle.

Inside the small bathroom, the manicured fingers of a man reaching back for his youth pulled the medicine cabinet open. They were careful to leave the mirror without prints. The hand took out a tube of Mortebarb. The other hand reached for the shaving brush on the counter and pointed it under the spigot of steaming water. It squeezed a spoonful on the brush and then whip-creamed wet cheeks. He took his safety razor and slashed at his face like windshield wipers under a thick pour. Meet Pazo "Pap" Fanti. Age: 44. 6'0". 215 lbs. Worked with his mitts before his feet learned to walk. Carried a candy-coated shell around his waist. Lean legs, one half-bum. Prominent beak, pointing to a mild mouth that smiled when upset. Paper thin 'stache. Eyes sky-blue behind bottle caps. Salt and pepper feathers slicked to his neck, tulip ears. Well-groomed even while asleep. Uttered in undertones. Father to "Angel #1." Charged: rum-running, racketeering, heading up illegal joints. Still at large. Occupation: nightspot baron. AKA Chameleon; AKA Night Fox; AKA Cap'n Pap; AKA Mr. Magic.

After his shave, Pap rubbed his cheeks. He owned the taut skin of a man who never saw the sun. Then he made for the kitchen. The gas stove and Electrique refrigerator looked unused. He opened the fridge. There was enough space to hide a body. Fortunately, Pap hadn't picked one up at the grocer. He reached for the pitcher of ice water, lodged between a can of Shiloh's powdered chocolate and a box of Cubongo puros. He poured himself a tall glass and guzzled it down. Then his ears measured a change in air pressure just outside his front door. He restricted his movements to none before floating back to the bedroom.

There was a single mattress on the ground. It was unsoiled and robed in silk sheets. A radiator heater snapped warmth from its coils. Twenty painted silk ties were racked by the closet. Stretched inside, a wooden rod hung ten suits, each a different shade of blue, and five tuxedos, three black and two dinner jackets. A dozen dress shirts maintained equal breathing room. Pap removed his bathrobe and picked out a ten-pleat with an attached collar. Mid button down, three wraps on the front door caused him to change directions. It sounded like a monk passing out free Bibles. He finished closing his shirt and made quick work to wrap up his legs. Then the wingtips. He went for the top of his strong box and took hold of his Colt .38 snub like it was covered in thorns. Then he slid footless towards the door. His eyes shifted up to the transom. It was opened when he thought he had left it closed. With a minty breath of space between his head and the entrance, Pap remained silent and waited. He crossed the virgin gun over his heart. Though it had never fired a round, it felt hot against his sternum. It was a gift from a friend who figured he could one day use it even if he was new to the game.

"It's me," said the visitor.

Pap let the air out of his lungs and unlocked the door, starting with the safety chain and ending with the deadlock. He flushed it open and let the "Salmon" wiggle in.

Basil Demur. Age 48. 5'8". 160 lbs. Olive skin. Two black pages parted down the middle of his head. Educated in the best schools. Homburgs, three-piece suits and leather briefcases, a real clotheshorse. Cigarette holders. Heart divorced his mind ten years ago. Connected in all the right places. Charged: aiding and abetting, racketeering, being too slippery to hold. Occupation: lawyer. AKA Salmon.

Pap called off his gun and sealed the door shut. His gait loosened up. Basil followed, dressed like he was headed to a party, top hat and tails. Pap returned to the bathroom to collect a set of gold cufflinks on the sink. The letters C.P. were engraved on them. He reappeared in the bedroom and noticed Basil looking out the window. He needled the links through his wrist cuffs.

"You know I don't get as jumpy with a telegram," Pap said.

"Not for what I'm about to say. Time to sell the farm again," Basil waxed urgent.

"I don't have the gas in the tank for another one."

"That's how dead people think." Basil fingered inside his breast pocket and pulled out an alpaca cigarette case. He cracked it open, clamped a fag and tapped it repeatedly over the top of his wrist like he hadn't a care in the world.

"You remember how it used to be?" Pap clipped a black bow tie around his collar. It was semicrooked.

Basil lit his smoke and breathed in a puff of ease. "The pachyderm in my brain forgets nothing. That's why you're still around."

"Dunfer's is the best we've known. It's a miracle they followed us out there."

"The miracle is the reason they followed, and they'll keep following, but in case you need someone to shove you into the deep end for another swim lesson, the Hangman's cut loose." Basil watched as Pap gave back what he had tried to swallow for eons. Just the mention of the name wrung the juice out of

Pap's heart. "He knows you pulled a Lazarus and is hep to the club."

"And the kid?"

"We're all on borrowed time, right?"

"Who leaked?" Pap slowed his fingers around each button on his double-breasted jacket hoping it would delay the seconds that took a sudden fondness to speed. His eyes wanted to discharge anger through Basil's, but he couldn't bring them up far enough.

"I'm working on it. Could be a dozen gees, but that helps you none now," Basil said.

Pap rotated his blinkers to Basil's just to see them slow roasting in their skull bowls. "Nix on the move."

"How long you think before his torpedoes are knocking at the door? You think they'll come with an arrangement of reds?" Basil asked.

"He would have done it long ago."

Basil grew tired of Pap's resistance. As he spoke, billows of smoke plumed from his throat like a volcano before climax. "It's a new contract, Pap. And it's a big one. If you ever took a tip, take this one," Basil said. With each word, Pap appeared to grow weaker.

"You seem to have an arrow on the bullseye."

"Better than through the heart if you don't take me serious. Hell, what am I trying to do if not protect you?"

"Things are getting too hot. We gotta get out of the Oven for good."

"Then what? You never struck me as a mountain man."

"I'll make do. Always do."

"Only there won't be any place you can go where another human being puffs the same air. How long you think that lasts? Stay with me for a second. I've never let you down."

Of all the things Basil said, Pap was hard-pressed to deny the last. "I'm ears."

"The old Calloway on Twenties Slip," Basil said, noticing the somber change in expression on Pap's face.

"Pity. The kid loved their chocolate." Pap's focus was still on the part about the renewed contract.

"I'll take care of the members. Forget the name change. We don't need one anymore. It'll keep you in the shadows until we can figure a permanent fix."

"Don't believe the shrinks. All age does is make you older," Pap muttered under his breath, "I can't do this anymore." How many more times would he hold death by the hand and not yield to its charms, he thought.

"Is that what you'll tell the kid?" Basil heard him. There was a breath of silence. Pap's mind retraced things he thought might never come back, but it was like snuffing out the midday sun. He grabbed hold of his lapels and raised his head high. After all, men in monkey suits didn't crack.

"Exits?" Exits ranked higher on Pap's checklist than entrances.

"Water surrounds you. As failsafe as you're gonna get without taking the whole joint on the high seas," said Basil. Pap offered a cagey nod. "I know you're scared," Basil continued.

"Only not for me anymore."

"Nothing will happen to the kid if you heed my advice," Basil reassured.

"Find the leak before it follows us."

"It's my next order of business." Basil nodded with a straight face and a sealed mouth. Pap motioned to the door. It was time for everyone to leave.

Basil turned for the door. Pap followed him like he had issues of mistrust. After all, Basil was Pap's lawyer, but formal relationships aside, he was also one of Pap's closest friends. They went back to the old days, long before Basil chose law and Pap enrolled in the school of hard knocks. Pap gave a lukewarm shake of Basil's hand. He needed to preserve what little strength he had for the night ahead.

"Sorry I wasn't the bearer of better tidings, but look on the bright side. You'll never find a live snake in your shoe," Basil said before a cool departure.

Pap inched the door shut. He let his head hang forward until it was leaning against it. He stayed there only a couple of seconds wishing he could deny what he had feared for years. Then he moved to the window. Pap nudged the shutters from the wall, just enough to peek through and spot Basil walking to his Dues Model J. Basil left the top down, and his wheel was frosting over. Pap returned to his medicine cabinet and pulled out a bottle of downers. His hands trembled to twist the cap off. He shook two powder drops to his hand and cupped them past his lips, swallowing both on saliva alone. He then moved back to his room and produced a suitcase from under his bed. He plopped it open. He unhooked the suits, three at a time and folded them into the case. Then the ties and a couple of pairs of shoes. He took the small roll of cash from the safe. It equaled over five large. He stuffed it in his pocket, removed the bedding and balled it up tight. A few toiletries, his cigars and the can of Shiloh's. Everything else could stay. It was time to head to Dunfer's and break the news.

- 3 -

A gumshoe he never was, but he sure played the part like it was tailor-made. DC Stiles. Age 33. 5'9". 160 lbs. Manila skin. Unblemished face. Eyes pinched close but alert. Cropped hair, long bangs, parted to the side. Famed by accident. Charged: aiding and abetting known fugitives, burglary, grand theft, extortion. Still at large. Occupation: private dick. AKA Dry Squirt.

Cracking the Lala Terre case was a fluke. Had he been anywhere but sulking over a failed career inside those porous walls of his dive in Victory Village, South Breaks, he would have missed that Terre's halfwit son was held ransom right next door.

Tonight he let his right hand dangle over the steering wheel of his Kissel Q. The other he held out the window. The cherry of his Lucky battled the cold air. His was the only car on the road, and that made him feel secure. The potholes on Banter Way did a number on the axel, but there were mechanics for that. Stiles had made this drive many nights over the last few months. The Thread District in Lower Leaf where even the factory buildings smoked. Every time he entered this tangle of brick and concrete, he was reminded just how much a person, of the wrong persuasion, could get away with. He checked his rear view, and his easy mood was instantly challenged. A pair of yellows stained the mirror from about three blocks back. He didn't care for the tail and neither did his foot as it smashed on the gas. The tail was holding like a railcar on a train. Stiles crumpled his brow like a sheet of paper and gunned his engine. The whole time, his eyes were stuck in the mirror. He was instructed to come solo. Any company was bad company. And the car kept following like it had a reason. Stiles had to think quick. He passed one, two, three more intersections, then cut a quick left onto Cotton and an immediate right into an alley where he doused his lights and stopped. He looked to his watch. It gave him 10:20 pm. The whiff of company had him out of sorts. He continued down the alley, brights out and navigating by instinct. He glanced back once and noticed lights flashing past like a shooting star. It was the tail, and he had cut it off without leaving a trace of blood. He hit his lights again and continued until he came to N Street. The abandoned industrial houses started to look like a string of paper dolls. He took another left at the fourth intersection. Then after driving a quarter mile, he decided it was time to retrace. But just to make certain, he shut down his car and had a ten minute conversation with a stick of tobacco. Odds were his tail had either given up or blown town, so Stiles started back to Cotton and then Banter. He continued southeast for a half mile and made the right he was supposed to take the first time. He was certain about the tail too. It had been lopped off. Up ahead he could see the yard and the depots lining up. He was back on course. His mirror was a blank stare. He cut in between the Textiles Depository and an unmarked stockroom. A handful of hod carriers appeared in his headlights. There was a checkpoint with a couple of night crawlers bumping gums. Past that was a series of warehouses. Dunfer's Linens Company. Stiles' final stop.

- 4 -

"I think he gave you the slip, Merlin," said the fancy man in the back seat of their Packard 740. He donned a cream-painted fedora with a wide black ribbon. His dark overcoat concealed a matching cream tuxedo and a crimson bow tie that pressed against his throat like a kiss stain. A sizzling cigarette clung onto the two first fingers of his left hand. He went by Chase Griggs. Age 35. 5'10". 175 lbs. Dimple chin. Eyebrows like fox tails. Eyes a shade from black to match a sideward slick of hair. Had his ears pinned back to look like the talkie star Mark Sable. Finest suits, all paid for by the missus. Cocksure. Mental two-timer. Charged: adultery on the only woman who could make it a crime. Occupation: land developer. AKA Hush.

The woman seated next to him appeared to come from the same clothier in her cream mink pill box. She was wrapped in a llama. Her wrists were cuffed in hoops of fur. A sexy-soft animal gobbled up her neck. Her ruby lips shrunk to a needle point. Vilma Griggs was her married title. Age 39. 5'2". 140 lbs. Bubble cheeks always three layers fossilized in rouge. Eyes under dark shades, even at night. Hair like a pile of autumn. Went in for a new chin, came out with a knuckle. A bit on the jowly side. Feared widths (of the waist variety) like most feared heights. Charged: aiding and abetting a known fugitive. Occupation: wealthy heiress, housewife. AKA The Bank.

"Not to worry, sir. We'll find it," said Merlin. His gray mustache made a perfect comb and stopped without fail at the crooked shoreline of his upper lip. His chauffeur uniform and hat covered him like layers of paper. He was stiff all over except in his kelpy hands, covered in black leather. They appeared to waltz on the steering wheel.

"Why couldn't we just go to the Dirty Spoon?" Vilma carped in private. She kept one hand on her hat to avoid upsetting her hair over each pot hole their limo met. The other hand gripped into the deep-buttoned leather of their bench seat. "Merlin, could you watch the holes?"

"Lay off the man. He didn't pave the street."

"I can't believe I let you talk me into this." Vilma was only getting warmed up. She glanced to the clock on the door. It was still early enough to salvage the night.

"Merlin, you'd better turn back."

"Sound suggestion, sir." Merlin made a long U and headed back to Banter.

Chase looked out his window. Vilma looked out hers. Their eyes refused to cross paths. A typical couple. She inherited the old man's fortune: one Congressman Worthton, who voted for the "mistake" just so he could consolidate his own racket. Of all the ironies, Worthton kicked the bucket off a bottle of tainted government blend intended for a bowery. And Chase, clad in a loin cloth, swung in to protect her from all the chiselers waiting to carve her pie. She believed him when he said he married solely out of love. People believe what they want. Chase negotiated his world with precision, even allowed Vilma to call the shots (with her own money). She even arranged their marriage, telling Chase when to tie the knot and how tight to make it. Vilma meant the one thing to him that he could have never attained alone: a reputation, the kind that only money could buy. She started out the breath in his lung, but over their four years had turned into the stone in his kidney.

"This will be better than The Spoon." He reached into his coat for a business card and took another gander to ensure it still said what he recalled. *Membership Card No. 74 & 75. C.P.*

"Why? Because that greaseball Jackson Reese told you?" Vilma hissed.

"Muzzle that tongue," Chase hissed back. A vein under his eye grew stiff with blood. Vilma had that special knack for giving Chase erections in all the wrong body parts.

"Don't talk to me like that," Vilma protested.

Chase pushed a button on his arm rest. The partition window rolled up. Merlin kept to the business of the road and its holes without a change in expression. "We're headed to the crème de la crème. If the law found what they got cooking in there. It's gotta be on the QT," Chase explained.

"Murder! A drum in a sweat shop." Vilma unwound her lips and laughed.

"And us togged to the bricks."

"You're the genius around here," Vilma cut back.

"Lay off the crust. It's more than another drinking fountain. I've been waiting to get in this joint for months if that means a lick," Chase said.

"That's what you said on our wedding night, and it still doesn't mean a lick."

"So that's what's eating you, Honeycomb. We can pitch woo when we get home if you don't come down with one your patented headaches."

"Maybe that's jam you feed your secretaries, but it makes me retch."

"Play nice, will ya? Let's just get there and see what's what. Can you at least wait that long?"

Vilma rummaged through her hand purse for a cigarette. Chase was quick to light it. She took in a deep breath of smoke and dabbed a flake of tobacco off the tip of her tongue. Chase employed silence.

Merlin attempted to retrace the movements of the car they had lost. And by accident, he finally found a place that promised a semblance of life. He pulled up to a boom gate. It was connected to a makeshift booth on the right. Vilma's eyes drew a blank. Beyond the rusted fence, there were textile workers pushing and pulling carts, driving forklifts and pallet trucks. A couple of large moving trucks with the words Dunfer's Linen Co. on their boxes were parked, one in front of the other. What kind of nightspot was held here? Chase rolled down the partition window to have a word with Merlin. "Wait a second," he said.

A fella emerged from the booth chomping on a sour pickle. He held a pen and pad with his other hand. He was larger than Chase but that didn't say much. The fella centered himself at the car's grill. He took down the license number and then flipped a page on his pad for a list. The headlights didn't make him shy, even with a face that seemed to have met the end of a tenderizer. He was clad in a collarless wool jacket that seemed a size to big. His brown wool cap hung off one ear because the other was missing from a knife fight. The fella curled to the driver's side and teetered against the car door. With his middle knuckle grazing the window, he suggested Merlin roll it down.

"What are you doing? Don't roll your window down," Vilma commanded, dread on her tongue. Chase blew a hush at her.

"Do what he says, Merlin," Chase contradicted.

Merlin rolled his window down enough for a finger to pass through.

"Salty Well," Merlin said through a clearing of his throat.

The fella shined his light on Merlin's hands and then his coat for any sudden guns. All he got in return was the bounced light off the coat's golden buttons.

He tilted his light up to Merlin's face and said, "Never heard of him. This is a work zone." His name was indeed Salty Well. His one job was to guard this very entrance. It was the only one on a paved road in or out of what lied ahead.

Chase rolled his window down and slid the same card he still held in his right hand through the slit in the glass. Salty flashed his lamp back at Chase. He left Merlin to himself and trolled back to collect the card. With quick eyes, he returned it to Chase, then shoved his light through the window at both Chase and Vilma. A corner of his mouth curved downwards.

"You got business here?" Salty asked with a tone of disrespect.

Chase fumbled through the first few words, "Making a payment. Order of linens from Dunfer's. Screen printing. Herringbone. But that's just pillow talk." He turned to Vilma and issued a half wink, but it looked more like a tick. Chase was no good at dealing with tough guys, much as he claimed otherwise.

Salty's eyes stayed long on Chase. "They're out of business. Stay to your right." He moved away from the car and walked around the back, beaming his lamp all over it for any hidden compartments. He semicircled the car till he was on Vilma's side. Then he marched to the boom barrier and gave it a robust military press.

"Shall I proceed, sir?"

Chase didn't need any more signals to know he had been granted admittance. "Go in. Stick to the right." They coasted under the barrier, passing grunts in dungy work duds and caps. The lot was a gravel pit. To the left was a building with corrugated metal walls and three loading docks. Other than a couple of straggler ants marching out, there was little action. Vilma kept her lenses to herself, but she could feel the eyes of the workers pasted to her. To the right was the only paved road. It was narrow enough for one car. Merlin slipped in. They passed a large warehouse. The bricks on the wall were shedding. Twenty feet up the wall, small windows, plastered in soot, ran parallel to the road. Vilma's mind ran through a million words, but none exited her mouth. Even Chase started reconsidering the whole thing. They cruised around the building and into what looked like a courtyard for the dead, but it was just another large lot. Warehouses surrounded them like a prison camp. At the far end, Merlin noticed a small sun shining about three feet off the ground. Vilma kept her eyes on her lap. If she raised them, her mouth would pop open.

"That's it. Go there," Chase said.

Merlin approached the beacon. It started to move around the end of another building. Merlin kept following to avoid losing it in the darkness. There was a gate. Beyond it were parked gems that could not have driven here by happenstance. Mercedes, Caddys, Rolls, all top of the line. On the near side, two black and white Ford Model A sedans fully equipped with drivers. The light stopped at the gate and so did Merlin. It revolved to Vilma's side and crept over the window. Her door flung open as though on its own. Vilma screamed before her eyes fully captured the culprit. An oversized homunculus in dinky overalls with the distinguishable aroma of liquid bleach. They called him Trunks. He had the head of a warthog and the body of a wart. A shock of fur gave him another three inches of hopelessness.

"Right dis way, mama," said the elf in Trunks' throat.

"Go chase yourself if you think I'm getting out," Vilma responded.

"What's crawled down your dress now? We're here," Chase said. Merlin exited only out of duty and tugged once at Chase's door. This was not Mrs. Griggs' milieu. Chase brushed his legs out.

Trunks remained stuck with his stubby fingers in his hands.

"Chase, get back. We're not staying here. Merlin, get in the car," Vilma said. Her eyes refused to look at Trunks, not because she was a snob but because she feared for her life.

"There a fuss?" Trunks asked.

"My wife's never seen a midget," Chase answered. "Where's the entrance?" Chase looked to teal acid salts scribbling the wall. Splintered boards nailed over doors weren't inviting.

There had to be a mine of diamonds on the other side to go to such lengths. He swung to Vilma's side, shooing Trunks away with a subtle brush of the wrist. Trunks stepped back a couple but he wasn't digging the piffle. "You need a highball," Chase said as he reached out his hand.

"I'll be having it here in a pig's eye. Why would you do this to me?" Vilma interrogated.

"Ten bucks says you have a good time. Come on, Snugglepuss. You know for a C a month I'm gonna get the goods on this place."

"Then I'll wait in the car."

"Baby! Give me your hand." Chase turned the chip on his shoulder to the midget. "Where's the door, mouse?"

"Right dis way, sir," Trunks said.

She held her breath and took Chase only by the tips of his fingers. Chase started ahead of her like usual. Vilma bit her teeth and went along. What choice did she have? They clip-clopped atop the slick pavement. One misstep and her red pump caught on a crack. Her left leg braked without the rest of her body knowing, and she tumbled to the ground, mopping the pavement with her coat. Puddles of oily muck sprayed another layer of rouge on her cheeks. Chase turned to the commotion. He snorted a chuckle and would later blame allergies. Trunks cracked up. Merlin kept a poker face, but the reality was that he would never laugh at such things to begin with. He rushed over to Vilma and helped put her feet back under her. Chase was late to the rescue, but he managed to get a hand around her arm and help Merlin straighten her up. Her heel snapped off and stayed in the crack. She was soiled and lopsided and had that "I'm gonna get at your throat" look in her eye. Chase kept a smirk on his face only because he couldn't wipe it off.

"Are you alright, Mrs. Griggs?" Merlin asked.

"Don't get into a lather. We'll find the powder room," Chase said.

"I'm leaving now. Merlin, get in the car." Vilma had yet to see the damage. She looked like a painter's overworked palette.

"What's the big idea?" Chase barked at Trunks like he had tripped Vilma himself.

"Hey, we can't have this out here," Trunks said. His head turned on a swivel like he anticipated the disturbance to invite prowlers.

"Now!" Vilma screamed. The waterworks went off in her eyes and muddied up her cheeks like an open hose on a clown.

Trunks looked to Chase in the gravest of ways, "Hey, mister, we can't have this,"

"Shut up!" Vilma barked at Trunks. "Both of you, shut up!" Chase had stopped talking, but Vilma could still hear him. She was gunning for a straitjacket and teetered back to the safety of the Packard. "I'm going to the Spoon with or without you."

Chase looked to Trunks as if he had any persuasive powers. The allure of what could be was too hard to resist, and the split second was too long to keep Vilma waiting. She reached for her door and slammed it shut. "Let's go," she blurted to Merlin.

"Take her home," Chase said.

"Yes, Mr. Griggs." Merlin returned to the wheel and pulled the car around and away. Chase stood in the middle of the yard like it wasn't the first time a date with his wife had ended before it begun.

"Talk about a bitch kitty. A real face stretcher," Trunks commented, ignorant to Vilma's relationship to Chase or just plain ignorant.

The snickering lump was pinching Chase's nerves. He produced a pack of wings from his coat, clapped one out and shoved it between his teeth. "Get me inside, half thought, before I belt the legs out of your waist," Chase said as he scratched a lucifer along the strike strip and lit his ciggy.

Trunks cussed under his breath. Then he spurted towards the nearest brick building. Chase nearly stomped on him in pursuit.

- **5** -

There were several washrooms at Dunfer's. This one was for plant workers only or anyone else with a desperate set of bowels. Only one of the four neon tubes on the wall had any spark left. The tile walls were smudged with neglect and trickled with every color except clean. Puke stains mapped the floor. They were only stains. A bucket of bleach and a dead mop did their best, but they were both pooped. Two faded stalls encrypted in love notes housed toilets beyond description. One of the stall doors was off its hinges and cast to the side. The other was closed with a wire. Hanging over the edge was a black tuxedo ready to be broken in. It was sized small in length but fat in width. To the left of the stalls, three urinals bled yellow. The whole room carried the faint but constant smell of egg. The large ventilation screens were on a long hiatus. A secondhand davenport of butterscotch velvet opposite the urinals curved its scuffed arms like it belonged. Next to the sofa, a Raveer cathedral whispered the gentle strum of a ukulele.

The quick knock on the washroom door pressed it open just enough to allow a set of lips to pass through.

"How you doin', Kid Cool?" a set of leather lungs asked from around the corner. His name was Lou Licks. Age 46. 6'4". 230 lbs. A cinder block on legs. White as ash. Moon-faced with a frog's jaw. Dirty black hair that couldn't decide a part. Gentle until pushed. Charged: murder 1 and attempt on another. Still at large. Occupation: club manager, confidant, cook. AKA Locker.

Lou heard the kid rinsing his mouth and knew he had to wait a few seconds for a response. Like clockwork, six swooshes on each cheek led to six gargles over the tonsils. The kid spat into the sink. "Quack, quack, ducky. How's the house?" Always with that joie de vivre in a gravel voice way past its prime, he could never be accused of being a jerk.

"Cats up to the gills," Lou said. "You're on in five. Need anything else?"

"Just putting on my munitions." Under the foggy mirror with a crack that bolted down the middle, the slim tin counter was organized like a surgeon's tray. From right to left on a stretch of towel was the full extent of his bric-a-brac: a tube of Gate's tooth polish, tooth brush with bristles in full bloom, a bottle of Hyperol, Dap's pomade. He was here. The kid spooned a nail of Dap's and ran it through his cotton top. He closed the jar and wiped it clean with a fresh hand towel, then folded the towel over the jar like a priest after communion.

"Shake a leg. It's moving night," Lou said.

The kid took the scissors to the left of the pomade and snipped in rhythm. The left side of his whiskers to match the right. Then the right to match the left until he figured to be out of whiskers. No one would notice anyway. "And I was just starting to get used to the joint."

"You're gonna love our new digs. Water as far as the eye can see," Lou said.

"Bacon-wrapped fish every night!" Off to the corner was the last morsel of a five-herb tuna and rice under a wide fork and knife. A tall glass streaked memories of chocolate milk. The kid set the scissors down and rolled up his stuff in the towel. Packed and ready. He took one step back and bent forward as far as his chubby waist would allow in an attempt to touch his toes. He could barely bounce his hands to his knees, but these stretches were part of the kid's routine, pivotal for onstage balance; this he'd swear by.

"Speaking of, you like the tuna?" Lou asked.

"And how!" The kid reached far left for his trumpet case. He nestled it open, took out his Elmer trumpet, custom designed with wide piston valves for his nubby digits, and burnished the bell with a rag until it winked at him.

Lou's smile was felt around the corner, but he knew there was little time to waste. He could smell the fury in the air, more pungent than the egg, and it was coming for them. The door eased back till it was closed.

- 6 -

"Keep your eyes peeled to the bone," Lou said to the dark statue of brawn by the washroom door. Ink Tambo had the eyes of a lion and the stoic expression of an Apache warrior on the range. He was a giant with steel beams for arms and known as "Bulwark." He was charged with multiple A&B's (assault and battery) and one count of rape.

Ink gave a casual but immediate nod of the chops. His only job was to stand by that door till the kid came out, escort him to the stage and never show his gun unless it was absolutely necessary. He was notorious for putting someone in place if they acted out of line. And if that didn't work, he'd just put them through a wall.

Lou plodded through the short corridor in a single-breasted soup and fish. He pushed through a set of double swing doors into a large room with ceilings far from reach. The only light came from the night sky and trickled in through the small windows high above. Stacks of disordered textiles, mostly scraps, mostly solids with an abundance of burgundy satin, were scattered about. A special detail of headless mannequins in birthday suits took their positions. Headed dummies scarecrowed the two doors. In their hands, cardboard gats. One double door was on the north side where Lou was headed. He slid a scarecrow over and pushed through the next set of swing doors and into another corridor that hooked right. At the hook was a freight elevator. He pushed the metal fire doors apart, then pulled the strap on the hoistway gate. It was scuffed to pieces. He pulled the gate back down and sealed himself in. The three buttons on the wall bore no markings. He pushed the one in the middle. The elevator descended. Opening the gate and the fire doors, the sounds of something that didn't belong. The sound frolickers made at a party. It was faint but growing louder. Lou followed it through another set of double doors. He walked through a room as narrow as a waiting lobby. A bare bulb jutted off the top wall. There were leather gig bags scattered around a metal table, some on the dusty floor. A bottle of rye, half topped, and a couple of ashtrays with smoldering leftovers sat on the table. At the other end, another door, this one with a handle and lock. Lou slid his key in and wiggled it right. He opened the door, and the sounds were deafening. A makeshift backstage and a set of scrim drapes separated what lied ahead. Two more mannequins guarded the ends. To the right of the curtains, a small swing entry led Lou to another short corridor that curled left. Lou bumped a fist against the final door. From its flip side another behemoth stepped out of his way. Turnip "Farm" Faymus had the head of an unpeeled potato covered in sprouting eyes and the strength of a rhino. His charges mimicked Ink Tambo's. They usually rolled together when they weren't taking turns at guard. Lou gave Turnip a look like they had gone way back and passed on. Turnip slid back to block the door, his real eyes set wide on the biggest party seventy-five people would ever know about. Club Polar: where miracles happened every night. Unlike every other corner of Dunfer's sinuous layout, this spacious hall was designed to impress, at least from a distance and only where it counted most. A raised bandstand of plywood was covered in black velvet. A two-foot trench separated the bandstand from the audience. It was marked off by skinny chains wrapped in sash. The Cats 6 from North Leaf were on. They all wore matching penguin skins. They were all street guys, sewer citizens. Not trained in fancy conservatories, doing ballroom parties, this combo cultivated its craft by trash cans ablaze on heatless nights, donning handkerchiefs as finger wraps. But now they were headlining one of the swankiest joints around. Starting from right to left.

Beans Fryer. Age. 40. 6'3". 260 lbs. Double bass. Double man. Skin shaded mud and a nest of cremated curls capped his crown. Eyes yellow on bloodshot. Twilight teeth. A peanut in a shell for a nose. He smacked his fiddle like a newborn bottom.

Pisto Leroy. Age. 42. 5'10". 155 lbs. Guitar. Sandy with freckles like stars on a beach, Flaming flattop. Finger nails thick as shoehorns. He tickled the strings, and the strings kept laughing.

Tots "Octopus." Age 38. 5'11". 160 lbs. Drums. A grape head with squinty eyes. Mouth agape, panting tongue. Wet towels formed a moat around his throne. His drumsticks quivered off his wrists like he had touched a live fuse.

Charmin. Age. 30. 6'1". 190 lbs. Sax. Black as pupils, dimples deep as pinholes, nose hooked over his figure-eight lips. He tipped back his sax like there was hooch in it.

Gumbie. Age 47. 5'9". 140 lbs. Piano. Skin mauve like a healing bruise, fingers like winter branches. They coddled every key, neglecting none.

Sas Parila. Age 39. 6'0". 175 lbs. Clarinet. Slicked weave of worms on a bromine dome. Skin like a banana peel three days removed from the fruit. Snakes had nothing on what he could charm.

And Clyde Davis. Age 41. 5'6". 150 lbs. Trombone. A cup of Arabica splashed all over him. Eyes set deep, nostrils wide as his smile. He jabbed his slide: right jab, right jab, right.

That made seven, but the name stuck just before Pisto Leroy joined them in the summer of 1929. All were charged with conspiracy and other crimes of turpitude. All were still at large and to be found here, under a puffy ceiling of burgundy satin and walls to match, where the invited could boast of the finest drinks and dinner, all on the house for a monthly cover of $60-$100, depending on their seats. Mind you, no seat in the house was bad. Basil Demur, the lawyer, had set it all up. He took credit for advising how the joint would be run and who would be let in. Most in attendance were friends, people Basil could trust which begged the question. None were underground toughs, but they all had the cash and clout to move in any direction they pleased.

Like Chase Griggs who sat at one of the small, round tables, cloaked in a white table cloth to the floor, a lamp shadowing his face in all the right places, a bottle of Label Azure, a short glass, and some cracked ice in a hand-sized bucket. He was packed in within two dozen other tables, each with their own bottles, cracked ice and polished faces, right in front of the Cats 6 and the High Legs, a trio of dancers that earned every letter of its title. Chase wanted nothing more than to be known in important circles and, for a few intoxicating hours, suppress the memory of Vilma. With their tables connected to make things more personal, Chase found his greatest enjoyment rubbing elbows with his chum, Jackson Reese. His hair and mustache were cut out of a magazine. Brown eyes sculpted to a twinkle when he talked from two moistened blades of grass that made up his lips. A thousand joints on the Leaf depended on ice to keep their drinks cool, and Jackson was the one to supply them. The cops never gave him a hard time because after all, it was only ice. Chase thought Jackson Reese a god in tails and groupies. Like the two peaches in strapless dresses and finger waves on each arm of his dinner jacket. None were his wife. Reese canoodled one, then moved to the other. It was a trait Chase admired as his eyes played follow the kicking leg. His lower lip hung loose. He was on his third Scotch & Sweet.

"Who's that?" Chase asked more to himself, but Jackson picked it up.

"That, as you so well put it, is death by ejaculation. Goes for them jackhammer types, you know, a million pounding miles an hour. A real sucker for dirty talk too. For each cusser, she'll pop you out another kid, so watch your salt shaker."

"What could be wrong with any of that?" He couldn't move his eyes from the lead dancer, waving her long feathered wings in front of her bare midriff. They made love in the space of a glance.

Her name was Holly "Hopper" Fountain. Age 28. 5'7". 125 lbs. Platinum waves pinned high. Northern cheekbones, an eyelash scar over the right side. Eyes like table spoons, Medusa-green, wide enough to fit a narrow nose with a bumped crown. Overbite of strong chompers, hardly sheathed by a baby's kisser. Her honey apple skin sparkled with crystals. Her gams were all beach, her head all clouds. Hips like bike handles with a swan neck to match. Charged: lewd conduct, abusing her pulchritude, gold digger. Occupation: dancer, seductress. AKA Heels.

"You better get through the intersection before the light turns red," Jackson said. His dates did nothing but giggle and drink, sometimes out of that order. Chase brought his glass to his lips and eased the tonic into a warmed belly. The High Legs foxtrotted off the stage but not before Holly wafted a smooch in Chase's general direction. The music enjoyed a brief intermission while the crowd serenaded them with applause. The band then picked up where it left off.

Jumping onto the bandstand was a voice too happy to come from a walking coat hanger. Ham Wails was a regular wag, pale but not pasty, bug-eyed with a shock of black hair skyward like a woodpecker. Tuxed with the rest, they called him "Fifty Fatlip" for a reason. He was the club's emcee and charged with cracking jokes that could make a statue gurgle.

"Man goes to the clinic and says: 'Doc, I think there's something wrong with my ears. I can't hear anything my wife tells me.'" The crowd introduced a chuckle. "The doc asked: 'Does this happen with others or only with your wife?'" The laughter turned up a couple of octaves. "The man looked to the doctor with that I've-seen-the-light expression and said: 'So I ain't sick?'" Cackle went the crowd. Even the women.

"But seriously folks, I know most of you wouldn't be caught dead in a dump like this unless you were killed in a dump like this." Another hoot caught the crowd by its throat. They would laugh at anything now. "Someone yank that buffoon off the stage before he hurts himself," Wails said of himself over the whirlpool of mirth. "He hates when I pat him on the back, but none of us would be here tonight without the special arrangements of our captain, the beloved Pap Fanti." The audience clapped hands, tapped glasses with forks and whistled.

On the opposite end of the room, jutting out from the corner of the wall was the bar. Pap stood by the last stool, his hands clasping the insides of his lapels. He batted a grateful lash. His eyes registered all in attendance. DC Stiles sat on the stool next to him like he was studying for an exam he was bound to fail. He was oblivious to Chase in the front row. Even when they crossed paths in the lobby an hour ago, neither had a clue that one had trailed and the other had slipped, and neither felt they should remember the other's face beyond the glance.

Dino Glass stood behind the bar and finished filling a tray with another round. He was nearing half a century and halfway between five and six feet, bore oily henna hair and grew cheeks like tomatoes. His potions earned him the moniker: Dinomite. Charges included: turning water to wine. He paid no attention to the runt next to him loading a small dolly with cases of liquid flame.

Anthony "Ant" Mound. Age 13. 5'1". 105 lbs. Orphan. Copper-coated. Pincer lips. Domed nose. Vascular as a rope. Could lift ten times his weight. AKA Barbell. Ant rolled the loaded dolly out the swinging door to the far right of the bar and out of view. On the other side, a dumbwaiter on the wall was his aim. He pried it open and lifted the case into it. Then shut it and pressed the button. The secondhand counted twenty, and the dumbwaiter opened at road level to another set of eager hands.

Moony "Bread'n" Butter. Age. 11. 5'2". 120 lbs. Orphan. Skin pink. Half-moon eyes. Whispered all his words. Moony removed the case and set it on a flat dolly with a strap for:

"Cheese" Burger Brasa. Age 16. 5'5". 170 lbs. Orphan. Stretch marks on his neck. Acne-littered forehead. Patch on his blind eye. Hair like sandpaper. Always eating. Perpetual joker. Burger pulled the strap through the short corridor. The exit door was within sight. He opened the door and checked both ways to make sure his eye and ears were still in place. They were. One on each side filling up the saline air with pirouettes of cigarette smoke.

Mack "Rabbit Stew" Loyter. Age 12. 4'10". 120 lbs. Orphan. Creamy. Sleepy eyes. Ears pinned back to his head. Fast as a cheetah.

And then there was Dradle "Dance Steps" Prestij. Age 14. 5'6". 140 lbs. Orphan. Tanned. Bangs that covered his eyes. Danced to kill stress. They surveyed the miasmic River Gorda through binoculars. Five abandoned sea freighters were docked. Beyond them, the water was crawling over itself. Nothing else, like say a police boat, was crawling over it. Gusts of wind shoved and yanked storm clouds into place.

Before Burger was a Dunfer's Linen Co. truck with its cargo hold opened wide. He lugged the dolly up the loading ramp. There were several crates stacked on top each other. Empty round tables and chairs and piles of silks and satins.

Organizing the stuff under candlelight was Bobby "Safecracker" Pin. Age 15. 5'7". 145 lbs. Orphan. White as a ghost. Quiet. Played with metal. Together they were known as the Gutter Gophers.

Back by the bar, Pap kept mental tabs on the passing minutes. Lou crowded him after having just filled his eye with a bowl of Rita Glass. She was the ginchy High Girl to Holly's right. Rita had noticed him in return before pulling her smiling gams off the stage.

"Everything jake?" Pap asked.

"You said it," Lou responded.

"You break it to him?"

"Front page. I still say we close ranks and hold down our turf."

"No more scrappin', Lou," Pap said. "Be a pal, will ya? Help out with the drinks. The boys are loading up."

"Sure thing, but I'm eighty-sixing 'em in an hour."

"Latimor's table," Dino said of the round before Lou took the tray into the crowd.

Pap connected an eye with Dino. They exchanged an entire conversation without saying a word. Something about getting out of Dodge in a flash. Then Pap slid over to DC Stiles.

"It's good you came," Pap said.

"You know I never miss a show," DC said. "Though I gotta admit, tonight has me on edge."

"Must be something in the air."

"Your legal eagle, Demur, he's clean," Stiles said. "I've been on him all week. He lives inside the courts and the cooler. That's probably where he got the tip."

Pap reached into his coat for his money clip and peeled off a C note for Stiles. "Stick around. I may need you again." Pap knew that any man who could find Lala Terre's son alive was a man he needed to befriend. Before Pap sent Stiles on Demur's trail, he had Demur do his own checks on Stiles. Turned out he was an ex-cop who was kicked off the force for doing too many favors for the wrong people. Pap liked him already. He knew that the police was heavily influenced by the Plagun and Cabra outfits, and if Stiles was doing favors for someone other than those two, Pap was a fan. Stiles turned house peeper and hung his shingle on the door. Hits and misses, mostly misses until Lala Terre's son put him on the map. Perish the thought, but he knew the value of a shamus with a bloodhound nose. Heaven forbid Pap would need it someday.

"I got no other commitments but to see the kid scorch the air. He's out of this world."

The words made Pap nervous. The whole set, everything they went through to keep it under wraps, it was all for the kid. Pap gazed across the hall to all the happy people in their silk suits and cocktail dresses. He knew why they were here. It was just like Basil had pitched to him long ago. A secret club for only the most distinguished guests, but what distinguished them from any other carcass with a pile of jack was Pap's guess tonight. Suddenly, everyone was a suspect, and Pap just wanted the night to be done, for things to quiet down once more. Pap tried to block out the hubbub, but the prattle only grew louder with the music. He was never a drinker, and maybe that was his problem. He appeared to need a relaxer just then. Instead he fished for his pack of butts and pulled out a roll. After a couple of drags, he was ready for the main event. Nothing had changed. Every time they put him on, it would always come down to this very moment, always predictable but just as surprising as the first time.

Holly was now in her evening gown, a slip that covered just a speck more than her feathers. Her hair was let down and bouncing on Chase's shoulder. They held hands to avoid saying anything stupid. Ham finished toying with the crowd and finally said the words that most had come to cherish those fleeting months at Dunfer's. Chase would hear them for the first time. "Now ladies and gentleman, the moment you've all been waiting for…"

"Hold on tight, and don't go bananas," Holly whispered in Chase's ear. He swore she took a bite of his lobe as she pulled away.

"…the angel that traded in his wings for a trumpet, come on out kid and dazzle us once more," Wails opened an arm. The kid waddled through the curtain blowing his horn like he had

31

invented music. He planted his rump on his stool and treated the revelers to a corner of heaven. The crowd responded with its usual kick of gaiety. Pap swallowed heavy nerves. Stiles closed his eyes and let the kid carry him to dreamland. Lou, Dino and Turnip fixed their senses on the crowd. Chase's peepers jumped in their sockets. Holly had to brace him steady lest he faint. He just saw a ghost.

- 7 -

A conveyor belt of fancy rides made the rounds to the arched canopy entrance of the Dirty Spoon. The marquee's neon salted the empty spaces of night and could be seen as far as Good Leaf Police, East 1st Precinct. Men in topcoats and hats, women in mink and cloches paraded through the front door without the slightest need for privacy. Three green and black RMPs loitered across the street.

Inside, a sprawling playground for the hoity toity who knew that to frolic with impunity one had to come here. The massive hall was divided into two. On the right, dozens of roulette and craps tables budded out from the Azul Bahia. Each one was chockablock with loudmouths and loose bill holders. Men flaunted cigars and finger gold. Women sparkled in neck pearls and bejeweled headdresses. Even the ugly broads had something going for them here. On the left, diners and drinkers tippled to the sounds of the big band, imported from Noola Quarter. The walls were masked with frames of every size, fames of every kind, local officials, stars of stage and picture shows, singers, dancers, wealthy tycoons; they all had their mugshots and autographs on display. And in plain sight of every budding turncoat, long bar tops of white granite, the walls behind each littered with bottles of top shelf scotch, rum, vodka, gin, cognac, brandy, you name it. White and reds of every pedigree. Ales and lagers, they had them. Standing room only. The blue-vested bartenders, three to each station, mixed and poured. The patrons dished out cash like it stunk. Waiters in red jackets and ribboned necks jettisoned silver platters of highballs to the high-spirited. A quartet of uniformed cops two-fisted shots of rye.

High above the pageantry on a second-story balcony, a single man in a chalk-striped suit put a flame to his stogie. It was the first free puff of air in three years for Buddy Plagun. Age: 29. 5'10". 170 lbs. Thick blonde mop. Brackish eyes, raffish style. Known for violent outbursts. Liked to challenge men twice his size and never backed down from a fight. Charged: rum-running, conspiracy to kill a G-Man, possession of an unlicensed firearm, attempted murder. Sentenced: ten years at Gastado Pen on Tracter Isle. Paroled on a three-spot. AKA Hangman. The smoke swam through Buddy's hair. He smiled and the origins of crow's feet sunk a dozen talons south of his temples. Three years had aged him triple. He gave a quick pick at the edge of his nostril and flicked the fleck on the crowd below. It was good luck according to him. Then he turned back and left the party to itself.

The private room was another haven of bad spirits. A flock of five full-figured floozies in frocks lounged on the white recamier and cherry sofas. Their see-through stockings stopped growing above the knee; stilettos dangled over crossed legs like live worms on hooks. Each fondled a martini glass of sediment and splash. Some smoked while others twirled tongues around skewered olives. They filled the air with mindless background twaddle until Buddy walked in. Their eyes stayed on him like he was a legend from the Old West returned from the dead. Sunken within the pillows of skin, Buddy's younger brother, Junior "Gentle" Plagun, gazed at him with the fearful admiration of a coward's eyes. He had assumed control of both the Dirty Spoon and the Champion Club when Buddy was sent up the river. He loved his chorus girls. "Dolls, go down and blow some money." Decked out in a short tuxedo and soft contours, he stood and handed a C note to each and watched his bevy of courtesans hop from the room, bubs sloshing in rhythm with their fringe.

"It's like you never went away, brother," Junior said.

With them was Jesse "on-the-take" Under. He was a small guy with a thimble nose and jumpy speed. They called him "Sanguine" but not because of his skin color. It matched a piece of toast. His widow's peak pointed to a chiseled goatee. His eyes were wide as owls, and he flashed a fade halfway up his head. "Strike first, strike last, no questions asked" was his credo. He had twelve kills under his belt but was never once convicted. The 'cuter was on the Plagun payroll and always concluded there wasn't enough evidence to put on a case.

And the last piece to the party, Basil Demur, the lawyer. Pap's lawyer. He sat on one of the wide lounge chairs like he belonged there.

"You did good, Junior. I'm proud of you. You kept us from sinking," Buddy said.

"Just keeping the seat warm for you," said Junior. Buddy reached into his waist and pulled out a burner, then offered it to Junior and got a polite but strict refusal instead. "No need for it."

"Some things never change, huh? Good to see you, kid brother." For what Buddy had in testosterone, Junior lacked. He hated guns, hated the rackets but loved the life. Thought if he could run the Spoon and nothing more, the party would never die. He loved catting women, the more the merrier like the actresses from his burlesque show, but Buddy knew he would never amount to more than a playboy with a few bucks and a fancy wardrobe.

"You see, Demur. History doesn't always repeat itself." Buddy searched out Demur's cagey eyes, but Demur kept his courtroom mask on. "What's your drink?"

"Nothing. I can't stay," said Basil. Jesse kept a watch on him like he was in enemy territory.

"My first night out in three years. I'm insulted," Buddy said.

Basil Demur pulled his cigarette case from his coat pocket and pinched another stick. He lit it in one motion and slid the case back in. Buddy and Jesse continued to press their eyes on him. "Scotch, two rocks," said Demur.

Buddy walked to the minibar and poured two scotches. He handed the short glass to Demur.

"A toast," Buddy said.

"To your freedom," Demur said.

"To tying up loose ends." Buddy took down his drink like a chug of water. He moved closer to Junior and placed a hand on his shoulder. "You been okay?"

"Everything's mint now," Junior said.

"That makes me happy. You look like your old man."

Junior didn't take it as a compliment. As far as he was concerned, their father was a curse. "How you doin'?" he asked Buddy like he genuinely cared.

"Gettin' ready for the best night of my life."

"Good. Anything you need is yours," Junior said with an air of arrogant affection.

Mank Mill entered the room with the cash bag in his mitt. Junior and Jesse acknowledged him like he was one of the boys. Mank's eyes bulged at the sight of Buddy.

"Hangman? You're sprung," Mank said.

"You don't sound too happy about that," Buddy acknowledged in a dry voice.

Mank took a few cautious steps towards Buddy like he needed to reacquaint. He wasn't certain who to hand the cash bag to so he defaulted to Junior as he had for years. He extended a handshake to Buddy, told him what a long time it had been.

"I owe you," Buddy said to Mank. Buddy then looked to Junior. "You mind if I steal your room for a minute?"

"Come join the party when you're through." Junior handed the cash bag to Buddy, then exited the room with Jesse. Demur got up from his chair and started to follow.

"Not you, Basil. Stick around," Buddy said as he pawed the cash bag between his palms. Demur stayed on his feet.

"Does he have to be here?" Mank's eyes pointed at Demur.

"Mr. Demur is my lawyer and friend. Maybe a better friend than lawyer. He kept the kites flying for us while I was away. You should thank him for that."

"He looks like a rat piece of shit to me," Mank said with unswerving eyes. The lawyer stood there taking the insults like he knew that to respond with verbal bullets would invite real ones.

"What's troubling you, Mank?" Buddy asked.

Mank made eyes to Demur like he wanted him gone or dead. Then he sauntered to the bar and overfilled his glass with ice. "Things have gone gashouse since you went away. Cabra's swallowing up the Leaf. Trying to muscle his way into Breaks. Over my mother's dead body." With two unsanitized fingers, he plucked the extra cubes out and tossed them back inside the silver bucket. Then he drenched the remaining ice in his glass with scotch.

Buddy looked to Demur and said, "Mank Mill is a respected man. He and my father used to break legs for Shotz the Shark way back when they were teens. He kept Junior out of trouble while I was in the can and helped our interests grow. I'll never forget him for that." Then he told Mank, "So I've heard."

"Now that you're back, I think we can make things right again. It's good to see you." Mank turned and let the glass slip from his hand without knowing it. It crashed on the floor. Buddy gripped his muffled hand canon. The silencer was pointed to the hole in Mank's gut. He groaned and ripped his jacket open to feel the blood soaking through his shirt. He reached for his gun. Buddy pelted him again an inch below the original hole. It stymied Mank's efforts. His brute strength kept him on his feet, but the spirit was fast fading.

Demur stood in a fit of fright. He held his glass in front of his belly like a shield should Buddy accidentally tilt his rod a couple degrees to the left. Jesse walked back in the office with a furniture cart loaded with suitcases and a body bag.

"Open the bank bag," Buddy ordered Demur.

"You shot him!" said Demur.

"Open it now."

Demur's fingers trembled on the zipper. Mank was down on his knees trying to catch the blood that was spewing from his gut so he could put it back in. "Wait a second."

"Pull out the piece of paper and read it to me," Buddy said.

"One jackass." Demur let the page slip from his hand. Witnessing a murder wasn't on his schedule tonight.

"Did Cabra give you the green light to clean out my father too?" Buddy asked. He nodded to Jesse. Jesse slipped out a switchblade from his pant pocket and approached Mank like an executioner.

"He's gonna drive you out! You're finished!" Mank screamed as he made one more attempt at his gun. Jesse lengthened Mank's frothing throat with a tug of his hair. Mank reached out to Jesse with a drained fist and got carved up for it. Blood gurgled through Mank's skin and poured over his chest. Jesse threw towels on him to soak it up.

"The floor. Jesse, watch the floor," Buddy said.

Mank sucked for air like a fish in a net. It was over in seconds. Demur did a damn fine job keeping it together when all he wanted to do was fall apart. He had no clue that Mank had switched over to Cabra's side, had no clue that he was robbing him blind. Mank Mill was once very involved in Plagun interests. Word had gotten around in years past that Mank Mill was a ruthless stick-up artist, a feared man who didn't care about hits. He got his start as a train engineer for the Eastern Union Railroad Company only because he had an uncle who put in a word. He was later fired when found "negligent" in preventing several train robberies. The authorities would never discover that Mank Mill would allow the robberies to take place, plan their locations and times, for a healthy cut that was divvied up sometimes weeks later. After Eastern let him go, Mank Mill turned in his engineer's cap for a bandana. He ran with a crew of five footpads turned horsemen. He'd park a flivver on the tracks to force the emergency stop. They jacked ten trains leaving the Leaf. Mank Mill would have done better to catch the last one himself, but like they say, sticky fingers respond better to an axe than to soap.

Demur should have known all these details, especially for the salary he was drawing, but right now Buddy's only concern was covering up the hit. He had just been released from the pen and nothing was going to send him back. He looked to Demur and the panic that crept over his lips.

"You saw the whole thing, clear as the nose on your face. He reached for his gun first. I defended you. You're either my lead witness or an accomplice to a murder." Then Buddy said to Jesse as though all of this killing was routine: "Take him out back. Junior will get all bent out of shape if he sees this."

Jesse bagged Mank up and hoisted him onto the luggage cart in between a couple of suitcases. He then rolled him from the room like a bellhop.

"You got something to tell me, counsel? Say it now," Buddy said. Demur had to remind his heart to beat. It had been years since he had seen Buddy at work and it got him wondering if he was next. "Keep your head. Take a breath," Buddy continued.

"Dunfer's. Thread District. Last I knew," whispered past Basil Demur's guilty lips.

"Tonight?" Buddy whispered back.

"How would I know? I'm not his keeper, and this well's run dry."

"You've lied to me before."

Two brains were drawing up battle lines. The only problem was that there were too many smoke signals on the map.

"I know you have no respect for the law, but rubbing me out would bring too much heat, even for a guy like you. I mean what I say. I know nothing more of Fanti except what I was able to dig up, mind you, at a remarkable cost, but I'm not your house peeper, so consider us settled in full. Don't call me again. I'm through." Demur did most of his sinning before noon so people would remember him by something decent at the close of the business day. It was too late to be bartering Pap Fanti's soul, but he had no choice. The thought of a hollow point massaging his back faded only after he closed the door.

Six months ago, Basil Demur had been summoned to Gastado Penitentiary, north of the Leaf, for a "conference." Buddy Plagun was doing hard time. Still, he lived better than most outsiders. He ate filet mignon in his own private wing. He had protection from inmates and guards, in part by Cabra, who had granted Buddy immunity while away. The olive branch was tribute for Bill Plagun, but Buddy took it as a slap in the face. He continued to control his southern routes and Crystal Plats, but this meeting had nothing to do with that. Word had gotten out that Pazo Fanti was still breathing. Demur denied it. Buddy buffaloed him for the truth. Demur stuck to his guns. It left Buddy with little choice but to issue this warning: "If he blows town, you better blow with him." Buddy had paid off Demur's secretary a thousand dollars just to let him know if Pazo Fanti stopped by. Demur would fire her the next day, but the cat was out of the bag.

When Junior later found out that Mank Mill had been rubbed out in his own private entertainment room he lost his marbles and let Buddy know the big shot he had become in the last three years. "I run a clean joint! What the fuck is this?"

"He's been banging you for years. That means he's been banging me," Buddy said.

"You don't think I was hep to it all the time?" Junior didn't mind the stealing as long as his bubble remained unpopped. It was the price he paid for safety. For Junior, it was better to be in the company of a thousand thieves than alone. "God, why did you have to come back?" It slipped out of Junior's mouth all by itself. "That was a big killing. You know Cabra's gonna repay us with a tank of droppers."

The hurt on Buddy's face was hard to conceal. Junior was a stage-door Johnny, but he never thought him to be just another spineless scion. Buddy had always hoped to have the loyalty of his only remaining kin if not his affection, but Junior didn't care to give it to him. He had taken too much shit from Buddy over the years and was now numb like a severed foot. He only prayed to not be implicated in another one of Buddy's shooting sprees.

- 8 -

The moon was a scoop of dirty vanilla over Crystal Plats Zoo. Clouds amassed to form a large sponge. The contents within were begging to be purged. Met rolled a hefty ice box through a dark walkway and in between the animal cages. His icy breath fogged the air. In the freeze he still found a way to get sweat into his eyes. Someone once told him that patience led to all good things. It also led to death if one waited around long enough. But Met had no choice anymore. He had to let patience teach him what she meant when she whispered *wait*. The stink of animal shit, even in the cold, courted his nostrils and stepped on his shadow, but he had to be patient. He had to be smart too. Each day for the last twenty years was the day his life would change. He had just finished shoveling hay into the troughs of the camels and mules. Bill Plagun loved his animals as much as his rackets. They were both gateways to the human condition. A functional zoo, complete with turnstiles, concession stands, Bill Plagun found a heavy duty washing machine for his liquor money.

Met moved on to the mountain lion den. Nothing more than a box in bars with a chute to a chasm. He clung to the remnants of a high he started hours back, but it was time for another hit. He toked his jazzer and then pinched the cherry with his bare fingers to preserve the rest. He opened the icebox and took out a set of rubber gloves and an empty plastic bag. He picked the food from the box. Chicken necks linked to their heads mixed in with the spines of rabbits. They were both plucked and skinned, so Met couldn't tell the difference. He took his sack and crossed the safety gate to the side of the den where a wall separated him from any danger. A ladder was fixed to the wall. He climbed up. When he reached the top, he opened the latch on the roof and tossed the whole bag in. It puked its contents all over the dirt. Lions lied in wait. The bloated clouds decided it was time to spit out some of their own ingestion. Just a few sprays to start, but this was just a sample. Met stepped back down and continued on to the other meat eaters. The crocs gave him jitters. They lurked in black liquid like loch fiends. Met couldn't see them coming, even though he was high above and out of reach. Soon the sky opened up with a heavy barrage of white noise and liquid hollow points.

Met's final stop was the chimp cage at the center of the zoo. The water drops danced off his hat and coat, his ice box. His shoes ladled mud. The tea he had smoked was now bringing him to peak, so the rain did nothing to stall his mood if not mystify the experience. He caught the sudden urge to whistle. It was one of his favorite tunes by the famed Dib Minty: *Someday Never Came*. It was like blowing out the candles to a cake smeared on his face. He spit water when he thought he was harmonizing. Met didn't care. To him, it was pure, a senseless escape in a dead-end existence while he rolled his casket of necks to the malodorous chimps. At this hour, they were dead silent. A single lamp post opened an eye to their enclosure. Dive bombers pelted the new puddles with reinforcements. It was another boxed cage as tall as three men. Pigeon holes poked the back wall about twenty feet from the face of the cage. Single occupancy only. Met counted ten holes, but not one of their residents seemed available. Maybe they were all on vacation. Maybe they needed some reefer in the pitchfork rain. He filled up another bag of fowl and bunny and tossed it down through the roof hatch. Half of it splattered all over the mud, the other half clattered over a large tin saucer. Thoughts of pole sitting entered his mind. He had never attempted it, but now felt just as stupid as the ones who would balance on high, days on end, in weather just like this, for the chance at a Saxon two-wheel. He started back down until a sudden vertigo jammed him up. His right hand slipped, but his left kept him stuck to the rung. The lower half of his lungs forgot how to breathe. He pressed his face against the ladder and shut his eyes. The water dribbled all over him. He was only fifteen feet up.

"Egg, what the fuck are you doing?" Jesse yelled. He stood right below Met under a large black umbrella.

Met snapped out of his funk and glanced down. "Taking a bath."

"Let's go."

Met climbed down. "What are you doing here?"

"Come to pick you up. Put that away. We're out back. Don't keep us waiting." Jesse started off. His gait was aggressive.

Met's eyes stayed on Jesse until he disappeared in a sheet of water. He stood with his thoughts and then shoved the cooler back to the storage room. It was right next to the warehouse. He entered and took in a breath of dry air. The frigid water continued to drip off his chin and hat. At least it washed out the sweat from his eyes. There were two large walk-in freezers to his right. He pulled the door open to the first and rolled the cooler in. The door sprang shut by itself. He shed his gloves and threw them to the ground. Next to the freezers a spigot grew out of the wall over the floor. He felt the need to rinse off the prior rinse. He leaned over and washed his hands and face. Then took a half fist over his hair and twisted the faucet shut. He turned out the light and headed for the back entrance and a third rinse.

A Triumph 15 Saloon purred at the gate. Behind it were two Divco milk trucks. Met picked up his pace. Buddy was seated behind the wheel of the Triumph with an unlit cigar in between his lips. Jesse was in the back seat. Met got in on the passenger side and brought his wet duds with him.

Buddy yanked the cigar from his mouth when he saw the puddles forming on his seat and footwell. "What the fuck is this?"

"Sorry," Met said. He kept the door ajar just in case Buddy wanted to kick him out.

"You're wetting the whole fuckin' car!"

"What am I supposed to do? It's raining out there." Met tried to wipe the water off his clothes, but it just made more of a mess.

"What are you doing, you dumb idiot?"

"Trying to dry off. You want I should get out?" Met asked with a foot leaning east of the door frame and a town-full of raindrops infiltrating the footwell.

"Shut the fuckin' door!" Buddy barked.

"In or out?" Met asked. He was as confused as he was petrified. Buddy was not a man he ever dared upset.

"Stay there and close the car! Are you stupid or what?" Buddy responded. Then he called back to Jesse. "Is there a fuckin' rag back there? Look at this shit."

Jesse couldn't produce one.

"Tomorrow you detail this car with your tongue," Buddy told Met. He kicked his sole against the pedal and pushed the gearstick towards the dash. The back wheels spit up soup and rolled off in a fury. The trucks followed suit.

"Where we going?" Met asked.

"You been puffin', haven't you?" Buddy responded with his own question.

"A little."

Jesse reached his arm over Met's collar and let it wrap around his chest. In his hand was a PPK. He let it drop on Met's lap. Met wrapped a wet hand around the heater. He popped the clip. It was loaded.

"A hit?" Met asked.

Jesse didn't say a word. Buddy shut his mouth around his cigar and kept driving. The trucks brought up the rear. They crossed Breaks Bridge into Lower Good Leaf. The rain was chucked down like spears from a squadron of hysterical cherubim warding off the skyward flames of hell.

Back at the zoo, the sky held back its tears. A cricket, mounted with a lion's courage, danced through the cemented marsh and under a lamppost. It made a big shadow, like a monster that should belong in a cage. It stretched a leg out and dusted the wet lint off the other. Then it chirped, alone just to see if it still could in this cold, wet air. Stillness resumed. Out of nowhere a voice as faint as yesterday whispered the same Dib Minty number Met attempted to whistle. But through the lingering rain, it was barely within the cricket's earshot. That didn't stop the hopper from satisfying its curiosity. It stared out to nothing in particular. A throat cleared itself clean, and the voice grew from a whisper to a tone. Through the filter of water in the air, the tone intensified until it drowned out any silence. The cricket scratched its head by the jiggling white foam of the storm drain. *"Someday may come tomorrow. Someday may come today. But someday for me was someday that never came."* The tin saucer was heard crashing against the cage bars with a violent bang. The voice died instantly. The startled cricket retreated to the last dry crack in the walkway until it flooded over with another shower.

- 9 -

Salty Well was getting pummeled from above. He footslogged back to his booth rubbing his thumb and forefinger on a roll of wet tens. It was for a job well done. The workers had cleared out and left their machines to rest. They wouldn't be back. Salty was about to do the same when he spotted a set of car lamps cutting the water. And then two sets right behind the first. All were approaching the boom gate. He wasn't expecting anymore traffic. He looked for cop markings on the vehicles. A sedan trailed by two fully enclosed trucks with no decals. He took a quick step into his booth and pulled the metal handle on the filing drawer on top of the small rusty table. Then he stuffed the cash in and took a pistol out. He met the car at the barrier. The men within eyeshot were perfect strangers and not anyone Salty would have over for dinner.

"Dead end, fellas," Salty yelled through the rain to the passenger in the sedan. It was Met. He flashed his gun at Salty's heart. Salty kept his piece by his side. He knew he wouldn't be fast enough to meet the barrel that was itching to greet him.

"Open it," Met said.

"Alright," Salty said in the middle of a suspended breath. The water running off his face was like blood. He treaded in reverse, always an eye on Met's burner. Salty picked up his pace. Jesse popped his back door open and spit bullets from his submachine gun all over Salty's chest. Salty splashed against the ground and retired with two exhales.

"You open it," Buddy told Met without paying a dime to the dead gink in the mud.

Met swung the car door open and threw a nervous eye back to Jesse who appeared to be gloating over his kill and craving seconds. The boom went up. Buddy drove through and Met hopped on a running board to avoid being left behind. They coasted around the bend on the right. Met crouched down as they took the corner. The three vehicles continued along the path until they were surrounded by large buildings and the fenced parking lot. It was empty.

Buddy stayed in the driver seat listening to the windshield wipers swooshing back and forth. His eyes traced the brick walls on each warehouse for the least obvious spot, but there were too many nooks and crannies, more loading docks next to more doors. Surely a place like this had back doors too. "Let's go."

Jesse and Buddy got out with choppers glued to their fists and no umbrellas. The rims on their lids created waterfalls over their faces. Met was the only one with a hand gun and no fedora to cut the rain.

The back door of the Divco trucks opened. A team of killers in Stetsons and slickers emerged. They gathered around their leader, Sert "Justice" Johnson. Age: 50. 6'2". 190 lbs. Ginger in skin but not in convictions. Green eyes. Brown hair. Nose like a brass knuckle. Mouth taut when he spoke. Shaved an enormous jaw between meals. Hard-boiled. Slept with boots on. Charged: being the best cop money can buy. Occupation: captain, Good Leaf Police, East 1st Precinct. AKA 11th Commandment. Johnson's right arm grew a sawed-off shot gun. He pointed it towards the warehouse on the eastern side of the lot. His deputies fanned the perimeter. Half went right, the other left until there were men stationed at every door.

One man flanked Johnson. His right arm supported the ambition of a full-size smoothbore. He went by "Itchy Lion," but his real name was Quick Coogan, a man of angry eyes and circumcized nostrils. His thick moustache hooked a lazy upper lip. He was "monkey see, monkey do" when it came to Johnson and one corrupt police lieutenant.

Coogan followed Johnson till they were huddled around Buddy and his crew. One glance between Buddy and Johnson acknowledged that their target was crafty. Buddy, Johnson and Coogan went east. Jesse and Met hoofed it west and hugged the perimeter wall until they met up with two deputies at a door dangling in the wet breeze. The exit was secured. Jesse moved to the door. Met lagged intentionally. Killing wasn't in his blood. Jesse pointed to Met with his eyes and fingered him to come closer. Met did as he was told. Jesse took one of the flash sticks from a clean-cut badge and handed it to Met. Then with a snap of the eye, he ordered him to break.

Met budged the door and slid his right leg inside. Then the left. It was darker than the night. The rain continued to drown out the silence. Met could hardly hear the water drops off his clothes colliding with the floor. He could hardly hear anything at all except his heart. The adrenaline drank up the booze in his blood and sobered him up instantly. He considered turning on the flashlight but feared what might show. On the other hand, standing still in the dark was like begging for a thrashing. He made an instant line of yellow with one hand. The other burst a bullet at something holding a gun. Met dropped his flashlight and plastered himself against the wall, emptying his chamber in the process. Jesse and company blitzed the entryway, blinking hot lights from their hands. They injected lead through everybody in sight. After a full sixty seconds of drum rolls they stopped. Everyone was breathing hard.

"Get a light on," whispered Met.

It was time to toll up the bodies. Jesse lit up the victims. A collection of mannequins, arms and legs torn from torsos, plaster heads sprinkled to sawdust.

"I swear they were moving," Met continued.

"You fuckin' junkie." Jesse had an idea to slap Met until he bled. Instead, he tossed him a reload and bossed the two deputies outside. Met switched out clips while Jesse trampled over the mess of splinters to the opposite end of the room. There was another door. Jesse's movements were hasty. He elbowed the door open and jerked his flashlight and Tommy in both directions. There was nothing in the vicinity worth wasting a bullet on. He summoned Met with a convulsive arm.

Jesse waved the flashlight from ten to two every few dripping steps. Met remained a long pace back. They continued down the corridor until they found a room much like an office. Jesse tapped the light switch just to see if someone had forgotten to cut off the power. Met raised his gun at the figure behind the desk. It was another dummy. "No," Jesse said. "We'll be lucky if they aren't in Jester by now because of you."

Who? Met asked in his mind. He had some idea.

Jesse skimmed the room and then shut the light off. He kept the flashlight on the mannequin. Then he pointed it to the phone and picked up. A switch operator on the other line asked what city just before Jesse killed the call.

They kept moving, this time through a set of double swing doors, from one large room of cluttered industrials to another. They passed a mess hall with a long metal table. There were no chairs. A couple of empty plates with scabs of mayo. They moved on and came to the workers' washroom. Jesse heard soft music on the other side of the door. He kicked the door in and sprayed a whip of lead into the black space before he flashed his lamp on the damage. An empty couch with fabric dust floating all around it. Met followed the light in with his gun at ninety degrees. The Raveer continued its sweet noise until it exploded under the barrel of Jesse's chopper. A blink in the stalls confirmed that they had missed here too.

They hustled out and kept moving through the corridor, the large room of scarecrows until they found a freight elevator. Jesse yanked the hoistway open and hooked Met in. Then he pressed the bottom button. No response. He tried the top. Nothing. Then the middle. The elevator shifted under their feet and sunk until it clanked to a halt. Jesse pointed his flashlight and machine gun where the fire doors met. He cut his chin through the air. Met got the signal and steadied his trigger finger. Then he pulled the doors apart.

- 10 -

Buddy blinded Met with his flashlight.

"Muggles went nuts on a dummy. Probably sent them scattering out back," Jesse said. Met held a hand up to block the light.

"They dusted out before we got here," Buddy said as he turned his back to Jesse and Met and continued into the gig bag room. The bulb was still on. The lock on the door before the theater curtains bore a kiss from a .45 auto. The door was hanging by a hinge. Buddy led his boys through. The scrim was cut down. Johnson stood on the wooden bandstand looking out to the empty hall. Satin drapes were scattered all over the floor. The ceiling and walls were peeling. What was once the bar was now broken in five pieces, each section folded over the next. There were no bottles, no tables or chairs, no cute lamps setting the mood, no pretty dames or High Legs or Cats 6. Just the dim light from the gig bag room, their Rayobeams and poor timing. A drift in the air of Belodgia Caron, cigarette smoke and scotch was all the evidence they needed.

"They had a line on us," Jesse blurted. He shot a live round at the ceiling.

"Had to come from the inside," Johnson said.

Johnson and Coogan started for the elevator. Buddy paced the hall as though his delayed hunt would yield fruit.

"It was that fuckin' shyster. I just know it," said Jesse.

Buddy, Jesse and Met found their way to the backside of the warehouse. The rain was demoted to a drizzle. It flew from east to west and snaked back without warning. Buddy and Jesse looked out to the river. The bows of the ghost ships glistened from fresh coats of wash.

Met minced back from the dock. "Nothing," he said.

Buddy and Jesse stood close enough to one another to make Met feel blocked in.

"Can someone tell me what we're doing out here?" Met continued.

Buddy windmilled the butt of his machine gun into Met's jaw. He buckled over with a splash, holding to his face like it had come apart.

"That's right, crawl like the dirty worm you are," Jesse said.

"Where'd he go?" Buddy asked.

"What the fuck are you talking about?" Met cried out.

"Let's chop him down." Jesse was jumpy to let a round off in Met's face.

"Don't go simpleton," Buddy said.

"I swear to God!" Met hollered.

"We don't need him. Come on, Mighty. Smash that roach," said Jesse.

"Would you put that thing away!" yelled Met at the sight of his impending cause of death.

"Why'd you do it?" Buddy asked.

"I'm gonna blow up this pigeon right now," Jesse said.

"Look, whatever that mutt told you, it ain't true. I swear on my mother. I didn't rat, I didn't tip anyone. I don't even know what the fuck we're doing here. Will you point that thing somewhere else?" Met pleaded.

Buddy set a hand on the barrel of Jesse's gun and eased it off its target. "We're just kidding with you, Egg Meat."

"You're busting my balls?"

"Get up, man. Who's gonna feed my animals if we dust you?"

Met's eyes shifted from Buddy to Jesse. He inched to his knees and feared making another step without permission. Buddy turned and left. Jesse marched to Met.

"Give me the rod," Jesse ordered.

"What?" Met had entered a state of delirium.

Jesse connected his heel with Met's ribs. He shoved his hands all over Met's coat until he felt the gun inside his side pocket and yanked it off him. Jesse left.

Met stayed on the ground, finally able to appreciate the pain that was forming around his jaw. He stuck a finger in his mouth to check for broken teeth. Just a couple of molars. Letting his head rest against the wet dock, Met shut his eyes, but that only made the ground under him gyrate. He got to his knees and wrapped an arm across his ribs while his legs pushed him upright. Looking in all directions for someone to yell at, he vomited his guts instead. Being offed wouldn't have felt as bad.

- 11 -

Getting a tri-wheel pushcart in and out of a tenement house brought its own challenges, but taking it up two flights of stairs to the third story was a brutal undertaking for any little lady, except she was no little lady. Sue "Rue" Sandloer. Age 34. A nickel and change above the ground. Lean and fit in her woolen slacks suit the color of pine needles and just about as rough. A thin black tie linked her shirt collar shut. Soft gray coat to her waist. A messy mane of flames brought to a low chignon was smothered under a wool cap. Never bothered to tear at her tresses like those normal gals did. Her spirited eyes hid many a wound, but she was no gusher. In fact, despite her raw beauty, she was rather mannish. Her lips in a stagnant state of thought. Charged: operating a blind tiger out of her Sunks District crib, Lower Leaf. Occupation: ladylegger, moll. AKA Little Man.

Sue left her *Dreamy Ice Creamy* cart at the base of the steps and opened the hatch to pull out a fresh case of Chingonwood single malt. It was none of that cheap Overheat one could pick up at Roth's Pharmacy and Drugstore down on the corner. She curled it like a barbell and marched up the steps without a single regard for the time or the pounding of her heels. It was two hours past midnight. At the third floor, she hooked around the railing and hustled to the apartment at the end of the hall. She backed into the chafed wooden door and stamped at it like a mule. Three times hard. The door opened.

"Had to detour. You know how it is when kids are chasing you around the block screaming for a Dreamy, especially at this hour. If you weren't so much of a geezer, maybe you could help." Sue plopped the case over to her super and took out a couple of bottles to lighten his load.

Kent "Rent" Quiler was old but on the up and up. He considered himself a moderate drinker. Two fingers. Ten rounds. A hard squiggle of coarse white hair on his lip. Another cracked wire on his head. Thorn bushes matted his graying eyes. He wore suspenders under his thick brown coat and a pair of trousers that fell off his waist, even with the shoulder straps clipped to his belt. The cold was his only enemy. He lived on the ground floor but did the town on the third.

"Don't make me grow your rent," Quiler said.

"You'd be so crass." Sue passed a modest room. There were two single mattresses made of more lumps than springs. One on each side. The beds were covered in gray fire blankets. A couple of lamp stands next to each. The walls exuded tobacco smoke. The rest of the place smelled like the oily head of an old man, or maybe that was just Mr. Quiler. There was another door on the far end of the living room. It was sealed shut and harbored a few secrets. Friendly voices could be heard on the blind side. Sue opened the door to what should have been a bedroom. Instead it was a bar. A long table along the back wall. Behind it, Sue's three-legged stool. A green leather couch and four blue linter felt arm chairs made for a tight fit, but that's all Sue needed to keep in business. There were four guests waiting for refills. One of them was a skinny man with a git box on his lap. He worked at the corner laundry where Sue sent the wash once a month. He only knew three songs, each composed of three different notes. Tonight he played the most detailed of the three for a young couple that just moved in from Ace Ward. Their baby slept inside a wicker basket on the edge of the green leather. The other man was a portly cab driver who would make the rounds every night just in time for last call. Sue twisted the top until the seal broke and spun it off the bottle. She slid behind the table and started pouring what everyone, save for the baby, came for.

Met appeared at the door like a wet housecat. His face was blackening from his chin to his ear. He kept a hand on his ribs. Sue's eyes greeted him with routine apathy.

"The life of the party," Quiler said.

"Can I talk to you?" Met's voice cracked.

"I'm in the middle of a shift," Sue answered as she poured a glass for the cabbie.

"You wrap your face around a truck grill?" Quiler asked like Met was actually acknowledging his presence, but Met kept his eyes on Sue.

"It's important," he said.

"When isn't it?"

Sue's eyes made contact with Met's once more. This time she noticed the purple blemishing the side of his face. Met retreated back into the living room.

"Mr. Quiler, man the bar a second, will ya?"

"It'll cost you another two fingers," Quiler said.

"Help yourself," said Sue. She slipped past her customers and into the living room.

"Can you get rid of them tonight?" Met whispered from one of the beds. His head was buried in his lap.

"That all depends."

Met nodded. He reached into his coat and handed her his keep. Twenty bucks for a whole month of crime. "Everything that's mine is yours."

"What's the proper word for these assholes 'cause I don't wanna offend no one." Sue spit out a chuckle and started back to the bedroom. "You should get some ice on that. Come on, I'll pour you a drink."

Met found a jolt of strength and pushed off the bed to yank at her hand. Her skin was rough as sandpaper. It was one of the things he loved about her. She was battletested and his only source of security. She went about-face more of her own will than Met's. Her hat slid off her messy head. She shifted it back in place.

"This is all you have to say for an entire month?" Sue asked as she waved the two bills in Met's face. "Met, you get me so evil sometimes."

"Give 'em the brush," he demanded.

"Why don't you give yourself the brush?" Sue left Met by himself and closed the bedroom door. He plopped on the edge of the bed and lit up what remained of his joint. He fit his lips around the end, careful to keep his jaw from moving, and sipped himself away. The voices in the other room had him thinking of all the parties he never enjoyed. He just seemed better alone, but even alone needed company every once in a while.

Fifteen minutes passed. The bedroom door was reopened. All four guests staggered out without a care in the world and without mention of the stink left behind from Met's reefer. Only the baby in the basket didn't seem to care for it. Its stentorian cry stabbed Met's eardrums. He turned to the basket under the man's arm and thought the kid deserved a better start than that. The father and his basket vanished around the corner and soon the baby's cries were nothing more than echoes.

"A couple skees, your face will be brand new. At least you'll know it's there," Quiler said as he passed Met by.

Sue met Quiler at the front door and transferred twenty bucks.

"The walls gotta sleep sometime," Quiler said. "Mind yourself," were his last words before he sauntered back down to his first floor. Sue closed up shop.

"Did you eat? I can fix up a sandwich," Sue said.

"Not hungry," Met said.

"Need some more mootah?" Sue asked. Met shook his head a faint once right, once left. Sue stood by the other bed. Her eyes grew tired. "You gonna tell me what happened?"

"I shot a dummy," Met said.

A built-up sigh escaped Sue, followed by one of her famous faces that only seemed to form when in the presence of Met.

"Why the face?" he asked.

"What face?"

"That face. The one that's filled with disgust, like you hate my guts and wish I was dead."

"I don't recall making that face. Not once. Maybe you're imagining things."

"I ain't imagining nothin'."

"How long are you gonna keep this up? Tell me," Sue said.

"What's with the third degree? You want me to leave for good?" Met asked. "I'll do it if that's what you want."

"You think saying that changes anything? You need to get out of those wet rags."

"Just let me lie here. Give me an hour. Then I'll go, okay? You don't need this shit anymore," Met said. Sue started for the kitchen without a word of notice. She knew when Met was out of his mind and into another. Met kept moving words from his mouth like his audience was still there. "I know who they were after." Met heard Sue scrambling through a drawer. The sound of silverware clattering, a plate clashing against the counter. "You hear what I say?" The sound of an icebox opening, the crumpling of paper, the kind used to wrap bread, an opened package of bologna, a squirt of mustard. Met squinted his eyes shut. The right side of his face ached. The corner of his upper lip gave a throbbing salute.

"So? What does that have to do with us?" Sue reappeared at the door.

"I'm in the business, Sue," Met said.

"That do anything for you? Look at this place. Look where we live. You think we make it through the month on your chicken feed? I mean you blow through that door like you've kissed a hurricane, toss me a couple of pin bucks and then tell me everything you have is mine? I may not have finished grade school, but I know what half of nothing is."

"The sun's gonna shine on us when you quit ritzing me." Met's desultory weather forecast did as much as the sawbucks he handed Sue.

"Same cold soup you've been feeding me for years. This ain't working no more, don't you get it? I'm tired of feeling like a fly in a jar. You think I like lugging a pushcart around in the middle of the night while you're out on dummy hits?"

"The sun's gonna shine." The chorus lost momentum.

"You're a walking stiff with a first-class ticket to the morgue."

"You're one to talk. How much did you pocket from your rabble tonight?"

"More than you and your big business!" Sue lassoed back her tongue just as it started to buck wild. She refused to lace up the gloves and get in the ring. "Listen, you can stay the night. I don't want you here by morning."

Met held his thoughts on the ledge. "You're all I've got," he said gazing to the window.

"For once I wish you'd act like it was true."

Met surged off the bed as though he were being drowned. He avoided eye contact and shot for the front door. Sue watched the door bang shut behind him. She counted a long second. Then walked over, turned the deadbolt and fastened the chain. Her eyes were plagued with remorse, whether for Met or herself, she did not know.

- 12 -

The Cats 6 made it a habit to meet at Gumbie's place after each show. Sometimes they'd have the High Legs over. It was all plutonic; no sex. Holly was the only one who rarely went. She enjoyed sleeping too much. But Claudette Calor and Rita Glass could go till sunup in those deep lounge chairs, especially when they were on the dust. Tonight neither had much to say, but they were all ears. The course of this discussion would change someone's outcome.

Gumbie shared a crib with Sas Parila and Clyde Davis. They lived in the northernmost edge of the Leaf where rates hovered around three bucks a week. But there were other costs in throwing jam sessions till dawn. For starters, the three a week was raised to six. To dress up their digs only meant higher rents. To downgrade meant heading to the sticks or back to a flophouse. They would oftentimes go till five in the morning. It was their private club away from the many spots they had known under Pap Fanti. They set up three metal framed beds like sofas inside the only room. If they needed a john, they had to head down the hall. Same with washing up. The place didn't even flaunt a closet. The trio hung their clothes on the window latches, the inside of the front door and over the metal backing of their beds. Their instruments were their only assets. The neighbors could file a grievance listening to bass and treble at all hours of the night, but the Cats made sure to water down the offense with a payoff of a couple clams a week. No one complained. It was a trick they learned from Cap'n Pap. When someone wanted to make a beef, offer them the frying pan and light the gas for them. In short, paying their bills killed their ills. The jams were always held at Gumbie's because he had the Hintz, and no one lugged a piano around town except Pap's club. Everyone agreed. There was plenty of round-the-clock traffic outside to muffle their music, so with the windows opened, they would throw caution to the wind, light up their jujus and bounce the room. Tonight though, they toned down their instrumentals and focused on the lyrics.

"All this scattin' around like gypsies," Tots said over a conga drum. He tapped it gently with the balls of his hands. A gasper hung off his southern lip. Tots started with a hammer and nail before he picked up a drum and stick. The pay was about the same, so the choice was easy.

"We headin' back to the ol' days, dig? I sees it in the Cap'n's eyes. Like he's packin' us up 'fore we empty the trucks," Beans Fryer said. He patted his bass fiddle with a slow draw. Beans and Tots were cousins, each from a large family. Before meeting Pap, they enjoyed putting on small shows during weekend BBQs and counting on their large families to eek by until they found their break. They met Pap at the City Hall subway station years ago while playing around an old hat. Pap gave them their break. It was small, but it felt like the world to them and, in return, they pledged their loyalty. "All fo' what? The busboy?"

"Ain't he worth the sweat?" Pisto Leroy asked. His belly-fiddle was still in its case. He was smoking a nico. Leroy was the newest of the Cats. He joined them a couple years ago after the club had started to pick up a decent following. Gumbie had vouched for him only because Leroy had backed him up a couple of times in street fights when they were teens. He figured this to be the best reason to vouch for someone. They spent a lot of time on busy streets and fights were common where money was scarce. Leroy was always quick to share his passions, dreams of recording for Neato Records, that kind of thing. The others thought him a cocky son-of-a-bitch, but he showed no incompetence when it came to the strings.

"Not for what he's shellin' out. You know Cap'n's in the money. I say we get a raise before anymore talk of hoppin'," Gumbie said. He was the only one of the Cats who attended music school. Only he never finished after learning that his mother was dying of an unknown disease. At her funeral, he played a requiem all his own. Pap was there to pay his respects. He had enjoyed eating at her small diner in North Leaf and even became a friend. Her fried chicken was some of the best around. When Pap heard Gumbie at the funeral, he knew he had to have him too. Gumbie was tinkering with a new melody on his piano, but his pinky kept getting stuck on the same G minor.

"And here I's thinkin' you cats had his back no matter what," Pisto said. The others looked at him like they had committed a mortal sin. All except Charmin who sat on the floor in the corner of the room. No expression on his face. He appeared distant. A pair of shades doused his eyes. The juju was buzzing his brain.

"You tell us what he's worth to ya, Joe Below," Beans said.

"I know I don't rat him out for a pair of jacks and that's damn straight on the level," Pisto Leroy responded. He was starting to lose his cool.

"I'm with Leroy," Claudette said. "No one gives up the kid for any price."

"That's my vote too," Rita said.

"What you gotta say 'bout it?" Tots asked Gumbie.

"Some things are hard to swallow. Leroy's right. A rat sinks the whole ship. You know I'd hit the sticks for the kid," Gumbie responded.

"What about you? You ain't spit a word all night," Tots looked to Charmin.

"We're all here. Just talking, chum-like, right? Anyone ever run it through their mind?" Charmin asked. He was the most reclusive of the Cats. Many nights he would skip out just like Holly. He boarded with an aunt who never got into his business. So long as he helped her with the bills, she didn't care what he did. She was already upset to have to take in her dope-swilling sister's son. But Charmin never gave her any lip or trouble. He liked his reefer and his popsicle stick. Only reefer wasn't free.

"Run what?" Beans asked.

Charmin took another drag from his jazz branch. "Come on. You know. The kid's worth a ton of dough. Pap grows an extra set of eyes in the back of his head just to watch him leave a room."

"He's right, you know. Worth a lot more than any of us could scratch, even if we gigged two years at The Spoon." Sas shared the same sentiment. Then he blew a wicked melody from his licorice stick to finish his message. "That's what they pay for, and they'd dish out tops for him." Sas pretended to blow in any direction, but it was all an act. He didn't have the courage to follow through on anything he said, except to play clarinet with the Cats. All he wanted, like the rest of them, was stability. The very thing that was crumbling before their eyes.

"You kidding me? What's the matter with you?" Pisto protested.

"Don't blow your top. I mean how long you think we can keep this thing under wraps? You don't think the members talk? I bet even Dino Glass, no disrespect," Charmin looked to Rita as he said it and continued, "Turnip Faymus, Ink Tambo, they probably all let it fly when they're sauced. The High Legs with their brains below the belt? You know you wanted to wash this in the papers ever since you laid eyes on him."

"This coming from a man who claims trees are his ancestors," Claudette scowled at Charmin. "Just 'cause you smoke them all day, honey, doesn't mean you are one." The rest laughed.

"That's real swell coming from a speed demon like you," Charmin snapped.

"Save the jokes, kids. Charmin gotta point. This is getting a little too hot to handle," Sas said.

"So you'd sell him out for a couple of C's?" Pisto asked. "After everything he's done for us? Ain't none of you got no heart? This is your brother you're talking about."

"He can't do much more than get us all nailed," Charmin said. He seemed to have assumed the lead on this conversation and his arguments made the most sense.

"I pray to the Lord to never turn my back on any of yous," Pisto said.

"Relax, Jack. We're just chewing the fat," Sas said.

"And what happens to him when the secret's out? I mean, I ain't down with getting him hurt, no matter how much they pay," Beans said.

"What else? Bright lights, picture shows, you name it. We split the finder's loot. Even kick some to Pap. He's a shoo-in for the easy life. Not this hiding in gutters like he was scum, like some sort of vampire. All of you know we can't keep him locked up forever. Times are changing. When would we ever feel comfortable putting on a show in front of seventy-five loud mouths?"

Beans came to his senses. "He right. If we don't do it, someone will. And that leaves us with jack squat in our pockets." The others nodded and made yes sounds. All except Pisto and Claudette.

"You're serious," Pisto said. His contemptuous eyes studied the others. He couldn't believe what his band mates were coming to.

Charmin let out a lazy laugh. "We're only pulling your chain, man. I mean who could we trust with something like this without getting gypped? The bulls would just tear him apart and leave us to rot."

"I know someone who'd pay whatever we ask," Clyde Davis said. They were his first words all night. His tram rested on his lap. His hand wrapped around a jug of hooch. He was the inveterate drunk of the group. He boozed before, during and after the shows. Claimed it kept him calm through the chaos. Only problem was that after each show he needed hibernation for a couple of days straight before he could go again. He met Pap through Beans Fryer, said he was doing vaudeville shows in West Leaf but needed something with more meaning.

"Yeah, who?" Beans asked.

"The man on Strobile Island," Clyde Davis said.

"Fuck you guys," Pisto said. He jumped to his feet and grabbed his guitar case.

"Hey, Leroy. Chill the yapper," Beans warned. "You can't stop what's goin' down."

Pisto Leroy curled up his cheeks in antipathy and started for the door.

"Wait up. I'll bounce with you," Sas said. They both left. The others went back to their jam session.

Sas and Pisto walked down the sidewalk. Even at this hour, there were alley cats who couldn't find a bed to sleep in, so they guarded their words with care.

"Don't worry about all that bushwa in there. They went down this same road years ago. Nuttin' came of it. Every now and again, they just have to get it off their chests or it makes them sick. You can dig that."

"I hope you're right. Life's gotta be more than a meal ticket," Pisto said.

- 13 -

Despite street names like Gem, Joy and Eden, Matanza Heights was the roughest borough in Good Leaf. Unfamiliar eyes never crossed. But for Holly Fountain, it was home, and when her tears didn't get in the way, she was proud of it. Long removed were her days from Bumpy's Burlesque, located smack in the heart of Flame District and across the street from Junior Plagun's Champion Club. The main part of her act was to sneak shady men to a dressing room, share a needle and get poked. It's where she once lived too, in the connecting apartment that belonged to her stage pimp, Bumpy Sarna. It's also where she met Pap Fanti. Pap relished her purer talents and believed she could pave a smoother road if she only got a chance. That meant no more needles, no more scurrilous sex jobs. Holly felt at home at Club Polar or whatever they were going to call it next. She took the news of the move to Calloway with bells on. Twenties Slip was about fifteen miles closer. That meant fewer chances at getting mugged in a midnight worm hole or raped in the back seat of a prowler's cab...again. But tonight, things were going to change, this time for the better. Her parents were dancers with a local theater troupe. They died in a train accident when she was just starting puberty. They had encouraged her to dream big, and maybe, with a little luck, she would one day be a celebrated star of stage and screen like Lala Terre. The charge of ensuring she stay out of trouble fell on her half brother,

Hendrick Fountain. He owned Heal Fast Pharmacy on 6th and Lake and was a part-time pastor at The Samaritan. Between the blind alleys and the backtalk, Holly soon became his least favorite person. He'd burn her ear with fire and brimstone every time they shared a line. Always pushed her to get a real job like that of a secretary at a bank, marry an honest man, a professional. His words were spoonfuls of Ipecac syrup, and she'd never hesitate to retch her dissent back in his face. One of these days she'd stuff his ear with a dose of: "Drop dead. I made it."

Tonight she slept like she hadn't in years. Her platinum locks made a pillow. Next to her was the imprint of another head on the other pillow, but the head was missing. So was the body. It was standing over the washstand in the next room. It was Chase Griggs.

He tucked his shirt back into his pants and erased his guilty face in the murky mirror. His five o' clock shadow was half past eight. But that did nothing for the red dime forming on his neck. A top button would conceal the evidence. He took out a business card and his Blanco Fine and found an inch of space among a dozen bottles of cheap perfume and prescription medications. He wrote a note on the back. "Next time I get a name. Mine's on the other side. See you at the club." Then he reached for one of the bottles. 4712 Eau de Cologne. He brought it to his nose for a sniff. Smelled like Holly. She did a lavish job of dabbing it in the most subtle of places. He passed on raised heels from the bathroom and slipped the card under the pillow. A gun discharged down the street. There had been at least three shots that night—a common occurrence among drug dealers and bootleggers in Matanza Heights—but Holly wouldn't budge from her sleep. She basked under a ceiling of painted palm trees that shimmied in the breeze of a new romance. Chase stared at the resting portrait of her face, the envy of the dead, hidden within a wreath of living sunflowers. He had fulfilled half the purpose of every red-blooded man: to sleep with a beautiful woman twice. The first was always for the exhilaration. The second would be to quell doubts of the first. There was an itch on his left wrist. He scratched it with his eye. His Grand Curvex read 3:30 am. Late even for him.

He floated into a living room that looked like it did the tarantella with a twister. Everything screamed rose-red. Lingerie and sparkly dresses poured sidewalks all over a chess board of black and white linoleum. Heels scattered about like miniature park slides. A couple of boxes of spicy egg noodles and pepper chicken with dumplings from Weeng Kee's mixed in with a dress or two. A rack filled with stacks of old magazines, Redbook, Candy Apple, Neopolitan. The needle on the Handley Osco spun against the edge of the record like a stalled hiccup. Chase left it spinning.

"4 Waterfall" were the only words Chase managed the whole cab ride home. He needed to iron out his story and practice his juggling. He was at the club. Check. There was something he'd never seen before. Check. He fell in love with another woman. Check. He shook his brain and lit a smoke. He was dozing off before he could alibi himself off the hook. Then again, alibi for what? He considered his pal, Jackson Reese, who went nowhere without giggly arm wraps. Like he told Chase many times, the wedding vows were meant more for the woman—even the priest that married Jackson had a couple of lady friends and priests were next to God, so what could be so wrong about tonight? Chase was a cat coughing up a hairball. Holly. Each trail of smoke was made to look like her, especially those pins in heels. His mouth went wet. *Straighten up, Griggs.* Passing buildings freckled in yellow appeared to close in on him. His timepiece showcased ten past four in roaring fashion. That was it. He'd talk about the wailing trumpeter. How he made him faint. By the time he came around, he was at Good Leaf General for a needle of Secotal. What was he saying? She wouldn't buy that bread if it was free. Maybe she'd just be asleep instead, and the new sun would burn away any traces of sin.

- 14 -

4 Waterfall took up an entire brownstone block on the rich side
of Good Leaf. It was the largest home in sight but that did little
to diminish the connecting castles. The cab was parked with its
idle engine clacking like a money counter. It was the only
sound within earshot. Chase remained in the back seat. He was
stalling and knew it. He looked to the house, the two lampposts
on either side of the entry. They stared back at him like the fiery
eyes of hell's gateway. In fact, it was the first time he had seen
those lamps at that hour. He paid the cabbie and tucked the door
in. He wished for the gusts of cars on Holly's street to filter his
movements—even the gunshots would have helped—but for
blocks around, it was a Sunday library and dark as chocolate. A
golden square on the corner interrupted the pattern. It was a
bedroom light. Vilma's. She was an expert in insomnia and
regularly required three martinis and a Valilow 20 mg to close
an eye. Chase brushed the lapels of his coat like they carried
cooties and started up the steps to a front opening of two
sculpted doors. He imagined Vilma on the other side practicing
her marksmanship with a flamethrower. He wouldn't see it
coming through the one-way pane. He inserted the key and
rotated the door knob like he was diffusing a bomb. Then he
passed through another door and into the foyer. Corinthian
columns held three walls together. Burrowed in the middle of
each, petite owls of glazed glass gave off warm light too weak

to show a living room that seemed to go on forever. A chandelier the size of a flying saucer hovered under a dark ceiling. Suddenly, Chase didn't feel secure standing beneath it. He passed swiftly to the spiral staircase and put his leg down on the first step without committing the full weight of his body behind it. Then the next step until he was at the second floor.

He glanced to his right around the curve in the long hall. The light he swore was on moment's ago was now off. He turned to his left and continued cat legs past another two long rooms. The sound of a door tapping its frame and Chase was inside his dormitory. He swore it was the only reason his marriage had lasted as long. But such processes, like growing crops, took time. As newlyweds, Chase and Vilma indulged in a one-bed life. They even faced each other. But soon the novelty had worn off like frayed undergarments, and face-to-face turned head-to-foot turned separate beds turned separate rooms. They were, however, still under the same roof. Chase flicked the light switch. It was a large habitat with a spread bed and wide leather chairs guarding a fire place. Tall windows with hand-carved frames and silk curtains touched a cathedral ceiling. Chase escaped into the bathroom, unknotted his tie, threw his shirt and pants into the hamper and snuck into bed without another thought. He still hadn't come up with a convincing alibi.

Morning was eager for Chase. It was a good thing he had places to be. He took a cold shower. It helped chill any memory of last night. He shaved off a fresh face and plastered his head with Tres Flores. He clapped a puddle of Zizane into his palm and spread it all over his neck and chest. The more cologne he had on him, the less Vilma would detect the markings of a rival mate. The hickey was screaming but another tight collar would shut it up. After a new suit, he was ready to impress. The question was who.

He headed down the hall and stopped to the sound of a cheerful song radiating from Vilma's quarters. He was hearing her right. She was singing. He didn't care much for it no matter that she had a voice quite lovely. It made Chase nervous, more so than when he had walked out of his room. If he strolled past her to the first floor without as much as a word, he would exacerbate the inevitable. He had to at least say good morning. He picked up his pace and tapped the door open. Vilma was standing over the baby changing table with a baby doll in a practice diaper. She placed the doll inside its Mahr Bufton which was large enough for twins, and here she didn't even have one, except for this plaything that Chase found scary as a clown in a closet. For Vilma, bringing a child into the world was condition number one to marriage. She wanted nothing more than the marvels of motherhood. Chase pitched her with curveballs that sounded like he was on board with her mandates, but he forced her to abort when a New Year's Eve accident met the egg. Years passed, and he promised that when he was done with the Easter Tower, they would bring a bundle home. The empty baby carriage was the down payment on the promise.

"What's with you?" Chase asked.

Vilma turned to Chase with great zeal. She rushed over to him and wrapped her arms around his neck. She came in for a big kiss but only managed a peck after Chase jerked his head back. "Zizane. You know it drives me crazy," Vilma said. "Make love to me right now."

Chase untied Vilma's arms from his neck and set them to her side. "You know I can't."

"Nonsense. It will only take a minute." Vilma lunged at him once more.

Chase flexed his shoulders and squeezed her grip off him. "Seriously, why the early-bird come on?"

"Maybe I'm beaking for a worm. Am I breaking any rules? You've heard why Indian warriors made love to their wives before they had their morning coffee."

"You planning for me to get hit by a street car before I get to work?"

"You got me thinking about last night," Vilma said.

"Forget it. That place was exactly how you painted it. In fact, it was so bad, I walked out when I walked in. Even mixed it up with the owner. Suffice it to say, they'll be crediting our dues, every last penny."

"I'm sorry to hear that."

"Went to the Spoon to meet up, but you weren't there. Won a couple bucks at the wheel and lost track of time."

"That's what I wanted to talk to you about. I came straight home. I didn't go to the Spoon or anywhere else. I think an apology is in order."

"Now, now." Chase went into his masquerade. The eyelids did a cloak job over his bulbs. His lips loosened like a snail.

"Let me finish," Vilma insisted. Chase's eyes swallowed a second of guilt. "You're my husband and that does come with certain rules. Last night I broke the most important one. Where you go, I follow. From now on."

Chase went from panic to vacation within the same blink. "I think it's a great idea."

"Good, now stop with the torture session and make love to your wife." Vilma tried to coil her arms around him one last time, but Chase flung his out like he was repelling crows after corn.

"I told you I can't. I have to get to the tower."

"Unless the tower sprouted legs overnight, it's not going anywhere."

"We finish up the last elevator today. Maybe I can be home early, and we can finish what we started, deal?"

"Keep me waiting too long I may just have to cheat on you."

"You sober?" Chase asked. He was starting to feel a little jingled himself.

"Don't insult me. You at least gonna have breakfast?"

"I think you've fed me enough sugar this morning." Chase turned to his trusty timer. "Let's make it dinner instead. Make a reservation at Venisons. Meet you there at eight."

"Don't welch on me."

Chase henpecked her cheek and left in one piece. Nothing to it. Vilma followed him out and stiffened at the top step. She went to his room for further investigation and found his soaked shirt, pants and jacket hanging over the shower door. There were very few reasons to wash dry-clean in a shower, but Vilma could suspect one.

- 15 -

The first thing Chase smelled when he walked into his office at the ground floor of the Easter Tower was 4712. Only hours ago he was swimming in it. The woman wearing it had her back to him in one of his office chairs, but he recognized that head of platinum waves resting on the shoulders of the red coat without once seeing the face. He could see the lower part of her left leg and a seductive foot inside a red pump. It crossed over the right and swayed like the branch of a weeping willow. His eyes punched the backs of their sockets. He glanced out to the raucous hall of secretaries at their desks transferring calls, subcontractors and blueprinters with long tubes stuffed under their arms. He couldn't form a thought to save his life and closed the door. She grew tall from the chair and cradled her body around. Neither would shoot the first word. A single bead of sweat appeared at Chase's hairline.

"It's Holly. Holly Fountain."

Chase was a board of wood and then limp as a noodle. He was in his office but out of his element. "Holly Fountain. That's a lovely name. What are you doing here?"

"I got lost on my way to heaven," Holly said. Chase swallowed for air. He didn't have a response. She cringed at the stupidity of her own line. "I'm out of line. Don't burn up. I'll go." Holly made for the door. Chase slid a roadblock in front of her. He didn't want her there, but he didn't want her to leave either.

"No, it's not that."

"Listen, I don't want you to think I'm fresh coming down here like this. I'm not one of those gold diggers. You left your card. Figured it wouldn't hurt to tell you I enjoyed whistling with you in person."

"Don't say a word. I liked it too," Chase said. When they had first arrived at Holly's place in the middle of the night, Chase was plastered and as smooth as a twelve hour shave. He had forgotten how to put the moves on a new woman, so he lied next to Holly and whistled the tune playing on the radio. His lips were an inch from hers. She did the logical thing and whistled straight back until their whistles met and created a flute. Then Holly cut the tune by planting her lips on Chase's.

"I like you." Holly started to undo her coat, top button first. "I don't know you from Adam, but I like you." When she unfastened the last button, she pulled open like a curtain. Her sunny nipples made eye contact with him like tacks through a poster. It was all the proof he needed to know she was naked. "I may be nothing more than a B-girl to a hep cat like you, but don't think for a second I won't kick you to the curb if you give me a reason."

Chase tried to blink but his eyes blew a fuse. His pupils grew plump. Other body parts copied. "I think it's better if we take a ride."

"We?"

Chase looked to his watch. It was 9:30 am. "All of the sudden I'm hungry for lunch. Do me a favor." He took the car keys from his pocket and handed them to Holly. "Meet me in the car. It's the red Lebaron around the corner. I gotta make one important call."

"You want me to cover up before I leave?"

Chase's fervent fingers moved in for a sample. That second serving of bliss was within reach. Holly stepped back and locked up the goods. "After lunch." Her 4712 stayed in the room.

The phone blared for his attention. Chase rushed to plead "not guilty." He lifted the top to the cigarette case at the same time as the receiver. His secretary blurted, "It's Mrs. Griggs."

"Tell her I'm on the tower and I'll see her for dinner," said Chase. He hung up and took another drag, then snuffed out his smoke and pulled the shades. His eyes followed Holly as she scooted a tight ass into the leather seat of his Lebaron.

When they got to Holly's place, Chase made one request and in no uncertain terms. Holly had never heard a man ask such a task. He certainly hadn't made the request last night, but then again, last night Chase couldn't have pointed to his feet if she dared him to—he was that corked. It was one of those things discussed after ten years of marriage. But what she had seen in Chase she didn't want to lose, so she let the shock of the petition roll off her tail and went straight for the washroom. She was not a dirty girl, but if this brought peace of mind to Chase, so be it. She came out of the bathroom with squeaky thighs, droplets of water kissing her navel. Her face asked for approval. Chase waved her over with two fingers and rewarded her.

An hour later, Holly rested her head on Chase's chest. She had forgotten about his request. All men had their quirks. Chase liked to keep his wares polished. What girl could frown on that? She twirled her finger through his chest hairs. They cooed to each other in her bed. A thin sheet shrouded aftertastes of salt on skin.

"You bugged I came by?" Holly asked.

"I like to keep work and pleasure in different drawers."

"Will you get in trouble?" said Holly.

"With who?" Chase asked.

"Is there more than one?"

"I'm the kind of man who looks down the ladder. That place you went to this morning. It's mine. I call the shots. Does that scare you?"

"Makes me feel secure." Holly buried her face inside Chase's chest.

"Why do you work there?" Chase asked.

"The club? I like it. It ain't Lights Street, but they treat me swell. Some people are born to the good life. The rest of us gotta scratch like dogs."

"My first spoon was made of wood."

"I can tell."

"How?" Chase asked.

"You don't take things for granted."

"Speaking of things. Was that thing real?"

"What thing?"

"You know. The Gabriel on the trumpet."

"What do you think?"

"I think they slip Mickey's in the drinks. I think I want to make love to you again." Chase noticed sadness pulling at Holly's eyes. "Why the funeral?"

"Nothing."

"Spill it."

"I don't know what a passing mark is anymore."

"Who cares as long as we both flunk together. I'll redo a grade with you anytime."

Holly met the trepidation in Chase's eyes with her own. "I met a man once. He was a gentleman. Treated me good. Took me to the classy joints, bought me things, you know. Even helped me out when I was hard on my luck, paid a couple months of rent, that kinda thing. I never even kissed him. I was taught that being a lady meant not giving anything away for free. This went on for a little while. He was patient. You know, a gentleman. Then he upped and disappeared. No promises. Never even asked. I never forgave myself. I didn't want to go through that again. I'm not chippy, and I don't skate around with every bird I meet. I want that clear."

"I could make a lot of promises to a tomato like you."

"You could lie to me and get away with it."

"Only then I would be heartless."

"You hitched?"

"Never found the right gal."

A knock was heard at the door. "Who's that?" Chase asked before the last knock. His voice went down a couple of decibels. "You got a boyfriend coming to beat me up?"

"Your guess is as good as mine." The wrap at the door was more pronounced just in case it wasn't heard the first time, and the door creaked open. Holly rolled her head off Chase. She wrapped a gown around and went out. Chase hopped off the bed and suited up. He had a sudden itch to find the fire exit. He slipped into the bathroom for a spell. A couple minutes later, Holly knocked on the bathroom door. "You in there?"

Chase opened the door. "Who was it?"

"One of my roommates, a chick from the club. We do each other favors. They owe me one. Will I see you there?"

"Like clockwork. She still outside?"

Holly shook her head 'no.' It was Claudette Calor, and she wasn't at all happy with being denied entrance. Holly had to bribe her with another Lincoln and a baggie of five B-drine tabs, AKA Nubes (methamphetamine), just to get her to take a second powder. "I promise not to stop by your office again, but I can't promise I won't get lost."

Chase grabbed his coat and a kiss and left. No one saw him go.

- 16 -

Chase and Vilma Griggs were received at the door by the maître d. Venisons was one of Vilma's favorites on East Leaf, and Chase knew it to be a direct route back to her good graces. They sat at their usual corner booth. Under candlelight, Chase noticed the vein cutting a hill down the middle of her forehead. He noticed her drooping eyes that she tried to raise up with an assortment of pencils, the small crook in her nose that was shaded crimson. He noticed the way her cheeks seemed to escape her face when she smiled. She had smiled three times since they arrived. They ordered bottles of Chablis and chilled caviar. When she ate, he noticed the tendons collaring her neck. They discussed topics from the Easter Tower to baby names. Chase veered the discussion off the latter. For every sip Vilma had, Chase downed a glass. It was by design. She needed to have a clear mind to interact with Chase tonight. She needed him ossified. An "influenced" man always divulged his hole card. Chase wasn't a goose to pour it on, but tonight he painted easygoing and paid little attention to the changes in his perception.

"Do you think I'm fat?" Vilma asked.

Chase lit a toba and had another swig of wine, then cupped Vilma's hand in the most businesslike manner. "Why would you ask such a question when you know the answer?"

And that was the problem. How could she know the answer to a question that Chase refused to answer himself? All she could remember was the increased frequency of requests to get her in full makeup, heels and negligees to even attempt love. But just in case there were any lingering doubts, Chase added, "I don't think you're fat. I think you're gorgeous, and I love you." He rehearsed lies like an actor rehearsed Shakespeare.

"You hate me," Vilma said. She needed much more than one taffied 'I love you,' and this was her way of coaxing it out.

"Doesn't matter as long as I love you. Why do you think I married you?" Chase asked with pudding eyes.

As though he had crawled through her ear and into her head, the question was the same one she had been asking herself for the better part of lately. Chase wasn't soused enough, but if Vilma reached for the bottle in the ice bucket and poured, he would suspect her up to something. As a main course, Chase had the swordfish. Vilma the duck legs. It was the most unsettling feeling to break bread with a man she couldn't trust. So many times she wanted to come right out and ask, "Have you ever been with another woman?" Vilma was over the bay before her brain let her know about it. The question slipped right out of her throat. She took her napkin and covered embarrassed lips. She hated laying it all on the table, but if not for loose lips what good was marriage? Chase removed the fork from his lips and kept the food between his tongue and the roof of his mouth. He kept his eyes on the silk cloth while digesting the question.

"I'm sorry," Vilma continued.

"No, no. You're my wife and you have every right to ask it," Chase said. His eyes were now aimed at hers. Vilma had no trouble meeting the stare. She would listen to the words that came out of his mouth, but the true answer would come from his eyes. If they twitched, if they shifted askance, if they blinked too much or not at all, they would be the preachers of veritas. "Have I been with another woman? I would appreciate

82

it if you showed the decency to keep such frivolous allegations to yourself because nothing could be further from the truth. You're my only squeeze, and that's the way it is. I may not have always been the sweetest guy, but I care for you more than you think, even if you can't see it. Maybe I can't either, but I know it's in there somewhere. I take you for granted only because I know I can, you see?" Chase said. He orated from a drunken brain, and his mood went sour on a dime. It was the only way he could control the spice on his tongue. He topped Vilma off. "I thought we were celebrating tonight."

"You won't believe this, but that's the most charming thing you've ever said to me." Vilma fashioned her mouth into a smile. The rest of her face remained contaminated with suspicion.

"Which part?" He raised his glass for a toast and gazed into Vilma's dewy eyes. "To my wife. I'm no one without her."

When they got home, Chase took Vilma to her bedroom and tossed her on the bed like a ragdoll. She was still in her dress. In years past, Vilma would even ask Chase what colors he wanted her to wear. Nine times out of ten it was blonde yellow. It never dawned on her that Chase not only liked angel food for dessert, he liked it in the color of his women, their skin, their hair. Blame the Maker, but such hues, Holly's, were etched into Chase's deepest desire. Vilma would always be a good sport. Tonight, Chase didn't care what she wore. There was no changing into something more comfortable, no peignoirs to obscure her cellulite, no stilettos on hooves. He left the light off and wouldn't be eyeballing her anyway, just balling her. She didn't wonder why. She didn't fight. Being in the dark made her feel safe from any snide remarks that found an easier egress when Chase was drunk. Besides, it had been a season since she felt the affirmation of his hands, and whether he was faithful or not, this would be more for her than for him. He took off his jacket and shoes. After he undid his belt and unzipped, he dove to the bed and wrestled her dress up her waist like he was ripping open a sack of potatoes. He hooked her panties clear and found entry. His thrusts were hare-fast, violent. Vilma let him pound into her. She climaxed in less than a minute, but Chase kept going until he was a sweaty, breathless mound of meat. He panted himself clear of a blackout. The wine had his head doing circles.

"Take your time," Vilma said. "I'm not the Easter Tower."

Chase pumped like an abraded piston. Twenty seconds later, he slapped the headboard and removed his wet body from Vilma with a couple of choice words. He didn't see the checkered flag. "I can't," he said as he worked his pecker flaccid. He just couldn't do it, not for all the money in "the bank."

Vilma stayed in bed like a woman freshly diagnosed with cancer. "Why does it all have to go down?"

"Because things go down, not up, down! They grow old, they die, and they go down," Chase was quick to temper with so much testosterone clogged up in his pipe.

"Well you need to keep it up!" Vilma wasn't talking about sex either, and Chase was fully aware of it. Vilma gave it one more shot. "I came out in high heels, not combat boots." Vilma remembered better times spent with Chase and realized the more they lived, the further away these times went.

"You coulda fooled me," Chase said. If he couldn't keep it up, he could always mix it up. If only she would be a bit more understanding, a little less demanding, know that Chase was nothing more or less than a male, eager to satisfy himself by pleasuring other women, relegated to playing the camper because Vilma came into the marriage with the picnic basket. But the spread was now crumbs for the pigeons. It wouldn't matter that Vilma was the most beautiful woman since Bathsheba, and she was not, he would always desire something new in his every effort to avoid reminders of things old, like death. That disregarding a passing eyeful of lust was no different than a touch of another's lips or the sporty genital massage that was exchanged with a complete stranger. What was the difference? But none of it would make a lick of sense to her. To her, love was quid pro quo with a noncompete clause. She wanted a man who wanted only her, and she could continue to delve into the delusion like all proud women did.

After Vilma heard the door slam shut down the hall, she got up and snicked on the light. She gave herself a wash and headed downstairs for a hot toddy. She didn't dare think it had anything to do with her. Such thoughts led to suicide. She had simply chosen a man with a rebellious groin. A woman couldn't have it all.

- 17 -

Holly went to answer the door. She couldn't imagine who would come calling as early in the morning and nearly bopped her conk on the door frame when Chase thrust a bouquet of pinks at her.

"Special delivery from a secret admirer."

Holly spread her arms long and wrapped him in a hug. "Oh, Chase, you've been doing somersaults in my head since yesterday." Chase invited himself in, but Holly stonewalled him.

"Don't tell me."

"No, not at all, silly. My roommates, remember? We gotta save our pennies somehow, you know. "Maybe we can go to your place instead?"

"I'll wait downstairs," Chase said. Holly ran to powder up.

A half hour later, Chase pulled up to the Werlick Hotel. It was close enough to the Easter Tower that he could make all the necessary appearances. Holly looked out to the marble frontage, the doorman in his pressed costume by the giant doors splashed in sculpted gold plating. Random rich people walked in and out. She could hardly believe Chase hung his hat here.

"What are we doing?" Holly asked.

"My place," Chase said.

"You're pulling my leg. You mean you live in this fancy hotel all by yourself like one of those picture stars?"

"Here and the office. Come." Chase wasn't a born liar, but he had perfected the art over the years. If he tried hard enough, he could see Vilma seated next to him, but that did nothing for his hard on.

The valet opened Holly's door. She slid a leg out. Chase opened his own door and handed a dollar coin to the valet. "Have it back here in a couple hours," Chase said. The valet thanked him with a nod of the head and took the car away without any unnecessary babble.

When they got into the room, Chase didn't waste time. She came out of her coat and made a beeline for the sheets. Chase joined her on the bed, but he kept his clothes on. Holly remembered the drill. She hurried to the bathroom to wash up. When she came back, Chase devoured her, wishing she had holes everywhere he dry-humped. The lovemaking lasted minutes. He was a regular squirt gun, and now that it was out, he was able to think with a clear mind. He lit a smoke and passed it to Holly. Then he lit one for himself. They were in a familiar position, both staring at the ceiling like it wasn't even there.

"Why don't you fix us up a couple mimosas?" Chase asked.

Holly scooted up and had a hell of a time uncorking the bottle. Chase offered a chuckle for help. When she finally popped the cork, champagne shot all over him. Then she laughed. They sipped, they laughed some more, they ordered room service, French toast with strawberries, veal cutlets, petits four, sweetbreads stuffed with truffles, shrimp skewers, roquefort cheese, grape salad, eggs Benedict and a cheeseburger with all the fixings. Chase dabbed a finger of whip cream on Holly's nose inciting a small food fight. They made love again. After they were spent and lying in each other's arms, Holly asked why Chase lived in a hotel.

"A real home gets real lonely. It gets lonely here too, but I can always mosey down to the lobby bar and listen to ten drunks at a time just waiting for a fresh ear to chew off." Chase sucked a puff from his cig. "Is that guy you work for dangerous?"

"Pap Fanti? He's like a father to me. Picked me up when I was in the gutter. Why do you ask?"

"Just want to make sure my future dame keeps good company." Chase leaned over and planted a smooch on Holly's lips. Then he got up and started to dress.

Holly stayed in bed with a glow on her face that she could feel. It didn't matter that he called her dame. He said it with such affection that she equated it with long-term.

Chase wasn't finished there. "If you're not too busy, maybe you can start looking for flats, you know, something big enough for two." He told Holly she could stay as long as she wanted, order whatever was on the menu, but that she would have to let herself out. He had business at the Easter Tower. Any more instances of hooky might come back to bite him. He left her in the grand suite with the memory of his kiss, a full bar and room service.

Holly picked up the phone, "East Leaf, 9-5627." She waited for the call to be connected. Her eyes grew nervous, like part of her wished the call wouldn't go through. The man on the other line disappointed her. He had a deep, diligent voice, the kind that always seemed to be working. Her fingers tugged at her to hang up, but she stayed on the line. "Hey, Hendrick." Her lukewarm greeting didn't draw much enthusiasm from the other line. "How you been?"

"Don't tell me you're out already. I gave you a three-month supply that you still haven't paid me for," Hendrick said.

"No. I'm fine. That's not why I called. You'll never guess where I am right now."

"If it's the city jail, I don't know you."

"I swear I don't know why I bother. For your information, I happen to find myself in the grand suite of the Werlick Hotel. I'm sure you've heard of it."

"How much is he paying you?"

"I didn't know they let pigs behind the pulpit. I called to tell you I met a special man. Someone you'd respect, if you respect anyone anymore. We're seeing each other. It's getting serious. It's all moving a bit fast, but I think he's going to ask me to marry him." There was a long silence on the other line. "You there?"

"This is why you waste my time? You met a man in arch supporters, and he drove you to a hotel?"

"It's not like that at all, V.I.P. He has feelings for me. You know what feelings are? And just between us, he's prime beef, a real biggie. In charge of major things. You ever hear of the Easter Tower? He's doing that. What do you think of that company?"

"Maybe I'll get my money soon then. He take you backstage?"

"Sorry to burst your bubble. I'm with another outfit. They treat me real good. Better than you ever did. Things are finally working out for me. Thought you'd be happy to hear. And you'll get your money. Don't worry about it." She hung up like she was squashing a giant roach.

There would be no big-brother speeches about why she'd never amount to a can of beans. No education, no ambition, no real job, no real husband or children, no life. Just reminders of how she would have played a better abortion. "Time to grow up and stop playing kiddie games before you find yourself busted," was his stick of charity, and she wouldn't let him beat her over the head with it this time. Heaven forbid Hendrick ever have a kind thing to say, a handout like other older brothers gave, instead of all the drugs and demands for payment. Why she felt the need to report her progress was anybody's guess. Deep down, she yearned for his respect just like any ingénue would. But she was done fishing for putdowns from a holy roller who was famous for saying that God wanted us to love him freely, and if we didn't, he'd send us to hell. Pap had called a special meeting this morning and she was meant to be there. At bare minimum, there were others who valued her just the way she was.

- 18 -

Calloway Cocoa was nuzzled among a dozen factories along Factory Island's eastern shore. This was both good and bad. Of all their prior stops, this one promised to be the hardest to reach. Basil Demur swore it wouldn't affect business, but it had Pap Fanti worried. Too many things had him worried this clear morning. Starting with who gave them up. Without knowledge of the leak, they would open up shop and lead the rat right back to the cheddar. He stood under the overhang of the boiler house, his wide eyes peering through his spectacles to the open harbor. It started right at his feet. One step in the wrong direction and he would find himself drowned. The water had a healthy flow. It was cleaner than the river back at Dunfer's. This made him happy in a worried sort of way. Last night's showers left the air with an original smell. For a second, he could forget that there was something old that didn't want to go away. Maybe here in the crisp of a new dawn, they would finally put that history to bed for good. Demur was right about the exits too. There were plenty, and still there were none. Not without taking to sea. Two bridges, one on the west, one on the south were all the connected the island to both Good Leaf and Jester. Everything else was a maze of roads that circled the island. To complicate matters, news of the Salty Well hit was ill received. Of all the things that might have made him happy this morning, this story had him broken in half. Lou could tell that Pap was disturbed. It meant that they themselves were that close to kissing the reaper's scythe a couple of nights ago, and there was no telling just how much better off they'd be here.

"I talked it over with Dino and the fellas. They'll throw in whatever's needed for the wife and kid," Lou said. Salty Well was a good man. No matter how ugly he might have been on the outside, he always made sure to protect his wife and baby. To them he was their handsome prince. Now Mrs. Well and her child were defenseless and would soon join the throngs of tramps at charity centers where the mortality rate for infants was one in three.

"I'll take care of them. Out of my share. I don't want you or the others to worry about this. It's because of me that this hell started. One of these days I'll have to face the music," Pap said.

"But not alone," Lou assured.

"I really thought the worst was over. Turns out it hasn't even entered city limits yet."

"They won't have bloodhounds that can track us out here. I can guarantee you that," Lou said. "It's a good spot. The kid will think he died and went to chocolate heaven." He tried to add a touch of light to an otherwise dire talk.

Pap listened to Lou with the side of his head, but his eyes remained on the water.

"They can box us in like rabbits," Pap said.

"Then we get a boat and never turn back just like your pal, Mercury."

Pap looked to his left. There was a main dock with three finger piers. A crummy skiff was moored to one of the piers. "Everyone here?"

"Inside drinking hot cocoa like the world ran out of everything else."

"Let's get it over with," said Pap. He was growing impatient.

Lou wasn't too eager to follow Pap back in. "I don't mean to be out of order here, but maybe you should keep this one under wraps."

"And add another serving of guilt to my plate?"

"They'll flee to save their own hides and then what? You, more than anyone, know how long it took to get to a stop, and we're still running," said Lou. "Do we gamble it all away now and go back to the days of fishing barrels?"

"Do you trust me?" Pap asked.

"What's that gotta do with it?"

"Just answer."

"You're the only one I trust, Pap."

"Why?"

Lou thought about it for a long second. "Because you're my friend. And you're supposed to trust your friends."

"Because they always want the best for you," said Pap.

"They wouldn't be friends otherwise," said Lou.

"And what would happen if all of the sudden a friend lost confidence in that?"

"Then maybe he becomes an enemy."

"Just like that," Pap said.

"It happens," Lou repeated.

"The leak could be closer than we think, and even if it's not, I refuse to wash my hands in anyone else's blood. If they want to walk, they walk in peace, and God decide their fate, not me." Pap turned his head and stared at Lou.

Lou nodded like it all made sense. He, too, was now staring at the water and listening to Pap with the side of his head. "You know my trigger finger cramps up with arthritis in this damn cold, but don't think for a second I wouldn't do it all over again."

Pap put a hand on Lick's shoulder. "Because you're a friend."

"The course of every man is set: He'll live, he'll sin, he'll laugh and cry. He will die. That's from a book I'm reading. Some jagoff named Machado. Good for a laugh. Let's break the news."

They headed down the narrow covered walkway, the harbor on one side, the boiler room on the other. Then around the corner and across a lot. Three Dunfer's Linens trucks kept still. There were four parked cars dotting the empty spaces around the trucks. A three-story building was right in front of them. A bridge high overhead attached the building with the boiler room. It made for a good lookout spot. They entered through the first door. Wide halls led to wide elevators. After making two rights, they came to a door. Stairs descended down to basement level. It was on their route. A short tunnel, about twenty feet met them at the bottom. There were a couple bulbs dancing off strings from the ceiling. On the right hand, another door.

They entered a large room. This was the basement. It was longer than it was wide. No windows and two ways out. A double-sided ruby red EXIT lit up over both doors. Incandescent fixtures were placed, three to a wall. Beams teen feet apart held the ceiling in place. There were pallets stacked in corners, empty burlap sacks with Calloway print. A few stragglers were still full. The tables and chairs from Dunfer's were the same, but they, too, were stacked all over each other. Except for the ones the Cats 6 and the High Legs used as seats. Dino, Ham Wails, Turnip and the Gophers sat on pallets or sacks of cocoa beans. Many drank cups of hot chocolate. Holly sat by her gals. Her mind still resting on Chase's chest two mornings ago.

Pap moved around the room shaking hands with everyone in attendance. They greeted him with an affectionate "Cap'n Pap." These were the people that had become the closest thing to a family he had ever known. They were loyal to him because he had been loyal to them. For Pap, it was never a matter of buying someone as much as loving them. Money was nothing more than love's expression. Money made friends. And friends loved each other.

"I know that everyone of you would take a bullet for me, but I can't ask that of you anymore. You all know the reason we travel light. Well now there's another. There are people who want me dead. Some of you know this." The crowd exchanged straight faces, some went reticent, some askance. Pap surveyed them all hoping to quash allegations of an inside job. "We'll stay here as long as we can. I know the moves are heavy and the rewards small. We'll continue to work. Work is all that matters. Hopefully we still have a following, but I'm proud of every one of you. We offer the finest entertainment in the three boroughs and all the Leaf and we don't do it at swanky buildings on the East side." The crowd nodded. Pap paused to hold back what was building up inside. Getting sentimental was an easy thing to do these days. "Anyone who wants out, I won't resent you for it. I only ask that you go in peace."

The Cats 6 kept shifty eyes under wraps. Charmin kept his shades on, so no one could see his. Pisto Leroy, spiffed out in his blue bow tie with minuscule yellow crosses and tweed jacket, looked to his leather watch antsy-like. He appeared to have places to be, but no one got up. Same with the Gophers and the High Legs. Claudette couldn't keep her twitchy legs still. Dino, Ham and Turnip remained on their haunches. Lou excused himself from the room without so much as a word.

"You stay, we stay. To the bitter end," Wails said.

"Let's shine the place up. Three days till show time," Pap announced. Turnip was quick to stand and leave before the rest of the group could disperse. Dino approached the High Legs and asked them to the bar for a quick toast. It was far too early in the day to start drinking, but he was insistent. The three gals gave in. Holly, for one, could use a drink. The Gophers scattered about the room and started cleaning out the spider spit on the walls, sweeping the floors and setting up ladders to arrange the satin ceiling. There was little time to waste if they were going to pull this off.

- 19 -

Sas Parila and Pisto Leroy exited the building and strolled to one of the parked tin cans. Sas took a subtle step sideways in order to avoid bumping elbows. In a shameless flash, Leroy's brain jiggled inside his skull, and all his circuits blew out. He tipped over like a tree on the final chop. He never saw the cudgel that cracked him where bone met spine. He was still breathing, albeit without knowledge. Turnip clotted the running gash with a plastic bag. Sas helped him scoop Leroy off the ground. They rushed him around the corner to the boiler room. Lou followed behind with the club in his hand and glanced back to make sure no eyes had taken account. When they were in the blind and on one of the finger piers, Lou and Turnip each took Leroy by his ankles and dunked his head underwater until he was drowned.

"Hurry up," Sas said. They brought him up. Sas tied a rope around Leroy's ankle. The other end was knotted around a cinder block. They heard faint footsteps approaching, far too connected in cadence to come from a man, unless that man was a woman. These sounded like the tapping of a dame's heels. Turnip went to meet the steps before they got any closer.

"Dump him," Lou urged in the same breath he used to snap the bat over his knee and chunk it into the harbor. Sas did his best to finish the knot. They shoved Leroy's body into the water. It disappeared into the depths in less than three seconds.

Down by the boiler room entrance, Turnip noticed Holly.

"Watch your step out here. It's not all that safe," Turnip said.

"The safest place I've ever been. You got a smoke?" Holly asked. Turnip reached into his coat and handed Holly a cigarette. Lou and Sas walked around the corner, doing their best to hide the mischief in their eyes.

"What are you boys doing out here? Dumping bodies?" Holly asked in jest.

"Seeing how far a swim it is to the Oven," Lou answered.

Holly stood next to Lou and Sas and smoked her flakes. She stood right over the dumping site and didn't think twice about it. There was no evidence of a murder. The men kept their cool. Like another cold day in paradise. She shared her encouragement for the new club and hoped that whoever was after Pap would come into a sudden heart attack. She talked about how crazy everything had been in the last couple of years, how this had to be the wildest place to set up shop, and how if everyone stuck together it would work out. They finished their smoke, and Holly went on her way. Lou, Sas and Turnip remained for another minute. When they were certain she was out of earshot, they looked around the area to make sure they left no sign. It was clean. The cleanest job they could have pulled. One minute Leroy was drinking hot cocoa with the rest of the crew, the next he was chugging saltwater at the bottom of the harbor. The Cats 6 was now a more conforming title.

- 20 -

Nightfall brought Met back to the relative safety of Crystal Plats. He was at the bottom of his second fifth of rye when he reached the apes again. He throated a song like there was no one within miles. It was horrible, but who among the comatose beasts would complain? *"There's no worry, there's no shame, can't you see, it's just rain on my parade. There's no trouble, there's no fuss, can't you see, it's just the two of us."*

He bagged the bald chicken necks and scaled the ladder. His movements were indifferent. No vertigo this time. The wintry air bit his nose. He looked up. The sky was undressed and broke out into a rash of stars. Moonbeams dripped till they evaporated. A sense of mortality slapped him across the face. Suddenly he felt as small as a seed. He slid down the ladder, but he didn't stop singing, not until he reached the warehouse to realize he had returned without the ice cooler.

Met reconsidered leaving it there till morning, but the thought of Buddy blowing his lid for any stupid reason made the decision for him. He strode back, long, relaxed steps. No rush. This time without his song. A sound caused him to brake hard. He shut his eyes so his ears could get a bead on it. Fear swept over him. Someone was singing the same song. They were inside the zoo. Met patted his pockets for a weapon. All he had was a dull blade. He took it out and ran his finger across the edge to the point. It could still stab through a normal man's gut. His first thought was to take off, but the voice wasn't of the repellant variety. On the contrary, it was inviting. The most beautiful sound he'd ever heard. He followed, his steps snake silent. The voice warmed the air. He started to think of all the people who could be pulling a prank on him. None he knew had pipes like that. If this was Buddy's idea of a hit, they wouldn't get him without a fight. Met kept his eyes open for business as he curved the bend and headed for the monkey cage. The open sky lit up everything in a cool blue, but he still couldn't make out a living soul. The voice had no quit. Met's breath grew quick. His eyes skipped to the bird's enclosure. There was no one there. The nested birds awaited the dawn. To his right was a pond of hippos. The water gave nary a ripple. Met continued towards the ice cooler. The chimp cage was within range. If Met's ears worked at all tonight, the sound was coming from there. He inched forward for a better vantage point.

"What the fuck is that," he whispered. His lower jaw separated from the top and pulled his lower eyelid with it. He feared his senses and cast all doubt on what appeared thirty yards away. He lowered himself behind a rail in the walkway and continued to take in what his eyes were giving him. Clearing the area without making a sound would be his next challenge. He didn't want to engage it in any way. He didn't want that thing to know he was there. It was singing like a man, but animals don't sing. They can't sing. They can't talk, not like humans. None of it was real. It was all the alcohol and reefer. His mind was playing tricks on him. Only there was no amount of intoxicant that could make him deny what was happening. It wasn't a man singing, and he was about to confirm it once and for all. He slid along the rail, each step closer to the cage until he got the clearest view he would get without tipping off the singer. A single cloud sailed across the moon and cast a shadow on the figure. It had a hunched back, long arms that touched the floor while standing. It raised its head high to the air and puckered its thin lips into a vibrato that rattled Met's bones. When the cloud passed, Met caught a glimpse of the simian figure in all its splendor. The voice was coming from it.

Back in the warehouse, Met slapped himself silly and abused a quick cigarette to ease unsettled nerves. It just couldn't be, but then again, he had heard of strange things once upon a time.

- 21 -

The Triumph Saloon idled in the back lot. Met headed out to meet it with another zip bag of cash. Jesse rolled down the window.

"Six tigers."

"Hand it over before your arms break," Jesse said.

Buddy passed a ten spot to Jesse as the relay point to Met. "That's for the other night. No hard feelings."

Met lowered his head to get a view of Buddy. "Thanks."

Jesse caught a whiff of Met's hundred-proof breath. "Hey! Point your dragon some place else!"

"Sorry. Just a little jumpy is all," Met said. He cupped his hands over his mouth for warmth.

"Don't worry about it. It happens." Buddy placed a hand on Jesse's arm to calm him down. "Just remember, the boozehound won't inherit the kingdom of heaven."

"I'll try to remember next time I'm on a bender."

"Need a lift?"

"Nah," Met answered.

Buddy nodded to Jesse. Jesse rolled up the window, but Met put a hand out and blocked it.

"Sober up, Egg," Jesse said. "Get your hand off the glass."

"Is there anything you guys wanna tell me?" Met asked.

"About?" Jesse said.

"About this place."

"What about it?" Jesse continued. Buddy kept his eyes facing forward.

"I don't know."

"Spit it already. We ain't got all night," said Buddy.

Met looked off to the side. He was trying to figure the right way to ask: "You ever notice anything strange here?"

"Strange? We run whiskey through a zoo. What's strange?" Jesse said.

"No, not that. Anything with the animals?"

"He's talking about the singing monkeys," Buddy said.

Met kept his mouth shut. He couldn't detect the sarcasm in Buddy's words, but Jesse's guffaw could only mean that they were kidding around.

"Lay off the tea," Buddy said. "I don't work with losers."

Jesse pressed the pedal, and the car rolled off. Met stood in place. His body was still throbbing with a buzz, but his mind was stuck on the singing chimp. It was stupid of him to ask Buddy about it, but it was all the confirmation he needed. They didn't have a clue. Maybe he was hallucinating.

He decided to have one more look and when he was within eyeshot, the chimp was finishing his last song for the night. It was a heartrending ballad. Met was his only audience, and the chimp didn't even know it. When it closed its last lyric, it headed back to its hole in the wall without even looking at the tray of necks. Crystal Plats would remain silent the rest of the night. Met had a plan to make things right with Sue, to make something of his life. The discovery was his and his alone. There were people who'd pay a pretty penny for something like that. Last he checked, he'd never read about a singing chimp in the papers.

- 22 -

9 am on the corner of Central and 10th did nothing to quell the migraine that Met hid under his cap. High rises surrounded him like a gang of enforcers. The garrulous growl of a thousand engines never stopped. Cars honked insults at one another and smoked the air with flatulence. The sidewalks were teeming with trench coats and Ulsters. Many wore paperboard overalls, replete with physical descriptions, exaggerated experience and "BORN TO WORK" greetings. The faces all looked the same, bitter and sunk; any remaining hope melted clean off the bone. That made Met feel out of place, at least now that he clung to his secret ambition. No way he looked liked these saps. He glanced to the Good Leaf Savings and Loans Building on the east side of Central and delayed not one second more.

A security desk was the first thing he saw. An armed guard in a blue jacket and tie was the second.

"Here to see Basil Demur."

"Got an appointment?"

"Sure I do."

"If you don't mind." The security guard signaled a pat down. Met spread his arms apart. The guard fanned him. "Fourth floor."

Met moved to the elevator and headed up. There were offices on either side of the hall. He looked on each door until he saw the name "Basil Demur – Attorney at Law." He opened the door in the most presumptuous of ways and let himself in like it was his own house. A pretty young thing with a bob sat at a desk.

"I need to see Demur," Met said.

"Your name?"

"Tell him it's a friend of Buddy Plagun."

"Have a seat." The secretary pranced back. Met didn't even bother checking out her backside, regardless that it looked like the lower bulb of a sand timer.

He noticed a tray of candies on her desk. His stomach griped for breakfast. He picked at the first candy within reach. It was a chocolate covered almond by Calloway, wrapper to match. He took two. One he slid in his pocket, the other he chewed right on the spot. The secretary pitter-pattered out. "I'm sorry. He's not available. Next time call."

Met stood from his chair and marched past her into the back offices.

She yelled, "You can't go back there!"

"Call security," Met said as he showed himself at Basil Demur's door. Basil recognized him like the onset of the flu.

"No more shills on old hags I take it?" Basil knew a bit of Met's history. Before Pap and Met went their separate ways many years ago, all three had known each other. Along with dealing dope and setting up crooked dice games, Met used to come to the rescue of old maidens. Acting as some sort of jewelry expert, he'd convince the widows that they had been duped into buying fakes not worth two bits, even the ones left to them by their dead husbands. He'd offer them a dollar and his heavy charm and then fence the jewels through a hockshop that made tens times as much. He got busted and sent to the big house for six months. Basil Demur was asked to come in on the defense, as a favor to Pap.

"If we're strolling down memory lane, it's only fitting to remind you all the bad money I paid you to get thrown in the can," Met said.

"I'm busy, and you're not welcome here." Basil grabbed the phone to dial security.

"I have something for Pap Fanti. You kick me out, I take it somewhere else. I'm here to do business, not waste your time."

"What makes you think I want to do business with you?" Demur asked. His hand was on the telephone receiver about to make the call. His other hand was on a glass of scotch whiskey. His tie was tight around his collar, and his navy jacket was buttoned around his waist even as he sat behind a fortress of a dark-finished oak.

"I stopped by his apartment. The super told me he was gone. It's the only reason I came here."

"I don't know where he is. Security, we have a situation. 403." Demur hung up. "Don't do anything stupid here, or you're going to jail."

Met knew his time had run out before the clock even started. His lips moved faster than his brain could process, but it was coming from the heart, so he didn't need any help. "Dig this, lip. You tell Pap I know all about his little secret and that there's a least more than one. He'll know where to find me if he wants to sample the goods, and I guarantee he'll wanna taste. But I'm only coming here 'cause I stand to make a buck. Otherwise, I take my prize elsewhere." Met disappeared from the doorway and left without any forced assistance.

- 23 -

Fire ants had nothing on Pap's crew. All four basement walls were cloaked in burgundy satin and gave off that Dunfer's feel all over again. The tables and chairs were set up to seat a serried seventy five. They wouldn't skip a beat. Lou installed electrical lines inside the walls. The guttersnipes sawed a bandstand from scrap wood. Turnip dug the trench that would separate the talent from the crowd. Dino dusted off the bar. It was a regift from Basil Demur. One of Plagun's tenants refused to tithe his weekly juice, so Plagun sent the bulls to light a bonfire after they cleaned out the valuables, including all the booze and a bar top cut of enameled travertine. It was a tribute to Pap that his crew was able to pull off such fine stunts with such frequency. The question remained whether the guests would make the trek out. Basil Demur opened the door and pranced in. Pap noticed him immediately.

"This place makes Dunfer's look like the city dump," Basil said.

"You take care of the guestlist?"

"Everyone. They'll be here for the grand opening right on schedule. You're in the clear."

"How do you figure?"

"Took care of the leak too."

Pap put a careful eye on Basil. "I'm all ears."

"Stenago."

With a rutted brow, Pap said, "Les Stenago? That's a line."

"He's gone. Heart gave out like a clock. You can appreciate the irony. I have to admit I snickered myself when I heard it."

"Stenago was square."

"Yeah, a little too square. The Spoon seemed to smooth out his corners. Ran up a marker he couldn't pay back. So he made a deal." Basil was eager to close the book on this and change the channel. He wasn't entirely convinced that Pap bought the line. He must have been slipping. It was true that Stenago was square. He owned a couple of large furniture stores. High end stuff. He had supplied Pap with all the tables and chairs for the club. Marked them down at the behest of Basil, who promised a spot on the V.I.P. list. But Les Stenago was the only man he could pin it on without putting a contract on someone still alive.

"People making deals everywhere, aren't they?" Pap asked.

"But you don't worry about that anymore. How's the kid?"

"You know this is the last time." Pap could often read Basil, and he knew that something else brought him out there today. Surely the news of the leak was intended to settle him down, but it was only a precursor to a spike in blood pressure.

"Your brother swung by."

Pap's face turned sour. "For what?"

"I don't know. Wanted to show you something. Said you'd be interested. He wouldn't tell me. I wouldn't tell him."

"What do you think?" Pap asked.

"What am I supposed to think? Such things are beyond my ken. I can't explain them. Can you?"

"Nothing to explain. He's a hard sell. Always has been. I'm not in the market for anymore of his ointments."

"Alright, but just hear me out."

Pap started tamping his toes on the floor. He kept his eyes on all his friends breaking their backs to squeeze special out of squalor. "You see that?" Pap tipped his head towards his crew. Basil took a pause. "You talk of miracles. They're the real miracle. To take a secret that could make anyone of them richer beyond their wildest dreams and swallow it just for me. That's a miracle."

"Yeah, well, maybe, just maybe the cat's out. I can tell you he was all over the place, like he had seen something that shouldn't have been there. You should pay him a visit. At least get it out of your head and mine."

"Anything else you got for me?"

"He still moves with Plagun. He tells you otherwise, he's lying," Basil said. Pap gave a slow nod. "See you in a couple days."

That night, Pap finished setting up his new room on the second floor of the main building. It was a former office with quick access to a stairwell and elevator. A tin desk remained. Pap covered it with a mantle of satin and spread three shirts and pants over it. He put his toiletries inside the desk drawers. There was a window coated with aluminum foil. It would keep the lights in and the snoops out. Pap poked a dozen holes so he could survey the harbor and parking lot. An army cot with a thin mattress is where he'd rest his head. There would be no more deep sleep. Vigilance. He was in full suit and tie, shoes laced up like he was leaving. He popped his head into the adjoining room. Lou was shading his windows. He, too, would enjoy a bony mattress. A rolling coat rack carried his three suits. He was in boxers and ready for some shuteye.

"I need you to keep a close eye on the kid tonight."

"Where you going?"

"Something I have to check out. I don't come back before dawn, you blow this joint with the kid. Go as far north as there is land, and never come back."

"I'm going with you," Lou said.

"No. I need you here. He needs you here."

- 24 -

Sue's neighborhood looked the same as it had years ago and that wasn't saying much. Tenements and electric lines met with strings of long johns and crispy sheets. Pap sat in his parked Model A Tudor juggling now, next and never. His hat dipped towards his nose, and a tinder stick grew from his mouth. His eyes looked for shady characters, perhaps a parked box of matches. All he noticed were steel gates over merchant windows. Sun Bros. Meats, LB's Discount Drugs & Donuts, Happy Hanky & Hosiery, even the 2 Cent Coffee House. After all these years, they were still standing. With the streets empty, that made Pap the odd man out. He snuck across and sifted into the apartment building.

The revolver came out of his coat pocket, awkward as a held sneeze. His feet turned to feathers, but old wood was like old people. Each step was met with a whine. When he got to Sue's floor, he started for the last apartment and knocked on the door. The deadbolt clanked from the frame, and the door cracked open.

"Pap Fanti?" Sue questioned.

"Where's Met?" Pap kept the gun at his rear.

"Asleep. What time is it?"

"Late."

Sue unfastened the safety chain and opened the door wide. Pap put his eyes inside the room before the rest of his body.

The thought of walking back out with the stench of that place on his suit gnawed at him good. Pap was a man who refused to deal in refuse. And there to his left, stinking up the bed, was some of it. Met's chest was an ashtray. An empty bottle rested its neck on the same pillow. Pap always dreaded the pain Met must have endured for so many years, a woe that continued to haunt him to this day. It seemed like every time Pap fucked up, Met took the beating. Where was the justice in that? Pap ran and was spared. Met stayed and was crushed as displayed by that face, those bruised bags folding under each eye. He was busted by drugs and unrepressed fists. Pap felt responsible for not being able to secure a safer path for him, but such emotions were only tapered by a stronger, more natural desire for self-preservation.

"You got company?" Pap asked.

"Just a family of roaches, but they're paid through the month," Sue answered.

Pap slid the gun back into his coat and kicked at Met's mattress. "Met. Get up. It's your brother." Met swung his head side to side. "Pin your diapers," Pap said. He tossed Met's coat over him. Met got up and rubbed his face alive. He lit a smoke to clean his mouth.

"Long time. Where did it go?" Met said. But to Pap it was only yesterday. Either way, people didn't age fast enough to realize they were already dead. Funny how when the time came, they always spouted off some dumb line like "where did the time go?" It had been three years since Pap last saw his goldbrick brother. Sue still couldn't see the resemblance.

A silk suit, new face and hair versus greasy dungarees and a wife beater reeking of onions two days old. She could never figure how these two were harvested from the same womb, could never understand why she gravitated towards the loser. But she could always tell the difference. Winners were winners, even when they appeared to lose. And a real loser could never become a winner, no matter how many times he boasted otherwise, no matter that he claimed trivial prizes along life's byways. Mrs. Madra Fanti (their mother) died giving birth to Met. There were no hospitals, no doctors or midwives. Just a landlord, his chambermaid and buckets. Met went into one. Madra's lifeblood went into the other. Their father, a nameless son-of-a-bitch who was getting plastered at a local tavern, blamed Met for his wife's death and disavowed both boys. It was easier than picking one son over the other. At least this way, they could never blame him for playing favorites. Pap took Met under his wing, even before he had grown his own. They were thrown into kid coolers until Pap was old enough to plot their break. They wandered Lower Leaf, staying at local Y's. It's where they met Lou Licks. He invited them to live with his grandmother on their small ranch house in South Breaks. For the price of a half-day of chores, Pap and Met would get room and board and all the cream and cornbread they could stand. Pap agreed, and they left the Leaf and headed across the Gorda to what was still mostly countryside. When the skies dried up, the crops died quickly. To score new bread, Pap and Lou would steal wandering pigs from neighbors and sell them in the city. Some went to slaughterhouses, some door-to-door. It was their first taste of the green. They even got Met into the act, passing him off as a retard. He would distract neighbors with dimwitted faces and buckling groans while Pap and Lou cleaned out their sty. Pap always watched out for his kid brother, but Met was growing up too fast. Stealing pork lacked panache, and pushing a plow was up there with catching a cold. As soon as his legs steered him, he would wander from the ranch house and take the train into the Leaf with spare change he had stolen from Pap while they slept. If there were no trains, he'd walk, no matter that it took him all night. He met up with the Sunks Boys gang in South Leaf. They tutored Met, showed him what the public wanted more than their bellies filled. A quick fix. Met showed Pap how much he would make off dealing dope. He'd come home with twenty smackers in a night. Pap had never seen such money, but it didn't sit right. There was no grammar school, no structure, no boundaries. In South Breaks, it was easier for Pap and Lou to avoid truancy cops, but Met found himself in and out of juvenile halls. When he was caught stealing from the drug gang, he spent a month hiding in Bigup, roaming the streets and rummaging through trash barrels. He was only 11. He returned to Lou's place one more time. Pap didn't say a word. He knew Met only came back to regroup, hopefully get a handout before he left for good. A note with a promise that he'd keep in touch was found under the front door the morning he took off. It would be years before Met reached out to Pap again.

"Can I get you a drink?" Sue asked.

"No thanks," Pap said. "Sorry to wake you." He heeled back out and shuffled down the steps before the smell could stick.

"What does he want?" Sue asked.

"Search me," Met said. He put on his coat and shoes and followed Pap out.

Met spotted Pap getting into his car. He stopped for a second to wake his mind up. His whole life was about to change, and he needed to make sure that the he was in full control over this change or he'd lose it all to his more wily brother. Met started for Pap's car and got in. Pap had the windows rolled down and fire in the engine to drown out their conversation.

"I see you're still out on the roof," Pap said.

"What can I say? I find inspiration at the bottom of a bottle, usually one in every case and damned if I guess right, it always happens to be that last one. But you didn't come to give me a physical. How you been? You look like you're hitting on all eight. Running your own rackets now?" Met asked.

"Tell me why I gotta hear from Basil Demur that you're sniffing around my door?"

Met showed Pap his joint. Pap glanced at it without a word. Met lit up and took a hit. "She's the only one that truly gets me, her and her ginchy cousin rye," he said of his reefer and booze.

Pap wafted his arm to send the smoke scurrying out the window.

"Nice wheels," Met continued. He loved owning the seconds, slowing them down to a standstill, especially when Pap was there to speed them up.

"Cut the act. What do you want?" Pap didn't come to bump gums.

"You believe in angels? Not like demons with scary faces, but angels with pretty voices?"

"You drag me out here to teach religion?"

"Just the part that talks about angels."

"You wanna quit the doubletalk?"

"I saw one. To this day I always wondered what the hell happened that night. You never gave it to me straight even though I was the one who brought you into the biz. I guess trust is a hard thing to come by."

"You still with the Hangman?"

Met kept his mouth shut. His eyes looked ready to crack. They made no attempt to connect with Pap's.

"Get out," Pap said.

"I gotta earn, don't I?" he said.

"Get out, I said."

"There's something at the zoo. You need to see it. I don't know what it is, but I need your word that I get paid first. If not, I pull the deal off the table. You won't believe it, or maybe you will. It has nothing to do with this," Met said as he pinched the joint in the air. He was talking fast, and his words didn't make any sense.

"What are you saying?"

"It's my way out. No one has to know. The past is in the history books."

"The Hangman's still gunning for me."

"I know, but you haven't heard a word I said. We go there right now. It's empty. Then you see it with your eyes before you call me liar. Deal?"

For years Pap and Met drank from the same bottle, but one night changed all that, and now they were complete strangers if they weren't enemies. Pap studied Met, his faces, the way he drew his mouth, the way he shifted his eyes, east to west. Was it another setup? "You put me against a wall, I kick till the chamber's empty. If you're in on it…" Pap stunted his breath. "Just don't be in on it."

"What happened that night? Tell me. I know I heard something. What was in the box?"

PART II

- 25 -

1927. July dripped all over the still waters of Breaks Harbor. It was dark enough to hide a body or a shipment of scotch. Bolts of lightening cracked the sky in half, but there was no rain, just sweat. Pap and Lou sat at the bow of a cigarette boat retrofitted with a V12 Libertad and plenty of empty compartments in the hull. They each had more hair, more color and less baggage. Almost like kids on a first adventure, only this wasn't their maiden voyage.

"Anything?" Pap asked with his flashlight throwing a glow at the sea ripples.

"No soap. Black the lamp," the man on the stern said. His razor voice could chop up waves. Oleg Mercury was a marine gypsy. He walked around with salt in his eyes and a fire of curls for a beard. His knuckles were decorated in warts. He held a wooden pole with a large meat hook over the water and appeared prepared to tangle with leviathan.

"You sure this is the drop?" Pap asked, his eyes stuck on the snaps of placid surf.

"This is it. Keep your nerve," said Oleg. He wasn't sure himself anymore.

The minutes turned into an hour. Nothing surfaced. The clouds grew obese.

"We're in the wrong spot," Pap said.

"Unless they didn't make the drop," Oleg said.

The sea spit up a couple bubbles. No one saw them. Then a couple more until a school of air fizzed around the boat.

"Here they come," Lou said. He almost coughed up a laugh in celebration. Pap had to quiet him down. Theirs was the only sound for at least two miles. And this is what they were here for. Thick red balloons burped over the surface, one after the other. They were attached to barrels and crates of timber.

"Pay dirt!" Lou exclaimed.

Pap hushed him once more. Oleg stabbed at the first barrel within reach and slipped his hook inside the rope wrapped around it. He gave it a sturdy tow and fished it to the side of the boat.

"What gives? It's empty," Oleg said as he curled it in.

"You're just stronger than last time," Lou said. "Get it in."

"I swear there's nothing in it," Oleg pulled another one out, then another. Each new barrel was brought on with ease. They dripped seawater all over the boat floor.

Lou felt the same weightlessness on his side. "Must have a sprung a leak."

"That's impossible," Oleg said.

Pap hooked the last crate. It was three feet each way and heavy enough to stall his efforts. "This one's got something. Give a hand," he said.

Lou helped pull the crate over the ledge with one grunt. The three runners sat under the dark rings of swirling skies with an insatiable curiosity.

"Makes no sense," Oleg said.

"Let's beat it," Pap said.

"I'm opening one first."

"Nix. You can't."

"They're hollow, I tell you."

Pap shook one of the barrels. It bobbed to a corner without a fight. He exchanged a glance with Oleg and Lou. It was all the authorization Oleg needed. He jimmied the face off. Nothing but hay, sopping wet. The insides of the crate walls were coated in a thick salt paste. It's the only reason they stayed down as long. But no bottles or booze. In other words, fucked.

"We've been had," Lou lamented. He was angry and wanting to kick ass.

A soft growl came from the crate next to Pap. His foot took a sudden step backwards and nearly sent him overboard. "What was that?" he blurted. He took a seat and braced himself against the ledge.

"Sounds like a drunk," Oleg said.

"It's an animal. Maybe a shark," Lou guessed as he reached for his gun.

"Sharks don't make noise, you ignoramus," Oleg said.

"Then what, sea king?" The growling came in waves, but there wasn't much power behind it. It sounded weak, like a ewe's bleat for help. A rod of lightning shot overhead. Two seconds later thunder drummed the clouds like a crack of hunger pangs.

"Throw it back over," Oleg said.

"It doesn't sound evil," Pap argued. He reached out a hand for the crowbar. "Let me have the iron."

"You're gonna let it out?" Lou asked.

A different sound came from the same crate and caught the trio by surprise. It was the sound a bugle makes in the hands of a greenhorn. "You hear that?" Pap said.

"It's a damn clown. I'm telling you throw it back before it starts pumping lead," Oleg said. He aimed his shotgun at the crate.

"Give me the bar. Watch my back." Pap took the crowbar and slid it into the seam. Lou and Oleg kept a firm hold on their firearms, ready to spit lead at the jack-in-the-box.

"Watch your face," Lou said.

Another couple of pushes and Pap split the crate open. Lou clenched up. Oleg poked his light inside the cavity. Bundled up in a soggy shell of hay was an animal, no larger than a medium dog. But it wasn't canine. It barely moved, and its eyes remained shut. A rusted hunting horn was tucked in at its side.

"What's that?" Oleg asked. The animal bleated again and stretched out its paws to Pap like it was trying to hug him.

"I don't know," Pap responded. He couldn't take his eyes off it.

"A message from a rival," Oleg said.

"Could be coppers," Lou surmised.

"This is bad," Pap said. He took the horn out of the crate and studied it for a clue. He couldn't even guess what this meant. The waterlogged creature appeared to drift into an instant sleep. It was covered in a pallid fur slicked into clumps. It had a small snout that connected to a black button. Its ears were two lumps of ashy coal on each side of its head. Four paws curled into themselves like it was the only way to provide warmth.

"Throw it back over. It's dead," Oleg said.

"It's not dead," Pap said. He had no clue. He slipped the hunting horn into his coat pocket. It was small enough to fit.

"Then kill it, and let's get out of here." Oleg was growing increasingly worried.

"We take it ashore and let it go," Pap said.

"Fine." Oleg fired the engine and turned the boat back to shore. It was just a few minutes away. The whole ride, Pap stared at the creature inside the crate, peaceful and asleep.

- 26 -

Parked at an empty wharf by Crystal Plats, Met waited inside a flatbed truck. A glowing gasper below his nose revealed the first signs of aging. The runners were late by at least an hour. He got out. His legs needed to stretch out the jitters. The sky was filled with clouds but still no rain. A strange stillness allowed Met to pick up the fragile trace of the Libertad racing in. Something about its cadence hinted that it was traveling lighter than usual. He jogged to the dock, past Oleg's trawler, and watched them coast up. Met knotted the rope around the fenders. "You're late," he complained.

"We met with a brodie," Pap said.

"What?"

"Glaumed the whole shipment. Left the boxes as a gag."

"What's the grift?" Met looked to the boat and noticed two opened crates. "Where's the hooch?"

"That's what he's trying to tell you. It ain't there. They came up empty," Oleg said.

"Pull somebody else's leg." Met was growing tired of doubting that their lives were about to be on the line.

"Check for yourself," Pap said. He hoisted a crate onto the dock, then tossed the crowbar on the floor next to it. Met pried it open. Nothing but wet, salty hay. "They're all twins."

"What am I supposed to tell Mank Mill? You think Plagun will pass it off with a laugh. Maybe send me on vacation?"

"I'll take it up with him," Pap said.

"You ain't gonna leave me holding the bag on this," Met said.

"I said I'll take care of it."

"He's gonna have a curse on someone, you know that?" Met said. Pap's assurances carried no weight. A lost shipment was tantamount to mutiny, and mutineers were hanged.

"As long as it ain't you," Pap said. "I'll go see him tonight."

The creature in the crate spouted off a soft growl. Met turned his attention to the crate thinking he heard something worth listening to, but the animal went silent. Instead Met gave devil eyes to Pap and then stormed back to his truck, fired the engine and cranked it in reverse. He would be making the short trek back to the zoo with nothing but an impending fear of retribution.

Pap and Oleg got out of the boat and sized each other up.

"I don't want to know what happens," Oleg said.

"Nothing's gonna happen," Pap assured. What else could he say?

"You know how long I live off three hundred smacks?"

"Can you trust me when I say we'll score again?"

Oleg shriveled his eye lids and spit the venom from his mouth. He needed to blow away, but he didn't walk from Pap without a nod of decorum. He still respected him no matter the disappointment he carried back to his empty Cruison. "I'll have to sell the gig," Oleg said.

Money was so important to Pap that he knew how much others needed it too, and he always tried to take care of them when he could. He reached into his pocket and pulled out a humble roll. He rubbed a C note between his forefinger and thumb and separated it from the rest of the bills. They were ones and totaled ten bucks. It's all Pap would keep. "Here." Pap handed the hundred to Oleg. "That's a third. I'll get you the rest as soon as I can, alright?"

Oleg took the cash from Pap. The embarrassment didn't let him raise his eyes. Instead he kept them focused on the hundred dollar bill. He didn't want it to come this way, but he didn't deny it either.

"Don't sell your boat. It's all you got," Pap continued.

Oleg gave a more courageous nod and plodded to his Cruison.

Lou stayed with the crated creature. It remained dormant. "What do we do with this?"

Pap returned to the speedboat. "Put the lid back on. We'll leave it in the woods."

"I don't think it's doing too good," Lou admitted.

"That's not our problem. He'll have a fighting chance like the rest of us."

Lou closed the crate and tipped it on its side so that the cover wouldn't slip off. Pap helped him lug it onto the dock. They stood on each side of the crate and squatted. In harmony, they lifted it and made their way off the dock and into a patch of trees.

They set the crate down and opened the lid. The animal within gave its best impersonation of stillness. Its head curled into its body. Pap stared at it once trying to figure out what had happened tonight. Each moment that passed without finding a cure was another moment closer to their end. "That's all we can do," he said. They cleared out.

- 27 -

Bill Plagun immigrated to Good Leaf at age six. By age seven he was busted for assault on the neighborhood bully with a tire iron. By age eight, busted for robbing a baker. Age nine, for firing a gat at a cop. He was yoked into a reformatory for five years. Busted out his first weekend. His boyish face followed him into adulthood but not his innocence. Tonight he was holed up inside the Arm Hotel on East 33rd. Just a couple notches down from the Ritz, but it had all the amenities he needed: murals on the walls, thick rugs, soft beds, plenty of hot water and quick fire escapes. He took up the two top floors, one buffered the other. No one but his family and crew was allowed up. The elevator operator was paid an extra hundred a week to make sure. He had a mental list of maybe ten who had access. And just in case one slipped past, two large men with guns strapped to their shirts would make sure to send the mislaid traveler back on his way. There would be no eavesdropping on these floors.

Pap appeared through the open elevator. He was allowed. Mank Mill recognized him without any formal or friendly greeting.

"We lost a shipment," came right out of Pap's mouth.

Mank smacked his teeth with his tongue. If he said another word he would shoot. Instead he turned and led Pap down the hall to Plagun's room. Mank knocked on the door.

"What?" Plagun said from the other side.

"Tonight's drop," Mank said. A brief moment of silence let Mank know it was okay to enter. Pap followed him in. Fancy copper drapes blacked out large windows. Plagun was lying on a king-sized bed. He wore a red robe with a silk napkin in the pocket. A Fumaroll cigar sent curlicues from a crystal tray.

His oldest son, Buddy Plagun, sat in a corner chair. He was his old man on adrenaline. A master sailor, Buddy ran rum into the Leaf from the north, east and south, all for his father's growing empire. Their next order of business was to force rival, Commodore Cabra, out and consolidate the trade routes. When it came to rackets, might made right. He looked to Pap with a glint of malice. Pap acknowledged Buddy first and then Bill Plagun.

"We lost it," Pap said in one shot.

"What!" Buddy yelled.

Pap's heart climbed up his throat.

"Buddy," Bill Plagun issued before asking Pap, "What does that mean?"

"They came up empty. All ten of them. Barrels too."

"But they came up?" Bill asked. He blew the tip off his Fuma. It sprinkled ash over his robe.

"I'm still scratching my head," said Pap.

"You and me both, Fanti," Buddy said.

"You're the storyteller. Make us believe whatever you want," Bill Plagun said.

"I found this inside one of the crates." Pap reached into his pocket.

Mank and Buddy went for their rods. "Easy, sailor," Mank said.

Pap froze his hand and smirked for permission, then slid the hunting horn from his pocket and handed it to Bill Plagun. Bill brought it to his nose and smelled the old salt. He looked to Mank for an answer. Mank's lower lip curled out. His brow furled ignorant.

Plagun turned the horn from side to side. "I got not kick. I know you're on the level. You and your crew. Even your dipshit brother."

"You think it was Cabra?" Pap asked.

"Nothin' doin'. The law wants to stop us, but the law's only as good as the man willing to enforce it. Get rid of that man, you write your own laws. There's a G-badge from a new outfit by the name of Fist. Used to lead the local vice squad or some bullshit. Can you believe that? We're getting so big they actually started a new crew to take us down, all backed by Uncle S. Fist jacks off to my mugshot. Joined up with the Coast Watch to make sure they don't take snacks. Apparently, no one else is as keen on enforcing some bunk booze law every decent citizen flouts. Word is he lost a wife to the booze and turned crusader."

"They were all sealed shut," Pap said.

Buddy Plagun rocketed from his seat and rushed Pap blowing flames from his mouth. He was fixing for a fight. "Bust this fuckin' cracked button right now for calling me a chiseler," he said. Mank turned into a wall and held Buddy back.

"I never said that. I just can't explain how they go in full and come up empty." Pap took a couple of steps back. He was nervous. At any moment, he'd be fitted for cement shoes.

"Buddy, ice up!" Bill ordered. He shot a dagger from his eye that landed square in Pap's. The cigar tremored between his fingers. Mank kept his hands on Buddy and his eyes on Pap the entire time.

"Maybe you had something to do with it," Buddy said.

"Don't say that. I swear to God, we were just doing the job. Mank, tell them. In all my years when have I ever pulled a stunt like this?" Pap said.

"Buddy, take a chair. Come here," Bill said.

Buddy didn't bat an eye from Pap. He never liked his cocky face. Thought his sissy act was a ploy to make others think he was dumb when he wasn't.

Bill continued, "Don't worry. These things happen. You did right coming here." He kept his eyes on Buddy. Buddy kept his eyes on Pap. "I promise you this won't happen again." Bill handed the horn back to Pap. Pap safeguarded it back inside his pocket. Bill's eyes told Mank he wanted Pap out of his room.

Mank cuffed a hand on Pap's arm and led him through the door and to the elevator, but before he pressed the button to summon the lift, Mank popped the question. "You ever kill a man?"

Pap knew what was next. He would be pressed for a hit on Fist even if the dots didn't connect. That's just the way it was with a man like Bill Plagun. Pap detested Met for making the introduction, even more so himself for taking the bait. He had never taken another life, let alone a G-Man, so he answered the only way he could: "Yeah."

"Then this won't come as a surprise," Mank said as he pressed the button for the elevator.

"No. No surprise." Pap's eyes hid their dejection.

"Need a hand?"

"No. I can handle it." Pap wanted no outside involvement in what he was already planning.

"It's settled. You do good, there's something in it for you." Mank didn't need to wheedle any further. Pap was in no position to refuse the order, and he knew it. So he gave a straight-laced nod instead. The elevator door opened, and he got in. Mank watched the door close and he headed back to Bill's room. When he got there, Buddy had questions for him.

"Well?"

"The crumb's made to order for it," Mank said.

"He was lucky to walk out of here on his feet," Buddy said.

Bill resuscitated his cigar with a flame.

"Was it Fist?" Mank asked.

Buddy Plagun's head went left to right. "Not this time," he said handing Mank the newspaper resting on a corner table. "Front page."

Mank grabbed the paper and flipped it open. A picture of Fist and a squad of Coast Watch gloating over another kill. His eyes followed the headline: *G.A.V. Head Ziggie Fist Sinks Another Cabra Rum Ship. Runners Beware.*

"Since when are we doing Cabra favors?" Mank asked.

"Will seem that way at first until they send in the tanks. Fist will be out of the picture, and Cabra will be a marked man," Bill said.

"He'll declare war," Mank said.

"Maybe. A man gets what he wants in one of two ways. Compromise or murder. One carries less consequence. To this day I'm not sure which one. Cabra is a businessman who knows that he makes more with Fist out of the picture. We want the same thing," said Bill.

"It's a pop fly with runners in scoring position," Buddy injected.

"And we're up at bat," Mank said.

Buddy handed Mank a leather folder, "Lieutenant Johnson dug that up. Hasn't made the press." Mank read to himself. It was a profile on Ziggie Fist and his intended targets. Next on the hit list: Bill Plagun and his associates.

"Johnson's a good man," Mank said.

"Yeah, he'd make even better captain. I'd like to talk to Buddy for a moment," Bill said. Mank took the hint and vacated. Bill waited a minute before he started talking. "How many routes do you control?"

"Ten if you count South Jester and the Gorda."

"I want you to stay out of the water until we straighten out this Fist business."

Buddy wasn't excited to hear the news. If there was one thing he loved more than rival hits, it was running rum into their harbors under black of night. What's more, with him helming most of the ships, he could ensure that none of the cargo would go accidentally missing or confiscated like Pap was led to believe. "Cabra thinks he can sail the Titanic on the row without getting nabbed. That lousy cunt deserves what's coming to him, but Fist knows better than to fuck with one of my ships. We're faster, and our plane-poppers would blow him into a chum slick before he could even blink."

"That's what I'm talking about. Once we set up our distilleries, we'll be out of the import business. We control the whole thing, production to distribution. That's where the real loot is. Beat Cabra to the punch, we'll swallow up his entire network. I'll need you and your brother strong enough to handle the operations. I'm talking about a major expansion here, and we all gotta be ready. I'm not gonna be around forever."

"Come on, don't talk like that," Buddy said.

"Just do me this favor. I've been worried about things. These are dangerous minutes. One slip-up and we're done for. If anything happened to you or Junior." Most fathers loved their children without rhyme or reason. But Bill had his. Buddy was as faithful as a guard dog, Junior reliant as a parasite. How could Bill ever think to turn his back on either?

Buddy watched his father, the conqueror, wishing to be just like him and greater, but now with a voice vulnerable and eyes humbled, he was afraid for his old man. Things had grown too quickly, and everything he spoke of was right. The daily dangers they faced simply to live at the surface were always present even if they weren't always spoken of. "Everything's gonna be swell."

"Your mother thinks we're bad men. She's never said it to my face, but I can tell when she looks at me. That's my burden. Everything I do is for the three of you, so we don't have to struggle like the rest of the bums begging for bread tokens. No matter what, we hold our heads high. Do this for me. Give your routes to Mank. Breaks, Strobile, all of them. When Fist is gone and Johnson's captain, we open the books. With the new money, we'll buy our votes and plant our own people in City Hall. Cabra will fall without a fight."

- 28 -

Pap burned rubber back to the wharf by Crystal Plats. An old rain left its clammy sheen on the ground. There was something he had to check on before he called it a night. He parked his Model T and got out. There was no one in sight. That's the way he preferred it. He moved through the darkness and back into the trees. The crate was still there. He couldn't tell if the animal was too. He glanced over his shoulder to make sure he wasn't tailed and moved in on the crate. Pap knew he couldn't leave the waif there. Even with his own life on the line, something told him he had to take it home and nurture it to health. It was the stupidest idea he ever had. He approached the crate. "Don't you bite me," Pap said. He tried to get a closer look. The animal was curled up in a ball. He couldn't tell if it was breathing. He thought to stick his hand inside but fear of a quick tooth told him otherwise. He got low and heaved. It was heavy without Lou's hand. He had to set the crate down a couple of times to catch a breath. He lowered the car roof and stacked it on his passenger seat.

The whole drive home, Pap considered blowing town. Bumping off a badge would put him on the hotsquat. Not going through with it would guarantee a contract on his head. Life had turned out badly. All he ever wanted was to earn his keep and live in peace. Pap found himself on the lam instead. There would be no hit, no fall guy, not for a shipment of panthers he was sure Buddy Plagun pocketed, even if he was stealing it from himself. He could never prove it, but that was the only explanation. The whole cop angle didn't add up. Why they were targeting Pap was a mystery. He had always worked hard, always remained loyal. Maybe Plagun just wanted Fist rubbed out no matter what, but this was the first time Pap had been asked to do a job like that. It was a night of many firsts. Pap drove himself into a headache. All he needed to do was get home and lock the door. He glanced to his right at the crate. The animal within was silent as an empty drawer. He wondered if it was dead. Pap pulled out a smoke and clamped it with his lips. The smell of burning tobacco would ease his troubles while he let his mind plot his next move. The drive to the slums of Lower Leaf seemed unusually long tonight but he made it without an accident.

Pap parked right in front of the tatty tenement he called home. His was one of the only cars on D Street. The denizens loved to poke their nose into his affairs, but the smart ones kept their traps shut. They knew he was dialed in, a professional runner. It's the only way he could afford that Model T. But that's as far as it went. For blocks on end, nothing but roach-infested motels. Pap had been on his way out, just like his brother, Met, for as long as he had memory. He always knew a better future awaited him, but he needed a night's sleep to keep such hopes alive. He lugged the crate from the car and with a swift kick on the busted building door, let himself in. The air was musty. The green carpet along the hall looked like a sweat-stained shirt and wore thin through the middle. Luckily, he lived on the first floor. With his arms under the crate, he leaned into the door and twisted the squeaky knob with a free hand. It was unlocked.

Pap set the crate down before his arms gave in. It brought the animal to a soft bleat. He was off his onion to lug it home. He shut the door and locked it in one motion, then turned on the light to his room. That's all it was and a boxy one at that. It had a toilet and a sink. They were both clean. A long leather sofa is where he slept. Summer nights often required nothing more than one's own skin. He took the hunting horn from his pocket and tossed it on the couch. Then he took off his jacket and unwrapped his sweaty shirt, throwing them both by a large duffle bag in the corner. His clothes were neatly folded inside of it. He had a small ice box by the sofa. Maybe there was something in there for the animal. All that remained was half a hot dog inside half a bun. They were both cold and hard. The frank bore a thumbprint of mustard.

"You want a bite whatever you are?" Pap removed the face of the crate. The animal was awake. His eyes were opened and staring at Pap with purpose. "You ain't gonna tell anyone what happened, right?" The animal continued to stare at Pap in a droll way. He tore off a piece of the wiener and tossed it into the crate. The animal sniffed at it and lowered its head to have a taste. It vanished within its mouth. "You are hungry, buster." Pap tore the rest of the hot dog into pieces and made a trail of it from the crate. The animal followed it, taking up each bite along the way until it was out in the open. The first time Pap was able to get such a clean glimpse. Its fur had dried out, but it was still joined at the tips. No more than two feet long, it wobbled on all fours, clumsy enough to tip over with a candle blow. Its body looked unfulfilled. The more Pap stared at it staggering aimlessly, the more he concluded it was a type of bear. One of those white bears that grew up to be two stories high. He'd never seen one before. Then again he couldn't be certain that's what it was either. What did he know from animals? The ones he dealt with walked on their hind quarters, wiped their asses and cursed in English. He was dealt another inkling of curiosity. Pap took the horn from the sofa and placed it on the floor next to the bear. It pawed at the horn until it was under him, then it dropped on its side and scooped it up like a bottle of milk. Planting the horn to its snout it let out air and with each breath, one nettlesome tone, sounding like C major, but that it sought to make such a sound was something of a phenomenon in itself. Pap didn't think to stop it either until he realized that they were encased in thin dry wall and it was the middle of the night. He snatched the horn from the bear's grip. It extended its paws to Pap and started bleating. Pap tried to shut it up, but the animal was begging to be cradled. He had never held an animal in his arms before and wasn't necessarily looking forward to it. Pap scratched the top of his hand and went at the bear like he was approaching a newborn. The last time he had this sensation, he was holding his baby brother, Met, while his father wailed over their dead mother. He rested the back of his hand on the floor next to the bear. The bear shifted its head to the hand and rolled onto the open palm. Pap took the other hand and scooped him up. The thing felt heavy like a sack of water and strong. It kept still but malleable in Pap's arms like it gave him full reign. Pap tried to pick up a scent, perhaps something foul, but the bear emitted no such odors. In fact, it had a hint of talc. Pap was in no position to adopt a bear, but he had taken a shine to it immediately. Within seconds it was asleep in his arms. He couldn't help but think it was a tender animal. He set it on the sofa and watched it snooze for a moment, then headed to the toilet to take a leak. He didn't have many days before Plagun would realize there was no hit on Fist.

- 29 -

The next morning, Pap woke up on the floor. He was so tired he had forgotten to get to the couch. He yawned and slowly remembered the most peculiar dream. It was about a bear that could play a trumpet like Dizzy Marea. He got to his knees, then glanced to the sofa. There was the bear, wide awake, a gentle eye on Pap. "Guess who's taken over," Pap said. The bear held its hunting horn and blew a morning salute. "Too early for that, buster." Pap snatched the horn away. The bear showed nothing in the form of a protest. It simply continued to eye Pap and each of his movements. Pap plodded to the toilet room without further attention on the animal. The bear hopped off the sofa and followed. Pap stood over the toilet relieving his bladder and without once noticing, the bear was standing within feet, his eye stuck on him. It stood on all fours. Pap saw him out of the corner of his face and almost felt awkward going in front of it. "I bet you're starving." The bear gave a sudden groan as if to say 'yes.' Pap nearly gave a double-take. The timing of the bear's response, in whatever language, was too precise to be incidental. But it was just a quick hum. "You'll have to stay here. Can you do that?" The bear responded with another gruff purr. "Bet it wouldn't take long for you to start talking English." He zipped up and turned to the bear. It continued to wait on him on all fours, patient as a tree, a tenderness in its eyes, almost human, that Pap couldn't recall seeing in another man. He knew nothing about animals except one thing: When they needed to go, they went, anywhere. He checked the sofa and the floor. The bear hadn't soiled a thing, and this had Pap worried. He took the sheet from the sofa and folded it into three layers. He laid the bear on top and wrapped the makeshift diaper around his bottom. The bear allowed Pap to do with it what he pleased in a display of unprecedented submission. "I don't know what you are or what I'm gonna do with you. Hang tight. I'll be right back."

Pap lifted a cushion from his sofa. Ten dollars hidden within. Emergency dough. He would have had more but for last night's failed job. He put on a fresh shirt, his pants, shoes. He glanced back one time at the bear before he shut the door. "No racket while I'm out, dig?" The bear almost shook its head "no," but that would have been too much for Pap to take.

Pap walked down the block to the Good Deal Grocery and bought a few cans of chop liver, a loaf of pumpernickel, quart of cream and some paper towels. He wasn't hungry. It was all for the bear. He hurried home, keeping an eye on guard at all times. Plagun could have buttons sewn on each corner. When he opened the door to his apartment, he noticed the bear seated on the couch like a well-groomed lad. It had the hunting horn resting on its lap. Pap closed the door. The bear brought the horn to its tar snout and blew. Only this time, its breaths were like Morse code; it seemed to be communicating something. And there was an added note to its repertoire. High then low, C to A, C, A, up, down, repeated until Pap said, "You're a regular goose." The bear stopped and looked to Pap.

Pap filled a bowl with chop liver and cream. He presumed it would be on the bear's menu. It didn't protest. But instead of attacking it like a wild animal, it was mild, almost calculating. The table manners of a prince, it took its time with each bite until the bowl was licked clean. Pap had nothing left to do but watch. "Are you sure you're an animal?" He remained in his apartment the rest of the day with the bear and the thought of what the next few would bring. He felt the need for backup and thought of bringing Lou Licks to stay. Only he knew that Lou never liked being anywhere except his own cave of concrete walls. He wondered if Plagun would truly send a hit squad on a bad drop. They were all criminals, but death for money didn't equal out in Pap's morality. But then again, if not money, what else?

Night fell with a tap dance of rain. The bear played his horn to the accompanying beat like it was a drum roll and he was seconds from crescendo. It seemed to bring him peace, so Pap didn't bother him. If a neighbor complained, they'd complain to the thundering clouds. The bear went for a whole hour before he dropped the horn and dozed off. This time it was on the floor.

Hours of thunder and showers and somehow Pap slept through it like he'd soon miss these respites. But a sudden flushing sound made him jerk upright. It was from his toilet. Pap got to his feet and crept to the bowl with nothing more than a can opener in hand. He had yet to own a gun. He peeked around the corner and turned on the light. The bear was standing by the toilet on its hind legs. A fear shot through Pap that was instantly quelled with awe. He lowered the can opener and stared at the bear for another few seconds. The animal never showed signs of aggression, but Pap remained mortified. He considered saying something to it, but what could he say to an animal that stopped acting like one. The bear dropped on all fours and lowered its head. It bleated to break the ice before shimmying past Pap who remained in place questioning whether he was awake. The signs were clear. He was starting to crack.

- 30 -

Pap let the radio play on. The bear seemed to be enjoying himself too much to stop it. For a few short thoughts, it made Pap forget he had a death-defying job to do for a very dangerous person. Thoughts of Met came to mind. If they learned that Pap went AWOL, they'd go to Met for an answer. When he didn't give them one, they would kill him. He had to warn him, hopefully get him to blow town. Pap turned off the radio. The bear stopped playing. He stared at Pap. Nothing in its mug told Pap that he would be trouble if left alone for a few. "I'll only be a second," Pap said as he started for the door.

With Pap's back to him, the bear took a seat on the floor and garbled out an "okay." Pap spun back on his heel, thinking someone was in the room with him and, out of instinct that he was about to get killed, ducked. Surely, Plagun had tracked him down without giving him a chance to make a move. The same word came from the bear again. Pap nearly gave up the ghost. His tongue went dumb. His knees wanted to give out, but they were too locked with fright to bend. Pap kept a silent eye on the bear for a motionless minute. The bear kept repeating "okay." On the third utterance, Pap broke his silence. "What the hell are you?"

The bear tilted its head into a nod. It never intended to scare Pap, but that's exactly what it did. With an absorbed gaze, it appeared to crinkle a smirk. "Buster," the bear said.

"Impossible."

"Buster. Buster okay," the bear repeated with the inflection of a child with sandpaper in its larynx.

"My God. This ain't real. What the hell's going on?"

"Buster okay."

"Stop that!"

"Okay," the bear whispered.

"I'm crackin' up. It can't be." Pap slapped himself across the face as hard as he could. This couldn't be a dream. It wasn't.

The bear curled up in a display of submission and closed its eyes. Pap could hardly move to escape, but he couldn't help but admit that there was nothing threatening about the bear. It certainly couldn't have come from Plagun.

"Say something again. I dare you," Pap said.

The bear lifted its head like it needed warmth and Pap was the sun. "Buster okay."

"Shit. You do talk." Then Pap regained his composure as best he could before a talking bear. "Alright. If that's the way you want it. Pipe this, Buster, or whatever you are. You try anything funny with me, I'll turn you into a coat."

Buster lowered his head and waved it like a ball of cotton. Pap felt remorse for his comments, even if a talking, musical bear would put him on the short list for the loony wagon. "Just pipe down till I get back. Can you do that?" The bear surrendered to a corner and curled into a ball, burying his face in the fluffy center. Pap got every assurance from "Buster" that things would be just fine, so he left.

It was 10 am. In 1927, Crystal Plats Zoo was only half complete, but it remained opened to the public for a cost of two quarters. Pap had never seen the zoo when it wasn't a ghost yard. There were kids, both with parents and without, love birds, old folks, the typical fare to make this the ultimate cover for a whiskey hub. He wondered if he would find Met at this hour. Pap paid his fifty cents to get in and wandered what must have been the worst zoo he could imagine. There were few exhibits. The ones that were housed few inhabitants. The chimp cage promised something worth noting, but Pap failed to see any life inside. Talk about a racket

Met tapped him on the back of the shoulder. "What gives?"

Pap turned. "We got ourselves into a little scrape."

"We?"

Trolling sightseers made Pap twitchy. "That's what I said. You got somewhere private?" he asked. Everything in Pap's life was about private. It's a wonder he didn't live in a grave.

Met turned and started for the warehouse at the back entrance.

Pap followed. "You alone?" he asked again.

"Yeah," Met said.

They bypassed the warehouse and continued to the back lot and the idle truck. It was empty. They entered each side and boxed themselves in.

"What happened?" Met asked.

"You gotta lam," Pap said. "I'm behind the eight ball."

"You never told Plagun, did you?"

"Not only did I break it to him, I pinned the whole thing on Buddy, right to his mug."

"They'll kill you for the drop alone. You got some sort of death wish?"

"It's a frame up," Pap said.

"You're crumbs off a table. Climb up your thumb."

"They want me to bump off a G-Man. Say it'll square things up. Maybe I'm number one for a fall guy, but I'm not going through with it. I came to warn you because you're my kid brother."

"I take a powder too, and we'll be as obvious as a whale in a tub. Try throwing strikes. Sometimes I wonder who the hophead is. I run out of breath the moment I take step one from this parking lot. You're lucky I don't turn you in myself. I bring you into this racket, and this is the payback."

Pap let Met vomit every last bit. He knew his brother was frustrated, but it never occurred to him that Met could imagine turning his own blood over. "I didn't fleece that booze," Pap said.

"I don't wanna hear another word. I don't wanna know what they do to you. I ain't going back to no asbestos plant, you hear me? No shipyards and no bread lines. You know I still got beef dating back to the Sunks Boys. With Plagun, I'm safe. If you give a fuck, don't bury me in your coffin."

Pap knew what it all meant. Met would be nowhere if he wasn't surrounded by booze. They didn't pay him shit, barely enough to tease Sue, but Met liked being able to slug off of the defects, broken bottles that would come in with each shipment. It was the main reason he stuck around. That and the respect he thought he had working for one of the mightiest gangsters on the Leaf. Pap opened the truck door and got out.

Met continued yapping, "Whatever they want, you see it through. I've seen Plagun dust a sap for a marked deck. No one makes him a Patsy and lives to sing about it."

"I ain't going through with it, I tell ya."

"Then I'll see you at your funeral. You made a bad move, and I only pray they don't mistake me for you."

"Get out while you can. We can get out together, forget any of this ever happened."

"You still don't know who you're dealing with. I ain't going nowhere, and if you don't get lost, I swear I'll tip them off myself."

Pap's stomach swished until he was nauseous. He shouldn't have come. "I'll never put the bite on you," Pap said as he dragged off. It was all he could do. He had gone too easy on Met over the years, given him too much rope. Now Met would tie his own noose.

- 31 -

Pap feared returning to his room and the bear, but the whispers kept telling him he needed to go back. It was the dark side of twenty-four hours, the only time he felt safe traveling around now. He checked the street. The peace of night kept things bitterly still. He put the crated bear in the car, and they drove to Lou Licks' place a couple miles west. Lower Leaf was rife with mouse holes. One could get lost for days moving from one room to the next. Pap hadn't introduced Lou to Plagun's crew. It's what made him feel safe there. Not to mention, Lou had no qualms about emptying a chamber in Pap's defense.

Lou lived in a dungy room with cement walls. He was a lonely man when he wasn't pulling jobs with Pap. There were earmarked books scattered all over the floor. They helped with the lonely times. Lou was married once, but it only lasted a few months. His life was cut from the streets, and that was no place for a milkmaid who wanted a herd of kids, so rather than stick around, she cut out and hitched up with a field hand. Pap always claimed she would but never interfered with Lou's personal affairs. They had been tied at the hip ever since they met at the Y as kids. The only successful business they held together was the pig-stealing venture. They tried a food stand, a corner grocer, even bookmaking, but neither had the capital to get far. They mortgaged Lou's grandmother's farm and soon found themselves in a bankruptcy court. The farm was lost, and the grandmother lived the rest of her days at a public nursing home. Lou didn't hold it against Pap. In fact, he reminded himself that the idea to mortgage the farm was all his own. Lou Licks' greatest strength was his loyalty to Pap. It was also his most glaring weakness. They vowed to get rich as a team, own their little piece of the Leaf, but what they had in heart they lacked in acumen. When Met brought them to Bill Plagun, Lou Licks thought he could finally get debt free with his grandmother, and he was chipping away at it too. Running booze was easy money for a roughneck like Lou. With one bad shipment, the dream was dashed, but as long as he had Pap in his corner, he wouldn't give up so easily. He laughed when he saw the bear next to Pap. They almost resembled one another in that portly, "it-wasn't-me" kind of way. He couldn't believe he had gone back for it but quickly understood why. Unlike Pap, there was no fear when Lou witnessed the bear doing unusual things like blowing its hunting horn. An avuncular bond linked them from the start.

"Don't ask," Pap said after thanking Lou for putting him up. There was a bed and a couch. Lou was paid up through the month from savings. All prior jobs he had pulled with Pap, so staking him a place to stay was the least he could do. He told Pap that Plagun would be a fool to try anything there. Under the bed, Lou pulled out a cache of lead blowers. There were hand pistols and automatics. He offered one to Pap. "It seems harmless. What is it, a bear?" Lou asked.

"I think so," Pap said as he declined the pistol. With a gun in his hand, he had an unnerving feeling he'd have to use it.

"What are you gonna do with it?" Lou asked.

"Beats me."

The bear had become something of an oddity, and it didn't take long for Pap to recognize that he had to keep it and for Lou to recognize another business opportunity. This was no neighborhood pig roaming free outside his grandma's ranch.

- 32 -

It had been ten days and not a word of a G.A.V. man being fished out of Breaks Harbor. Mank went to check on Pap and found that he had skipped right after the order. That could only mean one thing to Bill. And the penalty was long held. Open contract for all deserters. For Bill and Mank alike, cowards were equal to traitors. With the same ease that they ran, they would squeal. He set the bounty at two large to start. It had Buddy's name all over it. No one insulted him to his face and got away with it. Bill wanted Buddy to stay out, but it was hard to stop Buddy when he put his mind on something, especially killing. And to add injury, Fist continued to cruise the waters. He had hit two of Buddy's boats in the last two weeks alone and another Cabra runner. Bill kept Buddy on land until he determined it was safe to go back in. He sent Mank to Crystal Plats to have a talk with Met Fanti.

"He came by. I told him to wise up and do the job," Met said. They were seated inside the warehouse. Met choked all life from his cigarette.

"You're the one who vouched for that Nance," Mank said.

"He's a good earner. I've never known him to pull a stunt like this, but I couldn't tell you where he went."

"That leaves you up against a wall."

"He wanted me to jump ship, said you'd run the dogs on me. I stayed. I didn't run. I got nothing to run from."

"Tell me what happened."

"I was waiting in the truck like always. When they got to shore, they came with empty crates. That's how it is. I told him to fess up and get on his knees. You know, do the right thing."

"Get this through your thick dome. Your brother's a lammist fink. When we get a hold of him, we're gonna chop his legs off. Where is he?" Mank asked.

"I swear to God I don't know." Met's voice and nerve were coming apart. He was next in line for the butcher's block all on account of Pap.

"Plagun needs to know he can trust you. How can he?"

"He can. You can. I'm still here, ain't I?"

"Because you're smart enough to know that lamming won't save you."

"I had nothing to do with that night. I swear it on my dead mother."

"Hangman's gonna need a little more than that," Mank said. Men were rarely called to action without a threat. Met could feel one coming. "Be at the Breaks shipyard tomorrow, nine o' clock. Alone."

PART III

- 33 -

December, 1930. Pap hadn't been to Crystal Plats in years. There was nothing in it for him anymore except maybe a quick ticket to the afterlife. He kept Met in his peripheral while driving. Pap made sure he wasn't strapped before they drove off. He couldn't trust Met anymore knowing that he was still working for Plagun. When they got to the zoo, Met had Pap park in the back lot. There were no other vehicles. No witnesses had its benefits, but on a night like this, Pap considered the drawbacks. The air was cold and clear.

Met turned a cautionary head to Pap. "This is important. Whatever you do, don't crack up. You make noise, it goes poof into thin air."

"I don't know what language you're speaking," Pap said.

"You wouldn't have come here tonight if you didn't have some idea," Met said.

Pap became furious and reached for Met's shirt collar. "Listen hard, punk, I'm not here to bury the hatchet. You got something on your mind, then let me see it."

"Hey, go easy, mac. Just come on and try to keep quiet," Met said. Pap released his grip. Met straightened out his coat. They got out of the car and started for the back entrance. Met walked in front of Pap. Pap noticed that Met measured his steps. He was doing his best at playing it taciturn like whatever awaited couldn't know they were coming. They moved down the walk until they got close. But first it started with the sound of a voice. Pap's legs glued themselves to the ground. His first thought was to pull and fire, but he wasn't a shooter. To date, he had yet to kill a man and never planned on making Met his first. On the other hand, he didn't come out here to hand his head over on a platter. He whispered and then pulled his gun, "You set me up! Who's that?"

"It's a what," Met answered. "Don't go bats. There's no one here. Put that thing away, or you'll scare it off."

"If no one's here, you're the greatest ventriloquist I've ever seen."

"Bite your teeth." Met kept glancing at least five yards back at Pap. He stopped around the corner of the chimp enclosure. The broken moon and the lamppost were just enough to make it real. He turned back to Pap and waived him over with a quiet flick of the hand. Pap made slow steps and got within a couple of feet of Met. He pointed yonder. Pap peered around the corner of the rail. A flash of heat ran through his body. He knew better than to ask if it was a fake in a costume. He had run into this before. Pap's eyes couldn't blink, and then they couldn't stay open. It was a voice that man had dreamed to conquer. Anyone with pipes like that could write his own ticket, but this was no man. He glanced at Met. Met had a large grin on his face like he knew the singing chimp meant a life of easy sailing. Pap wanted to get closer, to confirm that it was indeed what he thought. Instead, they bolted back to the car where they could talk without whispers.

"What is that?"

"You tell me. Did I spot a dilly or what?" Met said. He could tell Pap was hooked. It was the score of a lifetime, and the best part was no one saw it coming. It wasn't like losing a shipment of booze or skimming the straw under the paints.

"When did you find out?" Pap asked.

"Just the other day."

"And you've told no one?"

"Just you," Met said. He could see the inspired look in Pap's eye, the way they came to a point like a million plans were building up behind them, but Met always spoke in exaggerations. Starting with all the money Pap would make running Plagun rum. This, however, was the first time he had undersold it, perhaps out of his own notions of doubt.

"I've never heard a voice like that," Pap said.

"So we got a deal?"

"This is Plagun's joint."

"That don't mean billy-be-damned. I told you, I'm the only one that knows and with you that makes two. I don't know what you got up your sleeve after that, but that's your business. You want him or not?"

Pap needed time to think things over, but of all the adversaries he had, time was his worst. "Yeah." Pap was back to a whisper. He had taken his eyes off Met and gazed through his windshield. "You sure nobody else knows?" He just couldn't get it out of his mind that something as unique could last a night without entering into the thralls of gossip.

"You think he's still sitting there if anyone knew? Have you ever heard a monkey with pipes that make Dib Minty sound like a tractor? Something like that can make you rich. You know something about that. Level with me, you've seen this before, haven't you?"

"Never," Pap said. Met didn't buy it. "Is it happy here?"

"Would you kick up your heels in a cold cage dining on frozen chicken beaks? Wherever you take him, I'm sure he'll be better off."

"We gotta do this fast," Pap said.

"Wait a second. What about me? You never asked me if I'm happy here." Met's voice went up an octave. There was desperation in it. Now that Pap knew where the gold was he could try to stake his claim, form a perimeter around it and shut Met out. He'd never get away with it.

"What do you want?" Pap asked.

"Enough to pave my roads for the rest of my life."

For Pap that was a pretty low figure. He knew he could keep Met happy with a couple of C's until things started to settle down.

"Alright, but this stays under wraps no matter what. You spill a word, you paint me red all over again."

"Again? Pull the brake. I didn't come up empty and turn into a shadow. Not once have you asked what I had to do to keep my head from getting popped. That ever enter into your calculation? I was on the boat when Fist went down," Met said.

Pap's stomach churned at the sound of those words, and his face turned a pale page.

Met continued, "Yeah. Bet you never knew that. Nobody went up to tell you 'cause nobody could find you. You're real good at playing the gopher, but when it's time to face the band, your kid brother took the rap. But I didn't come to leaf through family albums. I knew you had made it out, and Plagun still had you picked as his main course. None of it has anything to do with what you saw tonight. I didn't fold up then. Why would I fold up now that you're back in my corner?"

"When?" Pap asked. He wasn't backing out this time.

"You can have him now if you got the smacks," Met said.

Pap shook Met's hand, told him he'd be back in a few nights with a deposit. Met urged him to hurry. Couldn't tell what might happen in the interim. He hadn't bothered to think out the logistics of putting a singing ape on display. Pap was no carny and as far as Met knew, never threw up sideshows on country highways. In fact, Met had very little knowledge of Pap's dealings since he took to the lam other than a faint suspicion that he had run into something big, quite possibly like this before. But tonight, he let suspicions fall by the wayside and focused on celebration. He didn't care about all the formalities. Pap was dressed to the nines and drove a new car. Met couldn't stop focusing on his pinstripe suit, the silly silk rag that flapped an ear from his chest pocket. He wasn't sporting that kind of dough a few years back, so something had changed and in a hurry. And fast change was all Met cared about.

- 34 -

The men's washroom at Calloway was a notch up from Dunfer's. For starters the doors stayed on the stalls, and the vents blew when told. If there was any aroma to this air it was from a fine mist of cocoa bean that latched onto the invisible backs of migrating dust mites. The kid took deep breaths through his nose every chance he could. There was no mirror, but Lou said he was working on it. Before the next show for certain. He knew how important it was for the kid to have a mirror. Had nothing to do with a vanity trip. The kid had none. He simply refused to offend any guests with an unpolished countenance. Lou also promised a new couch, even another radio. The kid told him he needed neither, that his memory bank had recorded all he could want, that he felt bad if they spent another cent. He'd make paradise with a couple of chairs and a table from the basement. An old sleeping bag was waiting for a break in. The extra pillows from Pap would cushion his head against the cold tiles, but the kid liked the cold. Liked it so much he'd leave the small window cracked open all night till the washroom was rimed over. He sat at the table polishing his Elmer trumpet again. There was a soft tap at the door.

"Hey, kid. It's Lou. You counting sheep?"

The kid gave a lamb's bleat and welcomed his visitors. Lou entered with Pap. They had big news to share and hadn't once rehearsed how it was going to come out.

"How you doin', Buster?" Pap asked. That's what they called him.

Buster Horn. Age uncertain. 3'8". 115 lbs. Portly. Covered in a carpet of snow from crown to claw. Biped but could take to all fours. Two black marbles made eyes. Funneled snout. Lips of black rubber. A button of tar for a nose. Enjoyed tailored tuxes, jam sessions, fine meals, lots of chocolate milk and icy swims. Charged: masterminding a trumpet at a speako, killing with kindness, Pap's ace in the hole. Still at large. Occupation: trumpeter polar bear. Repeat: polar bear. AKA Angel #1; AKA Busboy; AKA Gatemouth; AKA Kid Cool.

"Quack, quack, ducky," Buster answered. "Have a seat, fellas. How's this for a new jingle?" Buster raised the trumpet to his snout like an extension of his powers, filled his balloon lungs and made that horn scream, mean, an alarm of life to the senses that had Pap and Lou forgetting their pains. The linchpin to their club, he could turn a funeral into a parade. When Buster finished, he looked to Pap and Lou with a smile that didn't belong on the Leaf, one that had either never known heartbreak or was simply immune to it.

"I think it's better if you take a load off. You're gonna have to for what we have to tell you," Pap said. Buster thought little of it and took a seat. He was never one to argue with Pap or Lou. They had never given him a reason to. Pap and Lou were the closest thing to family Buster had ever known, and he trusted them both with his life.

"Anything the matter?" Buster asked. His bottom paws gently swung off the chair. He was naked except the finish of spotless fur that cloaked him. It was white as a new tooth.

Pap stood still in his crocodile skins. He started towards Buster and put a father's hand over his head. So much he wanted to say. Thoughts of one final move, this time as far as they could get without ever looking back. Pap could have lammed off with Buster halfway across the world and made a mint. Only he'd have no way of controlling his environments the way he did with Demur's counsel. In order for this to continue to work, in order for the secret to remain contained and still provide a living, they had to stay in the shadows of Plagun's backyard. Pap felt guilty for not coming clean, for not informing Buster of the truth. He was a marked man because the bear came up from the deep instead of a standard shipment of booze. But how could he think to ever blame something as pure as Buster? He still couldn't figure out why he had come into his life. "How long we known each other now, kid?"

"Two, three years," Buster said. For a bear like Buster three years was a lifetime and a great one at that.

"And in those years, have you ever been unhappy with us? With me?"

"Never. Why, Pap?"

Buster clasped his hands to show submission. He was a tad uneasy with questions he had never heard.

"Everything is wonderful, kid, and it's about to get even more so, if you can believe that."

"I can believe it all."

"You know I hate moving you around so much, but it's for your safety. I want you to know that." Pap said.

"It's dog-eat-dog. That's what you always say," Buster repeated even if he had no clue what the phrase meant.

Everything Pap shared with Buster was done with an affection he simply didn't extend to anyone else. Pap had never married, never had a child of his own. He knew his friends were with him because they gained something in return, except for Lou, but even Lou knew he could always count on Pap. With Buster things were different. What he could possibly gain from Pap was incomparable to what Pap gained from him. The privilege belonged to Pap, and he did everything in his power to ensure Buster's wellbeing like a father would for his son. It's the same reason he couldn't bring himself to tell Buster that killers wanted him dead. Some things were simply too gruesome to share with blameless minds. "Buster, we would never do anything to hurt you. I need you to know that, okay?"

"I love it here," Buster said.

Pap tried to hold his emotions in check in front of Lou. Otherwise, he was a bowl of soup around Buster. Lou noticed the gloss forming over Pap's eyes. Pap removed his glasses and took a quick pass at the buildup. Buster, on the other hand, was used to Pap's tenderness. It was safe to say that he appreciated his raw side because through those tears, he was assured of Pap's love. It was the kind of love Buster always craved, and in Pap he was able to find it, that safe haven, a tower that made him feel not only comforted but protected from all the bad things in a world he knew little about.

"Do you think someone like you might love it here too?" Pap asked.

A spasm overcame Buster's lower lip, so he crinkled it, then bit it to hold it under control. He wasn't sure what Pap had just said, but he could have sworn it included the words "like me." Like me, Buster questioned. He never mentioned the differences he had with Pap and the others. He was the same as the Cats 6, as human as the next man, but he was no dummy. He always wondered what made him different. He looked different. That much he knew. The words kept ringing inside Buster's furry head.

"Like me?"

"I thought you were the only one. I just want to make sure I don't futz anything up. You're the world to me." To hear such affirming words gave Buster all the confidence he needed, yet he was as insecure as they came. The only time he held dominion was when he cleared his trumpet's throat and blew. That's when everyone knew who was boss. But otherwise, Buster was winsome, meek in inflection, ovine in nature and always watching that he never stepped on anyone's toes. Pap kept on. "I would never force someone here."

"Is he just like me?" Buster asked. Lou had nothing to say but watch Pap and Buster interact. He couldn't believe that another Buster was floating around the Leaf.

"I don't think anyone's like you, but I'm gonna need your help to pull this off."

"Whatever you need, count me in."

"Buster's gonna have a roomie. Can you dig that?" Lou said.

Pap thought to provide a better life to the singing chimp, but something about this adventure made him reconsider his motives. Buster came to him when he least expected it. With the chimp it was the other way around. He had to keep this clear, keep with his principles or the code by which he lived would unravel and turn him into a monster.

"Roomie?"

"Would you like that?" Pap asked.

"Boy, would I," Buster said.

"Get some sleep, kid and thanks. Thanks for everything."

Pap leaned over Buster and connected a kiss to his cotton top. Buster reached out with a hug.

"We're going to have the time of our lives, little buddy," Lou said just before they exited.

If Buster was about to turn out, he would have trouble now. His fur tingled with a life all its own. He returned to shining his trumpet. He could see the vague reflection of his face on the bell and wondered if that's what his roommate would look like. Soon his thoughts had him beat. He put his trumpet to bed, washed his face and teeth and slid into the bag. He stacked the pillows high and set his head to rest. Only he was too tired for sleep. He was fidgety. His legs meant to run when they should have held still. His body was at odds with his mind. A little help was in order. His only thought was what kind of friend he would be to the new arrival. Buster got up and stepped to the counter. A glass of milk on ice waited. It was for the morning, but morning would always be there. He slurped the cream and sighed. Then he gave his chops another polish and crawled back into the sleeper.

- 35 -

Basil Demur's word was his bond. Not many men could boast of such a track record, but when he promised Pap that he would pack Calloway with the same guests that called Dunfer's their hideout, he wasn't lying. They were called "consultations" and took place at Basil's law office, sometimes, though rarely, over the phone, on even rarer occasion via carrier pigeon. In person was preferred. Basil would simply tell the member of the new location and time of the next show. Phone calls and letters were as tricky as kiting messages from the hoosegow. The discussions were always about taxes, estate planning, corporate umbrellas, anything to encrypt the con. To date, his methods were failsafe, and the new spot at Calloway had turned out to be hotter than even he could have predicted.

The parking lot was once again smothered with Caddys, Rolls, Benz, cars that belonged as much as a rattlesnake belonged in a mouse hole. Yachts of all sizes and price tags were moored at the finger piers. They entertained bedizened revelers making the trek by water, partying on their private booze cruises. It was a perfect night for frolic on Twenties Slip. Burger Brasa and Bobby Pin patrolled the bridge. Trunks tracked the grounds. Dradle Prestij hovered on the rooftop of the main building with binoculars attached to his eyes, and Mack Loyter played shortstop inside the roof hatch.

The basement designated for entertainment now looked like a banquet hall at the swankiest hotel. Anthony Mound and Moony Butter returned to their original posts. They donned white waiter jackets and delivered drink orders with a smile. Only they never accepted a tip. It went against house rules no matter how much a guest ordered. Pap even had wash and powder rooms installed in the back, knowing no standard human could hold that much liquor. The same men and women who had sworn allegiance to their select society, crowded tables, drank top-shelf and smoked the finest leaves. Gunther Trilogy, chairman of Good Leaf Steelworks, Biz Ruphert, inventor of the Bestest Battery, there were bankers, stockbrokers, pharmacists, engineers, tobacco tycoons, lottery organizers, even a magazine publisher by the name of Preston Scriben who dared not leak the story. There were top dogs from the electric company, union delegates from the railroads, Daps Luger, owner of a string of movie houses, Germ Latimor, president of the Circle Equestrian Club, Sesha Lacy, headliner at Bolo's Vaudeville & Cabaret, ice magnates like Jackson Reese, and contractors like Chase Griggs. The women were either wives or mistresses. This was a safe place to bring a mistress. Under normal circumstances, anyone of those night crawlers would be quick to let gossip fly, but they knew it would be the last butter they ever spread. Basil had orchestrated the entire thing, told Pap it was the only way to ensure Buster's safety and a profit. Pap refused to go along but soon realized there was no other choice. Keeping Buster in hiding depressed the kid. The bear liked the audience, even though Pap knew none of the guests until they met at the club. They all came from Basil. He screened them, convinced them that the law would keep them on the move and then issued one stern warning. It was all it took. Said this joint was Buddy Plagun's best kept secret. They could drink in a thousand different gin joints or just go to The Spoon if they wanted to be seen under the lights. But these people wanted to stay in the shadows with

Pap and Buster. They had clean rap sheets, held reputable titles, but they all carried dirt under their nails and at Pap's, there was no better place to hide it. The place took men and women of affluence and made them stars in their own little universe. And if that wasn't enough to keep them from talking, Basil promised a steady dose of Plagun justice. They all had a choice, and they all chose to go along with it. There was no reason to spill the recipe. To this point, there had been no leak, other than "Les Stenago" as determined by a "reliable source." As Basil had put it, plant a fresh idea in a rich man's head, remind them of their boring existence, then make them feel like they were the only one privileged to partake in the novelty, and they'd follow you around the globe for a chance at being reborn. $60-$100 a month for cats like these was a drop in the pan. They came for the excesses in food and drink. Pap had each show catered by the finest chefs on the Leaf. They cleaned up the kitchen, once used to mix chocolate, and put them to work. The booze was from Cabra, of all people. Basil made the deal behind Plagun's back. He even footed the bill for the liquor as a favor to Pap. Without Pap, Basil would have never come to know Buster, and Buster was the only one that seemed to cleanse Basil of his iniquities. Jackson Reese provided the ice. As a result, his admittance was discounted by half. The music was the Cats 6, the High Legs spiced up the air, but more importantly, they came for the pill that was molded of a musical bear. Buster. He had that allure, like a snake charmer draining the fangs of seventy five vipers and leaving their jaws sore from mirth when they left. Where else could sophistication gather to enjoy one of God's finest accidents?

Pap went along with everything Basil said, but when it came to the operations the rules had to be his own. He couldn't pressure his crew into silence with lies that Plagun ran the joint. They knew Plagun was on Pap's tail. All men working for him had to be single, no children, no ex-wives. The only exception was Salty Well, but he had never actually known of Buster—

just thought Pap was running a popular gin mill. Pap didn't trust a married man. A woman armed with Pap's trade secret and without the direct threat of a Plagun counterstrike was a match at the gas pump. But he never expected his crew to turn monk or take vows of celibacy they weren't inclined to take on their own. He did, however, forbid mixing with the High Girls because love and business was a deadly tonic. Lou had joked on occasion how he wanted to put the moves on Rita Glass. Pap always said no. And for each of their services and loyalty, Pap paid as well as an underground nightspot patron could. Case in point: Trunks once shined Pap's shoes on a South Leaf corner. It was the worst polish of Pap's life—his cognac calfskins came out two-toned. Trunks couldn't grovel enough for pity, even refunded the dime. When the dwarf said he had no other skill set, Pap brought him on, moved him in to Dunfer's for starters. Now Trunks was lodged up at Calloway, all expenses covered, and he still cashed three Andy Jacks a month. He never polished another shoe.

At the club's highpoint (only months in the making), members of the Gutter Gophers took $20 a week, more than their school teachers made. Turnip and Ink each pocketed $175 a month, the going rate for a hired gun. Dino and Ham Wails were at $125, just like the High Legs. And the Cats 6 each banked $150 every thirty days. Pap warned everyone that it could end overnight and urged them to save for a rainy day. But as lip-locked loyal as his crew was, they were visionary spendthrifts. Fancy wears, dinners, drugs, gambling and twenty-dollar trips to the penny arcade were a few reasons why most still lived like they hadn't a pot to piss in. The only one who stuck to the advice was Pap, and his five large was proof.

Lou was Pap's right hand and doggishly devoted. As a result, Pap didn't feel the need to buy him like the others. Like Trunks, all of Lou's expenses were on the house. Sure, Pap threw him a bone every once in a while, nothing to brag about, but what seemed to make Lou happiest was the lunch trips, wherever he wanted, to gorge on whatever he wanted, all on Pap. Their outings were always brief because they couldn't leave Buster alone. It's not that they couldn't. Buster was a paragon in fur and taught to avoid all manner of trouble. But they wouldn't. And when they did, Ink and Turnip each took turns guarding Buster's door. Pap trusted both. They were cousins who took up prizefighting as teens but never made the big-time.

Pap first met Ink Tambo and Turnip Faymus at an amateur bout in a West Breaks church gymnasium. Ink was fighting Baby Bomber (his birth name), the pugilist who would one day become world champ. Bomber had a talent for wearing loaded gloves. It was a KO in the first. Ink flattened Bomber with a left jab that seemed to be shot from a canon. Only Willy Wring, rising promoter and Bomber's uncle, didn't take to the result. He "blacklisted" Ink on the spot and threatened to have him hauled into a back alley to have his fingers snapped backwards. Ink KO'd him too and left him blind in one eye. A couple of beat cops were called in to break up the fracas between camps. Turnip Faymus punched the heat out of both lawmen before they were able to draw steel. Pap offered a quick getaway and then a gig. Knowing they wouldn't be able to step inside a ring again without being read their rights, Ink and Turnip hung up the leather and joined Pap's club instead. The money was better. So was the respect.

Even the Gutter Gophers showed an allegiance not often seen in street kids with nothing to lose. When Pap came into his first scores running hooch for Plagun, he felt the need to launder some of it into more pious ventures. By eventually setting up a boys' home, he thought he'd be earning points above or at least cancelling out some of the ones below. He put a matron in charge, some ex-nun from St. Goodie's. Her real name was Catalonia Maye, but she went by Sister Second. She was the only kind woman Pap had known besides Lou's grandmother. They met at the Y when he was just a kid and Sister Second a kitchen volunteer. Almost forty years later, Pap would find her at the same Y, volunteering all over again. Now nearing sixty, he'd ask her to take on a new role, one she accepted all too naturally. She would be in charge of watching the Gophers, giving them one last chance at domestication before the wild streets of Good Leaf molded their manhoods. Sister Second rejoiced when she saw Pap, even if she didn't recognize him. She pronounced a benediction over his head which would free him of all sins, past, present and coming. When Buster showed his brilliance, Pap couldn't help but connect him to the sister's prayer. This benison was his alone, and he had to be very careful with it. He also had to be mindful of Sister Second and her double-face. After her soft side wore off, she revealed some gritty shades of power. A tyrant when it came to the boys' schedules, she objected to their all-nighters, said she'd sooner let them abuse a peep box and curse sun to sun. But Pap needed them like he needed his own eyes and always found ways to extend their curfews. The Gophers were the best perimeter Pap could have hired. These kids were men at their most potent point in existence, filled with stamina, stealth and spirit. They could weasel out of any jam. Their senses were acute; they'd pick up things that older men, like Pap, would miss. For them, Buster was like a best pal. They could spend a quarter and catch their favorite cartoon at the movie palace—something they did with regularity—but none of it compared to the real thing.

When most met Buster for the first time, they would react with fearful speculation, not knowing what to make of him, but Buster had an uncanny way of turning suspicion into joy. All it took was a smile, a word, a loving paw, a twinkle of his trumpet. No one could explain it, but after an initial encounter, those who were graced by Buster rarely questioned it anymore. He became one of the gang. Laughed at the same jokes, poked fun at himself, never showed hostility, was ignorant of cynicism. He lived free of rancor and was always the most important part of everything they did. The whole show, the club, all of it, was so that Buster could shine in a controlled setting, some place safe. They were private parties, and no one ever left upset.

After the High Legs finished their routine, Ham Wails pranced to the stage again and spun off another few yarns. "The mayor of Good Leaf just signed a new ordinance that states in part, and I'll read it to you so I don't futz it up," he unfolded the piece of paper from his coat. There was not a word on it. "Anyone caught within one hundred feet of a musical bear will be committed to an infirmary, beaten until they either regain their sanity or are dead, and here's the worst part: They'll be washed in the Daily Leaf as a cross-dressing marathon dancer." The crowd had nothing to do but laugh. Some blew raspberries. "If you thought that was rough, wait till you get a load of this. I sold my soul to the devil a couple mornings ago over breakfast. Today he swings by and asks for a full refund." The crowd rolled into a bouncing ball. Weak bladders marked underpants.

Chase Griggs was in full spirits. He couldn't wait for Holly Fountain to take her seat next to him. He hadn't seen her since the Werlick Hotel and wanted to apologize for not swinging by yesterday like promised. He was forced to work late at the Easter Tower which was code for Vilma having scheduled a dinner party at the house last minute with the admonition that he attend. It was the same explanation he gave Vilma tonight. He could never go wrong blaming his work. Holly was just happy to see him. She didn't care about all the pretexts. When Chase asked if she was available after the show, she acted insulted. She had made herself available ever since Chase came into her life, or rather since she threw herself into his. *Why wait?* was her new motto. Chase was all on board. In a couple of hours he would be strapping his waist with a belt made of legs.

DC Stiles sat towards the back with an eye on Holly too. House odds were most lamps were shining on her as she made tracks to Chase's side. All Stiles caught was the back of his head, which left him wondering what kind of face Holly liked to kiss. She sat as close to a man as a woman could without actually sitting on his lap, and it wouldn't take long before she was there too. Jackson Reese carried another set of peaches in spaghetti straps. They were a few years undercooked. Reese liked them young.

Ham Wails called Buster to the stage. He toddled down from the back stairs and through the curtain. His furry head glistened in the spotlight. He wore a sparkling red tuxedo that fit him snug. The onyx bow tie on his shirt collar barely connected around a neck that was thick as a hydrant. His slip-on brogues were square-toed and triple wide so his paws wouldn't feel cramped. He was shorter than everyone else, except maybe Trunks, but he was all polar bear. Pap, and Basil Demur for that matter, had worried that Buster would outgrow them all one day and develop an appetite for human flesh, but as he approached his final dimensions—in an alarming span of two months—he stayed put. As for appetites, Buster craved people food, spoke people words and carried out people deeds—the good ones anyhow. Other than his appearance, there was nothing animal about him.

Gumbie fingerprinted his ivories. Beans Fryer fractured his bass with those giant mitts, and Buster fluttered his trademark greeting: one strident caterwaul from the bell of his trumpet. It set off the band and boiled the crowd.

Only Chase was still having trouble with the whole thing. This was the second time he had seen the trumpet player. Words like freak, sideshow and monster waxed his thoughts, but as he looked to his immediate right at Holly's expression, he knew he couldn't use such profanities. In her eyes there was a strong caring for the creature, like it had graced her life with things money couldn't buy. He then glanced to Jackson Reese to see what he made of all this crazy talk. Reese's tongue was measuring the distance between freckles on one of his peaches' necks, and that told Chase all he needed to know. Maybe he'd never taken the time to set eyes on the thing they called Buster.

"That's not real," Chase told Holly. After three quarters of a bottle of scotch, the inference was obvious. He was at peak hallucination, and pixies would just as soon start flying around the room as a trumpeter bear would continue to bellow his tune. The first time, after coming back to his senses from his blackout, he passed it off as a midget in a suit. Holly bet him a grand that he was just as real as the tits he would be fondling later tonight. Chase took the wager. He couldn't imagine that something belonging in a zoo or in some icy forest could perform such wonders. Buster had gotten a lot of that in the early days, even some to this day, and that's why Basil and Pap had to show such care in how they arranged the business of the show. It was hard enough to let the scruples of every decent doubter decipher that what they saw was a musical bear. Those things only happened in fairy tales. For all in attendance, and this was all Basil's doing, there were plenty of explanations during the screenings and enrollment. Most of the guests reacted in a similar way when they first witnessed Buster, but routine had the power to dilute even the greatest absurdity. Chase was still shaken and struggling to come up with his own conclusions no matter what Basil had told him in his law office. Holly told him that some things didn't need to be rationalized. That's why they were the only ones to know of it. She had that funny way of making Chase forget about his doubts and focus on the long thumb gaining confidence in his crotch. No question it had something to do with the way she whispered into his ear and ran her forefinger along his thigh. A classic case of form over substance. For a split second, he felt emancipated from Vilma's purse strings. He was in the company of the fantastical bear who, with his trumpet, put the great Dizzy Marea to shame and had the woman of his dreams on his lap. The Leaf was known to harbor strange things. Rumors of sewer crocs and subway devils ran rampant among folklorists. Why not a musical bear? It all started to make sense. He poured another drink to underpin the logic and unnumbered thoughts whispered delusions of power. The man who spilled this to the world would make quite the name for himself, instant fame and a bounty of opportunities. The real mystery was how Pap Fanti was able to keep this under wraps in a world where gossip harbored the largest wings. He instantly remembered the "screening" with Basil. This was the secret that was to bind him to the cult, the select, the privileged. He wouldn't even share it with Vilma now, no matter that she serve him papers. Or just maybe that would be his breaking point. But any man who crossed Plagun could scratch his name from the census. He did recall Basil impressing this point to conviction. It was easier to focus on Holly's legs and try to forget all the hocus pocus of musical bears.

Music was the noise that kept man cozy while he bounced rationalizations about life on a detached dirt clod in the middle of a boundless vacuum. The music maker had a powerful gift in that regard and an equally important obligation to fellow ears. To quell a person's anxieties, to fill in the silence, to make a fella relax, to make him dream, to bring his mind and emotions to an easy place, a place he enjoyed often visiting. But instead of instilling such confidence, Buster played to keep the audience on their toes, to inspire in them a sense of their own mortality, that it wasn't all it was cracked up to be. This was the main reason they came. To dance with their fears, to know that whatever they claimed normal was turned on its head. People like Chase Griggs and Jackson Reese longed for such feelings. It's why they challenged the vows they had made to their wives. Changes to habit meant they could live a new life every morning. And during these obscure hours they needed to feel even more of what made them nervous, and this could only come when they embraced one simple truth: Of every whole second, death, in all its mystery and exhilaration, dominated half. This is how Buster played. It even provoked the jitters in Pap, but there was no shutting him down when he did his thing. Even when drifting into a session of improv, the Cats 6 knew how to keep up. Buster never let them wander into the musical wood alone. They knew when to let the little guy go solo and when to bring in the reinforcements. The melodies were deafening, but one didn't require ears for this brand of pepper. Pap even let his guard down for a few minutes. Dino could tell. He poured him a gazoz. Pap drank it like it was loaded, then put an arm around Lou. To him being drunk was all a state of mind anyway, and the buzz came from Buster.

One at a time, the players backed out from the set. Sweat trickled through Beans' sleeve cuff and down fingers that kept a steady pulse on the string. There was no Pisto Leroy. No one had missed him except Buster. Pap had told him he wasn't happy there anymore just as Lou had informed Pap. Buster was an understanding bear even if he couldn't wrap his head around this. He had recalled Pisto as being the most playful of the Cats 6 and never seemed down on the solidarity they had built.

Once during rehearsal, Pisto Leroy hid a whole salmon inside the bell of Buster's trumpet. Didn't leave it in long enough to develop any fishy smells but stuffed it deep enough so Buster wouldn't immediately notice. When Buster pulled his trumpet from the case, he felt the extra weight but paid it no mind. When Buster blew, the fish flew out and nearly gave Buster a heart attack. Pisto wet himself, he laughed so hard. They wound up wrestling on the ground while the rest of the band cheered Buster on. Only Buster never pinned Pisto down. He could have easily, but perhaps Buster didn't realize his own strength or if he had, never cared to employ it on his friends. To this point in life, he had known no enemies. But if Pisto wasn't happy, he could not be forced to stay. Buster remembered this being one of Pap's most fundamental philosophies.

Buster swallowed what oxygen remained in the basement, raised his trumpet high in the air and sounded the bronze siren, giving the crowd the works. The Cats 6 jumped back in, swinging their torsos left to right, the entire room swayed as though on a wave. Tots tingled the hi-hats and splashed the crowd with a stream of cymbal. Buster triple-tongued his way to a double high C so clarion, stray dogs started barking down the street. The crowd doused him with hoots, hollers, hands clapping, feet stamping, only life could be worthy of such moments.

"Just picture when we get the crooner up there," Lou said. Nights couldn't get much better, and still Pap wondered that exact same thing.

- 36 -

Pap and Lou sat in the automobile with the anticipation of targets over a car bomb. The wait shriveled Pap's innards. Any minute now, Met would haul his pallet truck out the back entrance. There would be no crates, no barrels. They weren't there for whiskey or beer. Pap looked to his watch for guidance. He was on enemy turf and if Plagun happened by, blood would spill. He considered blowing the whole thing just before Met appeared at the gate with the pallet truck. The burlap sack was resting on top, an inanimate bag of bones. Pap triggered the engine. Lou pulled his body from the back seat and helped Met hoist the sack in. It was a heavy, hanging, dull weight.

"He'll be out for the next four, five hours," Met said. He was jazzed off the tea but seemingly aware of his surroundings. He handed Lou a long steel pole with a wired noose at the end and two syringes filled with a combination of Thipentone and Propofol. "Use half a tube if he gets out of line. Any more will send it to that chimp tree in the sky. Good to see you, Lou." It had been a few years.

"Seems to me you already drained this battery dead," Lou said at the touch of the sack.

The larceny complete, Pap urged a swift departure. Met swung around to the passenger side and crawled in. Pap sped away. He asked Met if he had left any hints and whether Plagun would notice an absent ape.

"No one notices them during operating hours."

Then Pap went as far as to ask if Met had bagged the right one.

"You must take me for a boob," was Met's second reply. It was followed by a caveat: He had no clue how the chimp would take to new digs. A sealed enclosure and no escape routes were a must. After all, this wasn't a puppy they just picked up from the Good Leaf police kennel. Pap had more questions than answers, but he refrained from asking many simply to avoid tipping Met off about Buster. He knew that these special creatures had the ability to communicate in human tongues. But he did ask if the chimp went by any other moniker. "Chimp," "monkey" or whatever the hell they were seemed dry for a creature of such merit. Met confessed that "the crooner" was all his imagination could give. Lou looked to the sack of twisted limbs to his right. He thought to peel it off and have a gander but then changed his mind.

"What's this thing eat?" Lou asked.

"Anything but people, so don't lose any sleep," Met responded.

When they got to within a mile of Sunks District (Sue's place), a motorbike cop decided to pull Pap over. A carload of men dirtying up the night air usually meant bootleggers with hush money. The crooked flattie, named Dewer Mordi, had a sniffer for a payoff, and lonely nights were the perfect time to run into someone willing to stuff his runny nostrils. It was a purist approach to law enforcement. Pay the fine; keep the peace. Mordi parked, turned on his flashlight and stalked the car, one hand on his holster. These were hazardous times to be on the streets. Pap rolled his window down and rested an arm on the sill, his right hand signaled noon on the wheel. He knew how to make cops feel at home even when he was imploding under the pressure.

"What kind of work you boys into?" Mordi asked, his cool drawl belied his trigger finger.

"We ain't bootleggers." Pap was direct. He didn't care to mince words. Mordi was used to the script. He flashed his light on the steering post. The registration card read in pertinent part: J.D. McNole. Pap handed over his license with the same name and likeness. Mordi stabbed his light at Met and Lou. They kept their eyes clear of guilt. He then shined his lamp throughout the car until the beam made contact with the sack. "What's in the bag?"

"A dog. Ran in front of me. We didn't want to leave it there, so we're taking it to the river. You know, the proper thing," Pap said like he had planned for this very contingency.

Mordi held incredulous eyes. He demanded to see the carcass. When Met objected, the cop displayed his warrant with a cock of the hammer. Met peeled his teeth. Lou peeled back a section of the sack to reveal a black coat of fur and nothing more. No head, no hand, no foot, no leg, no arm, just fur, black, like any stray dog would presumably have if he wasn't a chimp and was instead a dog. Besides, detecting chimp fur wasn't in the academy manual. He kept his light on the hair without any suspicion that he needed to inquire further. His one big chance at a payoff was about to be blown. Mordi forced Pap to pop the trunk. When he discovered no evidence of liquor traffic and heard Pap threaten to leave the maggot-infested canine on his bicycle seat, Mordi dropped off and let them go.

- 37 -

Met couldn't even wait till the cop was out of earshot to howl out the window. Pap charlied his leg with an angry knuckle. He drove off before the cop decided to bust their balls again. "A dog? I gotta hand it to you, Pap. You always know how to cut me up."

Only Pap and Lou weren't laughing. Things were already off to a shaky start, and it had Pap on edge. "You wanna cut the crap?" Pap said.

Met brought his outburst to a simmer and then really started to get on Pap's nerves. The rest of the ride turned into a deposition. What was Pap going to do with the chimp? Where were they headed? Did they run some sort of secret club for people who paid big bucks and kept their mouths shut?

Pap didn't answer one and then answered them all with: "I told you I wanted him, but you gotta be patient. Nothing's gonna happen overnight."

It was like that every time and something that Met never got used to. Pap frustrated him to a boil with all his big-brother tenets, how he always had his shit together, how things could only ever make sense if Pap had decreed them to make sense. He made the rules, and others had to follow them. That's how it was when you came in second place by birth. But this time, Met was first in line because he, not almighty Pap, had made the discovery. There was always something to be said in being first to find what others wished they could.

They pulled up to Sue's place. There were random cars passing them to the left, late-night commuters, a cab or two, even a couple of night walkers prowling on the sidewalk. Pap was eager to get moving. He pulled his money clip and yanked a pair of C's. Met snatched them up but refused to extract himself from the car. Pap gave not a word. Neither Lou, but Met knew that allegiances had shifted, and he was now outnumbered. "Hold it a second. You gotta lot of moxie if you think I let you lam off with a million bucks without knowing where you're getting off," Met said.

"Don't worry about it."

"No, I do worry about it. You ain't gonna hoodwink me with a couple of hush-hush jacks."

"I gotta get this thing situated. See what we're gonna do with him. For all we know, it won't even work. But you can take him yourself. Maybe he can put on a show at Sue's. You charge at the door. But you gotta make sure that word doesn't get out, or Plagun and his bulls will be all over you like a case of crabs. So you'll either need muscle to keep tongues from wagging, or you'll need money to buy silence. Without either, you got a singing chimp for you and your girl to share. Only then you gotta worry about the super. That thing doesn't seem to whisper his arias. Before you know it, back in his cage will be the only place you'll know to put him, and then someone else can take a crack at it and leave you short. Unless you let me do it my way. With me, this thing stands to make us all a mint, but you can't know where I'm going. I think it's clear why. I already don't sleep at night. Are we still on, or do you take your missing link out of my car?" Pap had no governor on a snarky tongue.

Met's blood bubbled to a hearty froth. It was akin to the curve of having to take a shit in the middle of a romantic dinner, not that he would know anything about it. He suddenly felt claim-jumped, just as he had predicted. "You got anymore on you now?" He knew Pap had more cash because he had just seen it in his billfold. If terms were being rehashed, he might as well get all he can while he could.

Pap separated three twenties. "I need the rest for gas."

Met took the sixty and added it to his two hundred. Two hundred and sixty dollars. It was more bacon than he had fried in a whole year and still he felt cheated to death. The killjoy seated to his left didn't share the same blood. "Thanks," Met said knowing there was a thin line between "thank you" and "fuck you."

"There'll be more. You have my word," Pap said. "If you start going nuts because the days are clawing at you, you're gonna louse it all up. Can I trust that you won't take any wooden nickels? Can I trust you to keep your tongue tied?" Pap was looking to Met, searching his eyes. Met kept shifting them to new hiding spots. "Look at me," Pap commanded.

Met joggled his eyes to Pap's. "Sure. You know I'm on the level. Always have been." It wasn't convincing, but what else could Pap expect? They would part ways here, and Met would have no way of learning Pap's whereabouts.

Lou patted Met on the shoulder. "This thing's gonna do good for us all, okay?"

Met flitted his chin out. They were relieving him of the chimp's custody and fleeing. He'd never see them again. From friends to mortal enemies in one sour breath, all for the bargain price of two hundred sixty dollars. He jerked the door open and flung himself out. Before Pap could start off, Met glanced to the back seat. Something told him it would be the last time he saw his prize. Pap rolled from the curb.

Met straightened his spine and shot an eye at a zooming cab. He flagged it down and got in. "Follow that car, and step on it!" he said. The cab veered to the left. It was five cars from Pap.

Pap was headed north when a hunch told him to take a good look at his rear view. There were always cars behind him, but there was one in particular that had him on the defensive. Lou had mentioned that it was the same cab they had seen passing the Thread District. They were now passing Central Leaf and it was still there, not right on their tail but close enough to make Pap uneasy. "It's him. Thinks we're gonna give him the brush-off." Pap kept his turns smooth and was soon heading southeast onto the Jester Turnpike. The cab didn't lag. If they kept this up much longer, they'd be out of gas. What's worse, the chimp would soon snap out of his snooze. It was the long way to Twenties Slip, but over the Jester Bridge and into the Straits would bring them just south of Factory Island. Pap looked to his gas gauge. Less than a quarter tank left. He punched it a quarter mile from the Jester Bridge. The cab followed suit. Pap threaded through traffic and then it became obvious that the cab was in hot pursuit.

"I told you to be patient," Pap said to himself. He entered the bascule bridge, one of the last cars to be allowed before the red light started flashing.

"Run it!" Met yelled at the cab driver. But that's where the orders stopped being followed. The cab came to a screeching halt at the light. The bridge started splitting at the center. All Met could do was watch as Pap and his million-dollar cargo disappeared across the bridge and into Jester.

- 38 -

Dreams couldn't be as real, but Pap had his doubts as they pulled into Calloway. It was just past 1 am. Pap parked and helped Lou carry the sacked chimp inside. Buster had been moved to Pap's room, the office on the second floor. His washroom would now belong to the chimp. At Buster's insistence, they brought in a couple of mattresses where the chimp could sleep. They spruced them up with large, soft pillows, down blankets, anything to provide a nest of security and warmth. Waiting by the chimp's new bed was a rolling cart holding a covered tray of fluffy cakes, fresh fruit on ice, an assortment of dry cereals and clean water. It was the chimp's breakfast. If he had any other requests, Pap would stop at nothing to oblige. He wanted the new houseguest to be comfortable if not fully at home. There were toiletries of every kind over the sink, even a large washtub that Lou secured over the drain on the floor. They could boil water and fill the tub when the chimp wanted a warm bath. It was a trademark of Pap's to run a clean ship. He even had a small shower installed in the other washroom so that anyone calling Calloway home wouldn't have to go to a public bathhouse every morning. Basil had the utilities put in a fictitious name, even gave a sizeable deposit, so there would be no way to connect the place to Pap.

Everything in Pap's life had revolved around Buster's wellbeing. This included sleep. Since Pap shared the news of a new friend, Buster, who was known for 24-hour hibernations, couldn't doze off for more than ten minutes at a time. Buster held many responsibilities throughout his early years, but none as great as what was in store. He was excited in a frightened sort of way. He knew he couldn't fail Pap. He couldn't fail his new friend, and most of all, he couldn't fail himself. Buster enjoyed excellence in whatever he did. It was the reason he stuttered so much when first learning to talk like a human. Flexing his brain to get the phrases just right caused words to jumble as they teetered from his frontal lobe to his tongue. For Buster, the best was nothing more than improvement on the better. It wasn't enough that he was the cutest, most musically gifted polar bear in Good Leaf, if there were any others to compare. He wasn't showy, had no use for competition. He preferred to give all credit to his band mates, Pap, Lou, the punctilious people making sure the club hit on all six every night. But Buster did need some sense of accomplishment, rather involvement. If it wasn't for his mysterious talents and the preoccupation of keeping himself razor-sharp every show, it would have been a dozen other things. He enjoyed making model sailboats with Lou and then sinking them off the finger piers. He was always first to volunteer, anything from sweeping up after a show to moving furniture into trucks during a relocation. Only Pap wouldn't have him lift a claw in his own castle, much less show himself outside the walls without strict, personal supervision. "That's why I take such good care of them," Pap always reminded Buster every time he wanted to wash his own dishes.

Tonight, Buster waited for Pap and Lou to arrive. When he saw their car pull up, he zipped downstairs like a kid on Christmas Eve. When he saw Lou enter with a large sack flung behind his shoulder, images of St. Nick didn't materialize. He looked to each side waiting to see his new friend following on foot. When Pap told him his friend was in the sack, it caused Buster a hint of distress. Pap assured him that everything was under control and that he should return to bed. Buster didn't ask any questions, but the depiction of his friend sacked like contraband was seared into his memory. He returned to his room without a word. Pap and Lou placed the chimp on the bed. They left him in the sack. Once the tranquilizer wore off, the chimp would find an easy way out. Pap left Ink Tambo standing guard. He handed Ink the pole with the inoculants and instructions on what to do should the chimp throw a fit. There were no rules for something like this. If it turned out to be as cooperative as Buster, Pap would be a lucky man, but Pap was a man who got places by preparing for the worst. They had installed a special lock on the outside of the door to prevent escape. It wasn't Pap's intention to take away the chimp's freedom, but like Met said, they needed to make sure it was on the level before making his indoctrination official and giving him free reign over Calloway. After ensuring that everything was in order, Pap and Lou retired to their separate rooms and called it a night.

Pap flicked on the light in his office and noticed Buster asleep on the extra cot. The look of peace on Buster's face was the only thing Pap was proud of. He had kept his magical bear away from all harm. Pap changed into a pair of sweats and slipped into bed. When the snoring started, Buster could be sure that Pap was out. It was his cue to sneak from the office and head back to the washroom.

Buster noticed Ink in a chair, the bulb attached to the wall shining an eye over his Sunday funnies. There was a sleeping bag and a box of cheese puff snacks. Leaning on the wall was the steel pole with the wired noose. Buster didn't know what to make of the contraption.

"Hey, Ink," Buster greeted.

"Hey, little buddy. Sandman didn't pay a visit?" Ink asked.

"Can't sleep a wink. Is he in there?" Buster asked. Ink nodded. He didn't have a clue what else to say. This was just as new for him as it was for Buster. "Can I see him?"

Ink tried to persuade him to wait till morning, but inside these halls, it was just as dark during the day as at night. In all actuality, Ink was nervous for Buster's sake, but Buster wasn't going to move from that spot until Ink unlocked the door and let him in for a spell. Ink couldn't deny him other than to say: "He don't look like you."

Buster knew not what to make of that. Ink unlocked the door and let Buster in. He left the door cracked so he could keep an eye out. Buster pussyfooted to the burlap sack on the mattresses. The material was prickly. No real friend could find rest in that. Buster inched the bag back. What appeared rattled his eyes. Glancing at his own fur, white as toilet paper, he noticed the stark contrast with the encasing coat of coarse coal and ash on his friend. Buster doffed the rest of the sack and caught himself staring, as foreign a creature as he'd ever seen, it was beautiful, Buster thought, and it was now under his care. It had a callused ridge over its eyes; they were closed, dead to the world. Two holes wrinkled opened at the center of its flat face. Above and below its eyes, exaggerated raisin skin, more like gashes. There was no snout, nothing particularly protruding except those massive gums, the mouth as wide as a ruler, its lower jaw dangling apart from the upper, a chin that looked like it retained water. It could have grown quite the 'stache if its upper lip hadn't looked like a broad strip of craggy rubber. Those megaphones attached to the side of his head could surely pick up a whisper underwater. "What heavenly thing is this?" There was no snoring, not even the skim of a breath. Buster saw his entire future on the face of that creature. Its lean arms rudely sprawled out like it didn't care who was paying attention; the long fingers that looked like Pap's had they been dipped in cement. It was all grand. He hoped to make the best of friends, to show him the ropes, all the splendors of his home, his family. It was a wonderful place to be. He only hoped his friend would find it as welcoming as Buster did. Lifting the chimp's limp legs, one at a time, Buster pulled the covers over. Only the chimp's fur moved when the blanket passed over it. Then, out of instincts Buster didn't realize he had, he neared an ear to the chimp's mouth. A tiny but persistent breath was all the confirmation he needed.

"Sleep tight, friend," Buster whispered.

He took the burlap sack and folded it into a neat square, then placed it on the table. Ink kept his eye on the entire thing, always making sure that Buster's protection came first. When he noticed Buster curl up into a ball on the floor right at the edge of the bed, Ink was at a loss for action. Pap gave instruction to not have them in the same room until it could be better determined that such interaction would be safe. But no one put a hand on Buster either, and Ink wasn't about to yank him out. He let the door ease shut. If Buster wanted to sleep with his new friend, so be it.

The room was dark as blindness. Thinking had Buster's mind in a giddy twist. As each minute expired into the next hour it became apparent that he wouldn't be entertaining sleep tonight. He tiptoed towards the light switch. He needed to see his friend again. Buster stared at him lying in his bed. So many things crossed his mind, he couldn't contain himself. He thought the appropriate thing would be to rehearse what he would first say when his friend awoke. Buster only hoped he himself would be awake when this event took place. It was all a bit confusing; Buster had never known anyone like this. Would he get the words right? How he wanted to make the best of impressions, but therein remained the problem. Buster hadn't stuttered in a long time, but even before he could prepare the words, he conjured up a seizure of stammering so severe he thought to leave the washroom and come back in a few years when he had outgrown all his insecurities.

Suddenly, the chimp convulsed its lips into a pucker as though searching for a kiss. Buster was caught with delight. Was the kiss for him? What a pleasant way to start a friendship. The chimp rolled, turning his back to Buster without another sign of communication. It needed more rest. Buster's body was arguing the same. At this rate, he would be a zombie when the chimp came to and make a terrible impression. He hit the lights and curled back up on the floor.

- 39 -

Vying for the sky's attention was an orange peel of sun and an infestation of fog. The latter was a staple of Factory Island, and it shrouded the washroom window of all but a whisper of light. It was past time for the tranquilizer to wear off. The chimp's legs began to spasm beneath the sheets, and within minutes, he was coming to his senses. One of them was claustrophobia; the chimp threw off the blanket. He was woozy and warped. The first thing he felt was the texture of the surface beneath him, indulgent and warm and out of whack. The air was missing the ever-present whiff of animal. He sat up and shook the cobwebs clean. He couldn't make out anything in the darkness but could swear he wasn't home. He lowered one foot off the bed, searching for the ground. It came across something even kinder to the touch than the bed. The chimp ran his foot across the surface and concluded stable ground. He plopped off the bed, both feet landing square on Buster's side. Buster squeaked and rolled over. The chimp toppled with an edited scream. He scrambled for refuge in the dark and knocked his head against one of the stalls. Buster rushed to the light switch and made everything come alive. The chimp shrieked. It had defecated all over the floor and with one rapid-fire fist, flung a clod to Buster. It struck Buster on the chest and rolled off, staining his clean, white coat a nasty greenish brown. Ink opened the door.

"Buster, what's going on here?" Ink noticed the chimp rearing up for another assault. Buster was at a loss for words just like he predicted. Ink went for his pole and tranquilizers and flanked Buster ready to shove him clear of danger. "I think he wants to be alone now."

The chimp registered the image of Buster with one good eye. Buster appeared statuesque. He couldn't just leave, not on a sour note. The chimp's other eye burst open; it was bruised and thumped to the incessant beat of pain. Ink came into tangled focus. It was hard to tell who had the bulge. Ink would mince this ape if he had to. But then what if Ink got sucker-punched? The chimp never trusted man. His first encounter with them took him away from a place he vaguely remembered as paradise and threw him into a world of despair, all his days from one cell to another, only to end up at Crystal Plats. He stood petrified like a cliff wall. Buster tried to break the ice. "…" A timid grunt that was intended to say: 'Hello. How are you? My name is Buster. This is your new home. Did you sleep okay? Your breakfast is under the tray.' The chimp took the bear's cuff as fighting words. He flashed his eyeteeth. Buster took another step back. Ink kept a tight grip on the pole. He didn't want to use if he didn't have to, especially not in front of Buster. The chimp acknowledged that whatever Buster was, he needed to be reckoned with, like all the beastie neighbors at Crystal Plats, only here one of the neighbors had broken loose and entered his domain. Without warning, the chimp howled hell and fanned his arms like crooked swords. Buster dropped on all fours. It had worked to put Pap's mind at ease in the early days. He attempted another word, but they all failed him. The next cuff provoked the chimp into a blitz. He made a beeline and boffed Buster over. Ink swung the pole, grazing the chimp's head. The chimp turned and caught a glimpse of his worst enemy in the mirror, or was that only an introduction to self? It was ugly enough to be an enemy. Two canon balls formed at his wrists, and he lanced them both into the mirror. The image shattered and shards burrowed into his knuckles. Blood caked into his fur and dripped all over the floor. Ink came in for another swing but missed again. The chimp searched for an exit. The window high on the wall was too small to fit through and even if he could manage it, the swollen fog waiting on the other side was none too inviting. He catapulted off two arched feet, reaching for the top of one of the stalls and hurled himself over. Buster saw the whole thing unfold with horror. 'Don't hurt him, Ink. It was all my fault.' But Buster couldn't even let out a grunt this time.

"Go get Pap," Ink said through a grinding breath. The chimp had worn him out.

Buster hobbled from the washroom and stopped outside the hall. He had never known rejection but could only imagine its first sting as poisonous as its thousandth. He kept an ear on the commotion within. He wanted to return to help, but within moments, the warring chimp was silenced. A surge of emotion welled up behind his eyes and started to spill out in tears. Buster had never cried before. He hated this new feeling. He knew he had to get Pap, but all he could do was sink to the floor and scrunch into a knot.

- 40 -

Pap came to Buster instead and was mortified by what he saw, his most cherished friend, shaken, floor-ridden. "Did he lay a hand on you?" Pap rushed over to Buster and, with his good leg, took a knee at his side. He was not a man of vengeance, had never flushed its cool chill through his heart, but seeing Buster downtrodden had him flashing red.

"No, Pap. I made him bent is all." It was just like Buster to take the rap. What's more, he despised himself for allowing his friend's first experience to be such an objectionable one.

Pap noticed the brown staining Buster's body. "Go clean up upstairs. Everything's gonna be just fine. Like you said, he's just nervous. Remember this is all new to him, so nothing to be down about, okay?" Pap helped Buster to his feet, checked his snout and head for claw or teeth marks like he would any child of his, if he had any. An offspring of the streets didn't leave Pap the fortune of marriage and children, but he had family nonetheless and something that no family had. Buster was fine. "He'll be all right. I promise." Pap put a soft hand on Buster's head. Buster wiped the tears and started for the second floor. A good sleep would erase the pain. He'd wake up to realize it was all a bad dream. Pap shoved the washroom door open, didn't even bother knocking. A man didn't knock in his own home.

"Had to put him out again, but he's cool. You sure this thing is more than just a wild ape?"

Pap had no answer. He wasn't sure. If Ink told him that the chimp did nothing but scream, hiss and hit, what could Pap say that would convince him otherwise? It made him think again that Met had goofed and sacked the wrong one. After all, any thing that acted like such an animal surely held no dominion over the virtues of song. Pap looked to the shattered mirror. "Where is he?"

"In there," Ink said pointing to one of the two stalls. Pap opened the stall door and saw the chimp twisted on the floor next to the toilet. Suddenly the red in his eyes turned blue. He had no preparation for this, but one thing stood clear: Buster would not endure another traumatic encounter. "Maybe we should gift wrap him until we can figure what he is," Ink suggested. It was a logical idea.

Lou got his morning off to an early start. He was in the kitchen preparing Buster's breakfast when he heard a loud bang echo from the mixing room. It sounded like an accident and startled him to think that it could be anyone, a raider, the fuzz, even Plagun. He set the stovetop to a simmer and headed over. He made sure he was strapped before investigating.

When he entered the mixing room with his heater in palm, there was no one in sight, just massive copper kettles, drums where cocoa was once mixed and panned and a few straggler sacks of cocoa from the old regime. Lou paced around the room and in between the drums. He swore he heard a loud crash from in here. And then it was soft, like a snivel. It was coming from one of the drums. He climbed the short ladder and glanced down past the wide mixing paddles to the bottom of the empty drum. Buster looked back up to him with cheerless eyes. "Buster? What's the matter, kid?" Lou buried his gun back in his pocket.

"It wasn't his fault."

Lou was a berserker when it came to Buster's protection and turned from the bear like a cyclone, "Why, I'll fix that no-good varmint."

Buster opened the latch on the kettle and chased Lou down, begging him not to lash out at the chimp, assuming full liability, claiming that if he hadn't been there to frighten him, none of this would have happened. Lou had trouble buying a word. Seeing his friend in anguish blinded him. But he gave Buster the benefit of the doubt. There would be no retribution if Buster didn't call for it. Buster had only seen Lou lose it one time like he did that moment. It scared the bejesus out of him. The memory had been vaulted until today. But Lou's loyalty knew no bounds. This included inflicting pain on anyone who brought it to his friends, even to the point of death. Lou commended Buster on finding this neat little hideout and offered him a hot chocolate. It took Buster's mind off the chimp, even allowed him to nap for an hour.

When he awoke, he was on the cot in Pap's room. Pap was seated nearby. He had been staring at Buster the entire time, gnawing on so many thoughts. People were so accustomed to living in dark times that any glimmers of light were seen as nothing more than fool's gold, but that's not the way Pap spun it, not with Buster. It was because of the darkness that a light like Buster was needed. It was important that Buster be reminded of this often. The chimp, on the other hand, was a dreg, and it was easy for Pap to understand why he couldn't trust a soul. Now more than ever he would rely on Buster to confirm two things: Was it the right chimp, and could this thing work? A negative to any of those inquiries and the decision was already made: a one-way ticket back to Crystal Plats and no grudges.

"I don't want you to be alarmed when you see him," Pap said. Alarmed about what, Buster thought. He sat up on his cot and rubbed the sleep from his eyes. "You see, he was putting you in danger. We brought him here so he could sing with you and the boys, so you could become friends, to give him a home, maybe a family."

"He can sing, Pap?"

"Better than Dib Minty, but this ain't his bag yet."

"Is he okay?" Buster couldn't get over the fact that his new friend could sing better than Dib Minty who was the finest baritone to put his voice to a record.

"He's safe. He can't hurt you. More important, he can't hurt himself." Now Buster was really starting to wonder what they had done to him. "He's probably asleep. He's had a rough night, so you let him rest as long as he needs. When he comes around, maybe you should butter up to him. Give him the scoop on the gig, make him feel like one of the fellas. If for any reason you don't think it can fly, just the say the word. I won't be sore. I just don't want any harm to come to you or him. Okay?"

"Peachy keen, Pap."

"You're a sweetheart. You always make me happy." Pap continued with a stern warning. Whatever Buster did when visiting his new friend, he had to leave him as he found him until they determined it safe. Buster was confused with the last bit of instruction, but he grinned just the same and wended his way back to the washroom. He was eager for a second chance at a new beginning.

"Buster?"

Buster turned before Pater finished uttering his name. "Yeah, Pap?"

"Maybe it's time for you to show him what you got. You know." Pap winked. It was the only statement that Buster new without further explanation. It was the music that soothed the restless heart. Perhaps it would bridge the gap between new friends.

Buster approached the washroom with his trumpet case by his side. Ink wasn't at the door this time. He hesitated; a fresh memory precluded a rushed entry. He swallowed the nerves clinging to his throat, then closed his eye and whispered something to himself, almost like he was praying. He opened the door and braced himself for anything. Instead, he saw the aftermath of a demolition, the mattresses turned over, food shuffled all over the floor, the shattered mirror and no chimp. The stall door was closed. Buster set the case on the floor and measured his steps. He didn't hear a thing and thought it only appropriate to announce himself. He was a stammering, stuttering mess. "Hello?" Not a word was volleyed from the other side. "Are you busy?" Again no answer. Buster reached for the door handle and inched it open, slowly poking his head in. He hoped to avoid interrupting the chimp during his course of business. It's the only reason he could imagine him inside the stall but instead was shocked to see his friend bound and gagged, tied to the toilet, his eyes wide as bread plates and filled with panic, his body flexing to break free without any such luck. Evidently the sedative had worn off much faster the second time around. Buster was just as frightened when he saw the chimp in bondage. He was seated right over the toilet and yet had managed to soil everywhere except inside the bowl. It wreaked havoc on Buster's senses. He left the washroom for some clean towels. When he returned, he dabbed them under running water and wiped up the mess, flushing what he could down the other toilet and curling up the towels for a wash. The whole experience was stomach-churning, but now was no time to wimp out. If he was going to prove his worthiness, he would have to show the willingness to clean after him. As he mopped the floor, Buster kept thinking what the chimp could have done to merit such punishment.

Gimlet-eyed, the chimp could not break from Buster, the bulging belly, the slender snout, a glimpse of canine, the blacks of his eyes. At any second, this white creature would devour him whole. As Buster reached for the gag, he noticed the chimp's eyes shivering like they had seen a monster. After undoing the final rope, he ungagged the chimp and learned who the monster in the room was.

The chimp screeched and hissed, flashed his fangs and spit into Buster's face. Buster was so frightened he couldn't move if he could even breathe. The chimp was so terrified he couldn't keep the English from escaping. "Don't eat me! Help! Somebody help!"

This time it prompted Buster into a mad dash from the stall. He slammed the door shut, leaving the chimp to his privacy, still bound except in the tongue. He was afraid of the words the chimp just said. Eat him? The thought made his skin crawl.

Five minutes under any other circumstances would seem like a vapor in time, but for Buster standing in front of the mirror wondering what next to do, it was perpetual torment. Every time he sought to ask the chimp if he was alright, he withdrew the thought, and any remaining courage fizzled in his throat. But something told him that leaving the washroom again would bring him no closer to befriending this strange creature. With a final breath, he mustered the courage and fought through the stutters, "Excuse me, but are you alright?"

From the other side of the door, the chimp filled up a mad lung and yelled, "Do I look alright to you! Wait! What did you just say?"

Buster paused again. What had he just said? Hopefully it was nothing offensive. "I think I just asked if you were alright." Apparently having conversations with monsters was something this chimp had never done before.

"You talk?"

"Well, of course I do."

"How?"

"Same as you."

"What the hell are you?"

The chimp found it strangely peculiar that Buster could communicate in his native tongue, rather like the humans did. He had never encountered another animal that could do this. Buster, on the other hand, thought it as natural as playing the trumpet that the chimp could talk just like him.

"I'm Buster. Buster Horn, they call me. Pap says I'm a bear, a regular polar-type, but he's always crackin'."

Silence ensued ad infinitum. The chimp didn't want to understand; he just wanted to bust out. Buster didn't know what else to say; he just wanted the chimp to be happy. Considering his next move, Buster paced along the stall door. He wouldn't open it again out of fear. This went on for several minutes. The chimp kept his eyes on the paws skating outside.

"Excuse me," Buster said.

"What do you want?"

"I just wanted to say I'm not here to hurt you."

"Prove it."

"Okay. How?"

"Untie me."

Buster remembered Pap's instruction, to not free that chimp under any circumstances, but he couldn't mean it.

"I'm going to have to go back in to untie you."

"Only if you promise not to eat me."

The same words sliced at Buster's heart; he couldn't imagine eating his new friend if he was starving and the chimp was basting in bolognese. He caressed the door open again. "I promise."

"Fine, break a leg," the chimp said.

Buster entered the stall and noticed that the chimp was less terrified. Reason had told him that Buster was a logic-wielding being, whatever he was, bear, polar, miniature toy, didn't matter. It didn't seem like an imminent threat. He seemed too soft, especially in the eyes. Instead Buster worked to untie the chimp, one rope at a time until the chimp had his arms free and started helping his own cause.

"What am I doing here?" the chimp asked.

"Well…" Buster was folding under the chimp's questioning and soon found himself stuttering more than speaking.

"And why can't you work a straight sentence?" the chimp barked, his piquant words like acid on Buster's coat. Buster shrunk into his shell. He was well aware of his speech impediment, but no one had ever brought it up; they were just amazed that Buster could talk at all.

The chimp shoved Buster out of the way and stood unbound. "I'm sprung now, so scram!"

Buster escaped the stall without a shred of dignity. He wasn't the friend the chimp wanted, and the only thing he had managed to do was alienate himself with his sputtering tongue and unsightly appearance. He had even forgotten his trumpet.

- 41 -

The chimp's instincts warned him not to open the washroom door. There were men outside, and they would rope him up again, this time maybe worse. He evaluated his surroundings. The mattresses, bedding, the table and chairs, the trumpet case on the floor. He pried the case open the only way he knew how, bending the latches until they snapped off and pulled the horn out. It was an odd instrument, not spiked like a weapon, more like a metal vase, a container of sorts. Something went inside that funneled mouth. He pressed the buttons. Nothing happened. He suctioned the opening to his backside and relieved himself. When he was done, he tossed the horn on the floor and shifted his focus to the sink. There was a stick with quills on the counter. To the chimp it was more a weapon than the horn, but to everyone else it was a hairbrush. He grazed his fingers across the bristles. Surely this was used to slash and gouge. He brandished it in what remained of the cracked mirror, swinging it like the batons that were used on his compatriots at Crystal Plats. He caught another glimpse of the image before him and took his time with it. It was alien if he had ever seen one. There was neither acceptance nor embrace. The leathery parchment, cracked and peeling was only partially concealed by tufts of jet-black weeds. His prognathous grill was painful to behold. He opened his maw. An abomination. The teeth were jagged, out of place, decayed, blushed of death, his tongue was darker than his fur. There was no sense in leaving his mouth open. Something far more intriguing had his attention. Two worlds born below his forehead, a bluish hue that did not offend, he could only stare so long before becoming lost in those eyes. They were his.

Buster sat at Lou's side, watching him work his magic over the stove. A spoon of strawberry marmalade, a dash of cinnamon, swirls of whipped cream atop a heaping mound of bananas and bread pudding. "We go right through his stomach, and he won't ever leave you alone," Lou encouraged. Buster would try again this time with another recipe. He had confirmed to Pap that the chimp spoke in their language, so it wasn't a goof on Met's part. They had to continue their efforts to break the ice, and Buster would have to play liaison, one special creature to another, even if neither recognized the other as such.

When Buster returned to the washroom, he thought to knock first, but his tense paw projected the power of a mosquito's wing. The chimp sensed his presence, jerked his head towards the door and rushed back into the stall. It was quickly becoming his Xanadu. Buster filled his lungs and slid the door open as daringly as an infant in an incubator. He slinked along, nudging the tray with the chimp's breakfast to the table. The first thing he noticed was his trumpet dead on the floor. Glimpses of a mangled relic appeared to Buster, but he had overdramatized the incident—if there was one possession he valued over all others it was his bugle. The case was damaged, but he'd soon get over it. He secured the trumpet and pressed the buttons. There was a strange odor coming from the other end. He couldn't lie—it was downright disgusting and tempted his gag reflex. He gave it a flip and dropped the horn at first sight of the chimp's dirty business sludged inside the bell. He turned to the stall. There was no disdain in his eyes, just concern. He nodded confidence into himself and shuffled over.

"Lou prepared something special for you," Buster said to the door in one complete sentence. It surprised him that there were no breaks. What cured the stammers, he pondered. Perhaps the door acted more as protection for Buster than for the chimp. Perhaps he had more courage when speaking about his friends.

"Who the hell is that?" the chimp asked.

"Lou is my friend and yours too."

"I don't know a Lou and don't need any friends. Now why don't you take a powder, beat it."

How could the chimp not need any friends? Buster thrived in a world filled with them, and though he enjoyed many a moment of quiet solitude, they were only better when complemented with the notion that he would soon be in good company. And then another idea came to mind—Pap's idea.

Buster drew near to his trumpet. He wasn't too keen on making contact with it in its current condition, much less playing it, but this was no time to pull the covers over his head and pretend it would clean itself. He couldn't let Lou or Pap in on this either or they would give the chimp an earful. So he took care of it, the only way he knew how. A good soap scrub under the sink till it was good as new, and then he toweled it dry. A fine tuning with a couple of strong breaths, and Buster prepared to introduce himself in another language. He pressed his mouth tight against the piece and started to play, a crackle first, followed by a somber tune, one that bordered on heartache. How Buster, who had never known any such feelings, could interpret them so divinely was anyone's guess. But heartache was an emotion for which one needed no instruction.

"What's that racket?" the chimp barked.

Buster drew the softest of grins, pressed his snout against the mouthpiece once more and exhaled, smooth, sedative. The stall door made a gust of air; the chimp stood there, arms dangling, defenses dumped. Buster stopped.

"Keep going," the chimp uttered. His voice cracked with the sound of entrancement. Buster picked up where he left off. The chimp came closer. Never had he witnessed something like this before. He was one to talk, but around his parts, furry creatures didn't blow magical chords from brass horns, they blew rot from one end and hell from the other. Buster kept playing as he was told. He wouldn't dare stop now that he knew he had piqued the chimp's interest. He paced around Buster like a scientist upon a medical marvel and then came in and sniffed at the side of Buster's face like the greeting of tribal islanders. He smelled like a cloud of nothing.

"Doesn't add up," the chimp said to himself. Buster didn't stop to answer, letting his playing do all the uninterrupted, stutter-free speaking. After another spirited melody, Buster stopped and, for the first time, got a careful look at the conscious chimp. The ebony fibers, wooly as a steel pad, nostrils like snake holes, eyes, saucers filled with sky, the bottomless indigo in his pupils, surrounded by hard sand, wrinkles deep as gullies. Buster had never seen someone as raw, as powerful. He, too, sniffed at the chimp's cheek. The forgettable stink of ancient failures, but to Buster it was sweet as a kiss between dearest friends. When asked, the chimp knew nothing of a name or identity. He was curious about the trumpet and the meaning of the place. Buster explained it all, how he was born to a horn like others were born to a bottle, how he developed his tune under Pap's tutelage. How the place was home, among all the other undergrounds they had known. And then with one question it all went south.

"Can you sing?" Buster asked.

"What are you talking about?" the chimp turned on a heel. His arms tightened up.

"I'm sorry, I only thought, you see, they told me…"

"You thought what? What did they tell you? That since you can play some horn, I can sing? Whoever fed you that line is full of rotten fish. I don't know this," he snapped his fingers, "or that," snap, "about singing. Never have, never will, you got that?"

"Of course. I didn't mean to burn you up."

"Too late for that."

Buster's eyes dimmed to the floor. He felt the chimp's getting hot. "Why won't you look at me?" the chimp asked as though baiting Buster into a wrong answer. Buster was in a pickle. He felt the need to obey but fear kept him acknowledging the floor instead. Buster snuck an eye to the chimp. It was a docile eye, filled with warmth, his eyebrows frowning for approval. The chimp looked to Buster's trumpet. "That's a horrible noise. I don't care to hear it again."

It was a first in Buster's life, and something told him that the chimp wasn't altogether coming to him in truth. The chimp knew he was lying too, but he didn't care. In all the chatter, his appetite had finally given way to reason. But when he discovered what was under the tray, he branded Buster as jerk, a cliché, lashed out at him for being presumptuous and asked him to remove his furry carcass from the premises and hit the light. Just when Buster thought he was making a connection, the chimp reminded him that they had nothing in common. Bananas for the ape. How convenient. When Buster left, this time with his trumpet, the chimp grabbed the plate in the dark and climbed onto the bed. He took a nibble with his front teeth, allowing the tip of his tongue to peck a taste. His eyes melted in ecstasy. Bloody chicken necks phooey. What's more, he had lied to Buster about ever having tasted a banana. He lapped down the vittles, then tossed the empty plate on the floor and lied in bed, hands clasped behind his head. A burp broke up his chuckle. His eyelids filled with sand. Sleep. Voluntary sleep.

- 42 -

Pap was set on cancelling their second show. No one other than a small handful knew of the chimp. He suddenly wished that all he was running was another lowdown whiskey parlor. Humans were easy to predict. Pay them, they're happy. But this singing monkey business was more than he bargained for. It made him reconsider Buster, blasphemous as the thought was. Why these mystical creatures found their way into his life was something he neither had the strength nor time to contemplate, and with a show looming, the only thing that mattered was pulling off another miraculous night. They had all been miraculous. It was hard enough to evade the law. How they had managed it for as long without a single casualty, well, Pap was running out of time to think about it.

The Cats 6 had arrived early on Pap's request. They gathered a few tables in the basement. Lou and Dino sat by Pap. Trunks and Turnip were off playing dominoes. Buster was upstairs taking a nap, and the chimp was inside the washroom doing who-knows-what. He knew that Buster had untied the chimp that morning, but he was given assurance that the chimp would just as soon step foot outside the stall as he would kill himself. Pap was hoping to make the introduction tonight until he discovered that the chimp wasn't another Buster. How could Pap break the news that there was another creature with magical talents inside the washroom? Those who followed him this far might start to think him off his rocker if they didn't already. "Let's swing, Cap'n Pap," Tots said. The vote was unanimous. Even Lou disregarded the danger of a rogue chimp in the compound. Pap put everyone on standby. He'd get final word from Buster who'd surely give in to Pap's reasoning. Instead Buster came right out with it. The way to the chimp's heart was not through food but through music. He had explained what had happened when playing his trumpet in the washroom, how it was just a taste of something the chimp was starving to feast on. So, after all the deliberations, all of Pap's vetoes, the show went on.

The chimp had slept most of the day and into the night. What awoke him from his slumber was what he thought to be the continuation of a dream. It seemed to emanate from the floor. He sat up and snapped his eyes to the source. It was just loud enough to detect a cadence. Thump, thump, bump, bump went the tile. He hopped off the bed and let the beat massage his foot soles. It was like nothing he had heard before, and yet, he had been hearing it for as long as he had ears. He closed his eyes and snapped his fingers and then noticed his lips humming all on their own. Solace. He quieted to confirm the tune. It was still there, clear, unpolluted. His eyes opened. There were tears in them. He walked to the broken mirror. Ugliness stared back. But he couldn't help but start to sing. It frightened him to hear such a lovely sound spewing from such an unlovely grill, but that didn't stop him. He couldn't stop. It was the only medicine that could weaken the symptoms of his unsightliness. The chimp turned towards the music. He needed to become acquainted with it. He took the risk and opened the washroom door. It was unlocked. Then he left for the first time when, since his unbidden arrival, this is all he claimed to want. He poked his head out and noticed a clear coast. Ink was in the kitchen grabbing some grub. The chimp let the door shut without making a sound and then reopened it to make sure it wasn't locked. At least in the washroom he knew what to expect.

He followed the sound to the back entrance of the basement and was lucky to not run into anyone on the way. His bones rattled to Beans Fryer's bass line without even knowing who Beans Fryer was. Standing right behind the back curtain, no one in the club knew he was there. He was entranced by the music; his legs gave soft buckles at the knee. A smile crowded his face, and then the band silenced, leaving only exasperated cheers from an audience. Such sounds he had remembered from the zoo. They were nasty sounds, the type humans made when ogling at animals behind bars. The chimp was struck with fear and had one step in the opposite direction. But before he could break back for his washroom, Buster started a solo. It jolted the chimp from leaving. He reached for the drape, needing to know at once whether this was the same thing he had heard before. He peeled the curtain just enough to fit a squint. All he could see among the clouds of smoke and twinkle of lamps were the backs of men in dark suits making delightful intonations with a variety of tools. Just as indisputable was the bear in his tux and his horn. The chimp's eye locked in on the back of Buster's fat head. As extraordinary a vision as he'd ever seen. All the music he had ever archived flooded the stage. A strange feeling ran through him, a quickened pulse, a dry mouth, even a knot in his throat, like he shouldn't be having such desires, but he was powerless against the temptation. From this fruit he would eat forevermore. He shut the curtain and hurried back to the washroom.

Buster had released every emotion he had pent up over the last twenty-four hours. After the show he appeared spent. The Cats 6 gave Buster his due props and went home. It was a good thing because Buster knew that the chimp wasn't ready to meet anyone just yet. The poor thing had remained holed up inside the washroom since last night. Sitting at the bar, Buster was in no rush to head back there himself. It caused him guilt to feel apprehension, but the sting of hostility was fresh. Dino Glass fixed him another chocolate milk on ice and slid it over. Buster scooped and swigged it down in one motion, ice cubes and all. He didn't have all that much to say, only Dino sensed otherwise. The good times had ended and now it was time again to face the music. Dino served him another before Buster could consent. Buster swallowed it before he could arrive at his next thought. He thanked Dino for the drinks, patted him five and headed back to check on the chimp.

It was a quarter to two in the morning. Dino had taken the Gutter Gophers back home; Lou and Pap were up in their offices getting ready to turn in. Buster stopped shy of the washroom door and noticed Ink under the single bulb, fast asleep inside his bag. But Ink was a light sleeper, known to bounce an intruder during a catnap. He set Ink's mind at ease with a whispered announcement. Gently turning the door handle, Buster entered and glanced to the bed. The pillows were all over the floor, and the blankets were missing. A cart with two plates sat off to the side. One of the plates was licked clean; the other plate of spaghetti and meatballs untouched.

The chimp stepped out from the stall like he had just returned from a sabbatical. Buster smiled and asked how he had been.

"Been worse," the chimp responded. He wasn't steering clear of the bear like before.

"Were you able to catch some Z's?" Buster asked. The chimp nodded. He had a smug grin about him. Buster, on the other hand, was running short of ice-breakers. He glanced to the empty dish, then stammered, "Did you like what Lou made you?"

"You mean the mush drenched in prune juice? I'm not pushing up daisies, but I'll admit it burned my ass."

The chimp and Buster took turns exchanging glances. One would make eye contact and then break it, then the other way around. The reality was that the chimp had never eaten a meal so fine in his life but wasn't ready to concede an inch of ego.

The chimp climbed into Buster's bed. "You may want to get a boss to check that water bowl in there. Afraid it sprang a leak, but don't you fret. I plugged it up good," the chimp said.

Buster was so pleased with the level of confidence the chimp was gaining around him, he hadn't taken note of what he had just uttered. Leak in a water bowl. He must have meant one of the toilets. When Buster took his investigation into the stall, he noticed not just one, but both blankets, designed to keep the chimp warm, stuffed inside the toilet, a soup of excrement all over the floor. The oxygen evaporated from his head. Buster had to brace himself against the wall lest he faint in revilement. His new friend had turned out to be quite the ruffian, but at least they were on speaking terms.

- 43 -

The Arm Hotel was still under the same ownership, but the renovations upset Buddy's sense of nostalgia. New mustard walls, art deco furniture and metallic fixtures. Buddy knew the owners well; Friz Tunasco and B. Liever were friends to his father and V.I.P.s with open markers at the Dirty Spoon. When Buddy was released back into the world, he was reassured that he could go nowhere else on East Leaf to find the safety, the privacy he would find here. He rented out the same two floors Bill Plagun had once occupied, even took Bill's old room. It kept him in an unremitting state of discontent, and that's where he needed to be. He could hear the old voices, his father and mother laughing in the next room, arguing over where they would dine, all of it permeated through the walls like ghosts marred with unrest. He could still smell his father's cigar in the air. It blended with his Pana Bolivar. Just outside his suite, Buddy had installed a couple of large, scary men. The meeting was not to be disturbed even if Pap Fanti walked in with slit wrists, palms facing the sky and a bag over his head.

Captain Sert Johnson dressed like a layman. He wore a fedora and kept his black lenses on. Didn't matter that it was 2 am and the shades were drawn tight. He sat on one of the arm chairs, his leg confidently crossed over the other. Buddy paced the room with a drink in one hand and his Pana Bolivar in the other. He was a closed beer bottle inside a vibrating belt since the failed hit at Dunfer's. The time for a final accounting was well overdue and penalties were accruing by the second. When Buddy Plagun went to the can he lost his grip on the future of the Plagun Empire. Once an heir to the throne that controlled all ports south of the Twig Bridge, he was primed for a coup into North Leaf and the vast waterways that it afforded one Commodore Cabra. Cabra was known as the "Porter" because of his propensity to hang around the main exits of buildings in plain view of any would-be hitman. He was an ugly mutt, though he thought himself a regular Adonis. Slicked but scarce catgut was what he passed off as hair. He modeled snake eyes under textured brows. His skin was vulgar, noduled with tags. His most charming feature was the rake of four pubes that crawled over the bridge of his nose. Yes, they were on the outside and crow-black. Not tall, not short, he was of vapid stature, but his notoriety as a heavyweight boss was only rivaled by Bill Plagun and only flawed by his own lack of self-discipline. He had never killed a man with his own hands—some claimed him a coward—but he played the shot caller with aplomb. His first order came when he was fourteen, and it earned him ten blocks in Matanza Heights. He dealt in prostitution and gambling and laundered most of his earnings into coastline realty on a dream that alcohol would soon be outlawed. He was never seen without an entourage of ten strong, all expert life-takers. They had their way throughout the Leaf, excluding dwindling Plagun strongholds. When news of Bill Plagun hit the streets, Cabra seized on the opportunity and started devouring all of Plagun's former routes and protection. Even Captain Sert Johnson who owed Bill Plagun his life had accepted a new Cabra contract. It was Johnson's interpretation of equal protection. After all, why drink from the well when he could have the whole river? Buddy Plagun was up in arms about the lack of respect paid to his father and now to him. A declaration of war seemed imminent, and the peace the Leaf had known over the last three years would be ripped asunder.

"And what if by some brodie, one of them surreptitious acts of God, Cabra were to come into a sudden flatline?"

"There may have been a time when your old man could have put the entire Leaf in his knapsack, but you don't have the muscle to take him on, Buddy," Johnson said.

"So your loyalty ended with the old man?"

Johnson smashed his hat into the table. The surviving strands of hair wisped out of place. "You have the balls to drag me here and say that to my face? I respected him more than you or your brother."

"You're out of order."

"He took care of my family when I was hustling the beat, long before you fingered your first piece of pussy. How do you think I make it to captain in less than a year?" Lucky for Johnson, the former East Leaf captain was caught in bed with Mank Mill's wife. His "extermination" facilitated Johnson's promotion.

"So why are you protecting that bastard now? You saying we didn't keep you happy, even as I rotted in a cell for a three-spot?"

"The Spoon, it's still standing, isn't it? I even planted cars to show Cabra it was off limits. Breaks Zoo? The harbor? Junior Plagun, your own miserable, good-for-nothing brother. Cabra wanted him out of the game. I said no. And there he is, cradled in whores. As a favor to your father, Cabra left you both a living. He beat your father to City Hall, he's got judges on every bench, cops so crooked they put hits on their own mothers, but none of it is good enough for you. And to top it all off, you got us on a trip for biscuits, putting decent cops on the line for some second-rate hood?"

"For first-rate money," Buddy said.

"Just between us, Buddy, Pap Fanti had nothing to do with your old man."

"That's where you forgot the story," Buddy said.

"You put my men in harm's way. I can't go along with it. It's been over three years since the Leaf swam red. Things aren't like the old days. While I'm captain, I won't stand for another war. You keep clear of Cabra. I'll make sure he never crosses your path. And let go of that Fanti bullshit. He can't do anything to you. You're out. You've got the rest of your life to do whatever you want, women, money, all the things that make men happy."

"Is that your official resignation?"

"If you call a blind eye and a detail of protection resigning, then yes."

"You're right. If there's one thing the public won't stand for it's a crooked cop," Buddy insinuated through the crack in his teeth.

"Now you sound desperate, Buddy. That's one trait I never saw in your father. Overzealous, never desperate. He knew when to make concessions. You should learn from him. Wisen up. The moment people realize your desire to rule the world, they won't like you anymore." Johnson stood from his seat and grabbed his fedora off the table. He passed it over the top of his head twice.

"$50,000," Buddy blurted. The nickel and dime talk was getting cheap.

Five and four zeroes browned Johnson's pink cheeks like pork chops, but he knew Buddy Plagun couldn't back it up, not without the liquor plants and only one waterway. "For Fanti? You don't have that kind of dough," Johnson snickered.

Buddy started laughing at the top of his lungs; he almost choked on a gust of cigar smoke. "If only you knew what kinda dough we have. Enough to have you chopped up at a police ball without the papers typing a single word. Enough to make sure City Hall, all the way to the governor's house, never mentions my name again unless it's in a birthday card."

"What are you trying to pull here? You can't talk to me like that. You know what they'll do? You want to end up like your father? Better quit flexing your mouth before you pull up lame," Johnson said.

"If you can't beat 'em, join 'em, is that right?"

"That's fuckin'-A right."

"Well, I guess the horse is on you."

"You're losing it, Buddy. Take account of what you still got before you lose that too." What Johnson couldn't account for was that just an hour ago, as Cabra and his guns were exiting The Flamingo Club, Buddy Plagun had sent the greeting party: two car loads of bimbos, armed to the teeth and led by Jesse Under. Cabra and his top brass were splayed all over 31st Street in a lake of guts. The calls were flooding Captain Johnson's office, but he was sitting in Buddy's hotel room and wouldn't know the news until he read it in the morning paper. When the last hollow point burrowed itself deep within enemy flesh, all power was once again restored to Buddy Plagun. It was for Cabra's blatant disrespect for his rival, Bill Plagun, and everything he had sacrificed so that two empires could eat from the same trough. Soon the routes, the territories, everything that Cabra had adversely possessed would be back in the hands of its proper owner. Buddy Plagun had a new contract for Johnson. From now on he worked for Plagun only. Next order of business: put the squeeze on Pap Fanti. Johnson would provide all his resources in the department. He'd solicit the aide of neighboring states and the Coast Watch for an all-out dragnet. Fanti could start counting his last breaths.

- 44 -

In a few seconds, Buddy Plagun had undone everything it took Commodore Cabra over three years to accomplish. It gave him such a rush that he felt that he could locate Pap Fanti that very night and kill the demons once and for all. He had stopped at the Spoon and gotten drunk with Junior before he decided to drive the streets in search of Fanti. But if there was one thing Buddy knew, it was that Pap excelled at playing a rat. He lied like a rat, smiled like a rat, betrayed his friends like a rat, hid like a rat and was about to die like a rat. He was lucky that the man, known as the phantom, was even lingering around the Leaf, but with a $50,000 bounty, Buddy could stretch out. He'd have the chameleon soon enough and then skin him alive to see whether he still changed colors.

There was one source that Buddy felt could help him get the information he was desperate for. Sert Johnson was right about that. Buddy was desperate for justice, desperate to avenge his father who had no business meeting his end that night. Met Fanti. He could have whacked Met out when he first learned of Pap's treachery, but Bill Plagun said no. Over time, Buddy wouldn't touch Met because deep down he reminded him of both Junior and Bill, weak but loyal. Met proved his worth three years ago. "You're not related to that scumbag," he would often tell Met. "For your sake, you're not from the same dirty blood."

Buddy was on the tail end of his third divorce when he was sent to prison. He left two kids and a schizo wife who had just had about enough of his violent streaks. She took the kids out West. Junior took care of them while Buddy was doing time, sending them support once a month. Buddy even vowed to change his ways, maybe get some help and join them out West. But first he had to finish his business out East. Cabra was ground beef. After Pap Fanti, Buddy could sleep in peace.

He pulled up to Sue's in the Sunks District. Just a day before, it belonged to Cabra. He felt safe stepping from his car without bodyguards, but that was the alcohol talking. He pulled his handgun from his side like he was holding his penis. It gave him power. Maybe he'd take Met Fanti out too. His steps were bullish. Hiding was no longer an attractive trait. With the butt of his gun, he banged on Sue's door. It was too heavy a sound for Sue to ignore it. She feared the visitor would soon break it down if she didn't open. Buddy gave Sue a half grin and let himself past her.

Met was awake and sprawled out on the bed in a defenseless pose. He was back on Sue's good graces with the $260 he had scored off Pap but for reasons he refused to reveal, he wouldn't stop complaining about his pay. $20 dollar months never drew his ire, but now a $260 night had him crying foul. Go figure.

"You make as much sense as powdered water," Sue would say. $260 back into her speako could win over a few more customers; maybe expand into the living room. They didn't need much space for sleep, and Mr. Alquiler could always rent them a spare room from his apartment. But Met wanted nothing to do with Sue's rank-and-file ambitions. She was a small-time thinker. If only she had a nickel on what Met had come into with Pap Fanti. There were thousands of dollars due to him, maybe millions. He knew it and so did Pap. He was already spending money he didn't have. He had taken out credit at Marie's Boutique and bought Sue a few nice dresses. She wouldn't wear one, said she was more comfortable in her pants, suspenders and bowlers. He had started a tab at one of Cabra's old dives. The current damage was north of a football field in just two days, and if there was one thing to bring the dead back, it was an unpaid debt. Getting smashed was one way to dilute any paranoia that Pap had robbed him blind, but it also kept him from sleeping. Met was gassed from nothing.

Buddy noticed the way Sue looked at Met, her furrowed brow of concern like a mother with its child. "Let's take a ride," he recommended. The gun in his hand was the easiest thing for Met to spot.

"Come on, Buddy. It's late. Can't we do this tomorrow?" Met pleaded. He knew what "rides" normally entailed. He didn't have the nerve for another hit. For all he knew, he was the target tonight. All these moments continued to confirm to him what he had known all along, what he hoped to avoid when he brought Pap into a second opportunity. He needed out, but whatever remained of $260 wouldn't get him far.

"I got good news. Don't keep me in the lobby." Buddy walked out without the slightest acknowledgement that he had barged in on Sue in the middle of the night and without the second-hand courtesy of a farewell.

"Don't go. Just stay here," Sue said to Met as she scurried to her bar.

"And what? Have him come back and shove his gun down my throat?" Met's eyes grew wide when Sue walked into the room with both hands on the rifle. "Are you nuts? Do you know who that was? That's Buddy Plagun. He'll blank us both tonight. Put that fuckin' thing away," Met said.

Sue knew exactly who he was. Most of her inventory was Plagun stock before Buddy went away and her life fell into jeopardy. A couple of Cabra henchmen tracked her home one night, robbed her entire supply and raped her in the back of their car. She didn't fight them. Fighting would only bring her more bruises. Instead, she took her medicine like a cadaver being sliced up, no emotion, no interaction; she wanted her perpetrators to know that they would get no satisfaction from seeing her in the act. She never shared it with Met but learned a valuable lesson that night. From now on, she would only buy Cabra brand. What she didn't know was that Cabra was finished and she would have to switch suppliers once more. She stood her ground. "If you go, don't expect me to go after you," she said.

Met threw his coat on and torched some tobacco. When he got in Buddy's car, it reeked of whiskey.

"Cabra's with the devil," Buddy said, shoving his flask into Met's gut.

Met took it in his hand but waited to put it to his mouth. "You mean?"

"We're back on top," Buddy said. He closed his eyes and relished in the swift victory that death brought him.

"That's great," Met said lackluster.

"That's not why I came. I want to make your life easier," Buddy said. He pulled the gearshift and peeled the curb. Met knew better than to ask where they were going. He wasn't strapped. Even if he was, he was no match for Buddy Plagun, drunk or dry.

Met tried to butter him up without sounding like a kiss ass. Drunk people had a gift for taking a compliment as an insult. "You've done too much. I'm alright. Serious."

"You got a girl, right? She's a nice girl. Bet you fuck her everyday. That's good if you do. Some day maybe you want a family. You want that?" Buddy asked. Met tried to follow every word. Buddy was slurring his speech and driving faster than any drunk gee should have, but his intentions were focused. "Me, I never had much luck with family. I think when you're unlucky at something it means you're not supposed to have it. I see you, your girl. The way she looks at you. She cares. She deserves better. Anyway, I need your help, and I'm gonna pay you a bucket of coin." Buddy pulled into an empty parking lot.

The stores across the street were all closed. He called the flask from Met and took another taste.

"Sure, Buddy. Anything. You know I've always been here."

"I know, so what I ask you won't come easy. But I have confidence in you, and I know you'll make the right decision. I need to know where your brother is." Met could see this coming a mile away. He knew the target of the Dunfer's hit. "I got half the police after him. Those fuckin' pigs couldn't find shit in an outhouse. I'm not gonna hurt him this time. I just want to see his face."

Met didn't believe a word of it, but when Buddy offered him $5,000 for the tip, Met began to question all those he had trusted over his life. Sue was a saint. He could trust her. He needed her, but that didn't mean he deserved her. With five large, he may just deserve her a little more and convince her to stick around. Pap Fanti had left him hanging and with the knowledge that wherever he was hiding, Met was neither invited nor welcome. Buddy was the only one, after Bill Plagun, that gave Met a shot. Not even his own mother who died while popping him out. Not even a father who blamed Met and took the high road. Not even his older brother who took Met under his wing while they bounced orphanages. It had nothing to do with Pap's plans for escape from the baby cooler. Had nothing to do with the nights when they felt like kings, loitering local Y's in Lower Leaf and smoking alley walls into a migraine. Had nothing to do with following Pap to the Breaks countryside and Lou's farm. Had nothing to do with fleecing pigs, sometimes to the same dunce owners. None of that was Met's idea of a benediction. When he came across Bill Plagun at a gambling hall years later, he met the devil's agent. Met had squandered all the dope money he had, including a good chunk of his second marker. But Bill was always one to collect. Met asked if he could work it off and soon was introduced to the liquor traffic. He brought Pap along only as a return favor for their early days. By then Pap was hard up. Farmers got wise, put up barbed fences and booby traps. He tried his luck at running a gin joint, only no one drank the rotgut he and Lou made in the grandmother's bathtub. With the news of fifty clams a week guaranteed from running rum off the Breaks' coast, Pap enlisted. He once thanked Met for the job, said that working with Bill and Buddy Plagun was a promising start to a long career, that the Plaguns were stand-up guys.

"Just think about where that kind of money can get you and your sweetie pie. I'm talking about out of this stink. I won't ever ask where you went. You'll be footloose. You can have the family I had and lost and never have to look over a shoulder. Now I know I could ask you to give him up, and you'd do it for free. But that wouldn't be fair. After all, he is your blood, even if he means you no good. Every man deserves the right to make a living, am I right? You do this for me, Met." Buddy pulled up to Sue's and nodded. His eyes were on a black horizon. Met was waiting for more, but when more didn't come, he just got out.

When Sue asked for the dope on their dialogue, he blazed a Mary and got shit-faced. "Buddy wants me to give up Pap. He's gonna kill him."

"Tell him you ain't seen him in years, that you know nothin'," Sue said.

"Then he'll kill us both." Now more than ever Met had to find Pap and square everything away. This wasn't his idea of making a new life.

- 45 -

All the money in the world couldn't save Vilma Griggs from a lonely life. She never went hungry, never opened her own doors and never knew a true friend. She was wrong to fall for a man whose vanity was greater than her own, but a stupid heart always outmaneuvered the most cunning brain. Chase Griggs was virile and valiant, confident on a shoestring. When he first put his hands on her, she lost her sense of time. He would make the perfect father for her children, humble and hard-working. They would raise good citizens, and she'd never dine alone. It was her greatest fear. Buying company was cheap. Merlin was a loyal servant, but she hated to bother him every time she needed out of the house. These days it was often. She loathed staying in that palace of plastic. Nothing within reciprocated emotion. The furniture, the frescos on the wall, the chandeliers, the embroidery, the baby carriage or dolls, they were all insensible works. The sounds that little children make, whether laughing or crying, inventing their own dialects and grousing about the rigors of life, Chase wouldn't even allow the paw prints of a dog on marble floors he had adopted as his own. If the hum of his voice wasn't enough for her, then he'd give her the divorce. Only Chase's voice was now somewhere in the annals of a scalped memory. Some nights he didn't even come home. Blamed it all on the Easter Tower. So many times Vilma plotted spying on him. She'd follow him to his place of employment only to catch him detouring to some secret rendezvous. But she didn't have the strength to witness the manifestation of her own misgivings. She had invited this on herself. Chase Griggs was not a family man. He didn't care for children or parents. He had faked his love, or maybe it was genuine in the beginning. Who knew anymore, but Vilma couldn't imagine the whole thing a farce. Chase had to have loved her in the beginning. Who would go through so much trouble just for money?

Merlin offered to take her downtown this morning, but she refused. She would catch a cab. Vilma was not one to get behind the wheel of an automobile. Like most women of the day, she never learned to drive anything more powerful than her. This included men. Even when her father tried to teach her, as part of her independence, a new way of thinking that, as a woman, she could live a happy life without relying on men. But Vilma was never one to buck trends. She needed a man in her life if she was to stand any chance of completing the role for which was made.

The cabbie dropped her off right in front of the old Benson Building. She tipped him double the fare and made the driver's day. At least she could still buy people's affection. There was a smattering of cars and pedestrians on the sidewalks, all with their own journeys toward better or worse places. If she was going to go through with this, she could not stay standing on the street, staring at strangers who would never share a word with her. She entered the Benson and took the elevator to the second floor. The address was in the directory under Investigative Services. She had called a week ago to schedule the appointment but could never get someone on the line. Why she didn't go to someone else was by design, for such grave matters required the services of the best. And "the best" was only to be found in DC Stiles' office.

"You come highly recommended as one who can sniff out a man's heart and expose all its dirty secrets under the brightest light," Vilma Griggs said. She wore shades to control eye talk and a wide brim to temper her mind movements. Her lavender ascot puffing from her gray jacket and a skirt to her ankles showed she was not the type to toy with. Stiles was quick to light Vilma's cigarette. At least he proved to be a good waiter. Whether he was worth a lick as a house peeper was up for debate. His desk was old, small and cramped with open newspaper pages, an ashtray in need of a vacuum and a plate of snipes. There were a dozen lobby cards from Lala Terre's worst pictures tacked to the walls. Perhaps he was doubling as her press agent. Tabloid clippings of the day he became a national hero were taped to windows. He never told a soul how he happened upon Terre's boy and that his reward was just north of a bag of peanuts. He let the press make him a star. Soon, he had himself believing his own myth. He moved downtown into the Benson on a deferred contract and his newfound fame because he didn't have the full deposit. The office had a spare room in the back where he bunked. He put in a fridge and a water cooler. Stiles spent his time divided between the office and Pap's clubs. A self-proclaimed expert in incognito, Stiles got a rash of new cases from wealthy wives seeking to unmask philandering husbands. They paid him handsomely. He spent it to match. When the clients failed to get results—they rarely did—they fired him. Most demanded refunds and took him to court until he was tapped out with a drawer-full of unpaid judgments. Stiles was one month late at the Benson and in the hole to his neck, only no one except his creditors knew it. He never dared ask Pap for a spot. Stiles considered it carte blanche to simply be invited to his club. But he needed to land another quick score in a jiffy or wind up moving his office to his car. As it just so happened, luck would grace him again.

"That's the kind of eye I'm looking for," Vilma continued.

"So I've been told, but I still can't see through walls. Let's pin the tail on the donkey. It's your husband," said Stiles.

"I can see I came to the right place." Vilma had a hard time masking sarcasm. Stiles came across as cool as razor burn.

"Missing?"

"In so many words," Vilma said. "I'll pay good money, but there will be no publicity, no smears. My reputation is to remain unblemished. I'll require pictures, preferably in the act."

"I don't snap homicides." Stiles' cocky eyes hid a fumbling line of thought that Vilma was quick to detect.

"Are you sure you're a snoop?"

"I'm sorry, but I like to play word puzzles only after I've had my cough syrup." Stiles reached into his desk drawer for the scotch and poured himself a shot. He offered one to Vilma. She abstained.

"I have reason to believe my husband is having an affair with another woman. There is no murder, no missing person; there is only carnal lust, extramarital sex, acquiescence which was not given by this party during the exchanging of vows. Must I spell it out any clearer?"

"I'd say you put that in big block letters. Anything else you want to tell me about him?"

"He approached our marriage like a job."

"Never leave one till you have another, is that it?"

"You know, Mr. Stiles, when a person wants you to be strong, they always say 'grow a pair.' Only I've never understood the idiom. In my opinion, the balls are the weakest part of a man's construction. If anything, they should say 'grow a vagina.' They're far more durable and capable of quite a beating. I'll need pictures."

"Because you want to be able to blackmail him out of the scratch he'll need for the divorce lawyer."

"As job interviews go, I wouldn't call you back."

"Let me take another crack at it, toots. This time with a Louisville. You're not sure he's actually playing the switch, and you never will be because he washes the lipstick off his collars and soaks his suits in the tub when they should be sent to the cleaners. He tells you he's working late and when you call the office, his secretary always takes a message. Am I cooking with gas?" It was a lucky guess, but just because Stiles could rattle off the obvious, didn't mean he had the tools to prove it.

A rogue tear dribbled past the rim of Vilma's shades. She had shown her hand and it was a bust. "What's your fee?"

It had been ages since Stiles faced such a stimulating dilemma. He had forgotten how to quote a price. He looked to Vilma's dress, the fat wrist wraps, the blinding stones in her earlobes. Here was a woman of class. A random figure slipped from his tongue like it was the most natural thing to say. "$1,000, up front." Stiles was a man of limited vision.

"I know you're the best at what you do, and because of this, you'll have no trouble putting a big, colorful ribbon on this case. But you see, Mr. Stiles, this is the only way I conduct business. It's not a matter of money because I have enough to make a few banks jealous. Pictures first, then you get paid."

"Nice try, but that's not the way…" Stiles was cut off as he gesticulated a rebuttal.

"$5,000. Cash." Vilma's voice had no quiver in it which meant she could back up her words in a snap. "$500 right now. I'm sure you'll have expenses."

Stiles let his arms drop to the table. He had to retrace her words just to find the $5,000. Vilma knew the deal was done by the way Stiles wiped the tip of his tongue across his lower lip. She handed him a picture of the suspect. His eyes grew owl-large.

"His name is Chase Griggs. He works at the Easter Tower, but I doubt you'll catch him in the act there. We live at 4 Waterfall, East Leaf, so if your investigation leads you there, don't knock on the door. My number," she said as she scribbled it on a piece of paper. "Business hours only, or he may answer. Is all of this sinking in?"

"Your man doesn't shit where he eats, pardon my French, and if he answers the phone, I'll say 'wrong line' in Spanish."

"So that we are black and white, no pictures, no dice, and I'll be asking for the $500 back. I'm a woman who always gets what she wants," Vilma said as she counted five C's from her velvet wallet.

"Mrs. Griggs, for five large, I'll get you moving pictures with rolling credits," he said with the confidence of yeast in a hot oven. DC Stiles could surely play the part when the lights were bright. He could forward two years rent and settle with his other creditors. The question remained: Where would he catch this skirt-chasing gigolo of hers? He recognized the face in the mugshot from somewhere but couldn't, for the life of him, remember where.

- 46 -

Buster Horn found sanctuary on stage, and if ever he needed its soothing effects, it was tonight. The third show since the chimp moved in, and so far, the experiment had turned disastrous. He'd never admit it. The consummate professional, Buster knew when to minimize a domestic dispute for work's sake. Only problem was he had never had a familial spat, not until the chimp, spasmodic with emotive highs, lows and vibratos, started crowding his attention. Buster could never guess right with him, but at least he had the stage. The Cats 6 sheltered him with waves of swing. They detected nothing different about the bear, except maybe the mauve tux he sported for the first time. The audience detected nothing different about the bear. Chase Griggs and Holly Fountain detected nothing different about the bear. Chase spent most of his time detecting Holly anyway. DC Stiles detected nothing different about the bear. He didn't even notice his target seated in the front row. Neither Dino Glass, Turnip or Lou noticed anything different about Buster. But Pap did. It had nothing to do with how he played. Buster was a crackerjack and in top form even when under the weather, one of those rare talents that knew nothing of failure. Rather, it was what he played that tipped Pap off. Grief-stricken melodies, things his lips could never express through words were instead made by each passing note, but no one complained. The music was much too moving.

Pap was growing into the Calloway. All the measures he took to avoid detection had paid off. The club didn't even have a formal name. Members called it Hot Choc, Teddy Bear and ten other things. The old Club Polar, run by Pap Fanti, was "shut down" by the law. This was the story Basil Demur, under a blind tip, had pushed to his paper man. It was all a ploy to keep the attention off Pap, bury his infamous celebrity into the last page of yesterday's paper. Buddy Plagun didn't bite. He controlled the law and knew it was a false lead. But part of Basil's prowess as master of the truth was to have Pap believe that all their efforts would not only yield fruit but keep them safe. It didn't matter that Basil Demur had ties to the Plagun outfit; he had a deep affinity for his Captain Pap Fanti and Buster Horn. Pap knew nothing of Basil's back deals with Plagun. He trusted Basil Demur with everything, credited him with keeping them in business and alive. He trusted his crew, from Lou all the way to the Gutter Gophers. He trusted the Cats 6, including Pisto Leroy, who he could count on to keep peace and his mouth shut wherever life took him. He trusted Holly Fountain and the High Legs. Holly had a strong influence over the group. As she went so did the rest of the gals. He trusted Buster as a guardian angel who came to give him a few moments of tenderness in an otherwise vicious reality. The only one he couldn't trust was in the washroom. But then again Basil Demur had nothing to do with that chimp. This came from Met, another person he couldn't trust. Pap focused his energy on listening to Buster and the band. Such things he could control.

Ink Tambo's job duties, when it came to the chimp, had been relaxed. Keeping him locked away in the washroom was no better than Crystal Plats. Pap wasn't one for incarceration, not to anyone under his roof. So Ink's task now was to roam and make periodic checks. On Buster's advice, Pap would let the chimp do the same. Wander about, come and go just like Buster. If he employed his new freedoms, no one ever saw him, except maybe Ink once or twice. The chimp new that Ink hung around. A couple of times they even exchanged a glance. To Ink, it was the strangest chimp he'd ever seen. He didn't have the expressions of a brute but rather of something with more soul, something that idealized history as a scrapbook of suffering. And from such suffering any man could relate. It brought the chimp out of the washroom. Ink wasn't around. He had swung by the basement to chew the rag with Dino Glass.

The chimp had snuck all the way back to the stage curtain. It was as far as he had dared to venture unchecked. No one had seen him. His brain hummed to the tune, and he felt like singing. Only there was no way he would cross that threshold. The only audience he had ever known was celestial in nature, the starry jam of heaven, far-forgotten and never known to lambast a performance for want of heart. They were the only times the chimp could disrobe from the confines of his grotto and point his song as high, as loud as his dial would go. A washroom of creaking pipes, peeling dry wall and sheets of tin and brick an audience was not, but he needed to sing again before he lost hope in the one thing that brought him joy. The chimp continued filling his ear; his mind was unraveling with lofty propositions. This might be his only shot at the lime light, but then he wasn't sure he wanted exposure. Just to be left alone like before seemed a reasonable aim. But he didn't want that either. Stuck between hypocrisies, the chimp felt that the time would soon come when he was forced to make a move. After all, he wasn't brought here on a crusade to save the rest of his kind from a life at Plats. As far as he knew, and he knew more than he thought, he was the only one they siphoned out. He was still awaiting the bill on the relocation service. What did they want from him? The chimp closed his eyes. The song was ready to erupt from his gut. He snuck back to the washroom fast as he could with a container of melodies over the flame and moved to the cracked mirror. He raised his other hand, shuffled his fingers, cracking each knuckle, then snapped to the beat. With the other hand, he mopped back his knots. Bobbing his head like a lily pad on a pond, the chimp tried to bring back his lost glory. Dew formed in his eye, he cleared his throat and started to sing.

Fifteen minutes into his song, a random groan in the floor shattered his spell. He could have sworn there were people outside his door. Pap suspended his foot midair. It had given him away. He needed to corroborate the story before Lou and had hoped to catch the chimp by surprise like he had that night at the zoo. For now, they had to hold steady and wait. There was nothing but dead space on the other side of that door. Pap signaled silence with a raised forefinger. Then it started just where it had left off. The chimp sang. Pap and Lou manufactured looks of great disbelief. Dib Minty was an otter with laryngitis compared to this. For Pap, this was the second time he was walloped with such emotion. Such phenomena simply didn't occur within the realm of science and fact. But now was no time to compile data and run tests. He waved Lou away from the door. The two skittered back to the basement.

After getting all the gloomy muck out of the way, Buster worked his horn hot as an egg on a fryer. The Cats 6 picked up after his solo and stretched their musical legs. It gave Buster five to catch a breather. Pap sent Ham Wails around the backside of the curtain and straight for Buster's ear. Wails whispered something. Buster stood nonchalantly from his stool and followed him back. Pap and Lou waited on him with grins pinned to their faces. Pap apologized but said it couldn't wait. They crept back to the washroom. The chimp continued in song. Buster's snout went agape like a flytrap. It was all true.

When Pap asked him if he would like the chimp to join the show, Buster admitted he'd have no wilder joy. It started to make sense to Pap. Creatures like Buster and the chimp were tailor-made for him because he knew how to care for them, help them flourish and keep it all on the quiet.

Morning broke, and Buster paid the chimp another visit. Ink was in and out of his sleeping bag when he gave a half-hearted "yo." Buster brushed his paw against the door thrice, but when he didn't hear an answer, he patted it open and took his first step in. He was cognizant of the things he hoped to avoid, starting with the chimp's poor excuse for toilet manners. The memory of even the most trivial grief was inerasable. But an innocent heart gives too many chances and it cost him. A surging upper-cut of rank air popped Buster in the nose. His eyes leaked. His paws clapped over his snout, but the stench soaked through his fur. Wet towels dripped mud over the edge of the washtub, some off the stall door, the sink. There were puddles in different shades of brown and yellow all over the floor. The chimp had done it again, only this time worse. Buster couldn't see him yet. With teeth gritted, he sucked a straw-full of air and corner-eyed the free toilet. He had to figure a way to educate the chimp on sanitation or simply abandon the idea of walking into these facilities again. How a creature of such aptitude could play host to such defilements had Buster seeing double. He picked up all the dry towels, refusing to go near the toilet. Then he moved to the wet ones, not the toilet, the ones off the toilet, not the toilet, inside the sink, and over the lip of the tub but not the toilet. He gave them each a good Indian burn and bunched them into a corner. He was stalling and knew it. He couldn't dare stick a living arm inside that witch's cauldron, but then he wouldn't be a very good friend if he only chose to serve during peacetime. In for the charge, Buster double-toweled an arm and thrust it into the toilet's obscene mouth. Fist clenched, he punched through the clog and recoiled his arm like a rifle. Somehow his paw stayed a second longer, and he felt what was damming the toilet. It sent a shiver up his arm. He pulled the chain a couple of times, and the water flushed through. Where was his friend, Buster thought. Little did he know the chimp was inside the adjoining stall, his ass on the toilet seat, his legs folded up and off the ground. Buster exited the stall and moved to the washtub. The water was lentil soup. He could only imagine his friend one dirty fellow, but the chimp never set a toe inside that tub. He feared water as much as he feared man, maybe more. With a steady inhale, Buster dipped his arm towards the drain. It got stuck on what felt like fabric, but fabric didn't squish and dissolve. He pulled the water stopper and extracted his sludge-ridden paw. Buster then took a seat against the wall of the tub. He was breathing like he had just swum a mile. One day, when was an older bear, he could look back with pride and say the smell of war and death slapped him in the face and he survived with honors. He rushed to the sink and scrubbed his arms with the bar of lye for the better part of ten minutes. It was untouched until now. He had no clue that the chimp had snuck up behind him, his watchful eye alive with scrutiny. Buster caught wind of him in the mirror. His toes went star-struck and curled up.

"What's eating you?" the chimp asked.

With the eyes of an adoring fan, he held still until he had no recourse but to say: "I thought you were the cat's meow." The chimp took every word in like a matador under a shower of roses. "It was the most beautiful thing I've ever heard," Buster continued.

Then the chimp stopped time to gather his thoughts. He took quick notice that Buster had picked up the washroom. The notion of enslaving this Ursa soon dawned on him. He would make a swell servant. "Are you nuts?" the chimp asked.

"You can sing." He wanted the chimp to know how much he valued his gift. "I can show you some of my preshow stretches. They really help me loosen up."

"You looking for trouble?" the chimp asked.

"Well, no, of course I would never…"

"Then why do you say I can sing? You hear me sing or something?"

"Well, I don't…"

"You don't, and you didn't."

"I'm sorry," Buster confessed.

"Yeah, you're sorry. Let it happen again, and I'll pop you with two raccoon eyes." The chimp knew the jig was up, but he kept playing the hard bluff.

Buster fell into distress. The running faucet shaved through the slab of tension. But prior reservations about the chimp couldn't dissuade Buster from what he had heard. They stared at each other, the chimp with the eye of a gunfighter at ten paces, Buster like a stable boy. With such banter he was a virgin. He turned off the faucet and lowered his head, excusing himself from the room.

"Hey, you," the chimp called out. It was time to get to the bottom of things.

Buster spun back around. "Yes?"

There appeared a sudden mist in the chimp's countenance. "Are you blind or just stupid?"

In the most sincere of ways, Buster said, "I can see very well. Is there anything you need me to see for you?" He simply couldn't understand the chimp's idioms. It was like biting into a piece of glass just before it cracked.

"You see this?"

"I'm sorry, what?"

"You really are stupid. This." The chimp pounded his fist into his chest and then hammered an inflexible finger into his temple. "This!"

"Of course, I see you," Buster said. As the chimp grew hot, Buster froze up.

"Who in their right mind wants to see this? Tell me."

"Uh, uh, uh…"

"Uh, uh, uh. That's right. No one! I'm sorry we all can't be cute, little teddy bears, pure as the new snow, playing their stupid toys for a paddock of palookas." The chimp shoved Buster out of the way and put his body in front of the mirror. The crack split his face in half, one higher than the other. He was hopeless to make the image disappear.

Buster got his shakes under control just enough to say: "Well, I don't buy it." He knew full well what the chimp was getting at now. He may have not been a creature of vanity or known the evil ways of man, but he knew the pain the chimp was suffering was real, that he actually thought he was ugly, a monster, malformed and perverted by almighty God. These ideas were all wrong according to Buster, but the chimp had his ideas too. "What I heard was the most wonderful thing that's ever entered these ears, but if you don't want anyone else to know, I won't ever spill it," Buster said.

The chimp became an audience of one to his own imagination as he heard himself sing: *"Love may be four tiny letters that haven't got much to say, so why is it that love's little, tiny letters always get in the way?"* Then he returned to the washroom and the bear. "You don't get it, kid. I'll never get in front of those fang-toothed devils. If that's what you brought me here for, forget it." The chimp meant nothing of the sort. He dreaded the thought of returning to Crystal Plats. But what he seemed to fear more was the ridicule he would endure at the tongues of the same crowds that Buster thrilled. Still, he couldn't deny the prospect of showcasing his voice if just once. He knew what he housed inside that throat box. He knew how good it sounded. There was a reason he sang all those frigid nights. It brought him meaning. It wasn't vanity to acknowledge the beauties that fled the tormented heart. On the other hand, what wasn't vanity? And that's why the chimp would not be convinced to set foot on any stage, not unless he transformed into something less ghoulish.

- 47 -

Just outside the washroom, Pap heard the entire conversation. He was alone. Never had such human interplay taken place between animals. Talk of physical beauty, shame, talent, acceptance, applause. Animals didn't deliberate over such trifling airs and neither did angels. This was the vile rap of man, but it was coming from a chimp. Of all the junk Pap had to deal with, a prima donna ape with a complex was the last thing he needed. He left without either knowing and took the information straight to Lou. Their endless discussions netted superfluous vacuity. Returning the chimp to the zoo seemed as logical as leaving it to rot away inside a washroom. He needed it to join the family if it was to remain. Even more, he needed it to befriend Buster. Anymore of what Pap had suspected from the chimp to his kid and it was "curtains."

Several shows later—this made about two weeks—Lou took the problem to Dino Glass. He should have figured Dino to come up with something as brainy.

"Cap'n ain't gonna go for that. Not if you serve it to him on fine china with Worcestershire," Lou said.

Dino poured himself a short glass. He swirled it in circles and then scrunched his tongue around a taste. "Let me ask you something. What happened your first time in the sauce?"

"I broke someone's neck, threw up all over a cop and wound up in the hoosegow for two nights and not in that order," Lou said.

"You're worse than the chimp. I'm talking about normal people, like all the ones sitting out there enjoying the show. What happened to them? What happens every time? They get that first taste. It starts to loosen them, nice and easy, takes all the lies out. Next thing you know they're confessing murders to complete strangers and picking up scags that would shrink a sober man's dick to a booger. Liquid courage, my friend, has cured more ills than penicillin."

"Yeah, and what happens when you load him up and he goes ape shit on the joint? Maybe takes out a couple tourists before we can put the brakes on him? You know what Pap's gonna say about it? You think he goes for poisoning some innocent jungle Joe when he thinks about Buster? Forget it. We gotta come up with something else," Lou said. He made sure Pap was not within earshot.

The music was crazy cool as usual. Buster fought through all sorts of fatigue from pulling double shifts, but he didn't skip a beat. Pap was sitting in the Jackson Reese, Chase Griggs' circle. Holly played eye candy. They were having a jolly time, only Pap kept his laughter on a tight budget.

"Pap ain't gotta know every detail. You should trust me on this. He'll be up there bringing 'em to their knees if he's got the umph for it," Dino argued.

"You don't know what I heard. It was from somewhere else. Somewhere God likes to hang around. Not a voice for bums, you know what I'm saying? As lounge singers go, he's the best. We get him up there, you become a teetotaler. Let me talk to Pap about it. He makes the decision." Lou thought he sounded serious when he made the admonition, but he wasn't sure of it himself.

Dino Glass was brought into the joint through Lou. He owned a couple of nice restaurants inside of Plagun territory.

When he refused to pay protection money to keep Cabra out, four sticks of black powder forced him into a hot dog stand. That's where he met Lou Licks. It's where he told him if he could just get a shot at those Plaguns he'd stuff a stick of dynamite so far up their ass they'd have permanent heart burn. Lou thought Dino a funny man when behind the fortress of his bar. For every disease, there was a drink to cure it, he always said. He was a wizard at the Specter Spritzer and the Tortoise Tease, from a variety of infusions he had concocted during dry times, many of which made his restaurants all the rage. One hit you before the alcohol splashed the stomach lining. The other settled down for a game of poker before it wiped the house clean. Both left no residual effect; both could leave a terminal patient feeling mighty fine about his life, even during the reading of his final rites. But Dino Glass had trouble dealing with authority and Lou knew it. Pap Fanti didn't run the kind of joint where if a worker got out of line he'd get snuffed out. That was Plagun's brand. Pap believed in correction through inclusion. He'd bring the guilty party in, point out his error and encourage him to refrain from a repeat violation. Like a good teacher with his class. He'd leave the rough stuff to Lou Licks, Turnip Faymus and Ink Tambo. And rough could be an understatement when it came to that trio. Billy clubs, blackjacks, brass knuckles were all accessorized to the tilt when Pap's muscle wanted to make an impression. They all carried rods, sub machine guns, hand burners, but those were never meant to be used inhouse, only for "emergencies." Pap couldn't exile a worker once he was on board. It would make an instant enemy and send him blabbing to the cops. It left Pap in a tricky spot. Till now, his crew was stand-up, top to bottom. He was impressed by Dino Glass the first time they met. Dino had Pap sample a few drinks before he made the call, but since Pap wasn't a drinker, two Red Roosters put him to bed. Dino thought Pap a wise man with a weak arm. In the beginning he respected him only because Lou said he had to. Soon after he developed affection for Pap because he saw how good Pap was to him, to everyone at the club. He suspected it had something to do with keeping all those around Buster happy. A disgruntled man wrote a thousand books with his tongue. Whatever the case, Dino Glass proved his worth. He didn't see the need to fill Pap in on this. It was a minor experiment on a chimp, not deciding their next stomping ground. The members loved his drinks. Why wouldn't the chimp? But Dino gave his word. He would wait on Lou to talk it over with Pap. It didn't take twenty-four hours to get the green light. Only Lou never told Pap a thing. He didn't share it with Buster either. The bear was too innocent to understand the meaning of motive. Dino had won with reason. Worst case, they still had a couple vials of tranks.

- 48 -

Chase and Holly spent more time in bed than the sick. The night after the last show, Chase popped Holly with a diamond bracelet and then he popped her with his boner. It was the only way he thought—the bracelet, not the boner—to get Holly's mind off the confusion that occurred at the lobby of the Werlick Hotel a couple days ago. She had decided to surprise him after work and arrived at 6 pm on a Wednesday, hoping to catch him coming home. She wore whistle bait with white heels, white fur and cherry lips. The elevator man, a stocky figure with a puffy face and a cylinder hat, wouldn't let her up, kept saying he had no one by the name Chase Griggs on his list. When the lobby clerk corroborated the elevator man's story, Holly's first thought was betrayal. Her second was puzzlement. Chase had adored her over the last couple of weeks. One night stands could go on for three nights or more, but there was no need for him to blow all his dough on her just to lay a little pipe. The outfit she was wearing was on his nickel, and she came to model it for him and then let him take it off her. Chase had to come up with a strong defense. He had made plans to see Holly the day after the incident, and her surprises had him playing hopscotch at home. Vilma was already acting strange around him. There were no more theatrics before breakfast; not even pecks on the cheek before he left for work. When Holly called Chase out, he laid it on her book thick, told her that dangerous men were looking for him. It was the reason he had to stay at the Werlick under a pseudonym. He would even have to switch hotels, but it was all bullshit. She had trouble buying it too, but then Chase took her to dinner and then cuffed her with ice. When she asked him about these dangerous men, he insisted he couldn't talk about it.

"Pap Fanti can help you," Holly said in his arms. Their legs made a braid under the sheets.

"Katie, bar the door. He can't know about it. No one can know, see? I've got people working it out, and when it's all done, it'll just be you and me. You gotta believe me on this. Do you believe me?"

"Of course I believe you. I don't really know you, but I believe you." Holly moved her head to Chase's chest and stared off to the side as though she was searching for the truth in the air. The sudden fear of living without Chase became very real to her. "What would I do if I lost you?" Holly asked.

"You couldn't lose me in a crowd of panic. Have you been looking for flats like I told you?"

"No."

"Why not?" Chase was fifty/fifty at a fork in the road, so he had to make sure he had enough gas to go both ways at the same time. He wanted Holly like a gambler wants chips, but he wasn't ready to walk on Vilma and all she afforded him just yet.

"I don't know. It just all seems like we're driving a hundred miles an hour." She was guarding what little remained of her heart.

"In reverse," Chase said. That microscopic part of the lower intestine where the difference between right and wrong is cooked into gas made the words flatulate out of his mouth.

"Why do you say that?" She asked with sublime worry.

"Look, doll, I like you. I don't waste my time with dizzy dames that ain't hep to my beat. I only got designs for the girl that has it all. Body, face, ginchy even in the brains. You're a

Rolls I found at a Five and Dime, you've got everything I want. But I need to be serious with you for two seconds." Chase scooted Holly's head off his chest and took a seat. He lit a cig and collected his thoughts in the smoke. Holly sat by his side and looked like a girl about to be scolded by her father. "I want you to quit the pills. They don't let you think straight," he said.

"I don't take 'em anymore. They're for Claudie. I kinda sell 'em…"

Chase cut her off. "Listen to me for a second. I want to give you a future. That bracelet doesn't mean a thing. I'm talking about something serious. I'm not one to chew the fat over kids, but time ain't doing us no favors. You'd make a lovely mother too." He kissed her. "Are you getting any of what I'm saying?"

"I think so," Holly said.

"And that's why we need to take some time. I have some things I need to fix before I bring you into the popper."

"Those dangerous men that are out to get you?"

Chase got upset. He double-fisted Holly by the arms. "This ain't a gag. Are you on my side or not?"

"Yes," Holly whispered.

"Then back me up. No more surprises at the office or here. When I want to see you, I come to you. I'll want to see you all the time, you're truly the ginchiest. But the more they see me with you, the more they see another bullseye. I love you."

It was too early to be throwing phrases like that, like they were cheap candy at a rich kid's house. Why would Chase say that if he didn't mean it? Or was it just a barmy attempt to keep her nibbling at the bait. Holly wasn't going anywhere but Calloway. It was her only security until Chase had walked through the door. Now he was one step from securing her. But who was securing him? She wanted to talk to Pap Fanti about it, see if he could do something about the dangerous men that were poking their noses into Chase's business. He would never know that she went behind his back either. If she was truly to back

Chase up, she had to do whatever she could to help him out of trouble now.

Early the next morning, Holly took three separate cabs to Calloway. One stopped a couple of blocks west of the Twig Bridge, one south of the Jester Bridge. This was part of Pap's protocol to avoid being tagged. It cost a few extra bucks each time, but Pap reimbursed generously for the added safety. She mentioned the name Chase Griggs, but it didn't ring a bell. Pap showed enthusiasm for her new fling. Anyone who made an honest living and did it well was okay in his book. A man in construction, like Griggs, had a gift for building. Pap knew that Holly needed more building in her life. Another point for Griggs. When she informed Pap of the trouble Chase was facing, he said he'd ask around. He started with Basil Demur. Chase Griggs had come via his invitation like all the other club members. Holly didn't know anything about Basil or his involvement. It was none of her business. Pap discovered that the dangerous people trailing Chase were only one, a dreadnought of a woman, the typical all-big-gun, Vilma Griggs. If she even bore a shade of Buddy Plagun's temperament, they had all better duck. Pap used extreme caution when he said, "It's worse than you think. You should cut it short before either of you get hurt. I can't do much more than that." He simply couldn't bring himself to tell her that Chase was tied down—it would crush her spirit—and hoped time would work to bring their dalliance to a harmless end. But the word of warning backfired when Holly was driven deeper into Chase's embrace. Now more than ever she had to help protect him from these "dangerous men."

- 49 -

Claudette Calor wanted to be an actress more than anything, but when auditions led to dirty takes on the casting couch, she drew a line. The Leaf was at the height of its scandal in those days. And Claudette would not oblige. Pap respected her for this. Showed she had integrity and valued some things more than money. That meant she could be trusted around Buster. It was Pap's only precondition for joining up. Had he known about her drug habit, he may have thought otherwise, but she did a decent job keeping it from everyone. Claudette wasn't all that pretty in the face. It was one of the reasons she took to the speed, but that only made her look worse. She grew a squash where she should have grown a nose and her eyes were pinched together. She was, however, a spirited dancer with a lean and muscular body. Despite a blighted face, she had plenty of experience with men too. Just like with the theater producers, she remained chaste. She could never settle into a relationship that didn't bring up hanky panky within the first hour. This made her wary of all men. When she met Buster Horn, she was wary of any tricks. Like everyone else, she was sedated by his charms within seconds. He was too soft and sweet to illicit fear. He appeared to be male, though she never actually checked, but he was more angel than man, puritan in fiber. He seemed always concerned about others and never himself. This was novel to her, original to everyone, but because of her struggles with the opposite sex, Claudette found a special connection with Buster. She would shoot the breeze with him backstage after shows until one of them would doze off. When she was around the bear, she had no desire for the meth. Chase Griggs was another story altogether. She had zero for him, and she drilled into Holly's head until it throbbed.

"He's gonna leave you high and dry," Claudette said as she gave a verbal buffeting of her diamond bracelet. She was hopped up and hostile.

"That's some swell flash! You think it's real?" Rita asked.

"It's a queer I tell you. I've seen this character a thousand times. They buy you all sorts of two-bit rocks coated in nail polish. Next thing you know you're at the belly plumber, and he's booked first passage to the Bean Islands," Claudette responded.

"How much you wanna bet it's a real glow-worm? My guy ain't no cheapskate. He lives in the Werlick. You know the fancy place with giant hot tubs in the rooms and round-the-clock champagne service. You know he won't let me put my hand in my purse for a stick of gum. Says a woman is in charge of the love, the man is in charge of the money."

"Have you let him play with your kitty cat yet?" Rita asked.

"Rita!" Claudette blurted.

"What?" Rita kept a mischievous smile on her lips. "Well, have you? Give us all the juicy details. Does he take his time and set the table, or does he move in straight for the round steak? How's his kisser?" she asked Holly.

"I don't know anything about that," Holly responded, but she couldn't keep a straight face.

"Some men have money to burn so it don't cost them a nickel to blow it. Maybe he can buy you a maid to clean up around here," Claudette said. She was fed up with the chatter about obscene topics, with Holly coming in and out like a bat in a cave. Holly tuned her out.

"Is he chubby where it counts?" Rita asked. She couldn't get off the topic of male anatomy.

"Cut your tongue out!" Claudette rebuked.

Holly giggled and then hid her shame. The truth was that she was falling for Chase much faster than she thought reasonable or safe. But love was seldom governed by reason or safety, and that's what scared her the most.

"You hooked a real zinger. Don't forget to squeeze your legs extra tight so he can't wriggle free," Rita Glass said with a titter of her own. She was Dino's younger sister and once a waitress at his old restaurant. She was tall with legs like stilts, and that made her self-conscious. Her droopy shoulders accentuated the length of her neck and a swimmer's back. Her delicate eyes were her nicest feature, that and the bloom of her ears. Unlike Claudette, she loved men a little too much, especially their members, but after a night of passions left her burned with VD, she fell into depression. These days she preferred living her romantic interludes through Holly. Pap gave her a shot based on Dino's word that she was on the level. If he couldn't count on the girls, he would have scrapped the whole act. So far they had all accepted Pap's terms. To all three gals, Buster was a godsend. And because they revered him and Pap as his caretaker, they swore to forget he existed when they left the club, but it was impossible. They were trigger-mouths by nature and had an intuition about these things, much better than their counterparts did. They knew when they could talk without getting caught. After all, they were the ones who negotiated with the serpent.

"You're a filthy quiff," Claudette told Rita, but there was no malice in her words.

"I only wish I could do more to help him," said Holly.

"What do you mean?" Rita asked.

"He's got people after him. I don't know who, but they're the bad type."

"Did you tell Pap about it?"

"He's got his own problems. You can't bother him with this," Claudette said.

"He said to call it quits. I can't walk out on him now."

"What are you gonna do?" Rita asked.

"I thought about asking him to split town with me. He's got plenty of money. We can just disappear."

"Now you're sounding like Pap. What's the matter with you? You meet some salty egg, he buys you a string of pebbles and you're gonna run off with him just like that? I bet you a Ben Frank he's married," said Claudette.

"Not this man, sweetheart," Holly said. She was starting to lose her cool with Claudette.

"I really hope things work out for you, honey," Rita said.

"Yeah. Just as long as his troubles don't follow you home," Claudette added.

"Don't worry about it. In fact, forget I said anything," Holly said.

"Have you talked to Buster about it?" Claudette asked. She could tell that she struck a nerve with Holly but also understood that a chat with Buster might do wonders to set her straight.

"Are you nuts? How am I gonna talk to Buster about my problems? He doesn't know anything about the real world. I mean he's just a bear," Holly said.

"I talk to him all the time about things, you know, life, love. He gives the best advice."

"Oh really, like what?"

"It's always from the heart. He defines love in a way I've never heard, says if a man can't give me that kind of love and me to him, the kind that doesn't keep tabs and keeps on giving without take, then we'll never really love each other."

"You're high. That came straight out of Redbook."

"Shut up," Claudette said.

Rita giggled, so did Holly. They enjoyed siding with each other against Claudette. She turned a shade red. "I swear to you, Buster said it. He knows a lot more than you think."

"Have you ever wondered what he is? I mean besides a bear," Rita said.

"Don't waste your time, honey. You ain't gonna figure it out," Claudette said. Holly's mind remained on Chase. She loved Buster like everyone else, but she didn't have as hard a time accepting that he was just another magical bear with supernatural abilities. Things like that existed in her world without question.

"It's just sad, you know, what happened to Pisto Leroy," Rita said. If there was a dumbest to the group, she was it.

Claudette became sober as black coffee. "We don't talk of that. You know the rules." Then she switched gears on Holly. "Are you gonna pick up your shit today? You're not the only one that lives here, you know."

Holly stood up and yawned. "Are you gonna pay me for that last baggie?"

"The one you gave me to let you screw your fella in the bedroom?"

"No claws, girls." Rita tried to diffuse the tension.

"There's been two bags since, remember? What about those?" Holly said.

"I told you I would as soon as we got paid. What does that have to do with you picking up around here?" Claudette responded.

"Nothing. Just wondering is all." Holly gave a conceited grin.

"I'm sure everything's gonna be alright with your man. You just be safe," Rita said.

Holly gave a half-hearted okay, sauntered off to the bedroom, turned out the light and closed the door.

Claudette was now visibly upset and wanted Rita to be upset with her. Instead Rita started picking up Holly's leftover Chinese and a whole wardrobe of red undergarments.

"Leave that there." Claudette snatched the rubicund camise from Rita's hand and flung it back to the floor. "That's not your job. I swear, this fuckin' place is a pigsty." Claudette was known for sudden moods, especially when drugged up, but as Rita tended to the mess she couldn't help but think the same.

- 50 -

In a sky of stars, Lala Terre was a supernova. Her shows at Toucan Lounge and Theater Bay would sell out long before she'd get the 24-sheet treatment. Columnists, too important to chase baseborn agents or their show ponies, waited weeks for an interview. Writing anything about Lala Terre was tantamount to journalistic easy street. Some say it was that viola body and duck tail; others declared it was a smoky voice that made hard men noodle-kneed. When she sang, she made love to the microphone, and through it, thousands more made vicarious love to her. Everything curved in the right direction, including the amber rose petals that made up her eyes and the bushel of cinnamon finger curls that cupped the oval of her face. Starting out as a chanteuse, she would ascend the highest peaks of showbusiness. In 1930 alone, she was starring in ten pictures, three which would go down as the worst ever made: *The Kissing Conspiracy*, *Bread Kneads Dough* and *Mice Heads*. But she was piling on the duckets and nearing her first million when she won the award for best tightwad. When she got her son back, she paid DC Stiles with a jalopy, some lobby cards and a signed head shot, nothing more. She would have paid a mint for her boy had she loved him. But an accidental knock-up by one of her leading men, Aristotle Rocker, turned her into a cello and washed her out of the biz. When she planned a trip to the "clinic," Rocker threatened to smear her name in the tabloids as a baby killer and promised he would rear the child. So the boy came out, a little dimwitted. Rocker wanted nothing to do with a retard, so he signed with another studio and never saw Lala Terre again. DC Stiles would have never imagined falling into such instant fame without having anything to show for it but a car with a bad tranny and a string of mysteries he would never crack. This new case had everything he needed to put him in the high chair again, starting with five grand. Like the prized P.I. he claimed to be, he started with the obvious.

Stiles waited for eight long hours across the street from the Easter Tower. It was his second full day of spying. The first yielded a giant goose egg. The photograph of Chase Griggs sat on the passenger seat of his Kissel Q, Stiles in the cockpit with eyes on the hunt. After watching the sun move from one side of the sky to the other and a dozen gees exit the tower without one to match, Stiles decided to introduce himself in person. He had been told by a worthless receptionist that Griggs was out sick, to try again tomorrow. Griggs was shacking with Holly the entire day. When asked who he was, Stiles wiggled his cagey tongue into saying: "Elevator maintenance. I'll try back tomorrow." Today, however, he wouldn't be thwarted a second time. Stiles confirmed Griggs entering the Tower at 9:15 am and would wait the entire day if need be to see him walk out. Then he'd follow him to a meeting with his mistress, snap his shots and submit his invoice. When Griggs walked out at 6 pm, Stiles was a quarter-hour into a nap. Lucky for him, Griggs' Lebaron had a flamboyant motor. He awoke just in time and waited till Griggs was on the road. The next stop would surely be some cheap hotel or his mistress's place, but when Griggs wound up at 4 Waterfall, Stiles punched his steering wheel. He needed some help.

"You ever hear the name Chase Griggs?" DC Stiles asked. He had swung by Calloway the next day. He figured Pap Fanti to be a solid lead since he rolled with some important cats. Little did he know how easy this was about to turn out.

"He's a member of the club? Why?" Pap asked. They were seated in the basement at one of the tables. With the club vacant, it was apparent just how much work they had put into upscaling it. One would hardly tell they were inside a factory. Stiles had asked for privacy, said it was important.

"You're kidding me?"

"No, what's the scoop?" Pap thought Stiles had some dirt on Griggs that could bury the club.

"His wife paid me five grand to track him, get pictures with his lady friend. Can you believe that? I must be the luckiest dick in the Oven."

While Stiles gloated over what would soon be an easy kill, Pap sighed and lit a nico. He was slow about what he had to say, but when he spoke, it came out with authority. "You can't do that."

"What do you mean?"

"I mean you gotta give up the case."

"I can't back out now. It's five big ones. What's the deal?"

"I know the gal he's mixing with. She's a friend of mine. You do this, you'll tear her apart."

"I presume you won't even tell me who she is," Stiles said.

"Right."

"What about me, Pap? I'm late one month's rent. About to be two. The car's telling me she needs a bypass. I got a loaf of bread in the ice box that's growing flowers. I need this case. I'll even throw you a fee for the tip."

"Nix on all of the above."

"Look, I'm not the one taking dips in other people's pools."

"You're just the pool cleaner."

"What happened here? I don't tell you when to run a show. Why are you crowding into my business?"

"You asked me about him, and I told you what I know. Now I'm asking you as a favor to drop it. I'll cover your late rent."

"$5,000 worth?"

Pap admitted he didn't have that much to give but pleaded with Stiles to cancel the contract, said he would make it up to him. "Do this for me," Pap said as he handed him a hundred dollars. It would get him current on things. But to Stiles, a hundred was missing a few zeroes. He apologized to Pap while returning his money and promised he would do his best to not hurt the girl. He almost let slip that he would cancel the whole thing just to keep Pap off him.

Pap now had to figure out how to grow a third eye, one for Buster, one for the chimp and one for Stiles. He couldn't let him sink Holly, but then again how could he stop him? If he shut him out from the club, Stiles would feel insulted and suddenly a five thousand contract would turn into fifty with a sure leak about Buster. Besides, the lie Griggs was feeding Holly would surface on its own as they always did.

As soon as Stiles left, Pap planned a sit down with Chase Griggs at Basil Demur's office, well aware that by traveling the Leaf, he was playing with a fire of his own. He knew that his advice to Holly had not stuck, that she and Griggs were still clapping hips. It wasn't his business to be mixing in another man's affairs, but he would give it one last shot, for Holly's sake. He would tell Griggs that what he was doing was dishonorable, something that real men didn't mess with, and that he needed to redeem himself and break it off like a gentleman. Griggs was to tell Holly that he had to go away for a very long time because the "dangerous men" had upped their ante and made jokers wild. In other words, he wouldn't live through the weekend. He would not be able to take her along. He would have to be convincing because Holly was no goof. Pap would corroborate the story with new evidence he had discovered from the "bookie" Griggs was mixed up with. Griggs would have to use his own lies against himself. Included in the deal was that Chase Griggs was to gift Holly Fountain $5,000. Pap would be the one to collect and would then pay Stiles to drop the case. This was blackmail money that Holly was prepared to squeeze from Griggs in exchange for silence about the tryst. Holly never knew about such a scheme and she wasn't the type to blackmail money out of anyone, but Pap was laying it on thick. Chase Griggs felt the squeeze in Pap's words. For the first time he considered Pap Fanti a very dangerous man in his own right; someone capable of carrying out his objectives in a multitude of ways. Griggs stopped making appearances at Calloway, but he didn't stop seeing Holly Fountain. He reprimanded her for telling Pap Fanti about his secret, even threatened to break it off, but the sex was too hot to quit. If he was going to get killed, either by the fictitious men he had contrived or Pap Fanti, what better time than during climax?

- 51 -

Friendships like the one between the bear and the chimp should have been called something else. There were three shows that week at the club, another three the week after. On the last, Ham Wails had to rush backstage after Buster refused to show through the curtain. Turns out he dozed off and didn't even hear Wails announce him. The new life of a chimp's valet had Buster sleepwalking. Pap saw it coming and was determined to pull it from the root before it got any bigger.

While Buster slept in the middle of another cold day of gray, Pap marched into the washroom. No steel pole, no noose, no syringes. He was upset but showing it to the chimp would get him nowhere. The chimp made a sudden jerk to a stall and slammed himself in. Pap expected nothing less, but the chimp would have nowhere to hide this time. Pap swung the stall door open. The chimp threw himself against the toilet. Pap stood in place as a door normally would. He let his arms hang by his side, gently and without the persuasion of war. He didn't mean to muscle the chimp, but it was time to lay down a little law. Pap stared at him with those sociable eyes.

"I just wanted to talk you, if that's alright. I'm not here to hurt you. Okay?" The chimp kept a focus on Pap. "I was wondering if you could help me with something important. You know that little white bear, goes by the name Buster Horn, I've noticed that he's really pooped out lately. I think he's sad that he hasn't made a connection with you. He wants you to stay; we would like you to stay. He's really taken a shine to you. We'd all like to take that same shine. Do you know why we brought you here?" No response. Those probing eyes kept breaking Pap down. "You have a special gift. Something humans would kill for. Tell me it was you. Tell me that your voice made me believe in heaven." The chimp was a blank blackboard. "You know, when I learned what Buster could do, it took me a while to accept that he was real. Every morning I expected him to be gone, like some sort of illusion, but every morning he'd be there, waiting to greet me with his horn. I know you can understand me. I can see it in your eyes. I wish you wouldn't be afraid of us, of me. I'd be your best ally. Just ask Buster. Anytime you wanna talk, know I'm here. You wanna leave, you gotta let me know too. I don't read minds. You see, Buster, he's one of us. Wherever we are, he's home. I give him everything he wants, nothing I wouldn't do, and I need him to be happy at all times. When he gets stirred up, and I've never seen that, I tend to get a little buzzed, you know, cranky. I'll let you get back to whatever you were doing." Pap's eyes held dominion over the chimp. Then he nodded and left.

The chimp grappled the toilet. He understood every word. They were decent words; the likes of which he had never heard escape a man's mouth. But somehow it wasn't enough. The chimp's aversion to man, the decent ones or not, was simply too strong to become chums with them over a one-sided chat. The old man had made it clear enough, he could stay as long as he wanted and wouldn't be hurt. All the man asked in return was that he lay off the bear a little. What that meant, he pretended not to have a clue.

As the days carried on, the chimp's litany of demands weighed Buster down. "Get me another pack of Glazie Cinns." "How 'bout a bag of Cheep-Cheeps and a dog?" "More, more, more." "Hop me into a soda pop and a pie." "Now, now, now." "We're fresh out of towels." "I clogged your crapper again."

"Listen, we need to talk about the hour you come in each morning. I think it's best if you wait till after I wake up to come barging in. Try after 2 pm, see?"

Buster started spending most of his free time inside the mixing room. Lou would find him taking naps within the kettle drums. He thought that Pap would notice his grief if he stayed in the office with him at night, but it was hard to deny that Buster was hurting inside.

One morning, Buster had the most unusual request for Lou.

"A toy monkey?" Lou laughed.

Buster nodded. "As small as you can find."

"Is Saint Smooth giving you a hard time?"

"Of course not. I think he's real happy here." Buster wasn't a liar, but here he was pretending that things were jake.

That afternoon, Lou returned with a paper bag from Weelad Toy Emporium. He handed it to Buster, and the smile on his face said it all. Buster reached into the bag and took out the miniature doll, a plush little ape that had a striking resemblance to the chimp. "Oh, it's perfect, Lou!"

"You gonna name it?"

"I think I'll name him Mr. Crooner," Buster said. "Thanks all a million." Buster took his monkey and headed to the mixing room. He crawled into a drum, just him and his toy. He held Mr. Crooner in his lap, started to move his arms and legs to give it life. And then he made his introduction.

"Hello, Mr. Crooner. Do you mind if I call you that?" The toy stared back at Buster with unseeing beads. "I've heard you sing and I'm all to pieces for the day when you show off your talents to the nice folks that come and visit. I promise they won't laugh at you. But if you don't feel cozy with any of that, we can always think of something else you may like." Buster was hoping to get a reaction from his toy, but he knew better than to entertain the impossible.

"There is one thing I would like to bring to light if it's alright with you." Buster swallowed air. He suddenly felt as though the doll would channel the chimp's wrath. After shaking off such silly notions, he continued, "We need to do something about your washroom. If it is not too much trouble, and I would love to show you, just a quick demonstration is all, how to properly use the facilities. Is that okay with you?" Suddenly, he saw in the toy's face a ray of criticism, as though he were talking to the chimp directly. "On the other hand, we don't have to talk about this at any particular time. Maybe later or whatever you want. Even better, you just keep doing whatever tickles your fancy, and I'll be there to clean up after you. Don't you worry about a thing." Buster fumbled face first into a pie of jitters.

Every evening at the same time, Buster would cart in the chimp's dinner, now from a menu as assorted as the chimp's tempers. It was an off-night, so he wouldn't have to worry about doing a show. Good thing too because the chimp was in a foul place even if it wasn't directly noticeable from his lazing on the bed. "It's about time. A fella could die in here. You got my baguettes with ketchup?"

"Three, half-raw in the middle, just like you said."

"What about my mutton and vanilla cream?"

"Like maple syrup on a ribeye, says Lou."

"Don't you know how to keep a schedule?"

"Of course…"

The chimp cut him off. "I mean how will I know next time if I'm gonna get fed? Should I start hunting like they do in the jungle, or do I need to go back to my cage where at least I know the rabbit necks are never late?"

"Never…"

"Maybe if you spent less time spouting off how cool you are with that trumpet and more time thinking about important things like me, you wouldn't be such a mess, you get what I'm trying to say to you, snow cone?"

"Absolute…"

"You gotta a lot of problems, kid. Don't be pitchin' 'em my way." It was a tidal wave Buster didn't care to surf. The more the chimp bitched, the more Buster inculpated himself. It didn't matter that his friend had the patience of an epileptic mule kick. Buster would simply have to double his efforts and limit the slip-ups to nil. What the chimp demanded, he would have.

"I'm sorry for being late, Mr. Crooner." Buster was actually early but not early enough to put the clamps on his tongue when the name slipped out.

"What did you call me?"

Buster was stuck. He didn't mean to call the chimp that. Suddenly the name, which was as nice a thing as he could say, sounded like a squirt of lemon to the eye. It was the name of his doll. Buster felt like he had been caught in the worst treason. He tripped over the next few phrases, a rookie when it came to fibbing, but he kept the identity of his toy hidden and deflected to the dinner.

Lou had told Buster to keep a special eye on the chimp tonight, especially his balance. The chimp blew the whole name calling off. His stomach was suffering from hollowness. He uncovered the tray. It was what he ordered, but someone was skimping. It looked like half rations. The baguettes were puny. The pork looked anorexic. There were no fries, no slabs of cheesecake like the night before. The chimp felt punished. He reached for one of the glasses and poured it in. He cringed in disgust, but that was all an act to show Buster that no matter what he or his crew did, nothing would make the chimp happy. If he kept them on their toes, he could get the best out of them. After all, what else was he doing there if not feeding off the generosity of these idiots? Let them wait on him hand or fist or send him off. The reality was that the chimp loved the drink. It had a fruity taste he couldn't get enough of. Little did he know that it was Dino Glass' famous Busted Cherry, a tincture of feminine appeal with enough kick to bring out the naughty side of Carrie Nation. The chimp had no clue, but in a couple of moments his jerkometer dropped. He let out a hiccup followed by a laugh. He reached for the other glass. After polishing his plate, the chimp sat there and stared at Buster. Buster waited for any other requests or to be summarily dismissed.

"Where's that golden sieve of yours?" The question caught Buster off guard. "Why don't you bring it over here?" Of all the firsts the chimp demanded, this one was the best. "I like the crazy sounds you make with that thing." There was a loose drawl forming on his lips. Buster rushed from the washroom, grabbed his horn and returned all in the same excited breath.

The chimp was free-wheeling. "What took you so long?" Teetering from side to side, a simpleton's glaze in his eyes, a smug grin proved Dino, too, had a special gift for transforming personalities. The chimp hiccupped again. "I'm feeling like a million bucks. Go ahead, Buster Horn, the white bear, play your horn. Play it loud. I want to make sure I hear it."

Buster lifted his horn to his snout and blew a blast of B minor. It was heard upstairs where Pap was catching a snooze. When Pap put an ear to the washroom door, he could hear the chimp singing alongside Buster's tune. Chills called the hairs on his forearms to attention. This was the destiny that any man would only dream to have. He needed to know more, needed to see the chimp with his own eyes. Part of him said that if he opened that door, the chimp would revert to his former self and shy away into a stall. It was a chance worth taking. Pap propped the door open and wormed himself through. Buster kept playing the trumpet without interruption. The chimp cast a glance at Pap, and suddenly it hit him. He braved a smile and said his first words to a human being, "What's the word, fatso?" He now felt like the dominant force among the three, but he wanted to sing some more. The chimp freestyled torch songs like a poet. Pap couldn't understand what had happened. The change was far too unpredictable to be gradual. It was the right chimp alright. He couldn't leave the washroom, but no one would believe him when it was all over. He had to get other eyewitness accounts.

Within an hour, those who got the message were at Calloway. They crowded inside the washroom watching the spectacle unfold. It almost made Buster seem more commonplace. This was a headliner's voice, the kind that could pack auditoriums, coliseums; people would forget to pick up their kids at school to get a load of this. This was John Henry, the name they had given him at Crystal Plats. He hated it, thought it made him sound more proper than his setting. Age unknown. 4'0". 85 lbs. Ancestry Pan. Charged: crooning like a god at a speako. Still at large. Occupation: saloon singer, chimpanzee. Repeat: chimpanzee. AKA Mr. Crooner; AKA Saint Smooth; AKA Angel #2. He was coming back down and started to notice men's eyes on him.

While Buster kept playing, the chimp slowed to a few syllables until he turned it off. Then he stood there staring down all the men. Dino Glass and Lou gave each other a conspirator's glance. No one else had a clue. "Don't stop," was the soft request made from the crowd. It came from Gumbie. The chimp grew chary. Whoever was singing a moment ago wasn't him. He took slow, geometric steps past everyone and back into a stall.

Buster noticed the Cats 6, Dino Glass, Lou, Pap, Ink and Turnip, even the Gutter Gophers had come down. He was happy to see them all. From all angles, voices rang out. "It that real?" "Where did he come from?" "He's got talent like Buster." "Impossible." Pap led everyone from the washroom and into the basement for a meeting. Buster remained, but when he asked the chimp if he wanted to keep singing, the chimp kicked him out.

Meanwhile Pap explained everything he knew. "Crystal Plats. Don't ask me how. But you all know what Buster does. He's never let you down. He's made our lives good. I hope we can say the same about him." The others couldn't wrap their minds around it. It would be the greatest duo of musicians the world had ever know, and neither were human. They asked Pap how he happened upon such things and whether there could be dozens, maybe hundreds more wandering the earth. "Have you ever heard of something like this?" was Pap's only reply.

It was six the next morning when the chimp was jolted into consciousness by a throbbing bass line inside his brain. He moaned until a sudden urge to gag grated his throat. Then he shut up, his eyes trying to control the room from spinning him off the bed. Then he yelled, and all the demons of hell yelled with him.

Ink Tambo heard it first. Buster was inside the mixing room and heard it second. It was the first night in many when he had slept a whole seven hours without once being disturbed, without once having to cater to the chimp. The club had enjoyed a night of peace. The chimp sat up on the bed and launched his entire stomach all over the floor. For the first time since its arrival, Ink Tambo was hesitant to pop in. He warned Buster to use caution. He should have prepared him for an exorcism instead.

"Call the undertaker!" the chimp screamed. "I'm dying!" The chimp's guts tried somersaults, and out came the results. Buster felt woozy and sorely afraid. He whispered words of encouragement. The chimp demanded he stop yelling. Caught in a jam, Buster left the washroom and fell into Ink's arms.

Pap and Lou hurried down. Lou told Pap that he would take care of it and urged him to take Buster away. Dino Glass didn't live with the crew at Calloway. He had his own small place on the border or Breaks and Jester. It would take him too long to get here and fix the chimp up, so Lou would handle it himself. He was no bartender, had never mixed a blood-kicker worth ingesting in his life. He failed miserably to make coffin varnish with Pap, but he had to do something before Pap got the picture, even if he had already suspected foul play. Pap wasn't dumb. Lou filled a glass of rye and added a splash of ginger ale without noticing he had just formulated a highball. He rushed it to the chimp and told him to drink. The chimp didn't resist. He was in too much pain. It didn't take but a couple of minutes before he started to feel relief, even good. It was settled. To keep this chimp on the level, his blood would have to be spiked around the clock.

When Buster returned to the washroom a couple hours later, he didn't see Mr. Crooner, not on his bed, in front of the mirror or in the stalls. Ink had confirmed that the chimp hadn't left the washroom, so Buster got worried. He noticed the small window on the wall. It was sealed shut. The tin tub was filled with clean, soapy, warm water. But the chimp hated water and refused to get in it. This he made clear from the start. No matter how much he stunk, if a talcum bath couldn't freshen him up, nothing would. Buster noticed bubbles popping at the surface of the tub and feared the chimp had drowned. He stuck his head over the surface of the water and called out to his friend. Mr. Crooner popped out like a geyser and menaced Buster's face with two cheeks of water. Buster thought it the most puckish display he'd seen from his friend. He couldn't recognize him. "I thought you didn't like the water."

"Is that what this is?" the chimp asked. He was smashed, and all his cares were at the wayside. He had pulled the old switcheroo. "Aren't you hungry, my euphonious, furry friend?" the chimp asked as he climbed out of the tub, drenched and dripping his way to breakfast. Buster did a double take. He had just been called "friend." "Go ahead, take a load off." The chimp slid over to Buster and guided him to a seat on the bed. He paid no mind to the water that was draining all over the covers. Buster crossed flabbergasted paws. The chimp skipped to the tray and slipped on the tile till his mirth set him straight. He rolled the cart over, uncovering the dish: scallop linguini and cupcakes with hot sauce—all the chimp's idea, but Lou didn't care. "Dig in. I'm not hungry," said the chimp. He was abstemious, even well-bred. He took a couple of towels and dried off. Buster did as he was told and took a bite of the linguini. It was delicious. He would avoid the cupcakes. "Mr.

Crooner," the chimp uttered. Buster could do nothing but keep his eyes on him. A mouthful of Lou's cuisine had him all the more chipper, but he retraced his last few words to conclude that he hadn't just called the chimp by that name again. "I'm tickled to the shins by it. Mr. Crooner. You can call me that whenever you want."

"You feeling okay?" Buster simply had to ask.

"Am I feelin' okay, he asks. What is that you say? Quack, quack, goose! I've been liberated from bondage and ushered into a musical paradise where white-gloves serve me at the snap of a wrist. You tell me how I'm feelin'. Now go on, take another bite," Mr. Crooner said. Buster did just that. He chewed quickly and swallowed, sometimes bypassing the chewing and just swallowing on the chance that he would be summoned to speak. "Tell me that was really you at the clam bake in front of all those shieks and shebas."

"Did you like it?"

"Did I like it?" the chimp repeated. He swung his head away from Buster and appeared to be having a conversation with others, only there was no one else. "It was copacetic! A real juicy time! Aces, kid! The snake's hips!" Buster's star-white fur went a shade of rosy. "You have these high-class butter and eggs in fine patterns cater to your every whim, I'll say you're sitting real pretty." That was the first time Buster had heard his life described in such terms. It embarrassed him to think that others were laboring so hard on his account. Mr. Crooner requested another duet, but when Buster returned with his trumpet and cheer, the chimp went cold. At the mirror again, his eyes glowed dull. "What are you so happy about? You shouldn't be that happy here." He turned to Buster and then right past him en route to a stall with a closed door to his rear and a long time to contemplate reality. Again Buster wondered what he had done to provoke the southern turn of the seesaw.

- 52 -

Mr. Crooner, FKA "The Chimp," wandered through Calloway without one to spot him. He had snuck past Ink who was busy working on a mid-morning nap. He was thirsty and had an idea where he could wet his whistle. He spider-crawled down to the basement and set his sights on the bar. Something about the glimmering glass against the back wall solicited deep patronage. He took one of the golden bottles and brought it past his nose. Acidic like car blood, it flared up his sniffer. He cringed, but that didn't stop a taste. He needed a taste. This was the stuff, concentrated and ready to work but still a trace too potent for an appetizer. He set the bottle down and tried for one of the chilled kegs. He rubbed his hands along the icy shell. There was liquid in here, and he was determined to find out what it was. He pushed knobs, twisted handles, pulled tubes until a foam, the type that forms from urine, frothed out. He grew a finger towards it, careful not to wet his fur. Freezing. He brought the finger to his lips for a taste. Delicious. It was time to have some more but he needed a container. He opened cabinets, noticed dozens of clean glasses, tall, short, curvy, all shapes and circumferences. He took a tall glass and filled it to the rim. Then he chugged it down and belched a clap of thunder. Suddenly, the chimp was charged and made quick work of getting into every opened bottle, flagons with every grade of alcohol, taking swigs from each until the bar was nothing more than a collection of trash, shattered glass everywhere, the floor awash with flammable elixirs.

Dino and Lou were outside fishing off the harbor. They couldn't hear a thing inside. Pap apparently slept through it. So did Buster. Mr. Crooner strutted around the tables, cracking jokes under his breath to ghosts. He turned his head to the stage, music stands, chairs, a microphone centered like a beacon and made his way up like he had done it a thousand times before. Facing a headless crowd, he looked over both shoulders giving eye signals to an invisible band. Then he wrapped a hand around the Shuffe 30S one-button. It had one knob at the carbon-graphed center. Pushed into the mic head meant on. It was out and off. He had no clue that there was a button or what would happen if he touched it. His instincts, however, told him that this was the magic wand, the amplifier of ear noise. Cradling the 30S in his hand, it seemed as natural as breathing, like he was born to hold it. He brought it to his mouth for what appeared to be a kiss and whispered a nondescript phrase. His head low, he opened up his imagination and out spilled song after song. Then he cast an eye upon the empty tables and chairs, the romp of hep cats that would soon not forget that the greatest baritone graced that very stage at that very moment. *"My pockets are empty, but my heart is full, you said you'd always love me, tell me I'm a fool. Take my days, take my life, take it all, I don't care. Take my winter, spring and fall, but not your lips, eyes'n ears, nose'n neck, navel nice, skin so soft, hair so fair, no, no, no, I don't care about anything else in this whole wide world, but don't you take your love from me, don't you dare!"* His dreamy voice carried through the basement and beyond. He had no need for the mic.

Lou and Dino started back with their catch, ten cross-eyed halies. They could hear the voice once they stepped foot inside the building. Buster was awoken from a dream of his friend singing. But the song continued while awake. Pap batted an eye. He heard it too. They were two floors up, and the ceiling of the basement was concrete two feet thick, but through it all, Mr. Crooner's voice penetrated the walls like they were made of mesh. They hurried down to the basement. Lou and Dino had beat them to it. Ink was with them. It bothered Pap that no one had thought to wake him with such news, but there was no time to fuss. He noticed the sack of fish they had just caught. It was now on the floor, the fish having spilled out when Lou caught a glimpse of Mr. Crooner. Some were still sucking air for a drink of water. Pap also regarded the demolition zone that was now the bar, but none of it compelled him to take his eyes away from Mr. Crooner who stopped his song and cast a critical glance on his audience, as though he was now the one grading them. Then he guffawed and continued intoning. It was all an illusion to Mr. Crooner, so he thought. Pap, Buster and the boys approached the stage. They stood within feet, watching him perform. He was a natural, never a lesson in his life, so they surmised. He didn't need any. Where the songs came from, they hadn't a clue. One after the other, a hit was born. They wouldn't dare interrupt. When the chimp was done, they would applaud. Pap would ask him how he felt and if there was anything he wanted. Then he would talk to him about doing what he did in front of a larger audience in a few days, if he was up to it. No pressure. The pressure instead came from Mr. Crooner's stomach. He stopped midsentence and offered a lost eye to his new comrades just before projecting a river of vomit all over them, not with mens rea, but simply because they were in the line of fire. He conked out. Buster was most mortified by the incident. He thought something catastrophic had happened to his friend. Pap knew exactly what had happened, and his face had trouble concealing his fury.

Buster and Ink helped the chimp to the washroom, cleaned up his face and then put him to bed. Dino Glass and Lou Licks remained in the basement. They were to shine the entire place on the double and then have a talk with Pap. Lou was nothing but loyal to the club, especially to Pap, but something about

Pap's barefaced orders turned him off. Pap was a master of many things. Boundless invective was not one of them.

When the chimp came to, his pains were off the chart. Head, throat, chest, legs at an eleven on the ten scale; his fingers tingled numb. He was trembling, and this frightened Buster again. He groaned for something, but no one could infer what. Pap brought a glass of fizzing water to the chimp's mouth, and he took a sip right from his hand. He had no aversion to Pap at the moment. When Buster asked Pap what had happened, Pap gripped his cane with a tight fist and said in a calm voice: "He's a little sick, but he'll be okay." Whenever Pap was nervous he would strangle his cane. It gave him support should he lose his footing on the world underneath him. Seeing Buster react to the chimp had him more uneasy than seeing the sick chimp.

Two hours later, Lou and Dino were sweaty and beat, but the basement was spotless. Dino was quick to confess. Pap was slow to forgive. But Dino continued to make his case. He knew the chimp only performed because of the booze. He wanted the credit for cracking the chimp's code. Pap had heard it all before. Get him a drink till he doesn't know it is one, and you've hooked him for life. And while Pap had his eyes set on some sort of bottom line, he now felt he was crossing it. He lambasted Dino and Lou for going behind his back. It was a first for Lou, but Dino absolved him, said he had no part in it. Then Pap warned them both: "If I catch you slipping him one more hooker, you better be just as primed when I find you!"

"And if he don't budge?" Lou asked. A combination of endorphins and Pap's atypical display of temper had Lou on the rarer side of impudent.

"If he can't come out of his shell without eel juice, then let him stay a tortoise. I mean what I say. You keep something as stupid from me, what's to keep you from double-crossing me when it counts?" Pap asked Dino. Then Pap turned to Lou without a word. He could tell that Lou was getting bothered by all the schoolboy lectures.

"Come on, Pap, I think you're taking it a little hard. We were just trying to help him out," Lou said.

"We're not animal abusers!" Pap couldn't believe he had just called it an animal, but he didn't know what else to name it.

- 53 -

The chimp was seated up on the bed with no particular purpose. The last couple of days had been hard on him. The door opened, but rather than shoot to the confines of the stall, he stayed in place and watched Pap and Buster enter with another tray of food and a drink. Déjà vu took seizure as his eyes locked in on the goblet. All suffering that had taken place flew out the window in an instant. Only the chimp would be disappointed. Pap rolled the tray to a stop. The chimp went right for the drink as if he knew that whatever had introduced him to his internal muse was to be found within that glass.

Pap roasted up a Cubongo and clouded his face in a stream of smoke. "My name is Pap Fanti. You can call me Pap, Mr. Fanti, Mr. Fatso, whatever you want. Do you go by a special name?"

The chimp considered avoiding an answer, but the questions were harmless, and this fat man seemed to be a pushover. "You think I can get one of those?" he asked pointing at Pap's cigar.

Pap tossed the request through his mind. The chimp smoked too? He passed the blunt like nothing out of the ordinary. "Try keeping it above the throat."

The chimp took a sniff, then shoved the cool end in his mouth. Buster was all eyes. Mr. Crooner looked like one of the fellas with that fat stick simmering from his lips. Then he took a determined drag and choked. Pap kept cool so Buster would do the same. When the chimp regained his rhythm, he offered a glossy eye and said: "John Henry. I hate it. They gave it to me a long time ago."

Buster smiled. He liked the name very much.

"Who?" Pap asked. If he could get an answer, he could possibly figure the chimp's origins. He was hoping to give his ears some practice during this conversation, hoping John Henry would come out with his story.

"I don't know. Moes like you," John Henry answered. As the minutes passed and the Cubongo shriveled, the chimp expected to feel lighter in the heart, that change from morbid to merry. He got nothing but a hunger pang and a spinning head. He stayed quiet and inspected his food. It was a bowl of tomato soup and a salad with a spray of vinaigrette and walnuts. His stomach turned queasy, so he pushed the tray away.

"What's the matter?"

"Why would anything be the matter?"

"I've been meaning to tell you this ever since you got here. It's been tough, if you can understand. Not every day I run into such things."

"I don't know what you're talking about," John Henry said.

"I have a confession to make," Pap said. The chimp continued to watch his soup exhale. He wasn't inebriated, and there was little motivation to anything else. Buster chilled by Pap's side, hoping to show John Henry that he, too, could be happy there if he wanted. "You see, the night we saw you at the zoo, the night I heard you, I couldn't believe it. I mean I've only been touched by one miracle in my life, and he's sitting right next to me. But I guess lightening struck twice."

The chimp manufactured ignorance to what he heard. He reached for his empty glass and held it in the air. "You mind?"

Pap felt shunted in the middle of his discourse. The chimp disregarded everything he had said. But being the host that he was, Pap stood, took the glass from the chimp's hand and started for the door.

"Pap, I'll get it. You stay here and keep talking with John Henry," Buster said.

"I said don't call me that," the chimp warned.

"I'm sorry, Mr. Crooner."

"Hurry up with that drink. Maybe you can see to it that it comes back with something different," the chimp directed.

It disturbed Pap to hear anyone barking orders at Buster. No one usurped his authority around here. "Have Ink take care of it, Buster. You stay with us, little buddy."

Buster opened the door and relayed the message to Ink.

"Do you know why you're here?" Pap asked. "To sing with Buster here, with his band, to make you the second star in our dark sky."

The chimp shook his head shut. "I don't sing."

"Cut it out. We've all seen and heard you now. You have the most magnificent pipes anyone's ever heard, so whatever you call it, the rest of us call it singing." There was no more denying it. The chimp stared at Pap with conflicted eyes, part contempt, part contemplation. "I know your special gift, and we want you to share it with our special place. No one else will ever know about it. It's just us. Nothing bad could ever come to you if you let me be your friend. You see how I take care of Buster, how we take care of you. You like the food around here, don't you? We can get you something else."

"What's the catch?"

"I'm pitching softballs right over the plate. No catch. In fact, I was talking about it with Buster and some of the others. If you didn't like it here, I'm open to suggestions."

The chimp stepped off the bed and started pacing. It was apparent he was gaining confidence around the fat man. He stepped in front of Buster's mirror and stared at himself again. "No, not back there."

"Then you'll stay?"

The chimp remained speechless. He turned and looked to Buster. It was obvious that Buster wished to answer for his new friend, but this was a decision for Mr. Crooner to make alone. Ink returned with another pop and handed it to Buster. Ink didn't like the chimp, didn't care to have direct contact with him. The chimp took it from Buster and slammed it down. With all his faith that this one would do the trick, he remained sober as a funeral. Pap told him to think things over. There was no rush to make a decision. Buster was a great roommate, and the others were happy to have him there. The chimp kept bouncing an eye in the mirror. Disgust was all he could come up with. He couldn't show such a deformed visage to the pretty masks of the human world. Pap reached out a gentle but firm hand. He sought to show John Henry that he was a man of his word. The chimp shook it. When Pap left, Mr. Crooner's stomach settled into place, so he drank his soup and ate his salad. Then he asked Buster if he could trust the fat man.

"With my life," Buster said. The chimp considered everything he had known since he arrived at Calloway. His decision had already been made.

- 54 -

Evening on Twenties Slip was introduced with a serving of snow and a side of mud. The Cats 6 started filtering into the club. They arrived in two separate cars. Beans Fryer and Clyde Davis each drove old Model C's. They showed up twenty minutes apart on Pap's instruction. They were mumbling wishes and wonderment about the singing chimp and whether he would swing with them soon. Pap preached patience. The more the chimp heard the Cats 6 and Buster together, the more prone he'd be to unshell and join the party. There would be no way the chimp could resist the music for that long. But he did.

"And one…and a two…swing with Mr. Croo…and a three, Buster, four, five, swing Cats 6," Beans counted. The band sounded off. Buster fell in line and kept a watchful eye on Mr. Crooner from behind the bell of his trumpet. He could do it. Everyone was rooting for him. But minutes into the set, and the chimp did nothing but stand at the mic with a gar cooking between his molars. He was struck with stage fright.

"Maybe he needs help with the lyrics," Pap said after rehearsal. He returned to the chimp's room to find out.

"I don't write songs, and I sure as hell don't read 'em. They just come to me. Sometimes I hear a tune and guess right. If not, I wing it, and it's still right. Doesn't matter, see? When I feel it, I do it. Never forced. If I want 'em to change it up, I'll let 'em know."

But night after night, it was the same thing. The band offered myriad melodies. The chimp refused to adopt one. When the music stopped, the chimp gave his unintended glances and made a dogged return to his refuge. He would have no part in singing with any human company. He just didn't feel up to it. Dino Glass took first notice, and it didn't take long for him to go behind Pap's back again. He knew Pap was all bark. If the experiment was controlled, he could monitor the chimp and keep him from the edge. That goddamn edge. It was the only thing precluding the appearance of Mr. Crooner.

Dinner came in the usual way, but the drinks were spiked, just enough to get a rise. No one else knew about it, not even Lou Licks. He had even made a deal with the chimp. "I'll pour you what you want. You wow us and stay in line. No rough stuff, or it's your ass and mine. Deal?" The chimp sold his soul to make it happen. Tonight, Dino thought, Mr. Crooner would take the stage with the boys for the first time, and Pap would be so overwhelmed that he wouldn't bother to ask if Dino had played a part.

The chimp took his meal down and drank his drink. It kicked his insides with warm pleasure. The Cats 6 started up just around the time he sopped up his last bite of bread. He was charged. His heart raced, and he needed to get groovy legs under him. He hummed until he sang and soon was headed for the basement, crooning the walls along the way. When he crossed the curtain, he didn't hesitate; he chanted his entrance. Those in attendance: Pap, Lou, Buster and the band couldn't believe their eyes. Dino knew it would work. The chimp evolved into Mr. Crooner with a slippery foot towards the mic. He glanced back at the band, starting with Buster. Surely Buster had full confidence in his band mates and the way Mr. Crooner was feeling now, so should he. His eyes turned to Beans Fryer, Tots, Gumbie, Clyde Davis, Charmin and Sas Parila. He spun around and sent his mic into a swoon. *"Doobie, dibbie, slick and skivvy, poli all my ravioli means I'm fond of you. Tripping tongues and loads of fun and naked gums for sunny hums means I'm fond of you. Don't think for just a minute, that I'm out and just not in it, 'cause you know that couldn't be more than a fib, doobie, dibbie dibs on spending time and all its seconds, give me all of you I beckons 'cause I'm fond of you!"*

Pap snapped his toes inside his wingtips. He guessed right. It was only a matter of time before the rhythms took root. No true gate could hold out that long, not that Pap would know by experience. But the chimp didn't need liquor like Dino argued. In an instant, it had all come together. Buster played his horn like it was his destiny to be sharing the stage with Mr. Crooner. This was the moment they had all been waiting for. The band kept on, and soon they found that the chimp was leading in ways foreign even to Buster. The torch was being passed. The Cats 6 and Buster were now in Mr. Crooner's hands. He ad libbed every song, but the band had no trouble keeping pace, especially with Buster counting the beats in Mr. Crooner's head. It was better than Pap envisaged. The only thing missing was a pair of pants. An audience would surely take notice that Mr. Crooner had another mic, much smaller but still very noticeable, hanging in the wind.

Saturday night came, but the next show was set for Monday. Mondays were the best nights to either extend a weekend or bring them closer to the next. Since most club members made their own schedules, there was no burden, not even on Chase Griggs, who only lied about how long he had to work. Tonight marked the third rehearsal with Mr. Crooner. He hadn't skipped a beat and was coming down in steady increments. Dino had him measured like a mad quack, and Pap was in the dark about it. Mr. Crooner had even gone as far as to meet the band he was singing with, even if the Cats 6 did all the talking. Mr. Crooner didn't flinch, didn't rush for cover. He clapped hands, offered a few smirking nods and went to work.

While the band swung, Pap decided to make a cursory inspection of the chimp's quarters. Nothing terribly out of play.

He noticed the empty plate and glass on the tray. He was certain what brought the chimp to perform, but what reasonable man denied a doubt its day in court? He brought the glass to his nose. The proof was 100 proof. His anger begged to come out. His first inclination was to send Dino Glass packing. He couldn't be trusted, and in this line of work, trust meant the difference between another night of music or death. He stood there, wrestling his rage into submission, the music playing in the distance and considered his next play. He took a seat on the chimp's bed and lit a smoke. The chimp was singing with the band, had been singing with the band for three days straight, and there had been no fiascos. If he cut him off now, he may never get him to perform again. If he came to trust whatever Dino was doing, he could complement the greatest show on earth. Buster seemed just fine as long as the chimp was singing. In fact, Pap couldn't remember the last time he had seen Buster as happy. But Dino was a traitor in that he did not obey his boss. What kind of example would that set to the others, to Lou? The fissures were starting to show. Whatever he did, he would have to do it soon. Against all his instincts and principles, he swallowed all pride and went on logic. The status quo now meant Pap could turn a blind eye to Dino's insubordination. Besides, Monday was around the corner, and there were lots of things to do in preparation, including letting the chimp know that he would be in front of a live audience for the first time. It was a safe bet that Mr. Crooner would have to be in an altered state just to break it to him.

- 55 -

The Yank was one of Vilma Griggs' favorite nightspots. A shot in the heart of Emporio District, she remembered going with her father to enjoy big bands and a brace of lamb. It's where she met Chase Griggs six years ago. He had come with Jackson Reese to discuss new ventures that might put Chase back on his feet. With liquor traffic booming, a fleet of trucks rented to bootleggers doubling as honest merchants seemed a quick score. They talked big, they drank highballs, Jackson went into the ice trade instead, and Chase Griggs remained an idle construction foreman. When Reese introduced him to Congressman Worthton and his daughter, Vilma, Chase Griggs showed etiquette but no dice. Vilma, on the other hand, kept making eyes at him from across the table, and soon they'd be dancing under the kind of lights that hid most imperfections. Who was he kidding? Mr. and Mrs. Worthton made a dreadful combination and then named it Vilma. He would swear to this day that she put the moves on him when he was ditch-dug drunk, no matter how many times he nailed her with the lights off. He would not deny, and he'd probably never admit, that she also put him right smack in the middle of the building world. Soon after they wed, Chase Griggs would be heading major jobs for the first time and be known as the man who bagged the congressman's daughter.

But now Chase Griggs didn't care for The Yank anymore or the people in it, including Vilma. The drinks were diluted; the company distilled. But the occasional Saturday night seemed essential to hold up his end of the nuptials. It would be a long many Saturdays before he would feel secure enough to take Vilma for all she had and split. Chase and Vilma stood in swarm of socialites with ties to her late father. Men, like the coutured Mr. Carmen Signia, who had far too much culture and clout to be swinging on vines with the likes of Chase Griggs.

"Those are the whitest dice I've ever seen. You actually eat with those sugar cubes?" Mr. Signia asked Chase. He was the kind of man that could call you an asshole and get a 'thank you' in response.

To Chase, the man's words carried the distinct sound of farts. He even swore Signia say that if Chase had his kind of money, he'd throw his all away. They wasted life spouting off claptrap until the conversation turned to Chase and his many erections. Vilma boasted of his projects, the Gibb in Brixton, the Easter Tower, and then she stuffed a foot in her mouth.

"The best part is that he secured those contracts all on his own, right honey? Tell them about the elevators at Easter. They're state of the art. Air-conditioned. Sixty floors in less than a minute and no swollen feet."

"Looks like someone's moving up in the world. Just careful with the swollen heads," Mr. Signia jabbed.

"I'm just lucky to have the undying support of an angel disguised as a wife. Speaking of which, where's Mrs. Signia?" Chase dug back.

Before making the introduction, Vilma had cautioned Chase to avoid topics of marriage. The Signias had taken up residence in a divorce court, and Mr. Signia was relieved to be spending a week in Good Leaf on business. He was a big-shot record producer from across the pond and was looking for new styles to take back with him. Maybe one would rekindle a broken marriage. When Vilma suggested that Chase chaperone Mr.

Signia and his entourage to some of the local spots he raved about, Chase became upset. When Mr. Signia agreed on the grounds that "they needed a chauffeur of experience," Chase nearly socked him in the face. It was at that moment that Chase remembered the full weight of Vilma's thumb over his head.

Vilma thought nothing of Mr. Signia's comments. After all, Chase did know the Leaf more than most. He had managed to find his way into the doldrums of most alleyways and "to this day, he swears the best music is found at a cloth factory."

"To this day, she still doesn't believe me," Chase said. Mr. Signia insisted he be taken there. Chase admitted that this would be impossible. Now he held the upper hand. The trumpeter bear was his secret to enjoy with his clique only. It had nothing to do with money. This showed Mr. Signia and Vilma both that Chase never had any. Only people without money thought that way.

The whole drive home was stagnant. Merlin sensed the tension from his driver seat. It was more than the customary cat hisses. Chase was itching to dump Vilma at the house and get on with his fantasy role. Holly was on his mind. Vilma, on the other hand, was used to rides like this. As long as he was in her sights, however, she could keep tabs. When they got home, Chase headed to his room to rinse The Yank off his face. He was soon on his way out.

"Where are you going?" Vilma asked.

"All this hanging around gold-plated pricks, I need to find some new thoughts," Chase said. Vilma could smell the alcohol oozing from his pores.

"With who?"

"What?"

"Who?"

"Jackson, some of the fellas. Grab a poker game," Chase said as he coated his face with plenty of Zizane and wrapped up in a fresh shirt and tie.

"Uh-uh. I don't buy it."

"I ain't sellin'," Chase volleyed.

"Tell me the truth. Who are you going to see?"

"You're nuts. Don't wait up. Go play with your doll. Teach it to say 'please'," Chase said, but his eyes couldn't meet Vilma's for a straight second.

"First look me in the eyes," Vilma demanded.

Chase forced his eyes to Vilma. They glistened with guilt and had to pull an instant retreat.

"Do you ever dread coming home? After the day is done knowing you have to come here and spend time with this person?" she asked. Chase had no response, and that was all he had to say for Vilma to finish: "Because I can tell you that I now dread when you come through that door."

Chase's eyes chipped like an egg shell. "Are you out of your mind?" Her words slapped reality into him. She could shut him out for good, and he'd be left with only what jingled in his pockets.

"Yes! I'm out of my mind! Every night you go off mollynogging with your filthy barflys, then you have the nerve to come here and call me your wife!" Her cheek clapped against Chase's open palm, without knowledge or consent. It stung. It was the first time Chase had put a hand on her. Vilma let it soak into her face while she contemplated what he had done and, more importantly, why. If anything she said was false, he would have no cause to raise a hand. "You know what, now I want you to take me," Vilma dared.

"Anytime you want, baby. I got nothing up my sleeve. But you disrespect me like that again in front of anyone, it'll be your last." Chase grabbed his hat and slammed the door on the way out. Vilma ran to the phone to call DC Stiles. She would try him for an hour straight, and for an hour straight, she would get no answer. Stiles had been at the Yank the whole night, hiding inside a booth. All he managed to catch was a man and his wife getting along like water and oil.

- 56 -

Mack Loyter occupied a phone booth on a busy Leaf intersection. "East Leaf 5-3807. Basil Demur," Mack lowered his voice to the phone operator. Dradle Prestij went with him. Pap never sent the Gophers alone on an errand. There were no names exchanged. "I got pinched on a B&E," which was code for Calloway. "I see the judge Tuesday, 9 am," which was code for Sunday at 6 pm. Pap was suspicious of others listening to his calls long before tapping existed. If they could capture a man's voice for a record, they could capture it over the phone. He simply wouldn't mess with the devices unless he had no alternative. After the last excursion, he didn't dare enter the Leaf. He swore he saw Jesse Under at an intersection, and his heart had switched to the right side of his chest.

When Basil learned of the singing chimp, his mind jumped to the occult. Some form of divinity was intervening in Pap Fanti's destiny, and for this, he had no legal precedent. All he told Pap was how they could turn it into a profit for all, just like they did with Buster. It worked out for both parties. The talent got a nice living, as cushy as the men in charge. Basil knew Pap to genuinely care for his friends, whether man or beast. The men earned whatever brand of caviar they wanted. But now Pap needed Basil to have more involvement. First on matters of accounting. How to introduce Mr. Crooner to the club members. Could a crowd of drunks handle that much? Would it put Buster, the whole joint in jeopardy? Basil started with the things he could control. He answered every one of the questions with one single answer: "Don't worry about a thing." Basil was moved to tears when he heard Mr. Crooner and Buster perform together, like he had been touched with a power from another universe, a glimpse into the endless possibility of creation, something he could never understand. He would take care to convince the members how much they would want to pay for something as mind-blowing as they were about to witness. Never in the history of mankind would seventy-five guests experience this again. And if none of that was a good reason, it would just be another cool shindig with great music at a quaint little place. So price increases across the board. These high hats wouldn't care. But Pap didn't budge. It didn't matter that the glutton chimp had added to their operating budget. If they raised the price for admission to heaven, some would choose a night in hell instead and bring the whole thing down there with them. All it took was one call, followed by another and the scouts would know where to go. Prices would remain the same. In this tug of war, Pap pulled rank. In fact, everything would remain the same. This wasn't about clocking a fast buck.

"They came to me, both of them. Maybe to teach me some lesson I can't figure out," Pap said.

"Don't forget one came from your brother," Basil added.

As for the crowd's reaction. Some might wet their pants, even blackout. The Gutter Gophers kept cool just like when they had met Buster. Only sissies fell apart at things like this. Pap was proud to have these young men with him, no matter that they had the tongues of sailors and speech to match. When the High Legs saw the chimp sing for the first time, however, they showed Pap that they could curse with the best of them too. Accepting Buster was one thing. He was an easy pill to swallow. But a singing chimp with a barbaric flair and the occasional perverted eye was something else. The gals couldn't help but watch from a safe distance. Even the Cats 6 felt subjugated. Mr. Crooner was pompous and aggressive, but the hope became that repetition would eventually breed comfort.

As for Buster's safety, the Plagun angle, that he was the man behind the whole joint, especially now that he had snatched all power from the Cabra regime, would be his ace in the hole. Those in attendance wouldn't lip. It impressed Basil Demur that what he did with one hand, he could erase with the other, like the manipulation of enemies to serve each other, sometimes without either having knowledge.

But there was one matter that needed attention. Met Fanti was, no doubt, growing antsy. He was a nasty drunk and an unreasonable man according to his brother. He made decisions from his gut and was not to be trusted. He had failed to trail Pap to the club and knew that Pap was aware of the attempt. He had pocketed $260, and this was weeks ago. The new year was right around the corner, and they needed to ring it in right, with the least amount of heat possible. He didn't know where Pap went to hide with property that Met had a strict interest in, no matter that he stole it from Plagun. Met's argument was that Plagun never owned a singing chimp because he never knew he had one. How can one own something without knowledge of propriety?

"Just let me take care of it, will you? I'll cool him off. Tell him it's not working out. The chimp's been trouble, won't sing, won't talk, but that we're still trying to coax it out of him. If you pay him heavy, he'll get liquored and think he can split from the zoo. That will raise Plagun's antenna. A couple C's here, a couple there. That way he stays hungry, but since you haven't forgotten about him, he won't turn. We need more time to figure this thing out. Unless you're going to leave the state and turn carny, there's no more time, and even if you got out of Dodge, Plagun's appetite for Fanti steak is only growing. You'll be running the rest of your life." Basil made all the sense in the world. Pap was lucky to have such a mind on his side. And then Basil fell out of character. "I'm a man of the court, so this should never come from me, but have you ever thought about finishing it?"

"Finishing it?" Pap asked.

"You know, bang the Hangman."

That Basil Demur, respected attorney, would impress upon him the notion of putting a hit on a man like Buddy Plagun confused Pap. Surely, many people wanted Plagun gone, but unless Basil's love for Pap was that great, he couldn't think of a reason he would want him taken out. Men rarely asked for a hit that didn't in some way serve them directly. "I've thought a lot of things, thought about sailing away for good. I got button men to make him croak in a heartbeat, but then I wouldn't be the best example to Buster or his friend."

"Buster or his friend. You're going to keep risking your life for a couple of..."

Pap interrupted quickly, "Couple of what?"

Basil dialed it down. "Best to only have acquaintances. Knowing anyone beyond that only creates acrimony and heartache. Best of luck, Pap. I hope you find out why this happened to you. I'll take care of Met. He's the least of your worries."

Basil Demur scheduled the visit with Met Fanti first thing Monday morning. He had one of his couriers deliver the message Sunday night at Sue's. They were to meet at Demur's office. The walls were soundproof, and the security detail was reliable. Demur had acquired a couple more guards to keep an eye out. They patrolled his floor. Besides that, it was a sacred temple, where a man could confess his darkest sins and receive a pat on the back. Demur felt invulnerable here.

Met started most of his days fried and a few hours late; most of his weeks were ten days long to make up for the three he lost. Today he was humming on a wing, but the business was so important that he got there an hour early. On arrival at the Savings and Loan, he got jammed up on a fat gobbet of bubble gum. He went batty against the curb for ten minutes, but all that did was spread the gunk. It was easier to chunk the shoe and sport the solo-sole look. He didn't want his early entrance to be spoiled another second. But then it was Demur who kept him waiting. Thirty minutes, an hour, then two just to prove that he was nothing more than a flea on a dog's rump. Met uprooted from the chair and took pathetic steps to the secretary who sat there like it was perfectly normal to keep him waiting that long.

"I'm startin' to grow mold here," Met carped.

The secretary smirked, picked up the phone and whispered. She hung up and gave Met entry. Demur met him in his office and put out a hand. Met refused to touch it. "You got me out there two hours?"

Demur observed the pink film over Met's eyes and the stale cloud of air surrounding his mouth. Then he glanced south at Met's shoeless foot. "You're missing a hoof."

"It's at the curb, blowing bubbles."

Demur breathed through his teeth and pulled back to his bar. "Sorry about the wait. You know how it gets." Demur had been on the phone with club members all morning previewing the new Monday night attraction just like he told Pap he would, said it was another "splendid treat." Met never heard a word, and even if he had, he wasn't quick enough to pick it up. Apparently all Met was interested in picking up was the whiskey neat that Demur deposited in his hand. Keeping him fuddled would only make the lawyer's work easier, and in typical Met fashion, he washed his throat with it.

"I'll get right to the point. That thing you and Pap came across. The chimp. I don't know what you boys are into."

"I was three sheets to the wind, so you tell me what I saw." Met's tongue was spiced full of sarcasm. Demur had dealt with these types early in his career. The impoverished, oppressed by fate or the hand of sloth. Theirs was a powerful weapon, even if it was autodestructive. Mockery. "Why did Pap tell you about it?" Met wondered.

"He tells me because he trusts me just like he trusts you."

"Then he doesn't trust you at all."

"Level with me. Have you told anyone?"

Met shook his head. "I'm what you'd call superstish about ratting," he made sure to look straight into Demur's eyes when he said that. Demur wasn't moved.

"Good. It's real important that you keep it under lock and key until we tell you otherwise."

"We? Who's this 'we' roll?"

"I know you were expecting a larger score a lot sooner. It's in the works as we speak. Just have to stay patient, okay?"

"That's what you brought me to say?" Met asked as he put his glass out for a refill.

Demur refilled it. "Actually no. Apparently the chimp's got the blues. Home sick."

Met chuckled. "Figures when all he's known is steel and tendons."

"No one's losing hope just yet, but it may take a little while before he starts channeling his inner Dib Minty."

"He's ten times better than that mutt," Met said defensively.

"Pap instructed me to give this to you in earnest," Demur said as he passed a blank envelope to Met. It felt thicker than its actual value. They were small bills, adding up to $200 jacks. "It's to hold you through the month while they figure out that crooning business. Get yourself another pair of ground grippers."

"Funny guy."

"Remember, Pap trusts you and so do I. Anyone who doesn't take us seriously from now on we don't deal with. You're in the circle."

Met opened the envelope. It was all his, not like the cash bags he sent to Plagun. He kept his eye on the money when he said: "That's gratitude for ya, but Pap could have given this to me himself. What'd he need you for?"

"You want him to show his face all over Plagun turf? Then what? We can't do anything stupid here."

"Yeah we can't. Well, just give the chimp a little time. He'll come around. I mean what choice does he have, right?" He liked having the extra money. It wasn't a king's ransom, but he could buy Sue something nice with it and take her to dinner. The only downside was that Met hadn't believed a word Demur said.

It was half past one in the morning. The night was born in a deep snow and hundreds of skyscrapers were now sporting caps of white powder. Met wandered the streets, trashed and feeling the cold penetrate his bones. If rock bottom had a rock bottom, Met was touching it. His breaths were short. Thoughts of putting an end to his place in history surfaced. He glanced across the street to The Palais and the flashing neons advertising "DINNER & DANCING." Hermes Theater was a block down. He had worn out his welcome at both. He picked up a new suit and shoes at Zilk's right after he left Demur's office. No more shopping at Had Rags Wholesale. He was wearing it now, quickly marking the new threads with the scent of alcohol and smoke. He had even stopped by Tanfield's Department and picked up something special for Sue. It had been ages since he bought her a trinket. She didn't take to any of the dresses he got her last time, said they were tailored for quiffs, so Met returned them all and blew the cash on booze and reefer instead. Knowing he couldn't afford it, the snooty salesman pushed him into purchasing a Seafarer. It was guarded safely behind the glass counter. Met, however, had his sights on something more unassuming, a pair of silver-plated earrings. They were two grains of rice and bore the feminine appeal of pimples on a scrotum. Sue would love them. He had called and said he would be taking her out to a fancy dinner at the Saharan, with its beige camels all over the walls and its gypsy dancers, so she had better get out of those men's pants and into a dress. He sounded sober when he was on the phone hours ago, and Sue, like one too many times before, believed him. She got dolled up in an old ankle-length, yellow-dotted chiffon, buttoned to the throat that she'd cover with her brown coat. She was eager to hear more about this "singing chimp." Met had never displayed such zest for anything other than booze and jujus. Maybe he was changing after all.

When Met didn't show, Sue tried not to let it degrade her. She got out of her dress and back into her slacks. It was a business night anyway, and she could drown her sorrows by drowning the sorrows of Mr. Alquiler and the regular crowd of finks, including the cabbie, the guitar player and the couple with the baby.

Met took the subway to Sunks District and walked to Sue's place. He checked his pockets for the gift box and his remaining cash. All things considered, he was still sitting pretty. Things weren't as bad as he had made them out to be. He had forgotten about the dinner invitation, so there was little worry as he made his way up the stairs to the apartment. The door was locked, and Met couldn't find his key. He was gentle to tap on the door. Maybe Sue was asleep. He took the gift box from his pocket. No one answered. He knocked louder. Mr. Alquiler opened the door. He was ten fingers under.

"Look who's doing the town, singing chimp and all," Mr. Alquiler said.

Met saw red and with one straight fist, decked the old man on his ass, then started kicking the shit out of him. Mr. Alquiler yelled bloody murder until he was knocked out cold.

Sue ran out of the bedroom with an empty bottle of rye in her hand. "You bastard! What's gotten into you!" She screamed at the sight of Mr. Alquiler on the ground and Met vultured over him.

"What did I tell you about that!" Met exclaimed. He had no bearings. Sue cracked the bottle over his head. Had it been full, it might have knocked him out. Instead, it lit Met up enough to rear back and slap Sue on the chin with a closed fist. She collapsed on her bed. "I told you to keep it under wraps!" Met closed in for another round of fisted slaps.

Sue pulled a .22 from her waist and drew an imaginary dot on Met's gut. "I want you out of here. Never come back."

Met froze and time froze with him. Blood started trickling down the side of his head. The patrons in the bedroom shuffled out in dismay. The baby screamed as though it knew what was happening.

Sue slid up on the bed and started sobbing. Her gun remained straight-faced and kept its one black eye on Met. "All because some singing chimp. There's no such thing. It's not real."

Met plucked the cash from his pocket. It totaled over $200. He attempted to wipe the blood off his face with it, but all it did was smear it like paint. "Is any of this real?" He flung the wet bills all over her. "Is this real?" He took the gift box and tossed it at her side.

Sue fished in her pocket for the Calloway chocolate Met had retrieved at Demur's office. She threw it at him. "You want your brother. Why don't you go there? They've been shut down for years." Sue had no clue that Pap Fanti would actually relocate to Calloway, but she was so fed up with hearing Met bitch every night about where Pap had snuck off to with his singing chimp and his money. She had heard Met rant and rave about Pap's joint at the clothing factory and other underground clubs he'd frequent, how they were located in the most unusual places, like steel yards, schools, even an old shutdown prison. Met took the chocolate without much of a thought. His mind was on the aftermath. He saw Mr. Alquiler coming back around, squirming to find shelter under his arms. "Just leave now," Sue said.

Met took a remorseful step towards her, and she cocked the hammer. She could be a real virago when pushed, so he left. Mr. Alquiler then told Sue that she would have to find another place to call home and if she didn't want him to call the police, she would have to pay him the money that Met had just scattered all over the place.

The next day, Sue went to Buddy Plagun. She was tapped out and carried a purple map from her chin to the right side of her jaw. Buddy took compassion on her and promised to set her up in another place. He explained that Met was under a lot of pressure but didn't say why. Sue told him she knew and didn't care who he was after. It wasn't her concern. When she explained the cause of the outburst, Buddy laughed. "Singing chimps? We sell mules, tigers, iguanas, but no singing chimps. Not yet." That was never a code they used. Even in her anguish, her thoughts were on Met's wellbeing. Buddy assured her that he always had the zoo and could rest his head inside the warehouse.

- 57 -

As Mr. Crooner stood in one place trying to keep from coming apart, Pap and Buster's private tailor, an old, skinny man by the name of Byron Needle made the finishing touches on his tuxedo. Mr. Needle was bald except for the white wings he grew from the sides of his head that connected duck feathers above his neckline. His glasses were thicker than Pap's, and he had the nose and ears of a man that never stopped growing. He had known Pap for over thirty years and felt sorry for the Fanti brothers when their father took the high road without them. He had been tailoring Buster's costumes for over two years and credited the bear for keeping him in business when so many shops were going under. Buster was oblivious to such matters. He kept his nose out of things like economies and depressions, not by choice, but because he was kept naïve to such concepts.

Mr. Crooner was close to the same height, but that's where the comparisons ended. For starters, his hands could nearly touch the ground when standing erect. If he hunched over, he was predisposed to it, his fingers would sweep floors. In fact, his arms were longer than his bow-legs. He had a narrow waist—a miracle with all the junk food that fit in between it—so tailoring pants was a cinch. A tuck here, a couple inches off the leg, a snugger fit around the chest. Mr. Crooner rather enjoyed the pampering.

After Mr. Needle was done and gone, Mr. Crooner walked over to the vanity to check himself out. He had already had a drink and was working on his second. He cackled in Buster's face when he hunched over and tried to touch his toes, said it was the stupidest thing he could do before a show because all the blood would pool up in his head and leak out of his ears. The only preshow routine Mr. Crooner needed was to be found in these pretty flutes. Dino added just a little more to the potion. After all, this was the biggest night of his life. The dress was fine. It made him a new creature, one of human rapport. If only there was some way to sheathe or shed what remained above the neck. He simply couldn't get over his contemptible countenance. He took another hale and hearty swig.

"It's all wet," Mr. Crooner said.

The chimp tried changing faces, smiles, frowns, pouting his lips, then sucking them in. The only one that seemed to work best was when he shut his eyes tight. It hid all shame. But soon his skin was tingling, and his head buzzed in anticipation of what might be a night of pies to the grill.

"You look like a million, Mr. Crooner," Buster said.

The chimp acknowledged the way Buster addressed him. Mr. Crooner was starting to take root. He knew what a crooner was. They were iconic, the best, the voices that led bands into fame and brought young lovers racing into each other's arms. Mr. Crooner was right. He instantly had a recollection of that gal, the reason he held to his tune so fervently. It was a special day many suns ago. She came to a pause at the chimp cage. Only she didn't see any, and if she had, it wasn't through her eyes since they were of no use to her. The chimp, though, saw her from within the black of his dungeon. He couldn't stop paying attention. The most graceful creature he had ever acknowledged, she had not a clue what it was to judge the visual world. This brought him his greatest peace. Her face was a sheet of silk and honey, her hair a shawl of wheat. No matter where she shifted her head, her eyes would maintain their skyward direction. She would come to him in visions while perched up on his rock entertaining a desolate world. His muse to keep singing, to keep going, so he thought. Tonight, he would try to remember her all over again.

"Ten minutes to show time. You boys okay?" Lou was heard asking from the other side of the door.

"Quack, quack, double ducky," Buster answered. He was dressed to the nines and offered an encouraging glance to the chimp.

"Don't mess me up out there because it'll all be on you. Let me know if you need me to repeat that," the chimp said.

Suddenly Buster felt the air squeeze him at all sides. He had never known pressure like this and was never known to err while handling his horn, but tonight the chimp had made things very clear. Buster would pay special attention to his technique solely to ensure that the chimp had the debut he wanted. After all, the night belonged to him.

Downstairs, the band kept the vibe nice and easy. The basement was packed with the usual suspects. Quick-stepping along with Claudette and Rita, Holly Fountain snuck an eye to the empty seat Chase Griggs used to occupy. They had spent many a lovely night cupped from the rest of the world. The whole line about dangerous men on his tail had taken an unexpected turn when Pap got involved. Chase told Holly he would be waiting for her inside another hotel room when she was done. Holly wouldn't even bother sticking around for the main act. When she kicked her last cancan, she would catch a cab. Pap noticed that Holly left early and could only imagine where.

DC Stiles noticed the same thing. He had been filling his lustful eye with Holly for the better part of seven minutes. When Pap had told him that Chase Griggs was a member of the club, Stiles felt pennies raining down on him. And even though nothing in his practice was orthodox, tonight he would have to do it the old fashioned way. He had studied all the other men's faces in attendance. None fit the bill. But he had a hunch about Holly Fountain and decided to act quickly before he lost the trail. He was laid-back as he stood from the stool and slithered to the exit thinking no one would see him.

Pap had a bad feeling about the night. Things were going too well. In a few moments, two musical juggernauts would crown the stage and send the crowd into a buckle. Perhaps this would be the last night of Pap's life. Circumstances had turned his mind into a playground of paranoia. His nerves were racked just before Buster took the stage. He could never overlook that his magical bear might suffer a setback. Humans he could predict; bears with trumpets a different story. To this point, Buster had never once disappointed. He was a freak lip that could go every night if they wanted him to, but now Pap was falling apart on account of the new act, one that would surely leave the revelers to wonder if they had been drugged. Pap made his way backstage and stopped in his tracks when he saw Mr. Crooner giving music lessons.

"When I pick up the tempo, you drop in line. I sink into a lower octave, match me on the other end." It was as though the chimp had already performed a thousand times and knew all of Buster's tendencies. The chimp smirked to Pap like he was crowding them.

For the next five minutes, the band was on fire and Buster was pouring the gas. Jackson Reese grabbed one of his girlfriends and moved to the small space in front of the bandstand to cut the rug with the Charleston. Other couples took their cues until the Cats 6 slowed to a crawl.

Lou dimmed the lights leaving only a soft glow shrouding the stage, making the band members look like shadows from the past and Buster look like something out of dream. The circumference of the mic was an abyss. Buster screamed one high note and held it for an entire breath. When he went silent, a spotlight revealed Ham Wails standing at the mic. Beans Fryer kept the pulse on his doghouse.

Wails stroked the 30S, giddy and slack and addressed the crowd like any sauced showman would. "Ladies and gents, tonight we have a very special treat for you. I will admit it's something you've never seen before. Sir, put that back inside your pants. That's not what I was talking about." The crowd bucked in laughter. "We all know the privilege it is to enjoy Buster Horn, but they say misery loves company because he's managed to summon one of his friends to join us on this fine Monday evening. It is Monday, right? Don't you people work?" The crowd looked around, exchanged glances and started mumbling. Two musical bears. The notion that there was even one started to dawn on them as peculiar, and that was putting it mildly. "I want you to give the warmest of welcomes to a very special individual, one that will no doubt make you change the way you feel about saloon singers. Mr. Crooner, come on out, friend," Wails disjoined himself from the mic and departed. Just as the music picked up again, everything on and around the stage shined pitch-black.

Mr. Crooner's shadow grew towards the mic. The music ran through him like sugar. The audience couldn't yet see what was onstage, but when Mr. Crooner opened his voice, the audience opened its ears. Lou powered the lights, starting at Mr. Crooner's shoes and scaling up his pants, then his black jacket until the spotlight grew, revealing first a set of flat lips, then higher to the rest of the head and those oceans in his eyes. Pap constricted the nearest chair with his grip. When the light went wide on Mr. Crooner, several in the crowd lost their air; a couple of ladies fainted and had to be escorted upstairs. The rest gasped and gawked, some screamed. Several eyeballed their drinks. Despite this first wave of emotion, there was no nail-biting consternation, only awe. Buster they had come to adore. His humble manner was pleasing, but Mr. Crooner took a different approach. He commanded the mic and the audience like he alone was responsible for bringing everyone into their chairs and many to their feet. He giggled at the dozens of lamps on tables like rafts on the harbor. He could see teeth clapping in the shadows and smoke, incredulous fingers pointing, widespread chuckles and cheers. The lights warmed him like the sun. He bobbed his head, snapped cool fingers, loose and limber, the nuances of a seasoned pro. The cufflinked wrists kept his arms from flailing out of control, the bow tie wrapped around his neck like a leash of class, confirming to all that the singing chimp was indeed a civilized citizen. His pants harnessed those crooked branches. His shoes spit-shined. Mr. Crooner was not a man, and yet he acted so very manly. He brought the first song to a crescendo and the entire crowd to its feet. Buster had to stand just to get the full strength of his own cheers from his diaphragm. He was more thrilled for Mr. Crooner than Mr. Crooner was.

The band then slowed it down. Mr. Crooner seized an inner nostalgia. He paused for a moment of reflection, looked back to the Cats 6, eyeing their overheated mugs, then to Buster whose eyes locked on his friend as if to say, "This is what we were meant for." Mr. Crooner disregarded Buster and returned to his courtship with the mic. It was sad and slow. The words were waterfalls of vibrato, like a bard enthralled by a lost love.

A few unconvinced patrons approached Pap and asked him what was going on. They accused him of voodoo, witchcraft, mountebanking or at least some of the best costumes and sleight of hand they had ever seen. All Pap could say was that the chimp was as real as Buster. Where they got their talents he could not declare, and to each he would give a blanket statement, not knowing whether he believed it himself: "God works in mysterious ways."

As Mr. Crooner and Buster continued to rock the house, things took an unexpected turn. Against all protocol, Mr. Crooner decided that he would have a chat with Buster on the spot, in front of the crowd. He'd even take the microphone with him to make sure that everyone came along. The band could do nothing but improvise. For all they knew, Mr. Crooner had a new swing up his sleeve. He reached for Buster's paw, busy tapping finger buttons, and snatched it clean off the instrument to a horrendous honk. Pap glanced to the stage. Mr. Crooner was looming over Buster like a tutor frustrated with his pupil.

"You out to lunch? That's not how to carry a double ripple through the break. Do it how I told you. Keep it nice and low until it's time to belt out that heat and then blow, Daddy. Make it sizzle till it's well done, stop noodlin' around, and then char that rib roast. Dig?" The crowd laughed, thinking the banter a part of the act. Buster tittered. He had no idea what else to do but nod with the trumpet mouthpiece stuck between his lips.

Mr. Crooner headed back to the front of the stage. "Sorry about that, folks. Sometimes he needs a little kick in the nuts. Someone throw that bear a fish!" The crowd kept laughing. Mr. Crooner was channeling Ham Wails. Pap knew it was time to bring the show to a close.

"Cut the stage lights. Pull the plug on that mic," Pap told Lou. Then he ordered Dino to "slip him a Mickey." In doing so, he informed them both that he had known about the spiked drinks again. Now was not the time for either of them to clam up, but they could expect another talk. It never happened. Pap wouldn't bring it up again except to say that whatever they did, "do it safe." He knew the reality about the chimp. He was one of those losers who only came alive when they were slopped. If only human losers could sing like that.

Mr. Crooner kept at it like he had forgotten everything he just did. Oddly enough, so did Buster. He was just as good as Mr. Crooner—he set the standard for trumpet playing—but that wasn't the reason he played.

Lou doused the lights around the stage. Dino headed up with another drink. No one could see it. The band kept playing. The timing needed to be clean. So they waited. The band tried to end the song, but Mr. Crooner wasn't done. He was having the time of his life. The first time he had experienced humans eating out of his hand. In a flash he looked to the wonder tonic in Dino's palm and stopped midsentence. Pap gave Lou the signal. He cut the mic's juice. Ham Wails stepped through the curtain with the tease of a whole private bar if he would only step backstage. Lou and Turnip were waiting for him. They ushered Mr. Crooner back, said it was waiting in the washroom.

Ham Wails returned to the mic, "How about a round for Mr. Crooner!" Any louder and the crowd would have busted down the walls.

Lou made it a point to bring it to the chimp's attention. "You hear that? It's all for you."

The chimp grinned like he could care less. They made it to the washroom in one piece. Lou opened the door and let the chimp in. Now Pap's words started to make sense. Controlling his exit might be an important factor to consider once he started warming up to the idea of being around other drunks. Mr. Crooner noticed the food, but there was no private bar. He had no trouble filing a complaint and was suddenly becoming comfortable barking orders at humans too. He dug into his food like he had nothing better to do and waited for his drink. But it wouldn't come. Dino had slipped the chimp's last with half a syringe of Dorminow. Mr. Crooner would be singing in his dreams for the next twelve hours.

Halfway through his dinner, his fork fell from his fingers, and he went face first into his mashed potatoes. Lou would be back shortly to carry him to bed and tuck him in, tux on and all. He would remove the shoes. Only the dead slept in shoes Lou would always say. All in all a successful night until Turnip Faymus threw the door open, roscoe in hand. There was urgency in his quick words: "Trouble outside."

Ten minutes ago, the Gutter Gophers had spotted an intruder approaching on foot. The days of Salty Well and boom barriers were gone, but they did have an alarm system for such emergencies. For a walker it was at least four to six minutes, depending on foot speed, to get the word to the basement and clear through the small tunnel that connected the main building to the boiler room. Then one more that they had dug measuring fifty feet would lead to the getaway truck, in the event that the main lot was sealed off, or the small, motorized skiff Pap had bought on Lou's recommendation. If the raiders were on wheels, slice the time by 90%.

Bobby Pin flashed a single light from the far end of the bridge. It was visible only to Burger Brasa on the other end and Anthony Mound on the roof. Anthony hustled to the roof hatch and shot a beam of light down the long hall to the stairs. Mack Loyter caught it and flew to the basement to break the news to Pap. He said it was one man traveling alone.

Met Fanti had no clue that the trap had been sprung on him. The moonlight gave enough to see the words Calloway imprinted on the chocolate wrapper. Just as Sue had indicated, it was shut down. So what were all these fancy wheels doing here? Pap was good. Met wandered without a clue, but as he grew closer to the main door, Lou bulled his way out with a shotgun herniating from his midriff.

"One more step, you get wings," he said.

"Lou Licks? I'll be damned."

Lou squinted and started to identify Met. He kept the gun at the ready. When he got within range to know that it was indeed Met Fanti and his hands were clean, he dropped the man killer by his side and put a finger to his mouth. He led Met into the boiler room where they could talk. Shooing him away wouldn't do any good; neither would shooting him. Met admitted that he had his doubts about the place but was happy to locate Lou. Lou, on the other hand, was vexed with Met's insistence on finding them.

"Pap said he was going to visit you in exactly two weeks at Sue's."

"I ain't there no more," Met said. "Level with me, Lou. I feel like the dirt after a good sweep."

"No one's ducking you, but you being here now can blow the whole thing. You know all about the Plagun business. You also know he's tailing you everywhere you go because he doesn't trust you. He sees you here, he'll send the torpedoes, then the whole thing is dead, maybe you too. Just go. Pap will see you in two weeks. Crystal Plats."

"Make it one."

"Don't push it," Lou said handing Met forty of his hard-saved bucks for good measure.

"Is he singing?"

"The chimp? Don't ask me for an explanation, but yeah, he's singing, singing like a parrot with a split personality," Lou said.

Someone should have told Lou that Pap and Basil Demur had denied the whole thing. Lou would later tell Pap that it was some random bum who got lost. Pap didn't need anymore pressure. If he had known that Met infiltrated their hideout, he would have hitched up the wagon that night. Meanwhile, Met would do as he was told. He had waited this long. What was another couple weeks?

Across town, Stiles tailed Holly's cab, always with a two-car buffer. He had to eat a couple of red lights to avoid losing her, but this was his only shot. When the cab pulled up to the Grand Leaf Hotel, downtown, Stiles knew the booby trap was set. He took his time, watched her go through the revolving front door, noticed the square-shaped doorman and knew that busting in with his Graflex would only net him pictures of the lobby. So he waited in his car across the street, a constant eye on the entrance. He was a very poor detective, he thought. The famous Rax Beegle would have snuck inside Chase Griggs' room and caught five stills of them in coitus. But DC Stiles was no Rax Beegle. So he waited. He had no clue for how long. Could be ten minutes, could be till sunrise. He matched a snipe. On his third smoke, he witnessed Holly marching out again. She looked upset. Tears picked up mascara trails as they ran down her cheeks. It was safe to say, she didn't enjoy the after party. Stiles searched for Chase Griggs. Holly was alone and stumbling to the closest cab. The doorman came out to help. Another man pinballed through the revolving door and after Holly. His clothes hung off him like he had slapped them on in his sleep. He grabbed Holly by the arm. She pulled away. Stiles could see hostile words being exchanged. Chase put his hands together, pleading with Holly, and then they started walking down the street together. Stiles readied his camera and coasted his car from the curb. He kept a hundred yards back. Chase and Holly swung a right at the corner of Abyssinia Street and stopped at a red Lebaron. He opened the door for Holly and gently put her inside. Then he got in the other side and they sat there talking. The night was icy to the touch. Chase fired up the engine and let in some heat. This was as close as Stiles was going to get to both. In order to get a clear shot, he had to get in front of them.

He cut a U and drove around the block the other way. Then he crept around the corner, parked, and extinguished his lights. Chase and Holly hadn't noticed. Stiles grabbed his camera and flashgun. He was just within range to get a medium shot. His zoom lens was clear to twenty feet. What had Stiles nervous was the flashbulb. When he opened the shutter on his camera, it would catch flame and give off quite a light show. If his targets didn't notice this, they deserved what they got. Stiles peeped at Chase laying it on with both handles. He was petting her on the shoulder and caressing her cheek until she threw herself into his arms. Their lips searched for each other like starving dogs. Stiles, seated within his Kissel, raised his camera. This was his shot. He opened the shutter, and the bulb went off like a flare. Chase and Holly smacked lips through it without a blink. Chase got his shot and recharged the bulb with fresh ribbon. He couldn't have asked for better portraits if he had hired motion picture people to take them.

Soon Holly was back in Chase's hotel room, and Stiles was on his way to get his plates developed. Suddenly $5,000 for these prints didn't seem fair enough. He wondered how much

Chase Griggs would pay to keep them from seeing the light of his wife's eyes.

Days later, DC Stiles set up an appointment with Chase Griggs at his Easter Tower office. It wasn't for elevator maintenance. He'd have in his briefcase the judgment and the noose. What he didn't say was who had hired him to track Griggs and Holly, and that left Chase playing guessing games. His first thought was Vilma and then the club owner, Pazo Fanti, who had made it clear that he was to make a delivery of cash and break it off with Holly. But why would Pazo need pictures? Maybe to let him know that he had the drop on him. He wanted to blame Holly for putting him in a vice. He wanted to blame Vilma for not being the woman Holly was, but instead kept his cool and took the deal: $6,000 for all prints and the plates destroyed. He scribbled the check and ordered Stiles to cash it immediately. Then Chase Griggs closed the account thinking Vilma would never know. For a while she didn't. For a while DC Stiles lived it up. He knew that no matter how good Pap had been to him, he wasn't sticking his neck out for no one except himself and his bear. Stiles had to think about number one, and $6,000 in hush money was a good start.

Meanwhile, Vilma would continue see her husband coming home late, if at all. She would continue to act like nothing was wrong. She would continue to wait for so many things to change. Mostly, she continued to hold her breath for the clue that would tip the scales.

- 58 -

Mr. Crooner's mouth was a nest of chalk. His eyelids unglued into slits. There he was, Buster and that unbearable beam in his eyes like the sinful side of the sun. Mr. Crooner had to pay attention to his breaths. He took his eyes off Buster and circled them round his collar and as far south as they would journey before popping back. Clad in an outfit that he'd sworn he'd only experienced in a dream, he cracked his mouth ajar. His hand made feeble attempts to signal water. Buster was steps ahead of him and figured the first thing the crooner's throat would need after a night of serenading was a nice, refreshing drink of some crisp, clear, cool, sparkling…"Just give me the damn water!" The chimp wheezed. Buster put the glass to his mouth. The chimp took it down his gullet and shirt. He then throated a question about the events of the night prior.

"You sang your little heart out, and they just gobbled you up," Buster said. "You should rest your voice. Confidentially, you were simply the coolest."

The chimp lied still as a board and chafed his eyes shut, trying to recreate the images Buster described, images of a spectacle the likes of which he would have never envisioned possible, even if he dreamed it every night at Crystal Plats. The lights, the music, the jaunty crowds of hipsters and no-gooders, the jazz, the booze, the tingles on his skin, the candle-eyed gapes, the adoration and admiration for the world's greatest singer, all for him.

"It's all starting to come back to me, yeah, I can see it now. I know what happened last night. Every dirty ditty. We lit that stage on fire, and the crowd lapped it up like kittens in a tub of cream. We gave 'em the works. They begged for more. I can see it. They wanted to know who I was. Why I did what I did. When I opened my mouth, they all went dumb. Most are still scratching their noggins this very moment. I know it all. In my black tie, I was floating on the door of heaven."

Buster stared at Mr. Crooner with the same dreams pasteled across his stargazing pupils.

"I can see it clearer and clearer. It's like I'm living it all over again, something I know I'll be doing soon enough, and since I know that such events will become a staple, I also know that I must relay this to you because yes I know. I know how you deliberately made me look like a nincompoop, and complete ignoramus in front of all those lovely folks who paid good scratch to see me. I know all this! You don't have to tell me how it went down. I know how I was escorted off the stage like some goon in shackles because you simply couldn't follow my cues! I know all that! In fact, I know so much that from now on, we're going to be doing these jamborees my way, you got that?"

Buster wanted off Mr. Crooner's emotional pendulum. He was completely nuts if he was even a chimp. Buster offered no defense. Instead, he just took whatever the chimp dished out. It was coming in rapid succession, much too fast for it to compute as anything more than concepts that, while pleasing only a breath ago, were now rancid.

"When's the next show?" Mr. Crooner asked. Buster explained that he had no involvement in the schedule but would happily tell Pap that he was eager. "The sooner the better. Like tonight. I wait around too long, I get cold feet again, see? This is serious business. You ever play for someone of my caliber before? Of course not! Because there is none! That's why you better start fixing up right now. I won't play buffoon to some toy bear with a whistle. No more clams out of you or that golden toilet. Now if you don't mind, get that fat sap to fix me up some grub," the chimp continued, but the room started to spin like it was irritated. "Oh brother," the chimp whispered just before he upchucked all over his new tuxedo.

Buster leaped back again. Why was his friend doing this? Going through such agony? This marked the second time Buster had witnessed soup ejected from Mr. Crooner's mouth, and it paralyzed him with fear. "Oh, Mr. Crooner, what can I do?"

"Just leave me be! Take a powder! And don't come back till I tell you!" the chimp squalled. Ink heard the whole thing from down the hall. He wanted to tie that chimp into a pretzel, but instead let Buster take his medicine. Maybe it would toughen the kid up and force him to defend himself for once. Ink knew Buster could lick that chimp any day of the week. Buster was startled out of his pants and buckled towards the room exit with tears in his eyes. He bawled all the way to Lou where he mumbled his friend's dire condition.

Lou took Buster aside and consoled his runny heart. After a heavy night, it was normal to expel. "It's a poison that builds up from all that singing. If he doesn't let it out, he can really get out of order."

Lou couldn't believe he was lying to his best chum. There seemed to be lots of fibbing those days, but word had gotten around quick that the only way the chimp would perform was to get dusted prior to each show. With only one show in the books, it was a wonder he would ever perform again. Would Pap stand for it? Last night the chimp revealed some new vices. He was a greedy little ape. Hammed it up to the tilt and demanded full attention. The chimp was satisfied when no one else received due praise. He would have listed his name in front of his name if it helped him gain more fame. When he stopped his song to reprimand Buster in front of all, Buster was starting one of his burnin' solos and, like usual, drew love from the crowd. The chimp couldn't stand it. Pap saw a one-sided rivalry unfolding. But the crowd, with chants of "Encore! Encore! Mr. Crooner!" didn't care.

"I think it would be wise if you kept this under wraps. Not a word to Pap. He seems to fret, and that's not good for his blood pump. Your friend, don't worry. He'll be fine," Lou said.

"Isn't there any other way he can get rid of this bad stuff?" Buster even made the request that Mr. Crooner never sing again if that's what was expected each time.

Buster wandered off to the mixing room and squeezed into his kettle where his doll was "asleep" under a scrap of burlap. He stared at the doll with a pit in his stomach. His heart was a mélange of conflicted feelings. "Can you tell me why I'm no good on my trumpet?" Buster woodshed daily, practiced with the Cats 6 two, three times a week, but that's not where Buster derived his talents. It was as natural to him as being sweet. Now his friend was telling him he was all washed up. Perhaps he didn't say that, but if Buster was one thing it was sensitive to Mr. Crooner's words. If true, and he had no reason to believe his friend a liar, then he would need to straighten up. Buster shared another few confessions. He gazed into the doll's heartless, beady eyes and lost his tongue. Then he slid him back under the burlap and ventured out to meet Lou in the kitchen. The real Mr. Crooner needed his breakfast.

An hour later, Buster was back in the washroom. Mr. Crooner gargled over the sink. Lou had fixed him up with another stiff rinse of whiskey when Buster was inside his kettle. The soiled formalwear was rolled up in a corner. He stood naked with a coat of talcum bleaching his fur like nothing had happened an hour earlier. It's the closest he would get to a bath.

- 59 -

Against Pap's every wish, they would throw a second show two days after the first. But before letting the chimp take the stage, Pap made sure to have another word with him.

"When you're in the middle of a set and the crowd is going goo-goo, it's never a good thing to break it up. It's like leaving your audience hanging off a cliff when all they really want to do is fall."

"Whatever you say. Just hope that runt doesn't mess up. May make it difficult for me to want to go up there anymore," the chimp said.

Buster mess up? Pap splintered his tongue with a grin. "He's gonna be great. You're gonna be great. We're all gonna be great. Just do me that one favor. No more chastising the bear."

As the show started, everything seemed copacetic. The crowd had settled in, eager for more. The Cats 6 were happy to be playing again. Buster worked his horn. And Mr. Crooner sang with his back to the band as if they didn't exist. Pap kept a close eye on both Mr. Crooner and Buster. So far, so good. But minutes later, Mr. Crooner closed his eyes, shutting out everything but his own voice. He started to wince like some external energy was causing him internal pain. His voice was a nail on the chalkboard. His head brushed side to side, wiggling to a state of conflict. The band continued to play. Buster glanced at Mr. Crooner and paid extra special attention to what he was doing on his trumpet. The chimp tapped the mic four beats with his palm. It sent four hacking coughs through the speakers. He waived his hands into three crosses. "It's a train wreck!"

The band was reluctant to comply—it was out of character to break in the middle of song—but eventually Mr. Crooner's gestures were so pell-mell that they had no choice. The guests looked to each other, but Pap felt all eyes on him for an explanation. Buster stifled his trumpet and lipped a careful smirk.

"Can't you see I'm trying to sing up here? How's a jack supposed to entertain a crowd with you blowing bad fortune?"

"Was I playing to fast? Too loud?" Buster asked.

"Try too wrong and too bad. You're a disgrace to music. I'm no trumpet player but I'd swear I could choke a frog into better than the stink you're putting out with that kazoo."

The crowd chuckled. This was the fruit of a rehearsed comedy duo, an act of sheer genius to witness these two mule-kicking one another even if the only one with hooves was the chimp. Pap's hand suffocated his cane. Everything he had warned the chimp against was spit back in his face. After another few minutes of carrying on the chimp stomped off. All Buster could do was return to his trumpet, no flubs, no frills, all exactly brilliant. The Cats 6 trickled in one at a time. What else could they do?

After the show, Pap was in Mr. Crooner's grill. "What was that all about? Don't you remember our talk?"

"You're barking at the wrong cat, mister. Straighten your boy out, or I walk," Mr. Crooner said. Walk? Where was he going to walk to? The imbecile chimp really thought what he was and saw Pap as nothing more than a painting on the wall. Pap was two seconds from giving him a trank and returning him to the zoo where he could rot to death.

Later on in their office room, Buster shared a kind word and gave Pap one more reason to not quit on the chimp.

"You saw the way the crowd laughed out there. They think it's gold. Don't worry. Just give him a little time. He'll come around. It's just a great thing that he's with us. I meant to thank you for bringing him here," Buster said.

But the next request baffled Pap. Buster asked for a book. Pap wasn't aware that Buster read. It was on trumpet playing. Pap asked no questions. He had one of the Gophers bring over several from the Little Leaf school library so he could choose. Buster spent his nights soaking his brain in every word of each book and then informed Mr. Crooner he had straightened it all out. Only Mr. Crooner was never satisfied.

The next few shows all started out the same. Mr. Crooner would come on and do his thing. The crowd would expect him to slam on the brake and blow up at Buster. And just like clockwork he would. The band got to the point where they could now predict roughly when Mr. Crooner would come apart. After one such show when they were both inside the washroom and Ink was in the kitchen taking his dinner, Mr. Crooner had some choice words.

"What about everything you read, everything you said you memorized? Am I some kind of fool in your eyes?' Mr. Crooner reared back and bopped Buster across the snout, not just once.

Buster did nothing but take it. He was unaware of his own physical strength, and even had he known of it, he would never exert himself. He wasn't designed that way. Instead he bowed his head, wanting so much to cry but thinking that such a display would incite Mr. Crooner into a madcap rage. So he absorbed the pain, more in his heart than on his face.

"How many times am I going to tell you to not play that thing so loud when I'm up there?"

Buster would have no defense but to make a coward's exit. What he wanted to tell Mr. Crooner was that he was in complete silence while he sang. The trumpet was off to his side. Perhaps he would have to stop breathing too, just as he was doing now, his lungs in full arrest. Perhaps this was what upset Mr. Crooner so—the sound of his silenced breath, his very presence in Mr. Crooner's life. The only accompaniment while he sang was Beans Fryer's bass line, the twinkle of Gumbie's keys and the tick, tick, tock on Tot's hides. It was becoming evident that Mr. Crooner didn't want any of them on the stage with him. Buster had never known the touch of a hostile hand. No one else would ever know about it either until Mr. Crooner gave them a firsthand taste.

When Pap attempted another sit down, he was subjected to the chimp's unmitigated wrath. "Curse you, get the hell out of here!" The chimp hurled a plate in Pap's direction. He ducked just in time. The wall shattered the plate into a hailstorm of mac and cheese. Buster heard the scandal and hurried back to the washroom. He saw Pap and Ink Tambo in a standoff with the chimp. No injections this time. This was a war of wills, and Pap was set to show this lippy clown a thing or two about life.

"Pap?" Buster said.

"Take your handler for a walk around the park! I'm trying to rest!" the chimp yelled.

"Can you believe the way he's talking to me, Buster? Look what he's done to this place," Pap said. Opened bags of chips regurgitated all over the floor with chunks of raw cookie dough and sour pickles, ketchup and mustard muddying up the sink. Pap couldn't contain himself anymore. He hated that Buster had to see this.

"You blame me? Did I invite myself into your home? Did I? Hey, man, I'm just trying to swing with this the best I can, so cut me some slack," the chimp said. Pap was in a jam. He wanted to dump the whole act, but he knew, everyone knew: The chimp wasn't going anywhere.

"Come on," Pap said to Buster. He gave a nodding glance to Ink before they left. Buster sensed that something was out of place. Not the standard belligerence, but now Mr. Crooner was lashing out at Pap.

An hour later, Buster decided to go back to see if Mr. Crooner had calmed down. Surely enough, he was passed out. Ink had stuck him with another trank. Amidst all the squalor, something was fishy. He inspected anything he felt could contribute to the chimp's swings. He took one of the empty glasses and brought it close for a whiff. It was the same potent scent from the bar, the one Pap always warned him about, a "poison" only fit for human consumption. But Buster realized that Mr. Crooner was taking it down too. The poison that Lou told him about. The one that needed to be purged after each show and in massive quantities. He fell ill with grief. Mr. Crooner had no clue what was causing his symptoms. Buster picked up the trash, wiped the floor and rinsed out the sink before leaving to tell of his discovery.

"Dino, I know why Mr. Crooner is getting sick," Buster later said. Dino Glass listened with conviction. "It's the poison in his drink."

Dino took his time, lit a smoke and put his thoughts in order. He didn't feel comfortable justifying transgressions before the bear. It was time that Buster knew the truth. "If he doesn't have it, he won't go on. Takes away his angst. But you see how happy he is when he's singing, don't you?"

Buster listened with a patient ear and accepted, but he didn't agree. Pap scheduled another show immediately. He would work that bangtail into the ground. At least on the stage he could keep tabs.

As dinner approached, Lou rolled the tray to the washroom door. Buster was waiting with a secret plan. He had his trumpet case by his side. Lou joked that he was hiding "the annihilator," but Buster didn't get it. When Lou went away and the coast was clear, Buster made his move. He guzzled down the cocktails and replaced them with two ginger ales he had finagled from Dino an hour ago. The drinks hit him as soon as they touched down on his stomach, and he had to brace himself against the wall. He could hear the chimp growing agitated inside. Here went nothing, Buster thought. He placed his trumpet on the bottom shelf of the cart and rolled in.

The chimp threw his first placebo down the hatch. He felt nothing special. Maybe he was just growing into it like his shoes. The chimp noticed something peculiar about Buster, then asked him what he brought his trumpet for.

"Wanted to show you I've been doing my homework. No more clinkers. Those books really helped," Buster said as he fidgeted his paws along the trumpet and brought it to a kiss. If he was going to mess up and take his knocks, he might as well get it over with. The alcohol gave him armor to take it standing up. With the trumpet plastered to his snout, Buster positioned his paws on the buttons and started knuckling down. He knew he had to blow air to make sound, so he held his breath. The tunes were relegated to his head only.

"That's crackers, man. Looks like you're capable of groovy things," Mr. Crooner said in acceptance. "Do that tonight, we'll be squared away."

Buster remembered the first time he played for Mr. Crooner. How it brought him out of his shell. He was once drawn by the music, but now he was moved by Buster's silence. Mr. Crooner asked for a few moments of privacy so he could get dressed. He had a job to do. He didn't even finish dinner. The only thing he pined for was the audience. And now he wanted it alone. The stage was suddenly too small for the both of them. All Buster cared about was that Mr. Crooner had not taken the poison. What could go wrong? A hiccup was followed by a giggle.

"You sure you're alright?" Mr. Crooner asked. "You're actin' awful screwy."

"A million ducks," Buster said. "Let's knock 'em dead tonight."

Forty minutes later, Mr. Crooner sang with laser focus. He wasn't as freewheeling or wobbly. But Buster and his varnished eyes were. He jumped all over his horn in grand style when he was first introduced, but as soon as Mr. Crooner took to the stage, he went cold feet. He was going through the motions. He could recite them in his sleep, just like all the chapters he memorized. But Pap could tell something was off kilter. The chimp sang the whole song without laying into Buster once. Mr. Crooner glanced at his loyal subjects. He could now recognize faces. Jackson Reese and his vixens, Claudette and Rita, Pap, Dino, Turnip, Ham Wails. "Mr. Crooner!" he channeled into his stone-cold ears. His eyes went Narcissus; the crowd, a pool. For a split second he was even handsome. He touched the air with his chin. He was too important, too powerful to bow before any human, no matter how many pretty ones spread their lips to show rows of toothy reverence. Then came his solo. *"The greatest love I have, I have for you, forevermore, though I only saw you once, I know it's you, forevermore..."*

Buster continued to mime the illusion of sound from his trumpet until a belch escaped like the cackle of a crow stuffed in a girdle. Mr. Crooner's eyes stayed closed. He pretended to ignore Buster's affront. He was too enchanted with his own song and his own existence to bother. Soon the song came to an end, and Mr. Crooner remained unruffled. Showers of applause rained over him.

The Cats 6 picked up where Mr. Crooner left off, and soon Buster felt compelled to make noise with them. The silent act was wearing itself thin, and his buzz was starting to peak. Whatever Dino put in those drinks didn't feel like poison. He had forgotten all about the instruction he had received from Mr. Crooner. He was free to let loose, and suddenly Mr. Crooner's ear picked up a disturbance in the air. A masterful disturbance, but one nonetheless. A turf war ensued. Who would dominate the stage? Buster's ambitions had nothing to do with claiming victory, but some wraithlike force was taking hold of that trumpet and playing it in Buster's stead. He was a god of no pretense and couldn't help what he was doing any more than he could help wanting to please Mr. Crooner. But rather than stop in the middle of his song like he normally did, Mr. Crooner did something no one saw coming. A simple song became a competition to see who could carry it better, with superior style. He held notes longer than ever before, some as long as a fortnight. And Buster would match him, not to show Mr. Crooner up, but in that vain effort to follow his most treasured leader down any road. The quick steps, Buster wouldn't miss one. The volume of both voice and trumpet grew. The Cats 6 struggled to stay in tow. Mr. Crooner split the skies with his tuneful cries. He was aloof as he was sober. Buster, on the other hand, was oblivious, his bronze blowtorch turned feral, reaching for scales too reedy for human comfort. It was a fight to the finish, but whoever won didn't matter to the crowd; it was money well spent.

When Mr. Crooner's final song came, Pap slapped the raptness from his eyes. He had actually kept to the entire program, just as they had rehearsed it. No premature departures, no flare-ups. On cue, the lights were doused, Mr. Crooner unstrangled the mic and stepped off the stage, passing Buster without so much as a fleeting glance.

"How about that ladies and gents? Where else can you indulge in such a heaping hunk of heaven without it going to your hips? Mr. Crooner, thank you," Ham Wails said.

Mr. Crooner headed to his room, a declaration of war being drafted in his mind. Buster managed to step off the stage without much of a hassle. His buzz fizzled, and he grew weary. But it was all worth it. His plan worked without a hitch. Mr. Crooner avoided the poisons and sang his heart out. Kudos were in order, but an impulse of guilt overtook him. The words were all wrong well before they could form a stutter. He couldn't let anyone see him in this state. It would be a dead giveaway.

Sneaking to the mixing room, he slipped into a cocoa drum with his doll and tried to regain some normalcy. "Mr. Crooner, I can't tell you how happy I am with the way you behaved tonight. You don't know what I did, did you? Well, it'll be our little secret, okay? Just make sure not tell the real Mr. Crooner or he'll snap his cap." Another hiccup jabbed Buster's train of thought.

"Tell me what?" Mr. Crooner appeared out of nowhere.

Buster's skin tightened up as he yanked the kettle door in. Mr. Crooner wasn't fooled. He snatched the door back open. "What are you doing in there? Who are you talking to?"

"Me? Uh, no one, Mr. Crooner." The doll's head was in the corner of Buster's eye. With an invisible wrist he tried to cover it up. Mr. Crooner stopped Buster dead in his tracks and peeled the scrap back. The toy had an uncanny resemblance. He took it in his hands with a mother's touch.

"Who's this?" Mr. Crooner asked.

"Oh, him, he's just a silly toy. I found him long ago in a trash can. Doesn't mean anything. He's a ragamuffin of plush. You don't want nothin' to do with him. But I can get you one if you want. A nicer one. Would you like that?"

Mr. Crooner passed the doll from one hand to the other like a beanbag. He stared at that face, into those black eyes that seemed to say nothing. Reminders of brethren he left behind at Crystal Plats, who just like the doll, said nothing. But there was something about this furball that tickled Mr. Crooner. Even more that he happened to be in Buster's possession.

"Neigho pops, I think I'll take this one for a ride." He left Buster alone inside the kettle, even closed the hatch for him.

A new sensation overcame the bear. His stomach twirled like an electric fan. He thought of his doll's welfare. He had grown to love that doll. Whenever he was feeling low, which nearly everyday since Mr. Crooner had come around, Buster could go to his doll and talk his troubles away. But there were nefarious forces talking to him now. They had saturated his core, and Buster presumed the existence of only one antidote. He cupped his snout with both paws and rushed to the kitchen. Any of the washrooms, and he would have been caught. He couldn't imagine the look on Pap's face. Once over the kitchen sink, he let it fly. Poor Mr. Crooner, he thought, to have gone through so many nights of this.

- 60 -

"Are you alive? Do you have a voice? Do you have a soul?" Mr. Crooner played the shrink and the doll, the patient. The doll returned nothing but ideas, many that were prompting Mr. Crooner to consider the many tomorrows left in his new calling. If this was truly all he was, then the notion of changing into something else, perhaps something more or even less, was now imperative. But how? People lauded him, deified the name. He was royalty, and no one messed with him anymore. And still he was trapped inside that sarcophagus of dandruff-ridden hair. The frustration filtered into his fingers as he picked at the quills sewn to the doll's coat. One patch at a time, Mr. Crooner gloated over disrobing the toy.

"You say something? I could have sworn I just heard you say you don't want me to touch you. That wouldn't be a very nice thing to say. You prefer that stupid bear? Too bad 'cause you're stuck with me. So what you gotta say for yourself now? Diddlysquat. Okay, then just keep your yap shut while I decide what's best for you." Mr. Crooner plucked until the belly was threadbare. "Still chattering a storm. All you do is yap, yap, yap, but nothing good comes out. In fact, you yak it up too much. Let's try closing your head."

Mr. Crooner clamped the doll's head and squeezed in a measured, twisting motion. With one thrust he rented its seams and then with two more decapitated it. With an eye on a headless, hairless torso, he conjured up a new likeness. His vanity was calling out. The voice of a god could not be trapped within the face of an ogre. He took the doll's cranium and tweezed it till it was nameless. Not even the eyes remained. With body disregarded as refuse, he carried the head to the cracked mirror and placed the bust next to his own. No more would others hide their true intentions from him. From now on, he would show the world that he was beautiful inside and out. He couldn't wait to share his gospel with Buster, but when he rushed over to the mixing room he discovered that the bear wouldn't emerge from hibernation no matter what. Slaps to the snout, kicks to the belly, Buster was out cold. So the chimp returned to the washroom and tried to turn in. The ghostly night calm only worked to enliven his delusions. When dawn finally broke, the chimp was drained of thought and stamina and finally passed out.

By the end of the day, Mr. Crooner would be standing in front of the washroom mirror, Buster and Lou behind him, the remnants of his former self dressing the floor, his bare and pink dappled casing flaunting a thousand liver spots, exposed and pimpled from cold. Armies of stubbled roots cramped to break skin. His face was as melted gum after it had cooled into place. From bad to worse, he looked like a stinking pig. He had seen them at Crystal Plats and knew all about their kind. The wallowers of creation. What was even more shameful was his burning desire to cloak his naked flesh like the only other creature known to harbor this need: the human. Mr. Crooner whipped the blanket off his bed to disguise his tattooed exterior. But the face of a fiend had no refuge.

Lou swept up the hair, paid him a dry compliment and left to wash up for another show. Pap was bursting at the seams to replicate whatever had happened the night before. He knew nothing of Buster's bout with the queasies and had no clue that the chimp had shed its coat.

Buster had already switched out Mr. Crooner's drinks. He played leap frog with the clouds and greased Mr. Crooner on his new look. It was genuine praise, but to Buster, his old look was just as cool. Mr. Crooner couldn't get over what stood before him. He was nothing like the ones he entertained. Even though he sang like them, better, spoke their tongues, even had feelings like them, dreams, things that normally separated the species, he wasn't of the same cloth. Neither was Buster.

"You think you're one of them?" Mr. Crooner posited.

The thought never had time to cross Buster's mind much. For all he knew he was one of the guys. They treated him like he was one of them. But the way Mr. Crooner phrased the question struck him in that empty space where doubts originated. Buster looked different from his human compatriots, and he was intelligent enough to notice. He, too, could speak their language and play their instruments, live as one of them, but everything else was, well, different. It was the main reason he resonated as much with Mr. Crooner.

"Sure I do," Buster stuttered.

"I just don't get it. None of it. Mugs like us, we ain't supposed to get on like we do," Mr. Crooner said. "You ever see another bear?" he asked. Buster was at a loss for words. "Well, I've seen plenty of them, plenty of chimps too. They don't talk. They roar and scream and kill each other. They don't dress up and play instruments. They don't sing. They don't act like the boss," Mr. Crooner said. He wasn't used to the things that Buster was used to. He was a loner. He didn't have friends. When he was perched up in his cage, the moon and the stars were his only companions. "Where do you come from anyway?"

"Pap said he pulled me from the ocean. I was inside a box." Buster chuckled at the thought, but it was the alcohol that made the assertion absurd.

"See what I mean? Was it a box of corn flakes? What a bunch of bull. Come stand next to me."

Buster's eyes pointed to himself as if to say: "Me?"

"That's right, come on. I want you to look at yourself in the mirror."

Buster took his place and looked to Mr. Crooner first. Buster would have no trouble acknowledging his reflection while getting ready for a show because he was never truly focused on himself, not the way Mr. Crooner wanted. But now it was different.

"Look at yourself!" Mr. Crooner demanded.

Buster's eyes inched across the mirror until they captured the white thing with the protuberant, inky nose and cavernous, moonless marbles staring back. The ardor with which he once saw himself burned out. Like humans, he was mesmerized by his own reflection for the first time. He held an acute awareness of his existence and the dissimilarity from the others. He was nothing like Pap, not like any of the crew; he wasn't even like Mr. Crooner. He was a bear, rather a beast. The longer he stared, the more repugnant he became. Mr. Crooner studied Buster through the mirror and noticed a ripple of reservation form in the corner of his eye.

"What do you see?"

"I don't know," Buster said like a sad drunk.

"What are you?"

Buster thought long and hard. It was the first time anyone had ever asked him with such downbeat uncertainty. "Pap calls me an angel. He says that's a good thing."

Mr. Crooner upchucked a loon's laugh. "Oh, brother! What a roll that was! You really think you look like an angel? Do I look like an angel? Is this what angels look like?" The laughter kept breaking like whitecaps on the shore.

"I guess I've never seen one to know," Buster said. "Do you know what they look like?"

The laughter swung to tears of admitted struggle as Mr. Crooner recounted the mystery of his origin. "I was torn away from paradise with nothing but a song. It's all I remember. I was sent to sing. I don't know why. I don't know for who. It would be the only way I could get back to that place, but I don't know how that would happen either. I don't even know where that place is. It was filled with undying wonders, devoid of all suffering, filled with power, peace, happiness ruled forever. It was good. Everyday was a new heaven. Never got old, never ran out of juice. I can only remember it now in nightmares. When I sing, it's the closest I can come to getting back there, but my song is also the very thing that sent me away. Now I live in a constant blur, dark, wicked, where the paradise I once knew is something so outstretched from memory that to even mention it seems impossible. Now I'm what you see, gruesome and abject, no identity, no natural form, not even the knowledge of what that natural form once was, trapped inside this mold of decay, of aberrant design, this decomposing wrap of meat and bone, it stinks, it breaks, turns more villainous with each passing day, more vile as it approaches a sure death. And all I have to cling to is my song, and now the same unnatural form found in you. Angels we are not, buddy ghee. Try again."

Buster's head went dizzy from the overload of information. His friend was a regular Socrates. "Geez, I've never thought of it that way."

"Why are you here?" Mr. Crooner asked.

"Here?"

"Yeah, here as in with these cats."

"I guess to play my horn. It's what I love most, next to my family," Buster answered.

"That's where you're dead wrong. There's something fishy going on, and if there's one thing I know, it's that you're in the dark. If we're going to crack this thing open, I have to be able to trust you. You're the only one I know. I don't know about things like angels or fate, but whatever chance put us together, there's gotta be a reason. From this point forward, it's tops that your loyalty be to me and me only. I'm the only one you'll ever be able to relate to on this level," Mr. Crooner said. "Trust you with my life. That clear?"

"You can trust me with your life," Buster said with the utmost confidence. If he was nothing like his human companions, then Mr. Crooner made a point. They were the only two around that could relate on this level, and Buster knew how to cherish such a bond.

"I can't say the same about the outfit you run with."

"I can trust Pap and the boys with my life," Buster said. Just because he would ally with Mr. Crooner, didn't mean he would ever go against the ones who brought him in and showed him love.

"What's the catch?" Mr. Crooner asked. "What's in it for you? It's obvious what they get out of us."

"They take care of me. I've never gone without anything. I think Pap's too kind, but that's his heart. Wears it on his sleeve. Would you like to know him like I do?"

"I know him. He ain't my friend or yours."

Buster wanted so much to ask Mr. Crooner, "Am I your friend?" but he couldn't bring himself to it. Instead he asked, "Can I stop looking in the mirror now?"

"You understand what's at stake now, don't you?"

"I'm booted," but Buster just said it because he was agreeable. He had no idea what was at stake other than the next show.

"Good. Then since we're going to trust each other from now on, I guess I should give your toy back."

Buster smiled. What a gracious gesture. The chimp told Buster where it was, inside the stall. Buster skipped over and fell sick when he noticed the sodden body of his toy plucked like a chicken on the wet floor and the head playing Marco Polo inside the fallow toilet water with a couple of the chimp's turds. At least the chimp had learned to use the facilities. Buster pinched the doll's head out, picked up its body and rinsed them both in the sink. Mr. Crooner watched, half indifferent, half entertained.

"Would you like your dinner before the show?" Buster had to keep his mind off his broken toy. Focusing on Mr. Crooner seemed to be the easiest way.

Mr. Crooner took a seat at the table. Buster followed him. He avoided eye contact and dug into his plate like a battered housewife with no vacation home. Mr. Crooner left his fork on the table. His eyes were on Buster, especially the way he clicked his jaws with each bite. After a whole minute of torture, Mr. Crooner reached across the table and slid Buster's plate to the floor. It shattered, gnocchi and aurora sauce bled everywhere.

"Must you make so much racket? I can't keep on like this. I don't feel a devil's different! I want to go back to that place. I want a new head. Get me another one on the double. Make it a double," Mr. Crooner stood from the table. Before heading off to a stall he made sure to give Buster another thwack across the snout.

Buster froze his hams to his seat, alone and frightened to death. The food in his mouth balanced on his tongue until it dissolved down his throat. It was the last morsel he would have tonight. His appetite was shot. He could feel his heart beating like a frantic prisoner against his rib cage. He feared that if Mr. Crooner heard it, he would go ballistic. And through it all, Buster kept wondering what he had done this time around. Perhaps he wasn't sensitive to how loud he was chewing. Suddenly he found himself wanting another drink too. After a good while of exile, Buster took his doll parts and left.

Dino tended the empty bar, wiping it clean and organizing his inventory for the usual rush, due to start in about an hour. He spotted Buster sidling up to the bar.

"Buster?"

"Oh, hiya, Dino."

"You don't look too hot, little buddy. Everything alright?"

"I'm ducky, Dino. Honest," Buster said.

"A chocolate chiller before the show?"

"Actually, it's for Mr. Crooner. Says he needs another couple of your drinks. Doubles."

"Doubles? You sure he said that?" Dino asked.

"You know how he can get. I told him I'd have to run it by you first."

"How's he looking?"

"Oh, he looks solid. Got a new do. Looks real mellow," Buster said.

Dino followed Buster's shifty eyes and could tell something was amiss. Only Buster was the patron saint of truthtelling. If he said the chimp was doing great and needed a couple more highballs, so be it. Dino went to work.

"And a ginger ale for me, Dinomite," Buster said holding a hiccup from rushing the stage. Dino never had a reason to doubt the bear, and he wasn't going to start now. Buster took the highballs, promising to return for his ginger ale and lumbered back. A pit stop at the mixing room and he would forget all about the pop and the washroom. He had a show to prepare for.

Meanwhile, Pap couldn't believe what the chimp had done to himself. He looked fresh from the womb and refused to take the stage. Evidently he was now immune to Dino's full-proof punch. "If that's the way you want, but the show goes on. As far as your new look, nothing a silk coffin can't cure. You make the call," Pap said before he left the washroom.

Mr. Crooner paced like he was back inside a cage, wondering why the drinks had no effect. Was it all in the fur? Would he never feel alive again? He noticed the tuxedo over the stall door. Pap said something of interest. As he dressed, song leaked out of him. The voice was as pronounced as ever. The fur had nothing on it. Over his shirt he slipped on his jacket, his eyes speculative. After he wrapped his collar, he took a second appraisal. The bunion head was still an eyesore. Then he noticed the top hat on the bed, the one Buster requested from

Lou. Mr. Crooner crowned himself as he had seen others do. A tilt to the right and a couple seconds built tolerance. With each backward step from the mirror the vision faded. Twenty feet from a reflection stood a new likeness, a pinkish blur where there once was a face. Without pinpointing features, he conceptualized something appealing. Could it be? From distance, he looked more like one of them, one of those pretentious humans that he so vilified. Maybe, just maybe, he could sing tonight. Maybe his shave was an improvement after all. After another ten minutes, he decided it was time to take the stage. He'd hate himself in the morning, but he couldn't do without the crowd's mitt pounding anymore than he could without kicking Buster around.

Buster swayed on his stool and growled that horn like it was possessed. Pap knew him to be explosive, but tonight he was smokin' and strangely ungainly. The Cats 6 tried to match Buster's gusto. Never had the basement been as rambunctious. The crowd was loud. The dance floor sizzled under a dozen hyper heels. Mr. Crooner was an afterthought. Who needed him now? His fickle manias. Tonight the show would end as it used to, Buster trailblazing a record double encore and everyone leaving after a ten-minute standing O. But when Mr. Crooner swaggered through that curtain filling the air mic-free, the crowd cracked and made funny faces. Mr. Crooner couldn't tell if they were laughing at him. He didn't care. He raced for the microphone and blended in with the band, soon taking the lead and everyone with him. But Buster was on fumes and couldn't keep up. Pap's brow caved in, and a tear fled from his eye at what he witnessed. Buster's faculties were all for naught as the brunt of his being fell off the stool, crashing to the floor in a thump of loose limbs. The music hit the skids. Moony Butter yelled out the bear's name. Anthony Mound spilled a tray of Runny Rums. The crowd gasped. Its favorite mascot lay unconscious. Mr. Crooner carried his song a good ten seconds before he realized what had happened. Pap jostled the crowd without regard for anyone but Buster. Not Buster. Anyone but Buster. He fought to hold back his tears. The Cats 6 formed a perimeter around him. They hoisted him up and back through the curtain.

Ham Wails jumped out on stage with a quick mea culpa, even pitched a joke about Buster meddling in the medicine cabinet. The night was over.

A couple of hours later, Mr. Crooner sat in bed wide awake, wondering what had happened. For the first time, he was actually worried for the bear, not so much because of Buster, but rather for his own sake. What would he do without someone to boss around? He left the washroom and asked Ink Tambo where the bear was. Ink told him he was upstairs under Pap's care, but that didn't stop Mr. Crooner from venturing further. When he got to the office door, he made himself unnoticeable.

Pap and Lou were seated at Buster's bedside waiting for a response. The chimp didn't dare step foot inside. Pap sensed that he was nearby and corner-eyed the door. He made eye contact with the chimp just as Buster opened his lamps and yelled, "Please, don't hit me! No more! Please, I beg you not to sock me anymore!" Buster sobbed like he didn't know his surroundings. Pap secured Buster in his arms and pacified him with soothing words. When he turned back to the door, the chimp was gone. He ran back to the washroom and locked himself inside a stall. There he would stay till the next day without food or company. Surely, Pap and Lou knew what Buster had suffered at the hands of the chimp. Surely, they wouldn't let him live it down. What the chimp didn't know was that as soon as Buster had come around, the first question out of his mouth was how Mr. Crooner was doing. Neither could believe that of all the things Buster would ask, this would be the first on his tongue. He cared more for a creature that showed unadulterated malice than he did for his own life.

- 61 -

A swim in the icy harbor was just what the doctor ordered. Pap would try to get him out there every day, but since the chimp's imposition, their schedule had changed. Pap didn't care about the chimp anymore, if he ever did. What Buster had done in an effort to save his "friend" was unacceptable. He didn't even share a word about it with Dino Glass. Dino came clean on his own, begged Pap for clemency and promised that something like that would never happen again. This time Pap believed him. The bar was officially closed to all nonhumans. If the chimp never sang again, so be it. Pap got over Dino fast enough. Now his only focus was on nursing Buster back to health. They were lucky this was the worst of it. Lou had never seen Pap as worried as when he was weeping over Buster like he was losing a child. What got Lou more was that he also felt the same. Buster had grown on all of them over the years, and they had failed him when they brought the chimp in. The frost-bitten air and chilly water would do him wonders. He always emerged from a swim invigorated.

Pap stood on a finger pier watching Buster turn from a clunky bear into a lithe, weightless ribbon of fur. His paws made unhurried thrusts through the deep like he was moving through a dream. He was reeling from last night in the worst of ways, but with each dip into the icy water the pains were chilled. The water was clearer than usual even if the sky was not. It swooshed against the finger piers and wet the tips of Pap's shoes. He torched a cigarette and started to relax. Buster was back in his element and things would revert to normal. Pap would put the chimp in his place and warn him that if he ever laid another hand on Buster, he'd be kissing the gunner's daughter. But all that could wait. For now, it was about Buster and the water. He swam in circles, dove in and popped out. Pap could tell Buster was happy here. He made bubbles from his snout and splashed around in slow motion. Pap donned a smirk made half embattled with melancholy. Without Buster, where would he be? Buster turned on his back and let the water massage his belly. A thick stream of bubbles surfaced. They didn't come from Buster. Then something popped out. A head of cabbage. It still had hair, but the face was half pared to the bone. Worms slithered through the empty eye sockets. Crabs clung to the chunks of flesh dangling from the cheeks. The rest of the body rushed up like a barrel of air. It was fully clothed. A blue bow tie checkered with yellow crosses still secured the neck. Pap's peace was shattered; his face lost all heat. Buster felt the body rub against him, and he opened his refreshed eyes to the horror. A huge gulp of water rushed into Buster's mouth without consent, and he started choking so loud he couldn't even bleat. It was Pisto Leroy.

- 62 -

Pisto Leroy knew all about the man on Strobile Island. His name was Grandmaster Tragico Hosiah, and it wasn't entirely certain that he pertained to the human race. He was the wizard of weird, a connoisseur of degenerates. The most vicious nightmares could be found no other place than at his "House of Heroes" Carnival. When Leroy heard that the Cats 6 were starting to renege on their original commitments, he decided to beat them all to the punch and get first dibs on any finder's loot. Many had approached Hosiah with the promise of supernatural acts. Only when Leroy spoke of musical bears, he came across like a junk peddler and got laughed out. It was the only reason there wasn't a more immediate effort to bring Pap's club to light. Hosiah had the most remarkable things—things because they could be called by no other name—under his tents. "You think I run with the blood-and-thunder circuit?" A pygmy bear played a horn under virtually every big top around the Leaf. They wore clown hats, ribboned collars and shiny sash over their bellies. They pressed a series of honkers in a row for a tasty reward. At most they knew three to five notes. Big deal.

Sas Parila and Lou waited at Leroy's place the morning after Gumbie's. Leroy was up early enough to raise a flag. They had been casing him for months and knew it had nothing to do with Gumbie, the man who had vouched for him. In a dangerous world, a man could only close his eyes so tight before he was seeing through his eyelids; he could only vouch so far before realizing he couldn't vouch at all. And many times it had nothing to do with what one did to the other as much as what he didn't do for him. Gumbie got him a gig with the Cats 6 at Pap's secret clubs. A few bucks to live a month and nothing more. With word of the magical bear, Leroy could make out for the rest of his days, if he only knew how many he had left. Lou and Sas tailed Leroy for an entire hour. He was taking all the wrong routes, but he knew exactly what he was doing. He hopped a cab and went east instead of south, crossed Soldado Bridge into Jester, then cut down into Breaks where he ditched the cab and went underground for a subway ride back into the Oven.

When he crossed the Hoja Bridge into Strobile Island, Sas and Lou knew what he was going for. And even if it was just for a slice of deep-fried pizza and the dunk booth, Lou wasn't one to take a chance. Leroy's passions for truthfulness only worked to seal his fate as a great liar. Before he walked out of the carnival, the trap was set. The rest of the Cats 6 knew all about it. It was an easy set up. Show interest in the deal and see who would resist it the most. That would be the traitor. But it did blur the lines between trust and treachery. Who would be next to either resist or to simply go along with it? Buster had everyone turning truth to fiction, only he had nothing to do with their evil hearts and couldn't help it if they were born to sin.

"Keep this from Pap no matter what. I'll tell him he had a change of heart and wanted out. No beefs. That'll be that," Lou said.

Buster remained in bed the rest of the day. He didn't eat and he could barely sleep. He had never known such shock. The chimp was told to stay away, and he obeyed. Things were changing at Calloway, and they were about to get a lot worse.

"A change of heart?" Pap roared.

"I think you forget how easy it'll be when it finally gets into someone's head that this little secret we're guarding with our lives is worth a lot of money," Lou said.

"They were face to face! Close enough to kiss! Crabs pinching at his putrid flesh! Snails coming out of his eyes! Here I am trying to shelter the only pure thing in my life and this is what he gets?"

"He's gotta take his lumps sometime. This is life, Pap."

"Not for him! We've taken things too far. It's all over."

"What was the alternative? Lose the kid? Lose everything? Keep dockhopping like I know you love?"

"When in our time together would you ever go behind my back and do something like this?"

"You didn't seem to care when you were facing a barrel. And what do you mean it's all over? Since when do you get to decide that all of the sudden?"

Pap felt a surge of power leave his body and transfer into Lou's. Every decision they had ever made came down from Pap. He was a reasonable man, he would listen to all opinions, take each into consideration, but when all the sheep stopped baaing, the shepherd would point where the flock would follow until they decided it was time to follow their own course. To date, the only one had been Pisto Leroy. But rather than leave on his own accord as Pap would have decreed, he left on Lou's terms. And now Lou felt to circumvent Pap once again. Only Pap felt compelled to remind him of one stark reality.

"Get this. Buster belongs to me. You wanna take that jug-eared mongrel, then you do it, and God bless you. But this is not the way I run this joint!" Pap's voice was breaking up at the top.

Lou was visibly upset. He kept his eyes off Pap as he asked: "How much you make a month? Just you."

"What are you doing?"

"Everyone makes dough around here except me, right?" Lou cut Pap's sight line with his own eyes.

"Don't say anything you're gonna regret."

"Because you take care of me, right?"

"Shut your mouth. You know the heat we'll take for this? Or should we just sink his body all over again and pretend it never happened? Maybe we should take out the rest of the Cats while we're at it. How about knock me off too since you're making moves on your own now."

Lou snatched Pap by the collar and slammed him against a wall. "He was going to sell out the kid! Get it through your thick head since you seem to be the one with the most to lose around here. If you're not prepared to pull the trigger, you can kiss this, Buster, that chimp that's done more harm to him than anything else, all of it goodbye. Yeah, I killed Pisto Leroy, and I did it for Buster, and I'd do it again if I had the chance."

Pap knew he could never go to fisticuffs with Lou, especially when his eyes spoke so convincingly of death, but regardless of how scared Pap was, he couldn't take his gaze off him. It was the only weapon he had left, and a powerful one at that. No matter that he objected to everything Lou had just done, including the killing, deep down he knew that death brought the ultimate silence out of those who liked to talk. So Pap kept his eyes searing through Lou's, wondering if he could still break him or if the old ways were done. Lou let Pap loose and gave him some space. He paced around the room like a pug before a fight. Pap remained calm as a chess player but only on the outside.

"And just between us, before you go marking your territory, don't forget I was on that boat with you when he came up," Lou said.

"Fair enough." Pap was surprised that it took this long for things to escalate to this point. That's why he didn't make more of it; that's why he conceded. With a diffused voice, he uttered two orders and left Lou to his own conscience. "Start packin'. We're leaving."

Lou gave Pap a prickly stare before he walked out. He knew he had taken things a bit far even if there was no way around it. Trial and error and plenty of decamping had kept them all alive.

An hour later, Pap was at Basil Demur's office. He didn't care about the risks involved with showing his head on the Leaf. This couldn't wait. "You know I don't get tired of asking you for favors because you've never let me down," Pap said.

"There's always a first," Basil responded, half playful, half deadpan. "What do you need?"

"A boat, the nicest you can find. Enough to seat seventy five. We'll anchor east of the line so the coppers can't touch us. You can even increase the price to cover the extra costs. Hell, make it a cool buck fifty a head. They'll pay it."

"You're talking about a barge." Basil could tell that something bad had happened, apart from the usual constant threats of death, but something in Pap told him to keep it secret even from Basil Demur. Confidence or not, Basil was just another man to him now.

"I've got five large I can put into it. It's all I got. No one will spot us out there unless they can walk on water."

"I'm getting worried, Pap. Remember when I told you to enjoy this as long as you could and then get out?"

"Whatever doesn't kill you eventually does. I'm not getting out, not yet. I got Buster and now his friend, and they don't know anything else. Can you make it happen, or do I go it alone?"

"A swimming nightspot? Yeah, sure. Sounds like fun," Basil said as if he stood to gain anymore from Pap's traveling club. To date, he had netted a big, fat zero, but there he was, continuing to dole out favors. That's the kind of indirect influence Buster had. He lit a ciggy and chuckled out the smoke. This was the most absurd idea he had heard.

- 63 -

4 pm at Calloway. Sleep continued to toy with Buster. Pap had given him one of his downers to help him relax and hoped it wouldn't do him any harm. He was in the shower. Lou was in the kitchen making a couple of bean sandwiches and trying to keep his thoughts off his blistered pride. Now was the only chance Mr. Crooner had to get a word with Buster without anyone getting wise. He shook him gently by the shoulder until Buster revealed his blood-shot eyes. He made it through, a little groggy, but alive. The shakes were still having their way with him. Little did Mr. Crooner know what Buster had experienced. It didn't matter how many times Pap reiterated that it had nothing to do with him. Death, to a friend or stranger, was not something Buster was equipped to handle. His eyes wouldn't stop trembling, and he had no voice.

Mr. Crooner said, "You went cuckoo last night. I know why you did it. I get what's been happening. You know there are so many things I can say, but I never take the time to. I keep a lot of stuff bottled up. Just the way I am. But you, man, you really tore it up, every little thing you had to say came right out in one breath. Brother, if I didn't know better, I'd think you had a lot of junk inside you, and I want to help."

Buster gave a soft grin to avoid crying. He wouldn't dare speak of Pisto Leroy to Mr. Crooner. He was happy to hear Mr. Crooner coming to his aid.

"We gotta do something about what you're suffering. I mean this milquetoast attitude is just getting way out of hand. And I think I know just the trick," Mr. Crooner said. "You know, I think you're right. The only way I'm going to learn to trust your friends is to get to know them, sit down and have a heart-to-heart. I'd like to talk to that Pap fella. What's the worst he could do to me that I haven't already suffered?"

"Pap won't make you suffer," Buster strained to say, and then he started crying. Mr. Crooner didn't have a clue why. Buster reeked of alcohol.

"You sick or something?" Mr. Crooner asked. "I've seen what they do to sick animals," he continued. "Figures, being cooped in here morning, noon and night. Tell him for me then. I'll be waiting in the washroom. Don't forget to tell him." Mr. Crooner passed him a peppermint. "Here take this. You could use it." He had found it on Pap's desk on his way in. It stopped Buster's tears to receive such a gift from Mr. Crooner. Soon he would be within sleep's spell again.

When Pap heard of the chimp's request, he hurried to the washroom. There were a few things he wanted to lay out on the line. Between poor Buster and Pisto Leroy, it was a wonder Pap didn't come in swinging, especially when Mr. Crooner opened his mouth to say: "Mr. Fanti, with your permission I'd like to take Buster out. What he needs is some fresh air for morale. It could only help him kick all those phobias, maybe fix up his twisted tongue, get him to talk a smooth sentence. Who knows, might even help with his trumpet. Get him out of this dump once in a while, you know? Keep him from passing out on stage like he did last night." Mr. Crooner bowed his chest out and stood straight as his arched legs would allow.

"It's not like that at all," Buster said to himself. He had struggled down to the washroom and held the blanket around his neck like a cape. When he got to the door, he didn't dare poke his head through. Ink Tambo kept a close eye on him, even offered his sleeping bag, but Buster remained standing at the door. He could hear the two going at it.

Pap wasn't pulling any punches. "You son-of-a-bitch. You know why he passed out last night? Because of you! He was trying to protect you from harm so he took the shit instead and look what happened? Don't you have a vestige of a heart? You sing all these pretty songs like you know what it is to suffer and love and then you treat that poor creature like that and dare say it's the place?"

"Hey, I'm just making an honest observation. There's no bias in these eyes, but you're the boss around here," the chimp said.

"This ain't a prison, and I'm not your screw. Let's go, Smooth. Right now." It was time to curtail this chimp's term. Pap rushed the door and threw it open. It knocked Buster down by accident. He toppled over but was alright. "Buster! What are you doing here?" He helped Buster up. Buster said he was fine, feeling much better. He was good at hiding his symptoms for Mr. Crooner's sake. Pap redirected his eyes to the chimp. It continued to stand in the middle of the washroom. "I said let's go! You want to see places? Come on! Buster, you stay down here with Ink." Pap's voice was unwavering, and suddenly the chimp gave in. He wanted to see just how far Pap would go before retracting.

The chimp hustled to keep pace. Pap was hoofing it on that bad leg. He was mumbling curse words to himself the whole way. The chimp could tell they were curses because of the inflection as they left Pap's lips.

When Pap got to the front door, he swung it open and cleared a path. "There it is. All yours, *forevermore*. You want it? Go get it. But you will leave Buster alone, or I swear I'll kill you my own hands." If he couldn't expurgate the chimp, he'd excommunicate him.

The chimp took a step outside and sniffed at the air. There was an ocean nearby. He could smell the salt. He glanced left and right and then took another step out. Pap watched him, his arm holding the door open until the chimp was out. He took another couple of paces towards the lot. Pap let the door close on him. Good riddance. But instead of dusting his feet and moving off, he tarried around the door. He couldn't let the chimp go just like that. Buster would never forgive him, but suddenly something critically more calamitous interrupted his reasons. The chimp could talk. If he survived long enough to get picked up, he was liable to rat them all out. It wasn't like he was leaving on good terms. Why couldn't a chimp become a rat, especially if it meant saving his own skin. This was the paranoid mind of Pap, always at work. The chimp had to stay, but he couldn't bring another moment's harm to Buster. Navigating this minefield just became Pap's next priority. He wanted to open the door, to make sure a stoolie had not just been sent into the world, but a stronger part wanted the chimp to suffer for what he had done to Buster, to acknowledge that what he had was not to be taken for granted. A gentle wrap at the door caused Pap to reveal himself without delay. The chimp was still there, his arrogance tuned helpless. Not a word was exchanged, but each knew what to expect from the other from now on. There would be no rat on the loose just as there would be no further harm to Buster. Respect had just been earned. Pap led Mr. Crooner back, even called him by that name, and let him follow to the kitchen at a more leisurely pace. They both needed something to eat.

- 64 -

Lou Licks needed a break from himself. He was thinking evil thoughts and knew that nothing good could come from them. There was little else he could do at Calloway now that all future shows were cancelled till further notice. Pap Fanti was busy working with Basil on the relocation to a destination "unknown" as Pap put it. It was the first time in all their moves over the last three years that Pap had refused to tell Lou where they were headed next. He just told him he had it all under control and, when the moment was right, he'd fill Lou in. The same confidence wasn't there anymore. Pap was distrusting of everything and everyone now, and that didn't leave Lou feeling too good about himself. He had always been a faithful soldier, as lockdown as they came. But now he felt expendable. He felt like acting on some manly urges he had kept away far too long. This required a trip to the High Girls' apartment. Rita Glass. It went against the rules Pap had laid down, no fraternizing, but Lou wasn't listening anymore. He remembered all the times she looked his way with flirty eyes. What was the worse that could happen? She'd ask him to leave. Rita was there just as expected when Lou showed up with a bottle of rye and a couple cans of cola. A fresh shave and a new suit were meant to impress. "I hope you have ice."

Rita blushed. Her eyes gave a quick pass to Lou's face before she felt the need to pull them away. He looked debonair in a monstrous sort of way. She feared what he could do to her in the sack; he was large as he was strong. She felt her heart double up as she attempted to string a few words in order. "We doin' morning shows now?"

"Thought we could have drink, maybe chew the fat. You alone?"

"For now, but Double C will be home in a couple of hours. She's not too keen on visitors, especially large males."

"She a diesel?"

Lou's filterless tongue made Rita giggle. "No. Just one of those respectable-types. Isn't it early for a drink?"

"If you stand on your head, the sun's already going down," Lou said.

"You been tippin'?"

"Me? That's kinda what I wanted to talk to you about. See, I got this full bottle of rye here and no one to share it with. You gonna invite me in or leave me out here like some vacuum peddler?" Lou didn't take his leering eyes of Rita. They didn't seem to bother her. There had been too much suppression, too many lonely moments in the shower with nothing more than his member in a soapy hand and the illusion of Rita lathering him up where it counted. She looked good too. Like she had just woken from a long nap. Her big eyes were puffy in a cute way and so was her mouth. Rita couldn't resist any longer. Living through Holly's romance was one thing, but this large, protective man was giving off pheromones. She had a small crush on him too, his blue eyes that stood out of that ashy skin. He tried to slick his hair back, but like Buster, it didn't take to the pomade. Turning back into the apartment, Lou had a perfect view of her backside. She was in a pair of long johns.

"The heat's out," Rita said. It was cold in the apartment.

"All the more reason." Lou tapped the bottle against his chest. "Forget the ice."

Rita long-legged herself into the kitchen. Lou brushed the scattered clothes off the couch—they were all Holly's—and took a seat. He sniffed the air for womanly scents and waited, but he couldn't wait long. It had been too long since he had been natural, as in the business of men and women. The secret club, playing sitter to a bear and ape, he had forgotten what it felt like to be a real man. He took a swig straight from the bottle and watched Rita reenter the living room with a small plastic bag and two glasses. Her hair was pinned back, opening her face wide for all manner of kissing games.

"What's that?" Lou asked with an eye on the pills.

"They're Claudie's. Make her relax."

"Got one for me?"

She took a Nube and placed it under her tongue, then handed Lou another. He did the same. Then she held the glasses out, and Lou did the pouring.

"Here's mud in your eye." Lou clinked Rita's glass. She took a sip. Lou's was a gulp. "Nice place," he said.

"I'm sorry about that. It's all Holly's. Claudette says she belongs in the army. That she'd be cleaned up in a week." Rita balanced on foal legs, searching for that next step.

"Have I ever told you you're a great dancer?" He asked.

"I don't think so."

"A real looker too. Someone I like to keep my eyes on."

"Doesn't that go against house rules?"

"When the game changes so do the rules."

"Does Pap know you're here?"

"He knows only because I don't need to lie to him, but it's none of his business," Lou said. "You think I'm nice?"

"Maybe."

"How come?"

"Because you look like you always cared," Rita said. "I see the way you watch over Buster, all of you fellas, but especially you. You really love him, don't you?"

"He's a special little guy. Who wouldn't?" Lou said, pouring another drink before he could finish the last. Rita noticed him getting looser by the minute.

"I remember the first time I saw him. He kept calling me 'Sweeta Rita' and asked me to teach him how to dance. The other girls got jealous, especially Holly. They wanted all his attention, but I swear he kept asking me. I put him on top of a table. He wasn't as big as he is now. You shoulda seen the look on Pap's face. I'm surprised he kept me on. I'm sure my brother had to smooth things out."

Lou remained at full attention. "Things are about to change again."

"Where are we going this time?"

"To hell-and-gone," Lou said. "He'd have us cross the ocean. Only no one would follow. I just don't know how long Pap can keep this up."

"Maybe he should stop."

"Try to stop itching a rash, but where does that leave the rest of us?" Lou had Rita thinking what he wanted her to think. The club would shut down, and there would be no more work, no more dough. Soon Rita and Claudette would be kicked out of their apartment and then what? Back to soup lines? Back to burlesque with Holly and backstage rape jobs for drug money? The clock hadn't done them any favors over the years.

"You really think it's over?" Now Rita was taking healthier swigs from her glass.

"I don't know." Lou was ready to pour her another. "If anything happens, I'll watch out for you. What do you think of that?"

"Cut it out."

"Forget it. I'd do it because I like you. You wouldn't owe me a thing. Since you said you like me too, I think we can make it work. It's our own business. No one has to know. Wherever Pap takes us next, I ain't going."

"What do you mean you're not going?" Rita took a seat next to Lou. She was suddenly very comfortable around him and everything he was saying. It appeared to be coming straight from the heart. Bullshit. It was the booze and meth.

"You shouldn't either. I'm telling you I gotta bad feeling."

"We can't just up and quit. What about Pap? What about Buster?"

"Buster. He doesn't deserve this. His friend, maybe, but not the kid."

"That friend of his is a fiend in a monkey suit," Rita said. It got a laugh out of Lou.

"But boy can he belt it out."

"I don't care about any of that. I wish he would just leave Buster alone," she said. Lou topped her off, and she took another swig. He sat up and inched closer to her.

"He ain't gonna bother him anymore. If things work out the way they should, Buster will be safe the rest of his days, and all this scattin' around will be behind us," Lou said.

"What are you gonna do, Lou?" Rita asked like a small girl seeking a father's protection. It sent a wave of pleasure down his groin to hear her pronounce his name. He put his hand on her thigh. It made her lungs jump. She thought to brush it off but left it there instead. It wasn't moving further north, but then she might not stop its progress either. She took another quaff.

"I'm gonna take care of everything. Buster, Pap, you. No one's gonna get hurt. We all deserve better. We all deserve stability. You deserve stability." He gazed into her eyes. She had that manhandle-me look about her.

"I'm scared, Lou." There went his name again. He couldn't control what was happening below the belt. He leaned into her for a kiss. She absorbed his advance. He took her glass from her hand and set it on the floor and put two large paws on her shoulders. Soon they were petting her breasts. They both needed to release here. If there was no tomorrow, they needed this now. Lou worked her thermal off, and she was soon naked. He undid his pants, knowing he didn't have much time. Rita tried to slow him down, but she didn't try hard enough. A whispering "stop" meant "go," and Lou went. He was midstride to the finish line when the door opened, and in walked 'Double

340

C' cradling a bag of groceries. She dropped the bag, and a jar of ketchup shattered on the floor. Lou and Rita undid themselves.

"Hell no. This ain't a brothel. What are you doing with my pills?"

"You said a couple of hours," Lou whined to Rita.

"Claudie, this isn't what you think," said Rita. "We only took one."

"I told you to stay out of my shit," Claudette said the way someone who was about to attack sounded. She could barely tolerate Holly bringing Chase Griggs by, and that was only because Holly bought her off with plenty of pills. Now it was Rita and with Lou Licks of all men, and neither had yet paid the toll to use the apartment as a sex stop.

"What's shakin', Double C? You ain't gonna tell Pap about this."

Rita turned disenchanted eyes towards Lou. She wanted him to stay, to clarify the part about not telling Pap. Suddenly Lou didn't seem as in control as he was minutes before.

"Get out, both of you," Claudette said as she marched over and snatched her meth pills up.

"I'm sorry, Claudie. Don't get hysterical," said Rita.

"Get out of here."

"This is my place too."

"I don't give a fuck!" Claudette accosted her.

"Whoa, filly." Lou threw himself in the middle of both chicks. With pants bunched up at his ankles, he remained nibcocked. For a drunken second he thought to tag them both.

"Pull your fuckin' pants up, pig!" Claudette screamed. She had taken two B's before she went to the market and was jacked on high.

"Why don't you relax? Have a drink," Lou said.

"You rotten piece of trash. Cover that fuckin' thing now!"

Lou laughed. Claudette shoved a finger in his face. He returned the favor with a firm palm to her cheek. It was hard enough to knock the spit out of her and send her to her knees.

"Lou! What are you doing?" Rita yelled.

"You're dead," Claudette grumbled repeatedly with a hand dressing her cheek.

"It wasn't her fault. Let her be," Lou said of Rita as he buttoned his pants.

"Get the fuck out!" Claudette continued.

Lou gave Rita a smug smirk before pointing himself to the door. "So long." He would have to finish himself off with the old handshake.

- 65 -

When the sun buried itself under the horizon, Jackson Reese came out to play. Top hat, tails and a couple of gal pals in shiny fish scales and fox shawls marked his M.O. Jackson bent both arms at ninety degrees so his companions could hook their hands over his underworked biceps. Like a chorus line they approached the water taxi docked on the Harper East docks. It was a secluded spot a mile north of Twenties Slip. A watery moonlight and the premature glow of the taxi cabin were the only guides. Jackson handed the nimble boat driver three pine green business cards. On each card just one lower-case word: *fishtail*, followed by a different number. In this instance: 14, 15 & 16. There were four more passengers on board the taxi, two men in tuxes and two women in evening wear and furs. One of the men smoked his briar. They other introduced a flame to his cigar. It was 10 pm and ten days after Pisto Leroy popped out of the harbor. The ride would take about twenty five minutes. A minibar would help pass the time. The sea appeared as an arena of wrinkles; the eastern sky a chasm. The water taxi shoved off and rumbled into the harbor, due northeast for four miles where the ocean hid all manner of reclusion.

A half hour later, the water taxi approached what looked like a traffic light flashing green. It was the only light as far as the eye could see and was coming from a ferry. Pap Fanti stood at the center of the greeting party. He had the sudden urge to inspect each boarding face. Turnip Faymus flanked Pap's right shoulder. Jackson Reese and his dates boarded the fishtail. They were tipsy from the taxi ride.

"Mr. Fanti, you've made the adventure all the worthwhile."

Pap shook Reese's hand. "You the rat that's gonna chew a hole through my boat? How is it screwing around on the missus?" But those were just his thoughts. A man seldom said what was truly on his mind anyway. "Welcome, Mr. Reese. Always a pleasure," were his spoken words. Pap brought Resse close enough to smell his sharp cologne. "We've missed your friend, Mr. Griggs."

"I wouldn't worry much about him. His vices include arm wrestling with ginchy gams, not preaching on street corners." What Jackson didn't know was that Pap had a deal with Griggs and Griggs failed to deliver. No money, no backing off. When Pap asked Holly if she was still seeing him, she said "yes, thank you for the concern, and I know what I'm doing." They had been courting each other every day, usually in hotel rooms but now, with more frequency, at Holly's place to the increasing chagrin of Claudette. Lucky for Holly, she had plenty of pills to back Claudette off. Pap backed off too. Holly had no clue what was coming, and he had his own troubles to deal with. "Is Buster back in the swing of things?" Jackson asked.

"Everyone's back in rhythm. Let me walk you in," Pap said glancing at his sentinel out by the bow. Then he told Turnip to stay on deck with the Gutter Gophers.

Basil Demur had come through one more time when Pap Fanti needed him most. The Fishtail was a 100-foot passenger ferry he found retired at the Breaks shipyard. At face value it depleted Pap of all but some pin money. But it was in need of a facelift, so Basil dumped another five from his own pockets to make it both functional and presentable. This included engine work, a paint job, varnishing the decks, basics, all which took three long days. Any other sprucing he'd leave to Pap. It was either that or the honey barge. "This time I aim to collect on my loan," Basil said even if he would never have a creditor's heart for Pap. Pap had left him three Dunfer's Linen trucks as collateral. Basil stored them in a garage on the lower Leaf and had also made it clear that this would be the last of the favors. That was a lie too. Basil couldn't leave Pap and Buster floating alone on a ferry. The members would never guess the where, when and how. So Basil came up with a new system and imparted it to all members during a "final consultation." Green card, tonight's color, meant the ferry would drop anchor four miles northeast of Jester Straits directly south of Point Grave. Red meant another zigzagged mile southeast from there. He informed the members and the water taxi drivers that the club would do one-week tours in each location, three shows a week, all on the same nights to keep things predictable. Those members with their own yachts could meet the ferry directly on the sea. Pap frowned on that. A cruiser could be filled with law. Then again, so could a water buggy. To reduce the chance of bringing unwanted guests, the sea cabbies were paid a handsome advance to do one thing: pick up passengers with color-coded cards (green or red) and drop them off at the Fishtail. And now Basil Demur was out, his hands washed of the whole operation. Things were getting too dicey for him. "It's been an honor knowing you, Pap Fanti and your magical friends. Look me up in a few years when you're making flickers." Pap felt alone. The fate of Buster and Mr. Crooner rested with him, and he made sure to let everyone under his watch know it. Trips to shore decreased. Pap preferred to be at the mercy of nature more than man.

The skies cooperated for an hour, and then the winds started to run. Thunder shook the air, and bolts of lightning flickered fat drops of rain like liquid light bulbs. Lou Licks sat at the helm with his mind and his heart in each hand. He had delayed his promise to bail. His loyalty to Pap was that pronounced, but the truth was that he couldn't split without a better plan. Up to that point, he didn't have one. He would walk out on so much that so few ever knew about. Then the paranoia started again. Even out in the middle of the ocean, he could sense their doom. At least on land they had better escapes, and without speed boats, they were sitting ducks. Increasing sea swells blended with the sky, but the anchored ferry was determined to hold its coordinates. Lou knew that when the waves crested, they would spill onto the decks and sink the ship. He knew what Pap Fanti had told him. "I don't care if God's hand picks this dinghy up and turns it upside down. We take her in when I say." But Lou had had enough, and his head started to spin with sea sickness. The quart of rye he had ingested a couple of hours earlier wasn't helping. Lou was drinking, each time more than the last. It took his mind off of Pap. The old man was surely shedding his sanity. Never had Pap allowed an impatient tongue to run riot in front of Buster until they first took to the seas. It was with the best of intentions, but yelling at the bear to get out of the open and down to the lower decks could only mean he was coming apart upstairs. His words grew strident with Mr. Crooner too, and Lou now noticed that the chimp resisted little. He simply did as he was told. The environment had turned militant. Barking orders at Lou became the norm. Daily arguments about what routes to sail grew old fast. Lou's position was always to stay inside the harbor where the land could mitigate the weather. He had predicted the storms that were brewing tonight, but Pap remained unconvinced. But the thing that Lou couldn't stand, the thing that led him to the bottle more than any other was the constant reminder of Pisto Leroy. He once even threatened Lou with cutting him loose, did it in front of the others so he would know that Pap still carried the bulge. Lou jumped out of his seat and ran to the lower decks where the party was just as thunderous as the gathering storm.

The Fishtail felt like Calloway on a waterbed. Dino's bar was now inside the galley. Two generators powered lights, refrigeration and sound. The dining room on the second deck made a spacious club hall. Rusted portholes every six feet let in steady streams of cold, salty-flavored air which when mixed with tobacco smoke created the aroma of a pirate ship. The same tables and chairs, the same lamps, it all created a tight fit. Gold satin made curves on the ceiling. Pap put his signature on the Fishtail and other than being surrounded by angry seas, there was nothing different. Except maybe the stars of the show.

Tuxed and tapered, Mr. Crooner spread his arms wide and chanted his songs in front of a seated crowd of fifty. He never underperformed, but ever since they had taken the show to sea, this being their third, he had sung like he was responsible for the drop in the house. This had Pap worried beyond normal. That was over twenty souls who no longer felt a need to belong to the "secret society" Basil had limned during their "consultations." And this could mean over twenty souls who had seen two miracles and were now on the outside with their mouths and their stories. Souls like Chase Griggs.

Buster was back on his stool playing that trumpet like nothing had ever happened ten days ago on the finger piers. But there was something different about him. He had aged in days. The blinding bliss of ignorance was finally pierced by despondence, and his brio was all but gone. Things like death were now a reality. No matter how much Buster wanted to play his trumpet for Pisto Leroy, he would not be afforded that chance like he had with Pap. The topic was broached only once in the mess hall during breakfast. Buster and Pap sat alone to a salmon soufflé when Pap asked, "What do you think happened?"

Buster's answer was alarming. "It had to be an accident, Pap. Friends can't hurt each other on purpose, only on accident." The worst part was that for the first time he could detect the bear lying, changing. He slept more than ever. He felt safe when sleeping. When asked if he wanted to keep putting on shows, Buster said, "Oh yes, please. I couldn't imagine what I'd do with myself if I wasn't playing my trumpet."

Mr. Crooner had leveled off to lukewarm. No more huffs, no more booze, no more dive-bombing from highs to lows. He now approached his days like a virtuoso on the down slope of a decorated career. He was on cue every show, didn't interrupt Buster or the Cats 6 during a set and was in bed after the curtain was drawn. He respected Pap Fanti and his crew even if he didn't have much to do with them. He took his meals and his space with gravitas, even kept the food off the floor. He greeted Buster with courtroom decorum and didn't ask for another service. They each roomed on separate decks and unless Buster sought Mr. Crooner out, their paths never crossed. They moored at the shipyard on Harper East once every three to four days for provisions. Pap had left his car on a vacant dirt road and was always surprised when he'd find it there. Buster and Mr. Crooner would be given an hour shore leave. Mr. Crooner would take the most advantage of it, wandering as far as a couple of miles from the ferry unsupervised. Only once did he run afoul of local farmers who witnessed him mixing it up with their horses. But Mr. Crooner ran back into the woods, and that ended that.

Buster refused to disembark. He refused to get into the water again. He liked staying around his room and the club on the second deck. He had lost considerable weight since the incident with Pisto Leroy. His tuxedoes now hung loose off his shoulders, but he still had a Viking lung when it came to the horn and a heart that was quick to get away from him when he heard Mr. Crooner romancing the tears from his eyes with his song.

Lou entered the hall and noticed the guests vacillating like drunks with fists braced to their cocktails. The Cats 6, Buster and Mr. Crooner were in the middle of a languid set. It was a love song, and Mr. Crooner dedicated it to a mystery someone because he could not have invented such words had he not been graced with love's embrace at one time in his life. The lyrics told of a love that was pure and held no grudges. When Mr.

Crooner was finished, Buster's trumpet wept. The crowd cheered over the rocking floor.

Mr. Crooner and Buster headed backstage, it was just a gutted sleeping quarter where they would catch five. On Buster's request, the show was broken into two acts instead of the old ways of one extended set. Buster and Mr. Crooner sat by themselves in the room. There were a couple of chairs and a table with refreshments. A plate of mints, Mr. Crooner swore by them now. A jar of iced water and chocolate milk for Buster. Mr. Crooner took a seat and poured himself a glass of water. He kept aloof, almost like Buster wasn't in the room. Buster took a few swigs of his chocolate milk and complimented Mr. Crooner on a beautiful set. He made special mention of that last song. Somehow he couldn't help but feel that it was dedicated to him. Buster wanted so much to ask him that he couldn't look away from Mr. Crooner.

"You got something on your mind?" Mr. Crooner asked.

"That last song you sang," said Buster.

"What of it?"

"How do you know to sing of such wonders?"

"It's got nothing to do with you, if that's what you're aiming at," Mr. Crooner said. His tone was dusty. He handed Buster another mint and said, "Take the chocolate from your breath." Buster rolled the mint around his mouth but not before saying thank you twice to Mr. Crooner for what he considered another thoughtful gift.

Back at the bar, Lou whispered something in Pap's ear that made him perk up to attention. They headed out to the top deck and took cover under the overhang while the rain and waves tangoed around them.

"You call this a storm? You're slipping, Lou. We've run speed boats in worse than this. Do not weigh anchor," Pap ordered.

"We'll be ripped to shreds if you don't pull it up!" Lou yelled.

"You leave this ship here until I tell you. It'll pass, I say. We dock in the morning as planned. If you're sick get to a lower deck and take a nap. Cut that booze and stop burning your spoon in Rita's oven." Pap returned fire. Claudette spilled the beans. Lou wanted to hit someone, starting with Pap, but he held his fist by his side. Pap noticed it. Lou would deal with Claudette soon enough. That bitch. What he wouldn't know was that Rita was the informant, said she felt guilty and knew that Lou had gone behind Pap's back. Pap forgave her only because he didn't have time to hold the grudge, but the truth was that he had changed too. He gnashed his teeth daily and carried around his cane like a scepter. The only one that brought a tender touch out of him anymore was Buster.

Pap returned to the lower deck and prayed for the storm to subside. Within an hour it had. Lou was asleep inside the engine room. Soon the water taxis would be back to take guests and most of the crew back to shore. The only ones staying on the ferry overnight were Pap, Lou, Turnip, Ink, Trunks, Buster and Mr. Crooner.

When morning came, Pap weighed anchor and brought the ship ashore. Things were getting rough at sea, and Lou needed some firm land under his feet. Only when they got there, he wasn't as quick to get off. Lou had made sure that Pap was out of earshot when he approached Buster inside his room.

"I'm telling you, Buster, it's too dangerous for you out there. If you want to be safe, you have to come with me, and you have to do it now before anyone sees you," Lou said.

"Are Pap and Mr. Crooner coming along?" Buster smelled the alcohol on Lou's breath and noticed him stepping around like a trapped bird.

"They said they'll meet up with us later, but we have to split now." Lou put a hand on Buster's back and nudged him forward, but Buster wouldn't budge. He suspected that somehow Lou wasn't being as forthright as he had known him to be. Lou's maudlin desperation gave it all away. Buster's resistance came with soft bleats.

"Buster, you won't make out here. Remember Pisto Leroy. It's going to happen again. Please. Come with me now. We can make it." Lou heard the door open, and he reeled his tongue.

Pap stood at the doorway and noticed the uneasiness etched in Buster's eyes. "What are you doing?" Pap asked Lou.

"I was just talking to the kid. He was a little shaken by the storm."

"Baloney. What happened, Buster?"

"Nothing, Pap. Everything's quack, quack, ducky." But Buster's delivery wasn't compelling.

"I'm heading to the store," Lou said with a hidden glare. He started for the room exit.

"Don't you need my car keys?" Pap asked.

"I'll catch a cab." Lou left.

For the first time, Pap wondered if Lou would return. He needed to get a hold of DC Stiles. If one man could track Lou's movements it would be Stiles. The problem was that Stiles was M.I.A. and hadn't made an appearance at the club in some time. Pap drove to the nearest payphone. He put his change in the slot and gave the switchboard operator the number. The phone rang four times until someone picked up. There was no voice on the other line, not even a breath, as though the receiver was waiting for the caller's identity before giving himself up. Pap spoke. Gave his name, asked if Stiles could hear him, but for seconds on end he got nothing from the receiver. Pap hung up. When the line went dead, Stiles killed his end too. He looked to the manila envelope on his desk. Someone had offered good money for what was inside, and he was tired of letting clients down.

- 66 -

DC Stiles picked up the phone again and called Vilma Griggs. "Mrs. Griggs. Stiles. I got your meat, and it's getting spoiled. Better get over here fast. Bring cash."

Vilma hung up and hurried to put on her coat. She had to stop by the bank to withdraw the money. The moment of truth was at hand.

When she arrived, Stiles was three shots into a fresh bottle of rye. Lives were about to be shattered, and he was about to be another $4,500 up. The way he saw it, the deal he made with Chase Griggs was bad on its face because it violated the terms of the original contract. Vilma refused to take a seat even though Stiles warned her about the pitfalls of standing during tragic news. He offered her a drink, but she refused that too.

"You said you have something for me. I want to see it," Vilma said. Stiles slid the smudged envelope across the table like a death certificate.

"I'd make sure not to let those walk into a fire on their own. I know many women who might overlook something like this, even forgive something that's in a man's nature. Then again, I know others who would put a bullet in their brains after they cut their husband's throat. Either way, take it straight: Iron out your husband. There's not a good bone in his body." Stiles was talking too much. It was the only way he could stymie his guilty conscience from confessing that he had double-crossed Chase

Griggs out of six large. It wasn't out of some ethical duty he owed Griggs. The man was a scum filter. It was all based on Stiles own special code. He feared retribution and knew the moment Chase Griggs got the news, he'd be on a rampage.

Vilma took a tentative hold of the envelope, knowing full well she didn't want to unravel the contents within. She already knew. She reached into her purse and pulled out another small, white envelope and handed it to Stiles. "For a job well done." She started for the door without another word.

"Aren't you gonna inspect the goods? I don't give refunds," Stiles said.

"I trust you, Mr. Stiles," Vilma said. "Our business is finished. Good day." She left.

Merlin waited for her at the curb. Vilma's sightless eyes could only mean bad news. He remained mum as he opened her back door. She melted into his frigid chest. She needed to hug another human being, anyone with an ounce of compassion in their veins. Merlin felt awkward, his arms remained in their natural place until Vilma let him go and apologized for the scene.

"Take me to the Easter Tower," she said. Then she got in the car. Merlin skipped to the driver side, got in and drove off. He felt in better health when he was driving Mrs. Griggs to a specific location just like now. Vilma looked out the window to random faces, men, women walking down the street. She wondered how many had ever felt what she was feeling that moment. She opened the envelope and pulled out the photos of Chase and Holly joined at the lips. It reminded her of a time when she, too, was in love with the same man, but that time had eroded with each cashed check, each bank withdrawal. Their marriage was a fraud, a liquidation. She always suspected something like this could happen, but to gaze upon those pictures for the first time revealed to her that twisted visions could become reality. Her stomach turned, not because of the man she had lost long ago, but because the only reason he ever gave her his time was because he knew that he would be well compensated for it. Vilma felt cut-rate, unclean. She leafed through a couple more glossies, allowing the salt of her premonitions to sting her eyes and then slid them carefully back into their pouch. She wanted to vomit, wanted to cry but did neither.

The Easter Tower was a majestic sight, as tall as the Imperial but more like the big brother who had spent plenty of time under a bench press. It would be a symbol of Good Leaf strength and go down as Chase Griggs' most crowning achievement. Vilma stared at it from the back seat while Merlin stood idle at her open door. He gave her a hand when she reached for it. Her steps were those of a general who knew the war was lost even though she had won every battle.

Chase Griggs spoke into the phone, "No, don't come in. I'll meet you there." Vilma walked through the door with the eyes of justice. He hadn't noticed her yet.

"Who are you meeting?"

Chase clapped the receiver down like he had been caught stealing. "Subs want their money before they finish the job. Hard to run an honest racket out here."

"Are you quite certain she hasn't already done her job?"

"She?" The phone started ringing again. He ignored it.

"I'll give you one chance to fess up."

"What do you have there?" Chase asked like the envelope in Vilma's hand was loaded with bullets.

She kept her mouth closed and her eyes penetrating through his. It was morbidly rousing to watch Chase moments from bedlam. He was tired of beating around the bush. "Okay, you've had ideas about me for quite some time, I know this. So I'll tell you. Once I come clean, you drop it forever. I ran into an old friend. At the club. She's been going through a rough time at home, her husband drinks too much, that sort of thing. So I told her I'd talk to her. That's all it is. Just like you talk to Mr. Signia."

Vilma plopped the envelope on his desk like the prints carried leprosy. Somehow he knew what was inside. His eyes stayed on Vilma as if by doing so, the envelope would disappear. Just as predicted, he wanted to tear Stiles' heart out, but all he could do was tear the pictures in half and cast them to the floor.

"I want to ask you a question, and I want you to be honest. Did you ever once love me?" Vilma asked.

Chase couldn't answer. He wanted to say yes, but he never believed it. Money was stronger than anything he could have desired in Vilma, and yet, he stood by her side for years, knowing that the lost time should have meant more to him than faking love for survival.

"Alright fine. You got me dead to rights. But before I hand over sentencing privileges, let me state my case. It was all a setup. I swear to you that dame means nothing to me. I was drunk, upset, you know, burned up at the way you always talk down to me. Like I was your Cocker Spaniel."

"You still didn't answer my question." Vilma toyed with Chase. It would be the last time she saw his phony face, so why not? "But I'll spare you anymore anguish. I want you to know that I never harbored ill will towards you. It's not my nature to marry an enemy, but know that your take from this façade you called a marriage will be nothing but the guilt you feel for the rest of your life. Not even the glory you thought you'd bask in from this building. My lawyers will ensure the proper story goes in the papers, not because I'm vindictive, but because inside I'm dead."

"Vilma, you have my full concentration. Now you listen to me. You don't know what you're talking about. That meant nothing. Nothing at all!" Chase said as the sweat started to bead on his forehead.

"And now I know I meant even less than that."

"Don't I get a second chance? Let me fix it up. What do you say? We can go back to like it was. This time work on growing a couple of cuties. I know that's what you want." And even as he said the words, he knew he could never mean them.

"I wouldn't grow God's whiskers with you."

Chase knew he was dangling by a thread, and Vilma wasn't moving the flame away. He let out that last breath, like it was the only one he had left, slow and deliberate as he reached for a smoke. "What can I say? Maybe you should have kept a tighter leash."

"And maybe you should have been there the day you married me."

"So these are the dangerous men after you?" the voice came from the doorway.

Vilma turned. It was the same minx from the pictures, but her voice sounded like a child. "Time we all grow up and stop playing kiddie games," Holly preached Hendrick Fountain's refrain.

Chase stood abashed in the crosshairs of two bazooka tubes. His face drew a blank. There was nothing he could say that would fix this now. Holly connected eyes with Vilma for a split second before she turned and marched from the office.

Vilma remained for one second more. Her eyes were roiled with comic disgust. "Not bad," she said in reference to Holly. "There's a place on the outskirts of hell for jackals like you." Then she left just before her eyes went wet.

Holly hopped the first cab back to her Matanza Heights apartment to grab a bag, couple changes of clothes and what remained of her uppers. She wouldn't be staying the night. Claudette tried to keep her from doing anything rash, but there was no reasoning with her. Holly continued her journey back to Harper East dock. Her tears accompanied her the entire ride. She popped a B-tab and lit a straw. Hendrick was right again. The man she could stand least was the only one who had never lied to her. She should have known better than to believe a louse like DC Stiles.

It was a random afternoon after dry rehearsals with the chimp. Stiles waited inside his car just outside the Calloway lot. He floated in like a ghost and hoped to leave the same way. When Holly strolled out with Rita and Claudette, Stiles had to think quick to get her alone.

"Chase Griggs," were the only words that came out of his mouth. Of the three, Holly turned the quickest. It confirmed to Stiles who his mark was. "I got news."

"Stay here," Claudette warned, but Holly didn't heed a word. She dragged away from the others and minced over to Stiles. Rita's eyes urged Claudette to do something, but Claudette answered back with a look of her own, the kind that said "nope." They both kept their attention on Holly and the man in the fedora and long coat. Only they couldn't make out what either said.

"What do you have to do with Chase Griggs?" Holly asked.

"If you want to see him again, get in the car," Stiles said. "He doesn't have much time."

Holly got in. Chase drove off. They stopped on a Jester country road where no one could pry into their affairs. Stiles offered Holly a cig. She declined and pressed him for the dirt.

"You love the guy?"

"I do," Holly answered.

"I figured as much," Stiles said just as soon as he could think it. Each word came out faster than the last. "If you want to see him live, you'll do exactly as I say."

"Are you the man that's after him?" From the looks of things, Holly didn't figure Stiles to be a toughguy no matter that he dressed like one.

Stiles let his brain absorb the words before he used them to his gain. "No, but I know who is. A ruthless killer. He'll stop at nothing from banging your boy like that." Stiles snapped his fingers in Holly's ear. It left a ringing sensation that stayed with her long after the meeting. "But I also know his weakness. You see, he's a family man. Always cherished the simpler things in life. Swears to this day he ain't a widowmaker. Call it corny all you want. He's a sentimental jack when it comes to matters of the heart. That's where you come in."

"We don't have any kids. I'm not even married to the guy."

"Doesn't matter. I show him proof that you two are in love, you know, like a family, then he'll back off, give Chase some time to work it out."

"I don't believe a word you're saying."

"Believe what you want, doll. It's not your life on the line."

"Does Chase know about this?"

"You say a word to him, it's curtains."

"Why are you doing it?"

"As a favor to a friend who's in business with your boy. Look, nobody said it wasn't a craps game with loaded dice, but it's probably the only chance you'll have to save him. You do want to save him, don't you? Because you love him. Just like I'm sure he loves you." Stiles spoke with such conviction that he actually believed his own baloney. He had contemplated coming straight with it, confessing to Holly that she was tangling with a married man and that sooner or later the dominoes would fall. He would have had to offer part of his fee, potentially a majority part, to make the deal more enticing, but he neither wanted to give a cent of his keep, nor did he think Holly would be reasonable enough to follow through. Besides, saying a man was about to lose his life always worked to elicit some reaction out of most, and with a woman that seemed to do most of her thinking below the neck, he couldn't see this angle failing. Little did Stiles know that Chase had sold her on the same line.

Pap Fanti was no better at telling the truth, but she couldn't blame him anymore than she could blame herself. His words were of little consolation. Phrases like "life goes on" were hollow as a tree in winter.

When she arrived at the Harper East dock, she asked Pap if she could have an audience with Buster. Somehow she felt that

Buster would say the right things and, for a second, make her feel like life had one more beat in it. Pap arranged it, brought Holly to Buster's room. He was shining his Elmer trumpet when they walked in and doing very little else.

"Buster, how you doin', kid?"

"Ducky, Pap. Hello, Holly." Buster set his trumpet in its case and stood from his seat.

"Hi, Buster," Holly said. She remembered the first time she met him.

It had been a night of commiserating another session of debauchery at Bumpy's. Pap Fanti invited her to a late breakfast. She picked the place. A rundown tavern that fit her mood. A few rounds of Lemon Looseys, all for her, and she could forget about the night again. Pap was feeling her out, seeing if she could handle something like the bear. She was in need of a small miracle. When he asked if she could be trusted with a secret, she didn't become overzealous like those who blurted anything to gain confidence.

"I have a small club. I'm thinking of adding another act. A trio of dancers. All clean. What are they paying you now?"

"Enough to splurge on these," Holly said as she lifted her glass and took another swig. She kept talking about the good a change of scenery would do her. So Pap drove her right over to see Buster. All on faith. When he let her into their basement, Buster was resting on a nest of pillows, running a cloth over his mouthpiece. Lou was seated nearby cleaning out his gun. He stood and drew at the sight of Holly.

"Lou, she's a friend," Pap said.

She took an immediate seat at the sight of Buster. The bubbles had floated to her head.

"Can I touch him?" Holly asked.

"Go right ahead," Pap said. He winked at Lou as if to say "it's okay."

Lou relaxed. Holly took timid steps to Buster, but before she could get close enough, Buster was already hugging her. His head came to her belly, so his arms wrapped around her waist. He knew that before any words of introduction, this is what she needed most. She placed a hand on Buster's head.

"If you give him a good scratch, he'll fall in love with you," Pap said.

"I like it right behind my ears and neck, but you don't have to if you don't want," Buster admitted.

Pap and Lou laughed. Holly was caught off guard. "He can talk!" Gales of glee erupted from her throat. Her nails plowed back and forth over his scruff. Buster was in heaven.

Now there were streaks running south from her eyes. Buster ran over and gave her another hug. He knew the right medicine for the right time.

"You're gonna be okay. Stay on the ship now. Stay with Buster. If he can't pick you up, no one can," Pap said as he left the two in the room. "I'll be right outside if you need me."

Buster had Holly take a seat and took his trumpet. His song was the ultimate pick-me-up. Holly's mind was transported to another realm. There was peace. When Buster was done, he said, "I came up with that just for you. I hope you liked it."

"It was beautiful," Holly said. "Are you some sort of angel?"

"I don't think so."

"You're so sweet. I've never seen anyone as sweet as you. You don't belong in this world," Holly said. "It's an ugly world."

"It has a lot of beautiful things in it," Buster said.

"Like what?"

"Well, like you and Pap, Mr. Crooner, Lou, Dino, Rita, Claudette, the Cats 6, Ham, Trunks, the Gophers, Ink, Turnip, Mr. Demur for starters. Even Pisto Leroy."

"I'm sorry you had to know about that," Holly said as the tears resurfaced. "That's why this world is ugly. There's no trust, no honesty, no decency. I'm not a home-wrecker."

Buster hung on every one of Holly's words with ears attentive and eyes that wouldn't break, not even with a hammer.

He had tasted what she described, but wasn't ready to give up on hope like she was. Then he opened up like he had never known he could before. He spoke to her about all the things they had left to do, about the love she deserved and would have one day soon, about how precious it would be, about how she would need no safeguards for it because it would never want to leave. And when Buster finished, he played another song and gave her another hug. No longer did she feel the need to cry. Buster had lifted her spirit. Serenity mixed in with exhaustion. She would sleep the night on the docked ship. By first light, she would go to her brother, Hendrick, say she was ready to grow up and ask him for a job. She didn't say goodbye to anyone.

The following dawn found Chase alone inside a cheap downtown motel, the Staid Inn. He had no clue how things were going to play out, whether Vilma would cut him a break, whether he should return to the job at the Easter Tower, what would be waiting for him should he return. Vilma threatened all sorts of injunctions, but she didn't enforce one. If Chase wanted to finish his building, she wouldn't get in his way. But he didn't know any of that. He needed someone on his side; he needed to find Holly Fountain and smooth things over. He went to her apartment. The only thing waiting for him at the door was the cold shoulder of Claudette Calor.

"Holly ain't here no more. She ain't coming back. Why don't you do yourself a favor and chase a car before I call the cops."

He called her a draggle-tail. She slapped the grit from his teeth and called him a two-timing crook before slamming the door shut. His heart raced with the memory of his old man, the lecherous dirtbag he was, the proud stories he would tell about his days as a door-to-door salesman of wonder ointments and lucky trinkets. His name was Chester Griggs, and he would leave his only son, youngest in a litter of six daughters, with the very lessons that would guide him to this day. "If you can't believe what you're selling, no one will believe when it comes to buying. That goes for goods, services and broads. I know you 'yuck' them now. But one day, Son, you're gonna fuck 'em and fuck 'em good." Chase was only eight years old and a bit on the feminine side when he received those pearls of wisdom that forever changed his life. Now he had become a replica of a man he thought slimy to the touch. He sold his way into Vilma's life, and she fell for it. He sold his way into Holly's heart, and she gave it to him. Now the big jilt had sold him a nonrefundable ticket. He felt cheated just like all of his father's duped customers who purchased the film off rice water thinking it was snake oil. After all, snake oil was a certifiable cure in those days. He had grown to see his sisters all marry deadbeats who amounted to squat. Jobless roustabouts and line workers turned drunks. He aspired to just a little more if not a lot, and he got his chance when he met Vilma. She was his ticket to stardom.

Chase caught another cab to the Savings and Loan Building and Basil Demur for an impromptu "consultation." Demur was there to greet him, even let him into his office as a former "respected client." When Chase explained the situation and how he needed to find Holly Fountain, Demur went mum. He didn't disclose the location of the new club. To be honest, not even Demur knew any longer. Chase tried flexing, thought he could put the screws on the lawyer with his old man's hardball, but Demur had done business in Hades. What was some wannabe tough gonna do to him? He didn't have a gun, and his fists were polished with Vilma's knickers. He was never a hard-boiled construction man like he pretended to be. Vilma smoothed out his rough edges before he could form them. With her, he learned how to dress, how to act, a new way to sell. Without her, he was back to his roots, and Demur wasn't buying snake oil. So Chase Griggs did what any duped citizen would do. He went to the police.

"Who's in charge here?" Chase demanded. The rubbery deputy sat at the front desk feigning diligence by alphabetizing arrest sheets.

He looked up to Chase with serviceable eyes. "Can I help you, sir?" The deputy could tell that Chase was in a heightened state, like a victim of the Glim Hustle. "Are you alright, sir?"

"I got a hot tip, but I want to talk to the fuzzy in charge."

"The captain's not available. If you leave me your name and number, I can have a detective call you back."

"Ever hear the name Buddy Plagun? How about Pazo Fanti?"

The deputy's eyes grew rigid. He slowly stood from his desk. "One second."

"Keep me waiting, I run to the paper. It's the story of the century."

One minute later, Captain Sert Johnson strode out and greeted Chase with a policeman's grip. Then he led him back to his office for a cup of Joe and a smoke. There were plaques adorning the walls, letters of commendation from City Hall, family portraits, all the things that made Chase feel protected.

"Tell me, who are you?"

"The name's Chase Griggs. I'm one of the members of that secret speako Buddy Plagun and Pazo Fanti used to run out of Dunfer's in the Thread District. Don't worry. They're not there anymore."

Johnson kept his cards close to the vest. Buddy Plagun and Pazo Fanti didn't work together unless someone was pulling the wool over Johnson's eyes too. But the name Griggs sounded familiar. "You wouldn't happen to be married to the late Congressman's daughter, Vilma Worthton? Goes by Vilma Griggs now."

"That would be my wife. Ex, if you ask her, but we don't need to dabble into semantics."

"What's their fix?" Johnson asked. He would play along with Griggs' assertion that Plagun and Pazo Fanti were allies.

"There's an answer for that too. But I don't give tips for charity."

"Have you seen them together? Buddy Plagun and Pazo Fanti?"

"No. I just seen Fanti and his musical bear," Chase said.

Johnson snarled his brow. He didn't care for morning jokes, no matter who Chase called "ex."

"That's right, Captain Johnson. A musical bear. I thought it was a gag. Some gimp in a Halloween costume, but it's the real deal. A furry bear, about three, four feet tall, plays a trumpet like Dizzy Marea. I don't know what they're into, those criminals, but it looks like some kinda hocus pocus to me. I'm not supposed to share this with anyone, or they threatened to have me taken for a ride in the country, you know, killed. I'm sure you know that Buddy Plagun is a dangerous gangster."

"Musical bears, huh? Have you been drinking, Mr. Griggs?"

"I have, but that has nothing to do with what I got for you," Chase said.

"So you gonna cough it up?" Johnson asked again.

"How much is it worth to you?" Chase asked again.

"You know I can book you for conspiracy and aiding and abetting right now."

"That would get you the mayor's office for sure," Chase rejoindered.

"Why don't you give me your phone number, and I'll talk it over with City Hall. They give final word on any reward money. I'll call you as soon as this afternoon."

"I'm at the Staid Inn, under Griggs. Like I told your cadet out there. Take too long, it makes the front page."

"You can't do that. Once they get word of a leak, they're gone forever. Trust me. I've been tracking this vermin for a long time."

"Then I'm sure it'll be worth your while," Chase said as he took another sip from his coffee mug and stood up. Johnson escorted him out and closed the door behind him, returning quickly to his phone.

That night, Chase Griggs sat in his room at the Staid Inn with a bottle of scotch he had kept in his car for this very occasion. The room smelled like it was designated only for bad things, things he used to do, so he smoked to mask the licentious perfumes. The second night was always the hardest. It was a time of reflection. He couldn't believe the way Vilma talked to him after all he had done for her. She didn't deserve a man as genteel, as pleasing on the eyes, even if she could afford one. But her solitude would be her greatest punishment. Chase had bigger plans. He'd find Holly again and make it up to her, get on his knees, beg her for mercy and then marry her and give her those ten kids on the same night. He'd carry his weight as the former husband of the great Vilma Worthton and be hired to head another project. Besides, she couldn't simply take everything from him just like that. He had plenty of right to the wealth he had help built since they tied the knot four years ago. Four miserable years. He couldn't even access his bank accounts anymore. Vilma had them frozen to prevent Chase from draining them dry. When the dust settled, she would concede a generous severance package. She truly wasn't vindictive. Again something he wouldn't know about until the time came. For now he would fight her in court with his reward money for the tip. He would get back on the Easter Tower and finish it. He would ride into the sunset with Holly Fountain and her legs.

There was a knock at the door. Chase wasn't counting on company. He set his bottle on the table and went to answer. The police hadn't called him back like they said they would. Perhaps it was a detective with the reward cash. Perhaps it was Holly. She seemed to have a knack for finding him when he least expected it. There was a bounce in his step until he opened the door to a silencer. Jesse Under shoved Chase on his heels and let himself in.

"You have some information for me," Jesse said. Chase's knees urged him to drop. He was a startled dog with nowhere to run.

"Are you a cop?"

"Yeah," Jesse answered. "Where's Fanti?"

"Where's my money. We had a deal!"

Jesse through a C note at Chase's feet. "Where is he?"

Chase took the bill. A hundred dollars wouldn't buy him the public defender. "You insult me with this shit?"

"I ain't gonna ask again."

"Where's Captain Johnson?"

"Who?" Jesse Under cocked his pistol.

Chase pissed his pants. "Calloway Cocoa on Twenties Slip." Tears started spilling from his face. "Where's my fuckin' money for the tip?"

"Here," Jesse said as he pulled the trigger and pumped a muted round into Chase's forehead. Spurts of blood rosied the carpet and orange-checkered bed spread, followed by a vapor of magenta.

The police reported the homicide as a gangland killing between rivals and connected Chase Griggs to Pazo Fanti. Vilma shed a tear only out of respect for the man she once married, but she didn't make any inquiries and wasn't at his funeral. Instead, she packed a couple of bags and had Merlin drive her to the Jester estate.

PART IV

- 67 -

Bill Plagun had his own ideas about the law, what it meant to be a good citizen and a family man. He was the only son of Senior Plagun (dec), Good Leaf police chief from 1913-1919. Senior Plagun might have had a longer tenure had he not been implicated in the assassination plot of the teetotaler Bert Asbury, frontrunner for the mayor's office in 1919. Senior's level of involvement in the politician's death remained a mystery, but his stance against prohibition was firm, and it would tip the scales against him when a state judge sentenced him to the electric chair in 1920, citing: "A public servant turned mutineer in the most detestable of ways, his hands pulled the strings or his eye turned intentionally blind, either deeming sufficient in the death of a good man." His wife, Edith, was one of those wholesome women that didn't ask many questions. She claimed it was the only thing that saved her own life. But Bill Plagun always knew what his old man was up to. Soon he would be after his father's own heart. He looked up to him as a man of respect, one who had the courage to follow his own convictions even if it meant going against the grain. A man who always put his family first. If he wasn't getting what he wanted here, how could he be on his way to that place where everyone got what they wanted? Some called it heaven, but Bill Plagun held no such affiliations. Heaven was in the now. When his father was executed, any department benefits owed to the family were annulled. And Bill soon learned what it would mean to fight the law and win. He fought, fought for all the things he wanted, fought to keep a roof over his mother's head until she gave up and put a bullet in her throat from her husband's standard issue. Bill Plagun held the law responsible for his parents' death, for shutting his bars down, for taking the bread from his mouth. He swore to avenge his father by becoming the largest bootlegger on the Leaf. And he started out big. Many of his father's colleagues in the force became trusted associates, for a fee. Bill made more his first year of bootlegging than Senior had made his entire career as police chief, and he knew how to take care of those who had the power to make his life easier. His first order of business was to rub out the judge that sentenced his father. Bill didn't believe in sending others to carry out personal vendettas, so he took care of it himself. Judge Maurice Quashein enjoyed his brandy and Calabash. He presided over the South Leaf Supreme Court in Sunks District.

One sunny morning in 1922 while Quashein handed out prohibition violations like raffle tickets, Bill Plagun wired a bomb under his driver's seat. There were no witnesses. When Quashein turned the key in the ignition, his body blew apart. It was the last time a court parking lot was left unattended. When he was brought in for questioning, Bill Plagun admitted to running rum off Jester Straits the day of the killing. The public was outraged, but many rejoiced with a drink. After a police lineup, the district attorney pinned its case on a random colored hood they had at county to silence the masses and close the record.

Bill Plagun met Minnie Rupertina when he was eighteen. She was two years younger and the daughter of Good Leaf police sergeant George Rupertina. Mr. Rupertina made his objections known. He would never bless his daughter's marriage to a reputed gangster. Within two years, he would meet his demise but not to Bill Plagun like many might have suspected. George Rupertina excelled at keeping his crutch a secret—never kept the stuff in the house, worked long hours—but the inquest gave him away as a heavy drinker who threw in the towel to cirrhosis. To show his level of affection for Minnie and his grace for the late Mr. Rupertina, Bill Plagun made sure that Minnie's mother was set up right the rest of her years. He bought her an apartment on East Leaf and paid for a live-in butler.

A beautiful girl in Bill's eyes, Minnie was sickly and frail. She spent many of her early years in bed as a lunger and later contracted polio. As time wore on, her body shriveled but not before she was able to give Bill two healthy boys. Bill loved Minnie more than anything in the world. She was dealt a bad hand, but not one day passed without seeing a smile on her face. She was a fighter. It's what attracted Bill the most. In return, Minnie adored Bill. It didn't matter what he did for a living, even if she didn't agree with it all the time. Each man's life was arbitrary, and justice was as relative as his position in time and space.

In the summer of 1927, Bill and Minnie were expecting their third child. She had dreamed of a healthy daughter but knew chances were slim. Bill just wanted her to get through a day without crying. A small swig of heroine, the races at the Caurimare Hippodrome and the carnival on Strobile Island always seemed to cheer her up.

Of all the traveling circuses to pass through the Leaf, the House of Heroes Carnival was a fixture of fascination. It had all the motley mainstays of a mad scientist's living room. Miniature lions one could carry on their shoulders, trunkless elephant pyramids, fox-trotting horses, a terrier that killed a hundred rats in sixty seconds, three-legged acrobats, flame-throats, lively coffins, calliopes surrounded by janiceps clowns and plenty of pickled punks. Bill Plagun called them the born losers. Like Wanda Winger, the woman with slitlike pupils who grew feathered shoots from her shoulder blades to her wrists. She could suspend herself in the air from a standing position for up to three seconds. Then there was Piel Notengo, a man born without an epidermis, his entire vascular system open to the air. Only he never bled. And Nid Chara, the spiders' man. They lived in every orifice of his body. He'd reveal his arm pits to gardens of web spinners, his mouth, nostrils, ears, belly button and especially his groin and inside his buttocks. Even Blimp U, the male ton. His weight was only surpassed by his temper. For a nickel, a contestant could razz Blimp for sixty seconds straight, no holds barred, in the hopes of getting a rise. The prize was twenty-four ounces of arterial clog known as the "Corny Slurp" that most chunked in the trash. Digs at his mother, diet and bra size were most common. That is until Blimp got his revenge and unleashed the full weight of his rage. He took his steak knife and stabbed straight into his gut, exploding like a beached whale all over an audience of a hundred. They had to close down the carnival for two days to clean it up but could never fully get rid of the smell. These characters were all beautiful to Bill Plagun in their own grotesque way, but more importantly, they reminded him of Minnie in the greatest respect: They all fought for survival in a world that had already cast them out. There was little reason for any of those freaks to stay alive, and yet, they were there (Blimp U aside), year after year, proving to all why they still had a right to the same air. Somehow, Bill always thought that showing Minnie people worse off would make her feel better. But it wasn't the oddities that cheered Minnie up as much as her husband's undying efforts.

Bill rolled Minnie in her wheelchair. She showed a six-month belly. Her legs were weak and soft but not fat. In fact, for a pregnant woman of sedentary custom, Minnie was gaunt as a stick. Her hair was now brittle and thinning. Bill couldn't bear to see her deteriorate and knew that her days were numbered.

"Come on, sport. Let her have it. What's it hurt you?" Bill said to the *3 STRIKES* game operator. Minnie had missed every bottle by a mile. The game operator shook his head and said: "Better luck next time." This upset Bill. He rolled Minnie away, far enough to keep her senses guessing, and then returned to the sweaty man in pants too tight for his undercarriage. He leaped over the table, pinched the fat-ass by his scruff and ran his head through the bottles. Plenty saw it. No one said a word. "You made her day," Bill said. Then he stuffed the man's jar with fifty bucks—enough to buy every doll on the wall and pay for two booths. In exchange, he took one plush, pink bear in a red cup. It was the littlest one of the bunch and held a frownie where the smile normally went. Minnie's face lit up with color. She didn't ask how Bill had won it. She knew it was probably dishonest, but that's what made Bill a champion. After all, the rules, especially their loopholes, were made for those who made them. Seeing the smile on Minnie's face was all he could ever want.

They strolled through the carnival, the carousel, the clowns in a kaleidoscope of colors, balloons, the smells of roasted peanuts and caramel popcorn, a band of mermen and sirens playing hackneyed melodies on their harps and mandolins. It all transported them to a magical place, Bill right behind Minnie, pushing her into another day. Most would clear a path for them, some wouldn't, but Bill would keep his cool. He never made a scene in front of his wife. He simply rolled her around the obstacles.

They came to a seat on a bench. Minnie feathered her mouth with cotton candy. Bill stared at her with misty eyes and told her how much he loved her. She responded in typical Minnie fashion, telling Bill not to be such a sap. It brought a hearty laugh and even though he had a wife that was on the losing end of life, at that very moment, everything was perfect.

"How's your belly?" Bill asked.

"She's doing fine."

"How do you know it's a girl?"

"She talks to me when you're not around. Tells me she wants to be a gymnast in the Olympics, says you should stop smoking those cigars before they turn you into a wrinkled, old prune."

"Backtalking just like her mother." Bill chuckled, tossed his cigar to the ground and grinded it with a shoe.

Later that night, Bill, Minnie, Buddy and Junior Plagun sat to a fine dinner at the Arm Hotel restaurant. It had all the makings of a posh joint, namely because it allowed drinking, the booze provided by Bill Plagun. Bill sat at the head of the table. Buddy sat at the tail. Minnie drank club soda. Junior was on his third highball to fend off the boredom of sitting with people he was related to that he couldn't relate to. Buddy hadn't touched a bite on his plate, and Bill kept tabs. Mank Mill approached the table and whispered something in Bill's ear. Bill gave Buddy a furtive glance. Buddy popped from his place and followed Mank back to a phone booth in the lobby. Then Lieutenant, Sert Johnson was standing by. He was in civilian duds and hid his eyes under the lip of his fedora.

"Tonight. The row," Johnson said with a toneless voice. Buddy handed Lt. Johnson a small envelope. There was no confirming what was inside. Johnson knew the exact price for the information he had just delivered, and the expectation was clear that Buddy knew it too.

Buddy returned to his food and dug in like it was his first meal in days. His chop steak and asparagus disappeared in less than two minutes. He hadn't even bothered to look up once while he scarfed up his grub. Bill noticed. Buddy wiped his mouth clean, then turned his chin up and nodded to his father. He stood and went straight for Minnie with a kiss to the top of her head. Bill noticed again. He excused himself from the table and followed Buddy out. They seemed to be chasing the clock.

Junior was annoyed to be left with his mother. It was a habit he wasn't fond of. He knew his father thought him the weaker strain, and that's why he was never brought in on any of their important dealings. He finished his highball and stood from the table. There was no kiss goodbye. He just couldn't look at her with a straight face knowing that in an hour he'd be knee deep in smut.

- 68 -

Ziggie Fist loved denting the heads of hoods. He was a war hero in 1918 before joining the Good Leaf Police. He served another couple of years as commander on the vice squad, and his track record was unblemished. He took no bribes. The government took notice. "If you want a free country, lock up all the bad guys." That was his opening statement during his interview to head up the new agency called G.A.V. (Guards Against Vice). He was hired on the spot. It was the first program of its kind, and its sole aim was to cripple the liquor trade. The agency consisted of ten former blue coats and ex-warriors. Ziggie Fist was the toughest of them all. He was a hard man of a mustache on a clean shave. His square-rimmed spectacles gave off the glint of prosecution. His eyes wrath blue. He didn't care to put his life on the line for the sake of patriotic duty. He had lost a wife, but it wasn't to booze. It was to work. When asked to join up with the Coast Watch off the Leaf in an effort to put the Cabra and Plagun organizations out of business, Fist dove in head first.

Tonight Fist was on patrol in Breaks Harbor. They were four degrees west of Runner's Row. Their six-bitter skimmed the waters like a gigantic kayak. Any minute now they'd run into the largest bust in G.A.V.'s infant history. The tip from a reliable source was that a small armada of Cabra freighters was overdue. A Breaks police boat spotted the patrol vessel and flashed its main light ten times. It was a friendly gesture and kept police and Coast Watch from blasting each other to smithereens. The police boat trolled towards them. Fist noticed it approaching and warned his men to keep their wits about them. When the boat was within range, a uniformed policeman started yelling: "We got Cabra!"

Fist was charged like a predator on the kill. He needed to see the gangster's face because even though Cabra was known to sail with his own shipments, the chances of catching him on the waters these days were slim to none. The policeman moored their boat against the six-bitter. He kept his arms out in the open and an eye on the manned gun aimed in his general direction. Another coast watcher turned the large spotlight on the police boat. "We got Cabra on board. Two of his freighters slipped through, but we got the dock sealed off."

One of the coast watchers hooked a small ramp connecting the two boats. Two others, their shotguns firm in hand, boarded the police boat, followed by Fist with his large lamp blazing his trail.

"Show me his body," Fist ordered with an orotund inflection. This would make him a double hero and propel him to the highest ranks of office. The Breaks policeman walked Fist into the large cabin. It was dark. Fist pointed his lamp at the void and swung a leg in, followed closely by his two guards. The light shattered off, and Roman candles crackled blinding white throughout the black cabin.

A watcher on the six-bitter was heard yelling: "They hit Fist!"

Two "policemen" shot out of the cabin spraying their submachines at the six-bitter. The man at the main gun was cut down first, then the lamplighter. The police boarded the patrol boat and killed the remaining crew. Seven coast watchers in all, dead.

After the job was done, the two cops returned for their remaining partner. He was hit bad and streaking blood all over the boat. His two partners helped him onto the six-bitter and then onto the small speed boat anchored starboard. One of the cops cranked the winch and lowered his injured accomplice and partner into the water. He then climbed over the ledge and fell on board. They unhooked the boat and fired up the engine for a quick getaway. There were no witnesses, just like with Judge Quashein, but this time Bill Plagun had taken the worst of it.

"Just hold on," Mank Mill said in his blue coat. He pushed the speedboat to the limit. The Breaks dock was within range, but Bill Plagun was slipping fast.

An hour earlier, all Met wanted to do was hide from that ominous feeling that this was his last night on the Leaf, but the puffed-up moon highlighted him out and in the open. He had been pacing the Breaks docks for over an hour. He had kept his head clear. No jujus or hooch tonight. If they had called him here to be popped, then he needed to be about his senses if he stood any chance at making a run for it. He knew better than to bring a gun. If anything he would beg for mercy and put the whole thing on Pap. He didn't know what had become of Pap but was sure that he was feeding worms out in Jester. A car pulled up with two men inside. It was Mank Mill and Buddy Plagun. They got out. Mank Mill was dressed like a cop.

Buddy tossed Met a police uniform, complete with hat, belt and badge. "Smart you didn't disappear like that chickenshit pantywaist. Put that on." Met had questions, but he didn't dare ask. Instead he did what he was told, took his clothes off to his long johns and put on the copper outfit.

A police boat inched to the dock and came to a stop yards from them. Buddy and Mank observed it like it was right on time. Buddy handed Met a chopper. "You handle one of these?"

"Sure," Met said. He was relieved that he wasn't going to be killed on the spot. It was a hit instead. "Who's the job?"

"Don't worry, Egg, it ain't your brother," Bill said as he stepped off the moored boat. He was fully cloaked inside police issue, but he still harbored the face of a gangster. There was nothing honest about his eyes except the death they carried. He pointed to the open water. "Fist likes to park about two miles out and cutterize ships along the row. He never turns on his lamps. One of these days he's gonna crash into a freighter." He passed a picture of Ziggie Fist to Met. "Memorize that face. Wait till he's inside our cabin. He'll be traveling with at least seven strong. Mank will back us up. You unload with everything you got. If at any time, fear starts to settle in, remember: You can only get killed once."

"Can I talk to you for a second?" Buddy asked Bill. They walked off from Mank and Met. "What's this?" Buddy said observing Bill's police uniform. "You said Jesse Under was bringing a crew. You'd be waiting in Johnson's office."

"Change of plans. Evidently no one has the balls to square off with Fist," said Bill.

"What about Mank, that punk, Fanti?"

"Won't be enough. We're already underhanded as it is, and we won't get another crack at it."

"Then I'm going too."

"Nix. You stay in the car, and wait for us. That's an order."

"Fuck that," Buddy said. "You stay here. I'm going out."

"The hell you are," Bill responded.

"This is fuckin' bullshit! I swear to God…"

"Hey! Don't make me belt you. I still can, you know." Bill acknowledged the worry growing on his son's face. "It'll be plenty worth it. Keep everything on ice, and I'll be right back." Bill gave Buddy a hug and told him to be ready.

Buddy returned to the car and slipped in between an alley with a view of the dock. He fried a fag and thought about everything that was about to happen. He considered best and worst case scenarios. He thought about Cabra and all the promises he had made the night before. "We won't put a toe south of the Twig. We'll give up control on the Breaks/Jester border. You keep all your routes, and we'll fork over $1,000,000 so you can finish up your still." Bill Plagun assured that there would be no backlash against Cabra or his operations. They had two fall guys in Pap and Met Fanti. With Pap on the lam, Met would take the rap. Bill was willing to let go of Mank Mill too. He had been complaining too much, saying he wanted a crew of his own and thought it was time to break apart from the Plaguns. Buddy didn't trust him, called him the 'son of Judas.' Bill promised Mank that after the job, he could do whatever he wanted with Plagun's blessing. It was a lie. Mank Mill was too valuable to Bill to let go. He could kill a man on call and then sit to a meal like nothing had happened. It was not uncommon for Mank to enjoy a bite right next to his victims, blood still fresh on the same fingertips that clamped a sausage sandwich or a chicken leg. He was well suited for a more primitive time, and Bill needed him on the streets, shaking down businesses that wouldn't yield to Plagun's demands for protection money and hideouts for Plagun's growing enterprise. And that's the one thing that had Buddy in a twist. Aside from Mank Mill, they had a dozen button men that should have jumped at a job like this. Why did his father have to be so foolhardy? Just like Judge Quashein, Bill Plagun couldn't trust personal vendettas to other people. He hadn't even bothered putting the word out. His beef with Commodore Cabra was no longer just business. He knew that Cabra had more muscle in the police and would soon squeeze Plagun out for good. Plagun couldn't let his family go hungry, even if he knew Minnie didn't have much time, and that's probably what made the choice as easy. Something about burying his wife went beyond the pale of what Bill considered a tolerable life experience. He would rather sacrifice himself first in what was destined to be a suicide mission. He had the balls for it.

When Bill Plagun arrived on the dock washed in blood, he was moments from death. Mank Mill threw Bill over his shoulder and into the back seat of the car, then returned to the police boat and headed back out to the Row to dump bodies. It probably saved Mank's life. Buddy went ballistic, pointed fingers and gun barrels. He vowed to take Met out as soon as they got Bill to the hospital. Met pleaded, said he had nothing to do with the accident. Bill pardoned Met of any wrongdoing. He commanded Buddy to let go of all beefs and watch after his mother and brother. Buddy had to stick around to make sure the family had a fighting chance. Met sat next to Bill like he had never witnessed a man in the slow act of dying. In fact, it was his first. The dark blue uniform and golden badge were soaked in blood and long before they got to the hospital, the life was gone from him.

When Minnie Plagun found out, she vowed to fight on, give birth to their third child and raise a world champion gymnast. The child was a girl just as she had predicted, but still born. Minnie managed to last another two years on a steady dose of heroin before she joined Bill Plagun in that place where fights were of no further application.

- 69 -

Junior Plagun had one major problem. It would keep him from storming behind Bill and Buddy into the family business. He was scared of guns. As much as he hated his mother for falling victim to a crippling fate, he despised himself even greater that he walked with sturdy legs and a straight back and was more of a gimp. Bill Plagun never busted his chops over it. Though he spoke of courage and cowardice ad nauseam, he never wanted his own sons to wrestle with life's perils. They weren't educated men, didn't attend big schools, none of the Plaguns. As much as Bill wanted his heirs to be of influence with their words, he knew they had a few blood-stained generations to go. But Junior Plagun held to his own beliefs, and they didn't cause Bill any sleepless nights about him catching a bullet, maybe just syphilis. Junior liked dressing up in his flashy threads, his gourmet dinners and the lush-living of loose women.

Buddy, on the other hand, wasn't long for this world. He was the kind of man who would take on a group of thugs all by himself, win, lose or draw. He rarely lost. He roared like an eight cylinder and always hit first. The Plagun gene was cursed with aggression, which is why Junior's placid nature was equally anomalous and welcome. "You'll be bigger than me and your brother. You'll be more than a man with a gun," Bill would tell Junior. It was the nice way to say that his four-flusher son would be invited to feed off the kill only after it was dead. As things stood, he might just outlast them all and break the curse.

"Take it easy. The old man wouldn't want you to lose your head over some bum grifter. I say we stay out of it and let the gun-hips do their job," Junior said. He had a cold beer in his hand. The loss of his father hadn't touched him with the ferocity that it did Buddy. Junior was somber only because he was in the company of men he considered unappealing. He couldn't wait to get to a club, somewhere with plenty of fresh tail and celebration, anything to take his mind off this shit. Minnie Plagun was in the hospital being treated for a nervous breakdown, and Junior didn't care to follow her in. He knew if he kept around there much longer he might.

Buddy was a bull elephant in musth. It didn't matter that Bill Plagun decided such an easy fate. There were two others on that boat, and they walked out without a kiss mark. Why his father? It was a reminder to Buddy that their lives were not intended to last long. But while they were around, no one was going to fuck with them. He marched across the room and clapped Junior in the head, spilling his beer all over the floor. Mank Mill tried to keep a straight face. He had just lost a friend in Bill, but he couldn't help but grin at seeing Buddy paw Junior like a bitch. Jesse Under ignored the two like usual. He respected them enough to know that this didn't concern him. If he had to side with one, it would always be Buddy, but the night of the Fist hit, Bill ordered Jesse to stick around Junior for protection.

Jesse Under was another one of those small men that didn't wait on backup to strike a gang. He was half Mank's size except on the night he slit his throat. Bill had adopted him as a third son when he discovered him lifting a case of Cabra scotch at the age of 10. He had always been a dependable kid, and of all the enforcers Buddy ran with, he knew he could count on Jesse the most.

Buddy poked the barrel of his gun into Junior's cheek. "Stay out of it? Keep me under the covers? That's the respect you show your father? You lose your balls inside one of those drip holes? Or am I wrong to think you ever had a pair? The only reason your father's dead is because that breathing cocksucker failed to pull the trigger, sat in this very room and called us all pussy faggots. That means nothing to you?"

Junior let Buddy turn his head to the side as he kept shoving the rod deeper into his face. He didn't say another word. It would only heat Buddy up.

Mank's smirk disappeared. He kept a careful watch but knew not to gum up. This was between the brothers. Jesse glanced over to Mank Mill just to make sure he was checked. He had seen Buddy rough Junior up in the past, and if today he decided to raise the level, Jesse wouldn't stand in the way.

Buddy continued to burn Junior's ear. "There's gonna come a day when the steel will be your only friend, so you two better get acquainted before long."

He slid his piece away from Junior and holstered it back into his waist. He shot an eye to Mank Mill in a display of dominance. Mank was quick to move his gaze elsewhere. It didn't matter that he could snap Buddy's spine if provoked. He was smart enough to show respect when all eyes were on him.

Junior let a tear escape. It was for his father. It was for Buddy. It was for being born into a family of heathens. He stood up and excused himself from the room but not before saying: "I hope you kill him until he's dead."

Buddy stared Junior out the door and then gave Jesse the order. The contract on Pap Fanti was $5,000.

A week later, Buddy got the tip he was waiting for. Pap Fanti was holed up with Lou Licks in West Leaf. It had been a passive week, all things considered. Ziggie Fist and Bill Plagun cancelled each other out in the eyes of the law and public opinion. There were no other suspects in the paper but Commodore Cabra. Cabra's alibi cooled him off some—he was at a police function—but it tarnished his reputation, and he needed Buddy to know that this "favor" did more damage than good. The million bucks for the Plagun distillery was on permanent hold. All that did for Buddy was strengthen his resolve for justice or vengeance or whatever he decided to call it that day.

Pap had been promoted from mediocrity to marked man overnight. The only thing that brought him any sense of joy was his new bear and his daily marvels. He had learned to play a few notes on the hunting horn all by himself. Lou even swore he saw the bear reading one of his many books one random Tuesday. But the thing that got them the most was when the bear opened its snout and verbalized a completed thought, thanking Lou and Pap for a meal. It made Pap jumpier than it did Lou.

"Are you sure we're safe here?" Pap asked.

Lou modeled one of his guns and asked Pap the same question. Pap was lucky to have such a friend.

As night fell, Pap and the bear slept on the couch. Lou lied in his bed reading Don Quesilio until he was out. He kept the window open to let in the night's breath. The halls were hot and airless and quiet enough to hear a man's thoughts.

Thirty minutes into his slumber, Lou heard footsteps creaking down the hall. He shot up and thumbed the light. His face was dripping with sweat. He hurried to get his pants and shoes on but didn't have time to get a shirt. Pap and the bear slept through it. Lou grabbed a pistol and made the room go black. In less than one second, his front door was blasted at the handle and kicked open. Three shots flashed in. Two flashed out. The bear cuffed and bleated and panted. Lou turned on the light and looked to Pap. He was hit right below his hip and leaking badly. The bear appeared to be unharmed. It made a dash under the bed and started trembling. Lou looked to the culprit. Like father, like son. Buddy Plagun was popped in the stomach and through the clavicle. Lou threw his head out the door to make sure there were no more torpedoes down the hall.

Then he kicked Buddy square across the face before rushing back to Pap. He was fading fast; the blood from his hip was mixing with sweat. Lou hoisted him up and out. Buster grabbed his horn and followed them. They got into Pap's car and drove off without a second to lose. They left everything in the apartment and would now be wanted for the murder of Buddy Plagun. Lou Licks hadn't bargained for this, but he didn't run from it either. Pap was his friend, and he swore to back him up no matter what, ever since their pig-jacking days.

When the scorchers arrived, they found Buddy Plagun clinging to life in a cherry puddle. They rushed him to a hospital where he spent six months in recovery. He was booked and charged with possession of an unlicensed firearm, attempted murder and a few other gems for good measure, including conspiracy to hit Fist. Buddy would eventually learn that Cabra was the stool pigeon that sang him guilty. Lt. Sert Johnson was a surprise character witness for the defense. Basil Demur brought him in knowing he could help get Buddy off the hook. He wasn't cheap. Johnson testified that Buddy Plagun was only acting in self defense against violent street thugs that would soon pay for their crimes. Buddy was depicted as an honest citizen, caught in the wrong place at the wrong time. "Let's not impute his father's crimes onto him." But that's exactly what happened when the jury was switched out on the eve of trial by a judge with no affinity for Plagun politics. Buddy got ten years (reduced to three) and word through the grapevine that Pazo Fanti was dead.

- 70 -

The streets were nervous and painful to the touch. Each passing manhole was a vent on a pressure cooker about to explode. A shirtless madman, Lou Licks hid his large head behind the wheel. He kept clinging to the thought that a slug would pierce his windshield until they got over the Twig Bridge. The bear curled up next to Pap in the back seat, giving off soft, comforting sounds from his throat. Somehow the bear had known that the wound on Pap's hip was a bad thing. He applied pressure with the furry part of his paw in an effort to stop the bleeding. Pap had checked out, and Lou had no idea whether it had been permanently.

Within a half hour they approached the old farm where they spent the best of their childhood days. The farm of Lou's grandmother. When Lou pulled up to the entrance, there was a large sign by the mailbox: BANK OWNED - KEEP OUT! Lou ignored it and drove around to the barn. He screeched to a halt, sending clouds of dust into the stifling night air. The car's headlights shined on the barn door. A galaxy of insects hovered throughout. Moths and mosquitoes had a field day with Lou's bare top and Pap's wound. The door was unlocked. Lou shoved it open. Slices of moonlight crept through the decaying timbers. A stray dog was nursing pups in a corner. The bear noticed but would have no business disturbing it. It was worth ignoring. A nest of owls shrieked in the rafters and jetted towards the exit.

The calligraphy of a thousand spiders decorated the barn's walls and the old horse stalls. Lou opened one and set Pap down on the ground. Then he returned to the car. They had no lamps, so Lou drove the car into the barn and pointed the headlights into the stall. It was the first time he got a clear view of the gunshot wound. It was worse than he thought, right below the hip and lodged deep in the upper part of his thigh. The closest Lou had come to playing doctor was when he would deliver calves with his grandmother. If he didn't act quickly to remove the bullet and stop the bleeding, his friend would die. Pap was mumbling in and out of consciousness. Lou searched for something befitting a tourniquet. He broke off a piece of wood from the horse stall and slid Pap's pants to his ankles. His boxers were soaked in blood. Lou used the pants to fasten the stick around the leg. Pap wasn't resisting. Lou returned to the car in search of surgical tools. All he found was a wrench and a cross-head screwdriver. The bear wouldn't leave Pap's side no matter what. Lou dug up some rope from the adjoining stall and tied Pap's legs to the door handle as tight as he could. Then he popped the hood and touched the screwdriver and wrench against the exhaust manifold until they were red-iron hot. It was now or never. He took the sterilized tools and penetrated Pap's leg. It was the first time Pap came out of his coma. His roar originated in the lowest part of his diaphragm and frightened the bear and any other living creature within a hundred yards. He tried to kick free but the taut rope kept his legs secured like a calf. Buster could do nothing more than watch with misty eyes. With one gasp, Pap fainted. Lou had free reign to finish the procedure.

Five minutes later, he pulled the remaining fragments of the bullet head out and fell against the wall in a worn-out heap. He needed to clean Pap up before infection took residence. The bear kept a worried gaze on him the whole time.

"He's gonna be alright. Stay here with him," Lou told the bear.

The bear nodded. Again, it didn't surprise Lou much. He could remember animals nodding at him during his farm days. Lou took a crusty bucket and hurried to the faucet on the wall. It would be a miracle, but the water was still running. He filled up the bucket and rushed back, giving Pap a good rinse until the blood was off. Lou scoured the barn for something to cover Pap. He found an old horse blanket and shielded the wounded leg with it. Then he fashioned a poncho for himself. There was little more he could do but pray.

The rest of the night dealt Pap with an unbridled fever. He shivered in and out of light. Then a dream took him away. His bear was playing a trumpet as beautifully as he had ever heard. It was soft and soothing; the melodies spoke of a future where there was no more suffering. Pap felt like he was floating, leaving the world and everything behind it.

Two days later, Pap came around and opened his eyes. The bear was standing next to him playing his hunting horn in an incredulous way. Hunting horns were only capable of so many variations, but the bear ran the gamut of conceivable melodies.

"He hasn't stopped for two days. It's a wonder no one heard us," Lou said.

As the days moved on, Pap regained his strength. The bear continued to dumbfound them with his horn. He was now speaking in sentences. They were rough like that of a small child, but he could articulate most any thought except a complaint. The bear never complained. When he wasn't playing his horn, he was tending to Pap, bringing him wild berries or water. He had even learned to share a joke or two like Lou had taught him.

"Two Plaguns rob a bank. One cut a hole in the wall to get in. The other cut a new hole to get moving. I mean escape. I mean out. Oh boy, I think that came out wrong," Buster said. It had them busting up inside. The bear was more human each day. Pap called him an undercover angel. Without his calming tunes, he may not have made it through, swore it was the cool rhythms that chilled his feverish blood.

"Can you tell us what you are?" Pap asked the bear. Only the bear didn't have an answer. The question would cause more confusion than clarity. The bear was intelligent enough to acknowledge himself as a creature of thought. He <u>was</u> because he thought, but in those considerations he was no different than Pap or Lou. He had yet to come across the truth of a mirror, and even when he first set eyes on himself, he seemed to look beyond any reflection to something deeper, that trait that allowed him to bond with his human caretakers. Pap would soon stop asking the questions. He had taken it as simple fact that this bear-like creature was nothing more than a blessing in his life. He played his hunting horn like nothing he had ever heard before. It was obvious he had an ear for the sort of sounds that brought great pleasure. He told many stories every time he played, tales of adventure, romance and love. Lou saw money signs without appreciating the problem.

"What happens the first time someone sees him play that thing? Did you think about that?" Pap asked. The bear would be taken away, picked and prodded by the government until it was dead. They couldn't run with this act and expect it to last long.

Pap urged patience but knew they couldn't hang around the sticks much longer. They were once again living on the neighbors' hogs. Lou would steal them in the night, just like he did as a kid, and after they were sliced into chops and bacon, he would grill them over the manifold. The only hitch was that every time they cooked, Lou had to start the car and let it run. This required fuel, and they were running low.

A month later, Pap was back on his feet, gimpy and sore, but the wound had healed in its own primitive way. The bear's talents developed as fast as his frame. Now standing at over three feet, Lou credited his growth spurt to the bacon. Pap credited the bear with keeping him far from the clutches of a deep depression. In fact, it forced Pap to seek out a man he could trust as much as Lou but with the mind to maybe make a difference.

The lawyer, Basil Demur, was the closest thing to a brother Pap had next to Met. He'd go as far as to admit that, next to Lou, he trusted Basil the most. His family owned the local Y where he and Met stayed as kids. Basil would often come down and shoot hoops with the boys. Pap always accused Basil of cheating during heated scrimmages. Basil always denied. One day, Met and Pap found themselves on the wrong side of a hamburger stand owner. They had ordered a couple of burgers with all the fixings without the money to cover. The owner threatened to have them hauled off in a paddy wagon until Basil bailed them out. He paid the man double to cover any restitution. A whole forty cents. That act earned Pap's trust. Basil found a perfect calling in the law. He was a master at the slippery denial. 'Cutors couldn't get their hands around his clients. And when they finally did, he'd bribe the necessary doorstops with all sorts of concessions, favors and cash. Pap had no clue what had become of Basil's life. He left Lou with the bear and drove back to the Leaf on fumes. Pap found Basil inside the East Leaf Telephone Directory and made the call. After telling Basil he had something important to share, Pap received a warm invitation to his first office on the Eastside.

"Word on the street was you were dead," Basil said.

"It'd be better to keep it that way. You hear who it was?"

"It was all over the papers. Bill and Buddy Plagun, Ziggie Fist. Those names ring a bell?"

"Like a cathedral at noon. I see you done good for yourself. I knew you always had it in you." Pap sat across Basil and observed as the lawyer took to a breakfast of cocktails.

"I hit pay dirt when they dried up the Leaf," Basil said. "Pap Fanti, old pal, it's been years."

"Is Buddy Plagun dead?" Pap asked.

"Might as well be. Gastado for ten. That was in the papers too. Knowing him, he'll shank someone in the yard and extend his stay to life. Where have you been?"

"Out in the sticks."

"You got yourself some beef. What are you doing mixing with Plagun? I never took you for a gangster."

"I got a small favor to ask."

"This ain't Castillian's hamburger stand."

"I know. I got this thing. I want you to see it."

"I'm a lawyer, not a doctor."

"I'm serious."

"So am I. What is it?"

"I can't explain. You just have to come and check for yourself. I wouldn't waste your time if I didn't think you might take a shine to it, but it has to be soon."

"You find a spaceman or something?"

"Maybe. Oh, and I need you to bring a radio."

"We going dancing?"

"Just trust me. It'll change your perspective on things." Pap gave him the address.

Basil agreed and stopped by the farm hours later. Pap had him sit down on a flipped bucket, but Basil insisted on standing. He didn't come to dirty his duds. Lou was seated nearby. They were introduced for the first time, even though they had met many years ago at the Y. Lou was wary of the lawyer, even made sure to shake his right hand with a gun in his left. The bear was nowhere to be seen.

"Alright, whatever you do, swear you won't come apart here," Pap said.

"Pull the drapes off already. Time is money. I defended a woman once charged with cannibalizing her own baby. Trust me when I say I've seen it all," Basil said.

"Not this time, Salmon." Pap pulled the tickler knob on Basil's old Crosley and tuned it to a jazz program. "Come on out, Buster."

The bear hobbled out from the adjacent horse stall on his hind legs, his hunting horn stuffed in his snout blowing in harmony to the radio transmission. It sent a surge of electricity down Basil's spine. It should have still been shocking Pap, but he sat there like it was the only thing he expected to happen, a bear playing a hunting horn like he was part of the radio band. Pap looked to Basil. His reaction would tell him everything, whether he believed in God, whether there was heaven and hell, whether everything he had ever known was real or whether reality was nothing more than the illusion of some chaotic imagination. Basil took that seat on the bucket. He almost lost his balance; his eyes couldn't come off the bear. A cigarette was begging for him. He lighted it and inhaled with everything in his lungs. The questioned look in Basil's eyes confirmed to Pap that he was hooked.

"What's the roll?" Basil asked. It was his last attempt at calling Pap out on logic.

"It's no shrimp in a suit," Pap said.

"No, it's not," Basil said through a measured breath as he evaluated the bear. The chilled sallow clumps of matted fuzz, extending to their tips and branching out to threads, fine and reserved. Not explicitly coarse but thick enough to give a straight razor fits. Those committed hands that wrung the horn, like stumps, crawling under an albino landscape, nails pencil-black, pencil-points, yet soft as dandelion seeds parachuting in the breeze. Lips, made of tar, formed a seal around the mouthpiece with the fervor of a suckling infant.

"Put a paw on him," Pap said. "His name is Buster. He likes it. Doesn't bite. Doesn't fuss. I think he's one of those circus bears or something."

"Circus bear? I don't know people that can do that," Basil said with eyes fixated on the bear. Buster continued to play through their chatter and, with each stanza, seemed to gain another technique.

"You're not lit, right?" Pap asked.

"No, but I need to be and fast," Basil said.

"Then you got nothing to blame. Look at him."

"Where did you find this?"

"You wouldn't believe it if I told you."

"You're probably right."

Suddenly, the wheels in Basil's mind were turning. All feelings of horror and fear dissipated with his springs of cigarette smoke. Basil was at ease, almost humored by the beast. But such a refined creature could hardly be called a beast. "You need to get this Gabriel a real horn. He looks like a trumpet player."

"Nice call, but I'm on the nut," Pap said.

Basil pulled his wallet from his coat. It was another scorching day, but Basil didn't come out of his coat. He slipped a couple of twenties to Pap. Not once did he take his hypnotized eyes off the bear. "Get him something to eat too. He looks hungry. I'll be back tonight." Basil took out a pen from his pocket and wrote blind on the back of a business card. The eyes stayed their course. "Better yet, come to my office. Make it after nine when the halls are clear. Make sure you doll him up. I don't care how hot it is. I want people to mistake him for a midget." He handed the card to Pap and stood, but the eyes remained on Buster. His mind had completely lost track that Pap was just at his office a few hours earlier and knew the exact location without the card or the written directions. It was all the bear's fault. "Whatever you do, don't tell another soul."

"He'll make us all a mint, you think?" Lou asked. He felt like a passenger about to miss a train that both Basil and Pap were boarding.

"Remember, after nine," Basil told Pap, seemingly ignoring Lou.

Now Lou truly disliked the lawyer. But it didn't matter as long as Pap was in charge. Basil took a few close steps towards the bear like he was approaching some sort of deity. He got within a foot. Buster acknowledged him by prostrating his head under Basil's right hand. The whole time he was playing his hunting horn. Basil blew a girlish giggle. Pap had been running for his life, but the entire moment had just made him very stable. Lou rolled his eyes with a twinkle of envy.

As he drove off, Basil couldn't disengage from the image of that musical bear. He went straight to his office and tried to get ginned, but no matter how much he put down, his thoughts were straight. What the hell was going on? The government had been dropping hints about Martians invading the earth, but this thing was magnificently terrestrial. What's more, it filled Basil with a peace he had never known as long as he had been practicing. This could be bigger than any case he'd ever take. Somehow, he felt compelled to help Pap once more like he had during the Castillian hamburger caper. He had to figure a way to make the bear noticeable without jeopardizing the whole act and putting any of the players in danger. If Basil Demur knew people for one thing, it was their gift for gab. Once news of a musical bear hit the Leaf, Buster would be torn apart for the sake of science and religion. The press would be in a state of frenzy, and Pap would sleep on a bed of nails. For a split second he had wished he hadn't told Pap to come to his office. If Buddy Plagun knew Basil was mixing with Fanti, he could sound the death knell. The bear kept taking center stage in Basil's thoughts. And so started one of the most unpredictable experiments known to man.

Basil knew that in order to stack the odds in their favor, the environments for showcasing the bear had to be fully controlled, if one could regulate such a thing. Basil decided to start small. He moved Pap, Lou and the bear into the basement of the one apartment building he owned south of downtown. From here, the bear would play his horn for an audience of five, including Pap, Lou and Basil. The other two were Basil's cousins, trusted women who fell in love with Buster at first sight. There were no nerves, no squeamishness. It was a bear, both adorable and docile, with a talent for electrifying his trumpet. It took him one whole day to get used to the customized finger buttons. This cost more than the two sawbucks Basil paid, but he had no issue shelling out another $500 to make it easier on the bear. That was more than most new cars those days. When Buster finally got used to the valves, they had trouble shutting him up. Some of Basil's tenants started complaining, so he moved Pap and his bear to another place. This would happen once a week. Pap, Lou and Buster travelled light in anticipation of their next move. The shows all took place in basements. Basil scouted buildings around the Leaf, most were on the Southside where he knew he could control any dissenters through police intimidation.

Five turned to seven turned to ten. Basil charged a small fee to start. The invitations were all made under the strictest privacy. Basil would have candidates visit his office for a "consultation." They were people Basil felt would appreciate the novelty (who wouldn't?), who would pay money to see him (who wouldn't?), and who would keep their traps shut (who could?). That became the central issue with Buster and later with Mr. Crooner. After a few moves, Basil figured to accompany Buster's trumpet with a full band. Then Pap could start his own club and make it official. Basil would run it behind the scenes, and they could make a small fortune together. Offering exclusive memberships to a private club where only the privileged would be acknowledged. Basil pulled out his contact lists and went to work.

It was now 10:30 pm. Fans blew warm air throughout Basil's office. Pap and Buster sat side by side. Buster was inside of a fat woman's dress with a thick scarf around his neck and a baggy paperboy. It was the only thing Pap could snag that afternoon without needing a tailor. It looked awful, and Buster was panting to cool off. But he was hep to the drill, had even insisted they leave it on him until they returned to the barn. His speech was improving by the hour.

Basil had his whole plan scribbled on his brain, but when he saw Buster again, he couldn't help but attempt a conversation. He had forgotten the prior shock of witnessing an animal with human qualities for when Buster said, "How you doin'?" Basil answered, "Ducky." Buster fell in the love with the word and would use it ever since.

Pap was worried about putting on full shows on the Leaf. The exposure would carry great risk. Being around Buster, teaching him new things every day, like how to brush his teeth and get dressed made him feel like the father he once thought he had, one he wished Met had known. With these emotions came a sudden need to shelter Buster at all costs. Even without the bounty on his head, surely wicked men would kill to steal the bear from him.

"Plagun thinks you're a myth. You stay in the shadows, and you can ride this out for a long time. I'll be right behind you making sure no one messes up. Who wouldn't want to be a part of a club like this? Everything will be on the house. I'll front the money. You give me half the take. I'll set up the locations. We'll have to keep you on the move to keep the bulls guessing. I'll take care of all the food and booze. I hope you understand I really believe in this. You bring in a crew and musicians you can trust. I'll bring in the members I can trust. They'll all be swimming in dough, but they won't be street thugs. We'll create our own secret society. Three times a week to start. They'll pay what we say and won't think to talk because they won't belong to the club if they do. If there's one thing a man seeks, it's a sense of belonging. Feeds his most important organ: his ego. I guarantee silence." And surely Basil could make such guarantees, but not for the reasons he mentioned.

"Not sure how Buster will react to all the noise," Pap said.

"You've got a burning bush there. Just ask him yourself."

Pap knew that Basil was on the level. They had come into something special, one of those mysteries the white coats were always trying to unravel, and there was no telling what it all meant. Basil's ambitions wouldn't exactly go as planned though. He would run up quite a tab bankrolling the club in those early days and was still in the hole by the end of 1930. There were always extra costs, from paying off landlords and business owners to making sure the cops turned blind eyes to another illegal gin parlor. Mention of the musical bear was never part of the negotiations. Lucky for Basil, he had plenty of money from crooked defendants like Plagun to keep him around for a long time.

From one basement to another, they gypsied around town, rarely two shows in the same place, never a back-to-back. Basil would let Pap and Buster crash in his office whenever they wanted, but they had to promise to be out before 5 am the next morning. He grew fond of the bear and credited him with reinstilling a sense of loyalty, something he had lost soon after being sworn in.

Pap had gone shopping at Thread & Thrift Wears and picked up a few getups that could be knitted to fit Buster. These included disguises when traveling. They did a lot of it in the early going. Specially tailored baker boys he could fit over his wide ears and mammoth head, tweed jackets and baggy pants, and of course, the patent double scarf he would wrap around his face and snout when touring by car. Buster longed for the cooler days on the horizon. All these extra layers kept him lean as a fish that first summer. Shoes were always the hardest part, so Pap had special elastic socks made instead and gloves to match. The claws were the only problem, but they used bandages to cover them up. It made Buster look like a boy with an infectious disease.

While Basil was busy behind the scenes choosing new venues and putting all the members on notice, Pap was the battle strategist, making sure that each show went off without a hitch. Lou was the expert in guns, so he became chief of security. Turnip Faymus, Ink Tambo, even the Gophers became underlings. Pap had met the kids that would choose the name Gutter Gophers a few months after he found Buster.

Burger Brasa was a newsie by day and a one-eyed peeping Tom by night. Pap had seen him at the same corner every morning for weeks. After he'd deal his last paper, he'd bribe the local bathhouse attendant a checker to let him sneak a peek in the women's showers. That is until a flattie got wise and coshed the lust out of him. Moony Butter and Bobby Pin were his pals. They wandered streets, acting as tour guides to lost foreigners, but that was just their cover. They were pickpockets. When they approached Pap, he asked them if they wanted real jobs for real money without the risk of getting their heads smashed. Anthony Mound, Mack Loyter and Dradle Prestij were pin boys at Good Leaf Bowling & Billiards, but one night while Pap was playing nine-ball—Lou was watching Buster—he noticed their boss belting them with the leather for not replacing the pins fast enough. If there was one thing Pap couldn't tolerate it was a bully who had the bulge on a weakling. These kids weren't weak; they were just overmatched by a few years. What Pap would later learn was that the boys had cleaned their boss's cash register just before quitting. Pap made them mail it back in an unsigned envelope, saying they didn't need the karma or any new enemies. Then he promised to double what they took. When news of his own club materialized, Pap decided he would need a wide net of eyes. Who better than the Gutter Gophers to be trusted with someone like Buster? They were crafty where it counted, and with just the right amount of juice, they'd never turn. After all, that's what it was all about. The nectar of poverty was for chumps, and with his migrating club, Pap could ensure that neither he nor his friends would taste from it again.

Pap was planning to put on the finest evenings of entertainment in all of Good Leaf. With Basil fronting the cash and a fully vetted guest list, they couldn't fail. The members would come for the booze and stay for the bear. It took Pap a few weeks to gather his crew and the band. Looking back on it, he would admit it was the hardest part of the process because it entailed that pesky concept called trust. But if Basil's plan was to work, Pap had to act on faith. And if it didn't work, they would hatch one of Basil's many escape plans. Everyone could burn in hell as far as Pap was concerned, but nothing could ever happen to the bear.

Their first main spot as a fully stocked club was connected to a pizza parlor. Members would walk into the unisex bathroom and, behind one of the stalls, find a secret entrance. A bathroom attendant on the take, one of Basil's private courier's, would deter any unknown guests from entering that stall. "Toilet's broke." All those with privilege gained access by handing the attendant a blank black card and a five spot. No bank checks or charga-plates, there was never a paper trail—other than the books Basil kept in undisclosed locations—no bills, no receipts. They lasted five days before the owner of the parlor decided to have the toilet fixed and discovered the secret door. The number of guests, all thanks to Basil, was fifteen. Not much but it was a start, and if Pap could get fifteen to keep their mouths shut, he was doing well.

Buster had everyone seeing things, and Basil tried his best during his "consultations" to prepare members for what they would encounter. But it was easier to predict how Buster would react to guests than how the guests would react to him. He was an instant hit. For most and that included many of the gents in attendance, they thought he was delightful. Like some kind of unfledged kid who came out fuzzy and frank. He had a croaky voice like a toad after a Cubongo. And he waddled around like a plump midget. He wouldn't hurt a fly, and everybody knew it. Only once did things get strange around Buster. A portly lady by the name of Wilomena Fleming, the wife of Water Company President Casper Fleming, fell to her knees and lowered her face to Buster's toes. She started praying to him like he was a god. Buster was so embarrassed he lowered himself to her level and prayed for her to stop. It was the only time Pap swore

Buster's milky fur went rosy. Basil brought Wilomena and Casper Fleming in for a "special consultation" the next day. He had to impress on her more than him that she would not go to the church with this or the papers, no one, for the miracle was exclusive to her and those seated around her. She gave her word as a God-fearing woman.

As the shows continued, and the guests increased from 15 to 25, soon 45, Pap started to grow more suspicious of each invitee. When Basil reminded Pap that he had nothing to worry about, Pap questioned Basil's competence as a lawyer. When Basil told Pap that the whole club was advertised as Plagun property, Pap objected with every muscle fiber and wanted to call the whole thing off. But they had gone too far to turn back. While some became carpenters and doctors, Pap was quickly earning a reputation for throwing the best parties for white-collar law breakers, the ultimate hideout for wish-they-could-be tough guys. From Vie's Bookstore, Lou's favorite stop, where its large storage hall was renovated into the Maracas Lounge to Central Leaf Depository and G.J.s, each new venue came with a new moniker. Just when word wanted to spread, they'd switch out place and name. They spent a couple of months at the Sunks Sewing and Seamstress Shop under the alias Renfro Room and did a tour at the South Leaf Train Depot as the Choo-Choo until they wound up Club Polar at Dunfer's. The only trails left were the occasional strands of white fur that any nosy dick would have mistaken as Husky hair. But as the same "Husky" continued to be spotted in a list of joints as eclectic as their trades, others became suspicious too.

Buster was a bear, at least that's what everyone who knew him claimed, but all he had known with Pap was the inside of four walls, no matter that they were different walls every few nights, they were still walls. One night, Pap thought to show his friend what or where he might have come from. In the wee hours of a snowy morning, while the sun worked on the other side of the planet, Pap snuck Buster into Hub Park for a frolic.

A couple of hobos shivered in-and-out of sleep on frozen park benches, but Pap wasn't too worried about snoopers. Buster was edgy when he inched his paw into the fresh slush.

"Go ahead, Buster. Taste it. It's snow." Buster brought his paw to his snout and barely snuck his tongue out to sample the frozen crystals. He smiled and tried some more. "You like it?"

"Supermurgitroid, Pap." Buster skipped through the snow but not too far from Pap, just as he was told. It was one of his favorite days to date, but Buster was as cautious as Pap and was eager to return to the safety of their walls.

"With us, you're protected. Home. Anything you could ever want. We'll take care of you no matter what, but I'll never hold you back. You say the word, and you're free. I never want to mess up with you, and if you don't belong to me and know where you're headed...just know it's an angry world, and it ain't here to make sure any of us smile."

"I ain't ever leaving you, Pap. You're my Pap."

"I love you, kid."

Buster would never respond to that phrase, but he would squeak, like a hiccup, to reciprocate the sentiment.

Three times a week, usually on off-nights, Pap would invite the crew to a game of poker in whatever basement they found themselves in. Dunfer's ended up being their best spot. They would eat, drink and smoke. They would cheat, hide cards up their sleeves, make silly hand signals, but Buster, and his chocolate shakes, would end up cleaning house every time. When Lou held a full boat, Buster sat on four painted dames. When Turnip called on a straight, Buster showed flush, and on it went. One time Pap flaunted a staircase of spades, and Buster still beat him. Pap threw his cards in the air in defeat and went for another slice of pizza. The others gave Buster props. He hadn't a clue what a "blaze" was, but that was his winning hand. The pot never grew over a hundred beans, and after each game, Buster would feel compelled to return his winnings.

"I can't use this spinach in a salad," Buster would say. He'd have everyone in stitches. No matter how much Pap and his crew made Buster feel like he was one of them, no matter how much he acted like one them, the doubt that was only allowed to visit when the night stood still gnawed at his center. *I wish I knew someone like me*, he would think. And after spinning his brain to sleep, he'd hop the first train to dreamland and get ready for another day of adventures with his very dearest Pap.

"I'll wait outside," Pap would say each dawn before Buster's morning swim. The kid would never delay; he hated to keep anyone waiting but especially Pap. He had vaguely recalled a paternal figure that was as kind to him once, but deserting memories had him second guessing. Pap's presence was security. Buster knew that their operation required constant relocation. He never pinpointed the reason behind it, but the question did come to mind from time to time. Pap didn't want the burden on Buster, but he did inform him several times that he was special and that sometimes bad people took special for their own ill-gotten gain. The swims started at the Train Depot. It was right off Cangrego Harbor, and they continued throughout. Buster's waddle disappeared, and he would become aerodynamic, if someone his dimensions could ever achieve such form. Pap would stand on the dock with one eye on him, the other on the horizon, the hard brilliance of a city made of embers, a serrated skyline that sawed the air and stretched the world to shreds. There was nothing soft about anything he had ever seen, and then came the bear. What would he have been without Buster Horn? By late fall 1930, the club had grown to 73 members, ever faithful followers of the Buster brand. The next two would change Pap's life in ways he couldn't imagine.

- 71 -

Chase Griggs had heard of these "consultations"—some knew them as "screenings"—from his buddy Jackson Reese. But that's all he had heard. Not even Jackson Reese and his close friendship with Chase Griggs, not even his cocky money and manner, would let him talk about Buster until the time was right, and that was only while inside the club. When a member left for the evening, no matter how stewed, no matter how delirious, no matter that they suffered instant amnesia of every instruction given, they knew to never utter so much as a cuff about that bear. Basil impressed that on all the guests until they were dreaming retribution for a foul-up. Chase was dressed like a gentleman. His silk jacket was buttoned closed. His yellow tie in a fishbone knot. He sat with a splash of scotch in his short glass and one leg intersected over the other. He was impressed with what he saw. The office floor was a brunette oak. An art deco rug of pink and baby blue covered the center. Everything organized to both calm and coerce, two straight chairs on one side of the writing desk, one leather roller on the other. The minibar was fully stocked. Pictures of Basil Demur with some big wigs on the wall. A new telephone resting on the corner of the desk, a typewriter centered with a sheet of paper deposited within its clips, one leather squeezebox folder to its side, Chase Griggs' folder.

Demur paced behind his desk orating what sounded like a sermon. He spoke of the meaning of life, how man was king, how kings ruled, the meaning of a legend, the purpose of fulfillment, the introduction of a special society that was being formed among the elitists. When Jackson Reese had vouched for Griggs, he played it heavy, said Griggs was highly impressionable. So that's where Basil Demur did most of his work. Then after the "candidate" was moist as a newborn kitten, Demur would attack his credibility, see how far he could push him, see how easy it would be for him to talk. Demur didn't know Chase Griggs like he knew the other members, so he had to use all his powers of manipulation, study Chase's eyes like a doctor. If he had trouble making eye contact, he would rat. If he wouldn't look away or blink too much, he would rat. Demur looked for a relaxed set of eyes, even with the stress of being inside a lawyer's office. But even the tepid eye could rat. It's the best Demur could do. And then after dismissing Chase Griggs with a "we'll let you know," he would take his findings to Pap for a final answer. Pap asked a few questions about Jackson Reese again and then gave the okay. Chase would be invited back to Demur's office. This time Chase would stand and Demur would be seated, taking down every traceable piece of evidence for what he sold as an "entertainment contract." He kept the only copy. Names, address, date of birth, office, passport number, children, schools, parents, in-laws, even blood type. It was the genius of Demur's presentation, but the risk of spilling blood in a raid by a rival gang was real, and they needed to know what blood type for any emergency transfusions. Eccentric as he thought the whole thing, Chase couldn't stop soaking it in. Once he signed the dotted line and gave his first month's dues, Demur would bring down the sledgehammer.

"The owners of this club are powerful men, peaceful, but they can switch into warriors if provoked. Maybe you've heard of the Plaguns. It is the strictest policy that no word of what you see there will ever be shared with anyone outside of the club. Under no circumstances. The penalty would be severe. But we're confident that you won't feel the need to spill. Don't trust your eyes; they'll only lead to more questions. Just accept that there are things in this world that don't need an explanation."

Chase twitched a simper until he saw the arctic look on Demur's face. That's how Demur left him. No "welcome to the greatest party in history," no "thank you for your greenbacks." Their hands clasped like mismatching puzzle pieces. Once more, Demur exceeded a gaze into Chase's eyes. His pupils gave a slight shiver.

When Chase Griggs made his way into Dunfer's that first and only night, his expectations all became a reality. What a dainty hatcheck girl in a black, sleeveless one-piece, that left little to the imagination, could do to spice up Chase Griggs' blood. She stood on a pair of barracudas in fish nets, her feet in pumps, her neck in a choker and a red apron like the belly of a black widow. "Good evening, Mr. Griggs."

"Good evening," Chase blurted out of instinct. It struck him that this talking flower who he had never seen before just called him by name. Whoever ran this place had their chips in order.

"We were expecting Mrs. Griggs," she said. Her name was Sissie Demur, one of Basil's trusted nieces.

"I'm afraid she ran into a bout of cold feet." Chase handed his hat and coat and a two spot to the gal. He mopped a palm over his hair. She issued him a ticket, and with a wink, declined the gratuity. Griggs got his kicks from trading tongue with attractive women behind Vilma's back. Truth of the matter, any woman would laugh at Chase's dumb put-ons for a tip; he knew it. Buying attention was better than no attention at all. That he had learned from Vilma. But here was a real looker who would have nothing to do with his cold cash. It insulted and excited. An intoxicating effect was taking hold. Without an ounce of liquor, it started back at Demur's office. He fumbled the bill to his pocket and turned to the makeshift lobby, a specimen of glitz. Candles on long poles lit the way. The ceilings and walls were caped in golden fabric. A blood-red carpet flamed the path to the maître d', his white tux glistening under the soft lights. Arty Demur, another trusted nephew Basil put to work, stood behind a rostrum of cherry mahogany with brass accents. A couple with sculpted faces and garb to match allowed Arty to check their names off the list before passing through that velvet curtain to the mother lode of social circles. A rabid blend of jazz and chatter was heard from the other side of the drape. Arty scanned his list and clicked his silver pen twice, then checked off next to Chase's name. The headwaiter, also a nephew to Basil—he had a few he could loan to Pap—opened the curtain and in waltzed Chase Griggs, disappearing behind that red velvet. The denizens were drenched in the sweet scent of success. They ate caviar and drank bourbon. Men in pressed pin stripes donned cursive mustachios and slicked dos; ladies veiled in lip paint and rouge, flowers brimming off their hats, elbow-high satin gloves. Here, pretenses didn't exist. Everyone was equally better off than the next, just how Basil Demur orchestrated. They were glorious years.

PART V

- 72 -

Buster treated the roisterers to a belligerent horn. Pap had to catch himself midstride to the kitchen to see whether his beloved kid was, in fact, the culprit of those haunting intonations. He was on a tear. A melodic madness that mesmerized the mush between the macular and the magnificent. It's what those tall heads of haute couture came for every time, even if tonight the novelty had turned abrasive. It had Mr. Crooner and the Cats 6 scratching their scalps; they had never seen Buster in such a frenetic state. His horn had gone through many swings over the years but never the dreadful forecast that he struggled to hide. It was sheer instinct; he sensed something that no one else did even if he wasn't sure what it was. Perhaps he was calling to Pisto Leroy from the dead. With each long breath, he yowled, he blasted, he frightened the smoky air. It caused the hairs on Pap's neck to frisson. After his last gulp of air, both his apparatus and cheeks nearly exploded.

Mr. Crooner, busy fighting his mic, couldn't stop glancing back to Buster. The thought that he was once again on the spirits ran through his mind. He stopped in the middle of his song, like going back to the first few performances. Pap braced himself for the worst. Mr. Crooner headed to Buster's stand, but this time instead of bullying him into correction, he softened the words: "You okay?"

Buster snapped out of the trance placed on him by his trumpet's tantrum and grinned a gentle nod. "Quack, quack, ducky. Thank you for asking, Mr. Crooner."

Mr. Crooner raised a bandleader's hand and struck up the Cats 6 again as he pranced back to his post. The music between Mr. Crooner and Buster became united like no time before. They were in the pocket, a bond that could never be learned or rehearsed for such a connection came but one time and in one place during one's existence. This was that place and tonight, just then, on the second deck of the Fishtail, was that time. They could have interchanged skins and not known the difference. Their souls spoke to each other in a language exclusive to them.

Never had Pap seen such camaraderie between the two. He could only think that no matter the chaos, no matter that Lou had bailed, the complexity of his daily struggles, things were finally coming together. He now had two angels on his side. The only hint of a problem: He was still twenty devils up.

Turnip Faymus and Ink Tambo, the remaining muscle, wound up at the Champion Club the night before. They got plastered and ended up screwing around with a couple of chorus girls without paying the tab. When the girls bitched, Junior Plagun grew beet red and asked Buddy for help. It was the first time he had come to Buddy with such a request. It was the only time Junior felt such a sense of wrath, like a lion defending his pride and breeding rights. Buddy said he would do his brother the favor and show him that blood never changed colors. Buddy didn't even know who the guys were when he had them killed, chopped into pieces and fed to his crocs at Crystal Plats. He didn't care. It was enough that Junior had reached out to him and could only mean they would once again be close. There would be no police reports.

When Turnip and Ink went absent before they shoved off, Pap knew he should have called off the race on account of a sloppy track. His detail of security now came from the surrounding legion of waves, the Gophers, Dino Glass, Trunks the midget, and Ham Wails. None of them were trained killers, except maybe the waves. Dino Glass and Trunks could barely handle a gun. Ham Wails had never touched one, and six were just kids, no matter that they talked and acted like weathered dockhoppers. More than ever, Pap felt the need to push the ferry out further. Another mile, then one more until they were inside the Pony Currents. Anchoring the ship would prove a challenge, but so would getting a fix on them this far out. Pap made the phone call to Basil just before they shoved off. Basil said he would try one more time to convince the members to increase their travel times but soon knew that it was all in vain. And yet, the house had thirty guests. Even Jackson Reese and his gal pals had made the trek one more time.

Bobby Pin and Anthony Mound paced between stern and starboard—Moony Butter could cover the main hall with Pap's help now. Mack Loyter and Trunks covered port. Burger Brasa and Dradle Prestij kept near the bow with binoculars scanning the horizon. It was black as designed. If Sister Second had anything to do with it, this would be their last job under Pap Fanti, who she now regarded as nothing more than a street hood. It didn't matter that he put them up and even put the house in the sister's name. When the Gophers told him that Sister Second was threatening to go to the cops, Pap said he'd handle it. Of all the gratitude. He had picked the wrong gal. Sister Second, whose marker of good parenting was whether one kept their kids from suicide. It was a good starting point, but she was a hypocrite. Pap got the dirt on everyone, including Catalonia Maye. She became a nun alright, but not like most do. For starters, she had lied about being sexually unexplored just as she had lied about never taking a life. In fact, with one swing of the bat, she grounded into a double play. She was only sixteen, according to church records. Demur found a way to get his mitts on everything. It was a love story like many on the Leaf. Some slick gee promised moon and stars, then gave her the pump and dump. In her grief, she pumped her womb and dumped the lump growing within. Then she ran to the cloth until the truth found its way out. It's alleged that as part of her penance, she never let another man near her. Pap didn't toss a stone, but she had no trouble firing them back. Cause, no cause, didn't matter. Pap informed Buster that the Gophers wouldn't be joining them anymore. He couldn't risk bringing the ship down on account of a sister with a past. Buster gave each of them a bear hug and played one last solo for a special audience of six on the second deck of the Fishtail. It was something they would always cherish. Mr. Crooner wasn't interested in the mock gig. He called it petty and told Pap to wake him when it was show time. The Gophers were told that Mr. Crooner had a bellyache, but they knew better. Pap asked Sister Second to meet him on the Harper dock with the boys. He covered her fare but didn't let her on the ferry. She asked what was hiding on the boat. Suddenly, Pap thought the Gophers to be normal kids with loose tongues. Suddenly, he didn't trust them as much as he wanted to. This was two nights ago. "Keep a close eye on them. They're good kids," he told the sister, but she paid more attention to the hundred spot Pap slipped her to let the Gophers finish the week. "You boys grow strong. Never forget our secret." After tonight, Pap would have no way of knowing if another cat had gotten out.

The Pony Currents were calm for this time of year, too calm to keep Burger Brasa from catching a quick snooze. He had eaten a heavy dinner of franks and hoagies and couldn't keep his eyes open on the bow like he was supposed to. Dradle Prestij was in and out of sleep next to him with a snuffed stogy in his mouth. A quarter mile out, a disc of light came to life. Then another small sun a couple hundred yards to its right. A chain reaction ignited until a baker's dozen cordoned the Fishtail. Dradle shook Burger awake. "It's the pinch!"

Burger jerked open to the thirteen filled coronas gunning straight for them. They were getting larger. On the stern, Bobby

Pin had already relayed the signal to Mack Loyter, who was skidding down the bridge, through the main deck and inside the ship. He booked it with all the dexterity of an escape artist, barged into the main hall, skipping behind tables and thirty guests, unseen. Out of the corner of his eye, Pap noticed Mack crowding in on him. All it took was one glance into Mack's naked eye to know that the moment they had all dreaded for three years strong was upon them. Pap whispered back and sent Mack on his way as cool as the breeze. He wasn't as worried for the Gophers or anyone in the club as he was for Buster. He gripped his cane and bolted for the stage, trying his best to keep his emotions in check. He couldn't have anyone see what was imminent, even if avoiding it was impossible. He stepped onstage and went straight for Buster, ignoring Mr. Crooner altogether. He took hold of the bear by his midsection and plopped him on the ground. They hotfooted backstage. The members in the crowd pitched question marks off their brows but remained in place. Mr. Crooner took no mind to Pap and Buster's idiocies. The Cats 6 tripped over the beat like it was the first time they had rehearsed this drill, but just as swiftly, picked it back up. There were nerves in the air.

Pap pulled the snubnose from his jacket with one hand. With the other, he tugged Buster down the hall. "They're on to us, little buddy. You gotta go."

"What do you mean, Pap?"

A rivulet of tears formed from one of Pap's eyes. It was a sight Buster had never seen. Pap knew Buster would have to bury any thoughts of Pisto Leroy and return to the water. Stopping fast, he pulled his eyes in both directions. The hall was empty and deathly still. Pap turned to Buster and made eye contact like it might be their last. "Remember the bad people I told you about? How they would do anything to get their hands on someone as special as you. They're here, now. They'll axe this place into splinters, take you away from me, do horrible things to you, I'll never see you again. You gotta go, Buster. I love you with all my heart. Don't you ever forget it. You were my entire life. Whatever happens, keep under till the lights are all gone! You got me? Don't come up!" Buster was always a nervous sort of bear, but now he appeared still as steel. It was all he could do from coming apart.

Pap led Buster to the lower levels. He knew that if a glimmer of light hit them, they would not stop their search until Buster was fished out, alive or dead. Pap flung the door open to his room and checked for any lights penetrating the porthole. It was black. This was Buster's one chance to get away undetected if he could only fit through.

"Come on. You're going out. You've swam these waters a thousand times. There's nothing to it, okay?" What he failed to disclose was that they were miles from shore and Buster's endurance had never been tested. "Hurry. Take off your tux. You can't swim in that."

"I'm sorry, Pap." Buster got undressed.

"Don't you ever apologize to me."

"What are you gonna do?" Buster asked. It brought another stream of tears to Pap's eyes that his bear was so selfless, but he was growing frustrated with all the crying. Now was the time to maintain order. This was always a possibility. It's the very reason Pap moved the club so often, but of all the places to get nabbed, how could they have found them so far off the coast?

"You're too pure, and that's why I can't keep this from you any longer. The reason they're here is me, not you. It never had anything to do with you. It was all my fault, okay? I muffed it good, and I'm the one who should be sorry. Don't you worry about me, little buddy. Just promise me two things. You have to promise me this," Pap said looking intently into Buster's dark, glossy pupils. For a split moment he saw the reflection of a dead man staring back at him.

Buster couldn't wrap his mind around what Pap was saying. Pap could do no wrong in his eyes, but now was not the time to belabor the point. Of all the thoughts that crossed Buster's mind, his friend on the second deck was the loudest. "What about Mr. Crooner? I can't just leave him. He has to be safe. You can't let him get hurt, Pap."

"I promise you he'll be safe. Nothing bad will happen to him. Now get going!" Buster nodded both in relief and in fulfillment of all the promises Pap would ask of him. The gravity of the moment weighed a ton. He had never been far from Pap and even during those moments when Pap was not right by his side, he always knew the purity of safety. This was different. In a few seconds, Buster would be out on the open sea, alone. He couldn't quite comprehend it, but he knew that this was not one of those drills Pap had shown him back during their many tours. "Do not come up until they're gone, and make it back to shore. Promise me you won't get caught! Promise you'll make it!" Pap grabbed Buster and brought him close for a tender embrace, wishing he could hide him inside his tux coat forever and then vanish into thin air. Who said things had to end on a good note? Or does ending on one note or the other change the veracity of the entire experience, including all the bad and good notes in between? Pap released his hold and unlocked the side scuttle until a cough of cold air reminded him just how bad things were outside. Pap poked an eye out to the ambuscaders. They were gaining, but the coast was as clear as it would ever be. "Go now," he told Buster as he hoisted him to the hole. It took three strong shoves, an airless rib cage and a contortionist's spirit to clear it.

Buster splashed into the ocean without a light to eye him. He looked up one last time to the porthole and noticed Pap's woeful countenance. As the waves splashed against Buster's snout, he managed a smile of courage. He wouldn't let Pap down. He turned to the ships, now within reach, took in a lungful of air and plunged under the black surface.

- 73 -

Spotlights from a dozen plus police boats combed the ferry and surrounding water. Buster stayed submerged, but soon he was running short of oxygen and realized he might have to break the first promise if he intended to keep the second. He surfaced his blow hole just as a spotlight cruised over him. He was lucky to be mistaken for a breaking wave. The sea was toothy. Bobbing in and out, Buster wondered about Mr. Crooner and all his friends on board. He could see police boats anchoring to the ferry with grappling hooks and rope. Marauders in dark uniforms connected the gangplanks and stormed aboard with all sorts of large guns, the types he had seen once in Lou's cache. They infiltrated the decks.

Mr. Crooner sang for three more seconds. Then, with one shotgun blast to the ceiling, the hall fell into a din of hysteria. "Police! This is a raid! Everyone freeze! You're all under arrest!" Lieutenant Quick Coogan yelled. Thirty guests screamed for their lives.

Mr. Crooner made a mad dash backstage. Something in his recollection cried danger, and he wanted no part of it. He bolted down the hall and out onto the deck. To each side, he noticed the boys in blue and black blitzing. Scrambling for an escape, all the chimp saw was a body of ominous, dark liquid, the thing he loathed most, water everywhere. There would be no suicidal plunge. The ocean mist stung his face with irritation. He returned inside and galloped back to his quarters, slamming the door shut and finding familiar refuge within the head. He balled into a corner and cocooned himself with a towel. What he would have given for one of those drinks that made bad feelings go away.

The cops requisitioned the ferry in grand fashion. Patrons attempted to flee, some even threw themselves overboard only to be scooped out by trolling lifeboats. They were all cuffed and hauled onto the police vessels until all "innocents," including Jackson Reese, were off the ferry.

Pap and his crew did little to resist. Claudette and Rita were hooked to handrails. Quick Coogan took charge of the pat downs. He leered at both women for the weakest prey. He would save her for last.

"You put your mitts on me, I kill your babymaker," Claudette threatened.

It got Coogan's juices flowing. He slapped her across the face and stuffed his hands in between her crotch. Claudette pumped a mule kick at his balls. That infuriated and made him horny at the same time. There were cops everywhere, dirty cops, but still cops, so he moved on to Rita, who stood like a frightened doe. He fanned her with hungry hands, made sure she wasn't packing in between her tits. She didn't oppose. She just took her punishment with eyes shut.

"Curse your mother to hell!" Dino Glass spit at Coogan's feet. Coogan left the girls and bunted Dino's nose with his billystick. Then he fit him with a pair of iron bracelets and let him bleed a new drink.

Mack Loyter was peeled off the wheel. Bobby Pin threatened with a kitchen knife but was tackled and shackled. The rest of the Gophers were wrangled like jackrabbits and loaded onto one of the police boats for a one-way ticket to juvenile hall. After Sister Second learned of their fate, most of the boys begged to stay in lockup.

The Cats 6 dropped instruments and threw hands in the air. They were beaten to the floor and turned face down. A line of six murderous badges aimed their choppers at the backs of their skulls. Ham Wails went to his knees without a word. He feared getting hit in the face or anywhere else for that matter and couldn't wait to get on land and the light of a courtroom. Something about this raid, like the coppers who rigged explosives and poured gasoline all over the room, the walls, the floors, made him feel like they operated under a different set of laws. When they hung Trunks from a porthole ring, joking that they would stretch him to normal, Wails was confirmed of this.

Pap didn't run, didn't even think about it. He watched the beatdown unfold, dropped his gun and held out his arms for Coogan. For his compliance, he took a butt of a shotgun to the gut and crouched over ready to lose his dinner. Coogan yanked him upright, fanned him down and shoved him along to the top deck.

Inside one of the police boats, Captain Sert Johnson smoked a rollup over Lou Licks. They were unaccompanied. Lou was cuffed. His ankles roped, just like he had done to Pisto Leroy. He wore two black eyes and bled from his mouth. But he was fully awake, aware and alive. It was paramount that he live to see this, Buddy Plagun demanded. "That son-of-a-bitch dipped two bullets in me, so you put two in him, but only after that coward cocksucker Fanti looks in the heart of his eyes and knows who double-crossed him." For $50,000, half of which had already been delivered, Johnson would have them take portraits together before they got whacked.

Sert Johnson once had dreams of becoming mayor. He loved the law and hoped one day to use it to clean up Good Leaf. But his idealism was tapered with stupidity. He never finished high school. He enrolled in the police academy at 16. By 19 he was the youngest on the force, his mind still pliable enough to be molded au contraire his own predispositions. He learned that the people who ran society could afford to be twisted, that justice was bought. He would never hold the kind of power to exact any real change, and this frustrated two marriages and amassed thousands in support arrears. So he used the power of his badge to connect with people who could expedite his journey. In 1927, their names were Bill Plagun and Commodore Cabra and a little help from Mank Mill and a cheating wife. Today it was Buddy Plagun and $50,000. Johnson quickly understood that Plagun would get him places his taxpayer income couldn't. Plagun and all his syndicate ties, their workers, the ones who controlled the voting districts that would cart Johnson to the mayor's office. And $50,000 could buy a lot of advertising. So Johnson was loyal, loyal to justice and loyal to Buddy Plagun until an up-and-coming rival decided to take him out. He didn't take cheap bribes. He didn't blink. Never drank and tonight he had finally bagged the night fox. Soon they would cut off his tail and pin it to their trophy case at the precinct. It would be all over the papers as Captain Johnson's greatest victory.

From beneath the boat, Buster caught a glimpse of Coogan shoving Pap by the head onto the gangplank and into the police boat. Buster's heart beat with fury. It was something he had never felt before. These must have been the same people Pap warned him about so many nights. They weren't just bedtime stories. They were real men, with real guns and real malice in their hearts.

"Take a good look at your leak. One of many," Captain Johnson said.

Quick Coogan shoved Pap against Lou. Their bodies clapped and Pap fell over, looking up to Lou who was too beaten to say anything. His eyes were drenched with tears.

"Lou," Pap said. There were questions in the name. Like "why you?" and "was Met in on it?" There were doubts too. Lou had sacrificed his own life to protect Pap and Buster. He couldn't stand his current thoughts that somehow accused Lou of being a traitor. He loved Lou like the brother he had wished to have in Met, pure kin who would always go to bat for him. But now there was nothing but pain and one word: "Lou." Johnson's right boot kissed Pap's mouth shut.

"Where's Buster?" Lou gasped.

"Is that the musical bear or the chimp?" Johnson said before he gave the go-ahead nod to his lieutenant.

Coogan pressed his gun against Lou's head and juiced. The blast reverberated into the water below. Buster had heard gunfire before, but this shot announced a deafening tragedy. A massive weight belly-flopped against the water within feet of him. It bobbed momentarily on its stomach. Buster swam towards it and upturned the body. A river of thick blood oozed from his temple. Flashes of Pisto Leroy locked Buster's heart. He wanted to cry out to Pap but knew better. Lou, poor Lou. Why did they do this to you?

- 74 -

Busting the door down to Mr. Crooner's room, the cops noticed all kinds of odds and ends, the vanity, clothes huddled in small piles, the bed unmade. On the other side of the head door, the chimp continued to bide his time. He could hear men rustling about. They didn't sound like the men he had come to trust. They sounded hardnosed and dangerous. He started trembling under the towel but realized that it would give him away sooner. There was nowhere for him to go, so he would have to play dead in order to stand a chance. A cop reached for the door handle and yanked it open. He noticed an object underneath a towel and a foot matted in fur sticking out. With a couple extra hands, they accosted the chimp, pulled the towel from him and caught a glimpse. Mr. Crooner screamed just as the cops attempted to wrap him tight. The chimp fought to break free. He bit and clawed, but the cops were too many and his efforts too few.

Minutes later, Buster noticed the evil men carrying a paralyzed bundle. How he hoped that wasn't his friend and immediately wondered where everyone else was. He didn't see the Cats 6 coming out, not Rita or Claudette, not Dino or Ham Wails.

Once on board the police boat, the cops unwrapped the package for Captain Johnson.

"So this is the singing chimp," Johnson said gazing upon Mr. Crooner in his spiffy tux. The terror in his eyes said nothing of an intelligent being, much less one that could sing.

"I swear we saw him crooning, Captain," one of the deputies admitted. "He's better than Dib Minty." They chuckled.

"Can you sing for me? Go on, I'd like you to sing for me," Johnson said like he was trying to seduce a child into his car. "Yeah, I didn't think so. Send it to D.I.S.S. If they can't make it sing, I'm sure they can make it scream. What about the bear?"

Pap and Mr. Crooner shared eyes of defeat.

"What bear? We checked the whole ship. No more animals."

"We can rule out Noah's arc then. Let's get back to shore. Our work here is done."

The police boats unhooked from the ferry and rumbled to life. Buster was all alone in a gloomy sea. The water was dead cold. He didn't seem to mind that as much as being alone. He kept his focus on the police boats growing smaller in the distance. Within minutes, they were dots of light and then black. They had not noticed him. He thought to get back on the ship and search for Mr. Crooner until the ferry lit up in a giant fireball. It shot glowing chunks of wood and the remains of six colorful gates, two colorless hoods, a couple of unnamed chorus girls and one matterless midget into the water. No one would miss them on the Leaf. Buster swam for his life as fire rained down from above. This must have been what Pap meant when he made him promise to not come up until all the lights were out. The entire sky bled red and orange. He kept pushing himself, further from the sinking remains of the blazing ferry, all in one breath and without regard for the strain he was putting on his lungs. When he finally came up, he roared for oxygen. His lungs sounded cracked, his voice hoarse, wheezing breaths, begging for air. He had never contemplated his own death until now, and that just made him push on. His legs were quickly giving out. He hung his head in the water for a second's rest. He tried floating in place. The night was black, and Buster could barely see his paw in front of his face. The moon appeared to dissolve in the oncoming fog. He had no clue which way to keep swimming, but knew if he stopped, he'd be done. So he kept paddling until he couldn't anymore, and then he tipped on to his back and floated until he couldn't do that either. Soon he was being carried by the grace of the current and a wish it would lead him to some place dry.

A week earlier, under the chaperon of an inflamed moon that seemed to burn the passing clouds on contact, Met Fanti returned to Calloway. All that remained was a few sheets of burgundy satin and a busted wooden stage. The memory of spirits and cigar smoke confirmed what he had suspected. He had scoured the whole place, from the boiler room to the mixing kettles, had noticed the strands of black hair, chimp hair, in the washroom stalls. Even picked up some white clumps of fur inside the upstairs office. He bunched up the fibers and stuffed them in his pocket as though he was going to have them analyzed. Who did he think he was, DC Stiles? There were dirty dishes in the kitchen, glasses with the residue of chocolate milk. Pap and his crew were gone. They weren't coming back. Met felt the acids of betrayal corroding his entrails. All he could think about was all the money he was out and how he would never get back on Sue's good side again. So many nights in the stench of Crystal Plats meant nothing knowing that he could always go back to Sue. Life had been very unfair. They hadn't even left an open bottle of rye for him. Met had to get back to the Leaf. The silence at Calloway made him feel like a corpse strolling around a graveyard. He needed noise and a quick head change. He was still sitting on a few clams from Demur. The shyster mouthpiece. That was the ticket. If Demur couldn't explain what had happened or shell out enough dough to make caring irrelevant, he was a dead man.

Met hurried back to Twenties Slip Boulevard and flagged a yellow car to Crystal Plats. The whole ride he conspired with his heart and mind, wondering what it would be like to turn on Pap. Opportunities abounded, but Met had always stayed loyal to him in that most important of senses. The full moon pulled at his evil tides. This was the last straw. It was clear, if it ever was blurry, that Pap took no interest in Met's welfare. Blood was suddenly no marker of friendship. He could do it perforce. He could double-cross Pap for reward money or for free.

Met prayed for the morning hour when honest folks went to work. It was 8 am, and the same burly security guard was waiting at the ground floor of the Savings and Loan Building. He went by the name Mr. Stone, but Demur called him Sam. He had been the gatekeeper as long as Demur had been a tenant and had never let an intruder pass, not that many had tried. Met marched past him without as much as a courtesy eye. He had slurped down an entire fifth for breakfast and was now invincible.

"Where do you think you're going, mac?" Mr. Stone leaped out and blocked Met's path.

"Basil Demur. He's got property of mine. I'm here to get it back," Met said with a lazy tongue and one rough eye.

"Mr. Demur says he has no remaining business with you, left clear instructions. Says he doesn't want to see you here again. Kindly remove yourself from the premises, or I'll have to escort you out, face first." Stone stared at Met's brittle mug, making sure everything he said was sticking.

Met tried to swallow, but all he had in his mouth was a delusion of grandeur. Stone's eyes were lurid as lighthouses. He demonstrated a set of fighting teeth under his inwardly-fused lip.

Met arched up and threw his arms wide. "Do you know who the fuck I am? You have any idea who I run with? Step out of my way, hulk, or you gonna spit blood from your ears," Met said as he lifted an arm as a battering ram and attempted to plow through. He was half the guard's size and rapidly reminded when Stone curled Met into a half nelson and dragged him to the front door. Met garbled all sorts of threats, prophesying Stone and Demur's death by nightfall, their families burned to ashes, all weightless pie-eyed talk. Stone craned Met by his neck until his feet were a foot off the floor and caromed the top of his head against the front door until it opened. He did a quick pat down for guns and then gave Met the bum's rush.

Winded, Stone said, "Next time it won't go as nice."

Met was dazed and didn't dare make another go. He remained on the ground while bystanders did their best to bypass him.

Across the street, a flatfoot spotted the whole thing and rushed over. Stone explained the facts. Met barfed all over the sidewalk and was hooked and booked on drunkenness and disorderly conduct. His holding cell came with a couple of rascals from Cabra's camp waiting arraignment on armed robbery and murder. They had stolen a Plagun truck of whiskey and killed the driver and his passenger. When Met bragged about his boss, they beat him to a pulp. His one chance at freedom was snatched from him by the hands of his own brother just as he had done three years ago. As Met lied on the floor with wet bruises, he couldn't help but think that he was now lower than the caged chimp he discovered.

He was ordered to pay ten bucks in court fines but bitched such a storm that the judge doubled it. Released two days later, Met returned to the only company he could ever rely on. It was to be found at the Crystal Plats warehouse. Tonight he would crack another couple of bottles, pour out the contents into his stomach and write them off as defects. Tonight he would turn the clear mind careless. Sue was out of his life. Pap Fanti had raped him in a dry ass, stolen his one shot at glory and fled. And all he had left to show for it was a few stale lizards, enough to buy a car had he budgeted properly, but Met wasn't a planner. He hated being inside that storeroom and needed some air. He picked himself up and went out to the chimp cage, wondering if by some miraculous fate he might encounter another crooner. Lou was standing there instead.

"I'm a lucky man to find you here," Lou said. He, too, was lathered.

"You got my money?" Met was incensed, but he was also fresh off an ass-beating. All Lou would do is give him another should he ask for it.

"We ain't at Calloway no more."

"I trusted you and Pap, gave you the golden goose, and what do I get? Blackballed by a couple of dirty fuckin' roaches. You know I coulda made this happen on my own. Taken him to the hero hustler down on Strobile. He woulda paid me big. So where's my geetus?" The humid air suggested blood. But Pap had it coming. Lou, too, since he was in on it.

"I came to talk business. Just you and me," Lou said.

"You got a bucket?"

"Hack and foot."

"Let's take a ride," Met said.

They headed into Matanza Heights. Met's new dealer. It was the best shit he had ever gotten his hands on, some minstrel he ran into on the subway, or maybe he was actually black, Met couldn't remember anymore. He just cared for the reefer. Lou parked in the alley between the tenement buildings. The dope dealer crept out of the back door with a brown paper bag, rolled at the top like it contained sandwiches. He approached Met's window. Lou corner-pocketed the man with his eye and pressed the gas before the bird could recognize him.

"Who the fuck was that?" Lou asked.

"What are you doing? That's my supplier! He ain't no cop! Go back!" Met yelled. Lou slammed on the brake and ordered Met out, told him to meet around the corner alone. Lou kept a hand inside his coat and on the butt of his pistol. He kept looking for Met to reappear alone with his brown bag. When Met got back in the car, he was much calmer, toked up.

"You know who that gee is?"

"Some broke reeds player. What was all that about? You off your nut or somethin'?" Met asked.

Lou left it at that. He didn't bother mentioning that it was Charmin from the Cats 6 and if he had fingered Lou, word was already headed back to Pap Fanti that he and Met were in cahoots. Lou asked for a hit of Met's stash. He needed to settle his hops. They drove back to Crystal Plats, the warehouse by the Reptile & Amphibian habitat. Met hit the light, and Lou's eyes brightened at all the crates of booze. Met poured a couple of glasses of rye and handed Lou a smoke. They talked about the singing chimp and about Pap.

"He's coming apart. I don't think he makes it."

"What's the old saying? Get mad once, everyone does it. Get mad some more, you get pills. Get mad nonstop, you get an exorcism, ain't that right?" Met said.

Lou took another swig of his rye. It made his tongue looser. "You know your brother's in the ground without me. I fuckin' kept him alive."

"I just can't believe it's taken you this long to figure that out. That's how it goes, Lou. When one gives, the other one takes. Only problem is no one wants to give without taking double, and no one wants to feel disrespected. Not even the animals."

"Those two things have him running into walls. It's a wonder we're not all locked up in the bounce house."

"I knew it. I heard that thing on the boat blowing its horn. It was a thing, wasn't it? I knew Pap kept another one, kept it from me. Were you in on that too? How much did you score?" Met tracked Lou's eyes, but Lou kept them caged up.

"I didn't say two. There's only one, you got that?" Lou got in Met's face as if to say 'don't you dare' and then his tongue left his mouth. "If anything happens to the bear, I'm gonna make you suffer like you've never known you could, and then I'm gonna end your life." Met would have never guessed it, and he was still working through what Lou had just said, but there it was, out in the open. A bear, possibly with the same talents as the chimp, and Lou was too stupid from the booze and dope to know that he had just given him up. But no matter Buster's fate, Lou could always pretend in his heart that he cared for the bear to the end. Who was he fooling anymore? He was there to make a deal for Pap Fanti. The result would inevitably be a bear bereft of a home and any knowledge of the real world. The thought made his brain hurt to the point of dropping it. It was better to focus on the reward money. At this point it would come from Met's pot, now exaggerated to be over ten large. Lou would be told that he had to pick up the dough at an undisclosed location from people he had never met before. This meant that they wouldn't know a thing about him either. A guarantee of no retaliation was a must. In fact, Met went to great lengths to ensure that Buddy Plagun would never learn the identity of the leak because he alone wanted the credit. But Lou wasn't convinced. It was his first rat job, and he needed to channel Pap Fanti's cunning to ensure he pull it off alive. One prerequisite was that Met accompany him to the pickup spot. Another was that the spot be chosen by Lou. Met made the call, and all parties agreed.

Natural 8's was a dumpy bar in West Leaf. Lou knew it well. It was always crowded, so no one would pull a fast one, not in front of a glut of witnesses. When Lou and Met got there, a posse of strangers was waiting for them at the back corner booth. Jesse Under was with them. They sat, ordered a round of skees and went to work. Lou wouldn't talk until he saw the bread in his hand. Jesse Under accommodated and slid over a stack of cakes. Then they waited for the punchline. "Point Grave. Out at sea. That's where you'll find him. But if I know him, he'll take to the Pony Currents. Wish I could give you an address. You better move fast. He changes his mind more than the weather." The strangers got up and left Lou and Met to finish their drinks. Sert Johnson, Quick Coogan and a squad of sawtoothed buzzers entered the bar in their police uniforms. They forced everyone out and put Lou and Met in separate cars. Met was sent back to Crystal Plats without remorse. He would spill the news to the cops about the chimp and now some bear and instantly regret it. If word got back to Buddy, Met would be on the hook for theft. Lou was relieved of his loot and sent to a slaughterhouse to spill blood. Somehow, he wasn't surprised. What some would do for payback. Pap had ducked Met long enough and insulted Lou to the point of making something of it, even if it meant that he, too, would go down with the ship.

- 75 -

"Extry! Extry! Read all about it! Pazo Fanti and his musical monkey pinched, floating speako up in smoke!" the pint-sized paperboy chanted to all would-be passers.

Met heard the kid wailing news on the street corner but was tapped out, didn't even have a sou to buy the Daily Leaf. He had been mugged the night before outside a gin parlor but getting his hands on the paper was now more important than scoring reefer. He surveyed random birds taking turns and noticed one man in a plain suit cross the street and enter Hub Park. He shadowed him for a whole hour as he read the paper from back to front. The degenerate lowlife. Couldn't he see that Met had important news to check? The man eventually folded the paper shut and tossed it in the garbage can. The news was apparently getting trashier on the Leaf. Musical monkeys and gangsters. A likely story. Met hustled over and retrieved the crumpled paper, nearly tearing the front page in his grip as his eyes lapped up the headline: "BOOZE KINGPIN PAZO FANTI AND SEAFARING SPEAKEASY RAIDED! WORLD'S 1st SINGING CHIMP SEIZED!" He couldn't read fast enough. The part about police boats cordoning Pap's barge, the undisclosed source that brought the rip down. All guests booked with participating in an illegal liquor establishment. The ferry that caught "accidental" fire and exploded, killing most of the club's crew. How the police had nothing to do with it. How

Pap Fanti was being held without bail. Eyewitnesses, both club members and cops, who caught a last-second glimpse of the marvel, a chimpanzee in a tux standing on stage, handling a microphone and singing with a voice that defied interpretation. Met couldn't believe what he read. The words blurred into ink spots. He went illiterate in one shallow breath. Revenge was finally his, and for an instant, he felt the full glory of vindication. Throughout his days, he had assumed the position of the cheated, the victim of many injustices, overlooked, overshadowed, simply overmatched by life's muscle, acknowledged for less than nothing, undercompensated as a man and stamped out as a human being. Except now, written proof. No sooner would he seek to memorialize it, frame it, preserve it for all time as a memento of his magnum opus. This was the miracle he would have wished to avoid but one that was as necessary as rain to drought. Met had proven to himself, far beyond the discovery of the chimp, which to this day he credited as fully his own, that he was capable of single-handedly orchestrating the takedown of one of the most notorious characters, the self-proclaimed king of the underworld, the gentle and noble spirit and the pied-piper of freak animals with otherworldly talents. He could go to his grave saying he was responsible for helping the law win the day. Finally, in what was nothing more than a wrong life, he was on the right side. Now Pap would know what Met had felt for a million hours. Perhaps in the future, should a singing monkey come to him by way of some act of generosity, Pap might recognize how not to rub those who made it happen.

There was a glimmer in Met's eye, not of relief or even victory but of emptiness. He knew this was the end, and there was nothing more for him to do. He had exacted vengeance like an expert, carried it out without remission and was starting to wish that the newspaper article that continued on page two would read on for days. But the minutes went from endangered to extinct, and soon there was nothing more to look forward to.

All the angling had come to a wrap. He reread the part about the chimp, the singing—he needed to make sure that was in there, that he was not fictionalizing the entire thing. It was, so Met could put to rest contentions of lunacy. There were witnesses. An official probe would ensue, investigations, laboratory experiments, anything to determine the origins, the authenticity of the mutant chimpanzee. As Met came to the end of the article, wishing to reread it from the start, something continued to gnaw at his gut. In his moment of triumph, there was the nuisance of lamentation. To Met, Pap was dead. It was time to shut the door on this unmemorable history and move onto something new, something to help him forget about a tragic ending that should have been otherwise. But like Met kept reminding himself as he stared at Pap's mugshot, obese with guilt and red meat, and now known as Good Leaf Corrections #7410, he had it coming. Still he never happened upon word of any other anomalies, say a talking bear like Lou blabbed about, just the chimp, which made him wonder if that was the only freak out there. To their dying day and credit, no club member, save for Chase Griggs, ratted out Buster. And no authority figure took the notion of another musical animal seriously without further proof. It didn't matter anymore to Met. It was time to collect his reward.

A couple of hours and a long but inspired walk later, Met arrived at the Arm Hotel. The elevator man let him up and Jesse Under led him to Buddy Plagun's room.

"You think I can get a drink?" Met asked Jesse. Jesse didn't hear a word. He just left Met alone in the room.

Buddy was in the bathroom, in front of the vanity. He wrapped a red double Windsor around his collar and then slid on his pinstripe gray jacket. He eyes twinkled like medals when he came out. For the first time he showed Met a grin and poured him a drink.

"I remember my father, what he said the night he died. You fought like a soldier." Buddy handed Met the drink. Met took it down before it got stale. "I'll never understand family like he did. Take my brother, for instance. He wants nothing to do with me. I don't blame him, but he's stupid to think that way. You, you got the heart of Satan. Stabbed Pap Fanti in the back and didn't even have the courtesy of using a clean blade. You're a trooper, and I salute you for your service."

"Thanks, Buddy," Met said. He needed another drink. Buddy could tell, so he handed Met the bottle instead. Met poured another glass of rye and chugged it down. He was there to collect his money but didn't dare bring it up.

"There's no guilt here on your part. You did what was right, but I'm left with one, like an itch I can't scratch, question. A singing chimp. That some kinda gag?"

"You know them newshawks, always pulling flying frogs out of their ass to sell papers."

Buddy took the paper and read: "Several eyewitness accounts of a chimpanzee in full tuxedo singing with a human voice, but not any human voice. If Dib Minty idolized a voice, this would be it. Internal probe to follow at D.I.S.S. No evidence of hallucinogens on the witnesses in question." He looked up to Met with a whimsical look on his brow. "The first chimps in all of Metro were installed at Crystal Plats three years ago as a tribute to my old man. He always wanted 'em. Said he liked their funny faces. Thought they'd bring a little joy to my mother, rest in peace. They're the only chimps I know of to date in all the boroughs. My chimps. Not even the man on Strobile Island has any. After all, what's so strange about a chimp? You know anything about this?"

"I may be a cockeyed hophead, but I ain't never smoked nothin' to make me see a singing chimp."

"I don't know. Somehow I'm not swayed. Anyway, I'll keep an eye out, see what happens. If I find something like this is real and it had anything to do with my zoo, then you know where I'm going to point a finger. I mean this would be worth millions, and if I even suspected that you stole from me. What am I saying? You're right. Those fuckin' paper men. I'm better off reading about that boy who turned into a mule."

As the alcohol started to work on Met's courage, he blurted out in a tremulous voice, "You got Pap. I even gave you Lou Licks. Do I get my money?"

"Not so fast."

"What do you mean not so fast? I'm down to the felt, Buddy. I delivered for you. Twice. Did I get flimflammed or somethin'?"

"You callin' me a cross-roader?" The rush in Buddy's blood could be seen through his eyes.

"Course not, but come on, will ya? I was hoping to use the dough to get back on Sue's good side." Met said. He was treading on burning coals accusing Buddy of anything but good.

"You can forget about her. She won't have nothin' to do with you, told me to my face."

"You know where she is?"

"I seen her around from time to time, but I couldn't tell you where she went. You boxed her good."

Met stopped paying attention. He had given up his brother and didn't have the money to show for it. He felt like a beggar and almost wept right in front of Buddy. "Can I get some money? Please."

Buddy reached into his pocket for a couple of sawbucks, just like the old days when Mank used to pay up. He put them on the table. "Get yourself a scrub and some grub. Don't worry. We still have time. Gin up, and maybe I put in a good word with Sue." Buddy put a hand on Met's shoulder and applied just enough pressure for him to know it was time to get out of his chair and leave. With a pat on the back, Buddy saw him to the door. "Buck up. You're a swell fella. You can sleep with a clear conscience."

Buddy and Met shared one more glance. Then Met started back down the hall to the elevator with his twenty bucks.

Buddy waited till he was around the corner and heard the elevator bell ring before he moved to the next room and knocked on the door. Sue Sandloer opened and let him in with a kiss. She was out of her manly suit and looked much prettier in the red dress that Buddy bought her. It matched his tie. Her face was made up nice, her eyes were gem drops, her hair pinned up high to accentuate her cheeks. Her bruise was all but gone. She didn't look too happy, but she looked pretty.

"Was that him?" Sue asked.

"I ironed him out. He'll be fine. Is that the dress I bought you?"

"Do you like it?"

Buddy reached for her and started smudging her pink lipstick with his mouth. He shut the door and did what he wanted to her for the next hour. She let him. Not like she had ever let Met, but Buddy was a man of independence, and independent men could call shots, even for her. She would let them from now on. Sue had grown thin from fighting for her lot in a world where reaping what you sowed came more favorably to a man. And if none of that persuaded her to hang it up and take shelter under Buddy Plagun, at least she didn't have to worry about caring for an invalid, no matter that she sometimes missed the stupid faces he would make to try to get her to laugh.

- 76 -

The grilling room at the East 1st Precinct was narrow and windowless and smelled of old urine from many a forced confession. Fresh coats of paint touched up the white walls and the dried up freckles of blood from suspects who swallowed their tongues on the way in. Captain Johnson had the respect of the judges to do whatever he deemed fit in the name of justice. He also had Pap Fanti sitting at the empty steel table on a cold hot seat. His face bore the record of a beating less than twenty-four hours fresh. Cuts over his lip, parched blood on his mustache. Two engorged googs where his eyes once resided. His hands were crossed tight behind his back, fastened to the chair with iron hoops.

The door opened and in walked Buddy Plagun. He was alone and moved cautiously towards Pap, taking in air through the crack in his mouth to avoid smelling his filthy victim. Seeing him with his own eyes was all Buddy needed to do, but even then he couldn't believe who was seated before him.

"Pazo Fanti jazzin' up the Ponies. I would have never guessed it in a million years," Buddy said. "You remember me? You remember my father?" Pap would not make eye contact until Buddy yanked his hair and forced the eyes north. "Look at me when I'm talking to you, you piece of shit." They held a trounced expression but looked at Buddy's like he had won nothing in return.

"I know you're gonna kill me, but that won't mean anything, not anymore. I've already seen things you'll never know about. Things that belong in another world. That's the world you're going to send me to, so get it over with," Pap said matter-of-fact.

"Like singing monkeys? Tell me, are they really what the papers say? I mean I was never a big Dib Minty fan, always thought he sang like an old hen, but you gotta admit the guy sells records."

Pap was done talking. Buddy answered Pap's silence by face-planting him against the table. Blood dripped freely from Pap's nostrils.

"How did it feel to lay eyes on Lou Licks, to know that your own brother fucked you? To this day I'm convinced he ain't related to you. He doesn't carry that pussy gene. I'm sending you somewhere else alright, but when you get there, you'll beg to come back to this very moment." Buddy straight-legged the back of Pap's chair. He teetered like a domino to the floor, chair and all. Buddy then punted Pap in the head three times. "They say the anticipation is the best part, but I don't know that I'd agree." One more blast from his steel-toe and Buddy was breathing heavy.

Pap tried to faint, to lose consciousness to avoid the experience, but Buddy wasn't kicking him in the right spot.

"You know you could have at least invited me to the joint. I like good music too, but don't worry about your crooning chimp or whatever it is. He'll be with me soon enough. Enjoy hell, Fanti," Buddy said before spitting in his face and walking out. Pap remained on his side, strapped to the chair and then let out all his emotion with a roaring cry. He was writhing in pain and struggled to catch his breath. He didn't believe in killing another man, but Buddy would make an exception if he could only manage it. He'd be dead before he got his shot.

Twenty minutes later, Pap was led down the hall by a mechanical-type police guard. He had trouble limping at the guard's pace. Pap knew where they were leading him and was in no rush, anyhow, to get there. Inside the detention area washroom a couple of former Cabra goons with a promise from Captain Johnson that their police records would catch fire before seeing the D.A. would gut Pazo Fanti until he was dead. There would be no arraignment, not for the hitmen, not for Fanti. He was walked into a small office instead and told to wait on his feet while a by-the-book sergeant, a clean-cut transfer from West Leaf 2nd that looked a lot like his old man, George Rupertina, opened a folder before him.

"Sign here," the sergeant said from behind the counter.

Pap knew nothing of police procedure, but he never thought he would sign his own death certificate. He received a copy but was too distracted to read it. When he was lead right out the front entrance to the open air, Pap wondered what went wrong. Perhaps he was being released to Buddy Plagun for more of the rough stuff and a ride to the country. Why all the hassle of arresting him? The guard tossed him around and undid his bracelets.

"What's this?" Pap asked. Another thought was Basil Demur had worked one more miracle from behind the scenes.

"Ask the broad who bailed you out," the guard said as he closed the door on Pap.

He rubbed the soreness from his wrists, then stepped out to the street with the peculiar feeling that he would get torn down right in front of the station. Plagun loved making examples of enemies. A Packard 740 limo waited on the curb. The front door opened, and Pap clenched his raw teeth. He wanted to duck, but one throbbing leg and another bum peg wouldn't let him.

A tall, middle-aged man exited the car in a spiffy chauffeur's suit. "This way, Mr. Fanti."

Pap didn't say a word. He thought to run but would need to borrow another set of drum sticks. He started for the car and out stepped Vilma Worthton (formerly Griggs) from the back. Pap sprinted through his thoughts, trying to uncover the elegant woman's identity, and then it hit him harder than a rifle round. It was the same face in the pictures Basil Demur had showed him during his inquiry into Chase Griggs. He looked to her hands too. No devices that could spit a pill, not even a blade. He couldn't help but think that Vilma was set to ash him out for the alleged connection to Chase's murder. The news had traveled fast, but it hadn't come from Holly Fountain. She was still missing.

"You look just like your picture. Not as sad, but just as charming," she said trying to counter the effects of what was obviously a rough visit in the cooler. She was cloaked in a black fur hat and fur coat. "Won't you join me for a late breakfast? We can have those wounds tended to properly should you have the time."

Pap looked to Merlin like he was a threat, but there were no guns hanging from his hands either. So he got in the car, and they drove off.

The ride to Vilma's Jester estate was silent. Pap studied Vilma's face and manners. She softened her eyes in return, nothing to hide, polite, dignified. She raised her head and looked to the slowly forming country scenery, but Pap wasn't used to bucolic ways. There were no basements, no tunnels, no fire escapes, no scrapers a thousand feet high to shield him. Instead hundreds of naked sugar maples lined the empty road like mammoth fence posts. Pap understood that whatever was to be said was to happen under conditions far more private than he had ever known.

Merlin pulled up to the large double gate and exited. Something about it reminded Pap of Salty Well and his days guarding the boom barrier at Dunfer's. He wondered if Lou simply pocketed the dough he sent with him to Well's family. Lou had always told him that Mrs. Wells was grateful, but Lou was a liar. He wondered where Buster was. They drove through the gate and around the driveway that stretched another quarter mile through a row of red maples. Merlin pulled up and gave Pap his first glimpse of the face of Vilma's country house. It was a small Victorian castle surrounded by trees the length of giants. Merlin opened Vilma's door first and then went around to Pap's. If they meant to kill him here, no one would ever know. He knew he had to get out now.

"Merlin, do us a favor and return to the Leaf for some proper attire for Mr. Fanti," Vilma said. "What's your size, Mr. Fanti?" she asked Pap.

"I beg your pardon?" Pap wondered.

"You can't remain in those dirty duds, and I'm afraid you won't fit into any of my dresses, not without a girdle and two trucks to pull it shut," she said with a smirk.

Merlin approached Pap and asked for his jacket. Pap hesitated. This was all a new experience for him. Then he removed it but not without grimacing in pain. He felt like he was disrobing for an execution that he couldn't see coming. Whoever his lady was, she killed with class, not like the thugs Pap was used to, but more like the former members of his once vibrant, reclusive club. Again he thought of Buster. Pap gave Merlin his pant and shirt size and off Merlin returned to the Leaf.

Vilma waited for Pap at her front door. He took ginger steps. The adrenaline had dried up, and the aches were setting in just in time for breakfast. Once through the entryway, Pap took stock of all the ornate furnishings, chairs so rigid one would not dare sit on them, end tables of ivory, silk rugs imported from the Asina, Rembrandts and Angelis grew from the wall, each carefully displayed and lit from different angles, a virgin grand piano that hardly looked teased, much less touched. Plants made for an indoor jungle. Bookshelves from floor to ceiling with millions of truths and lies.

Vilma entered the kitchen. Pap couldn't help but follow. An old newspaper was on the breakfast table. Pap eyed the headline. "WEALTHY LAND DEVELOPER GUNNED DOWN. Victim of Gang Feud. Pazo Fanti…"

"I had nothing to do with your husband's death. I want you to know that," Pap said.

"I know," Vilma said. She was now in a long, gingham dress that showed very little but respected much. The truth was that Pap was in the direct causal link, and Vilma knew about it. She proceeded to dig out the first aid kit under her kitchen sink. "I'm sure you want to know why I brought you here. Why I bailed you out. I want to set your mind at ease. I am not on a vendetta to find my husband's murderer. I'm a horrible woman, but part of me actually felt relief the day he died."

"I'm sorry about the whole thing," Pap said.

Vilma put the coffee to brew and had a seat at the breakfast table with Pap. "Now hold still. This is going to sting a little, but we need to clean up those cuts and put some ice on those bruises." She dabbed a swab in a dropper of Merthul and made gentle brush strokes on Pap's cheekbones and above his left eyebrow. Pap's face contracted tight, but he let her continue. "Don't get me wrong. I did love him. He was once a real cake-eater. It hasn't been easy, but I've come to the conclusion that everything he gave me was a gift, especially the things he didn't give me. You may think I had something to do with it."

"Never crossed my mind."

Vilma then packed an ice compress and was careful to apply it to Pap's cheek. He winced but let her continue. "So why does a wealthy widow bail out a reputed criminal without any knowledge of his identity?"

"To be blunt, I thought you brought me here to snuff me out."

"Would you like some coffee, perhaps a cocktail?" Vilma asked. "That's the funniest thing I've ever heard. I've never even seen a gun. Neither had Chase."

"Do you have any family?"

"No kids. A couple of aunts that live in Bigup. Cousins, you know. And I have Merlin who is the best family any old Jane could ask for."

Pap stared at Vilma. She appeared to be the real deal, but he still couldn't figure why she bailed him out, and in doing so, probably committed suicide.

"Would you believe I did it all on my mother's advice?"

"I've believed crazier things," said Pap.

"Well, crazy she is, but to be perfectly honest, she would have made a better clairvoyant. Lives at Vallarriba Sanitarium. Her mind turned on her when Dad died. I hadn't visited her in over four years, since before I married Chase. She told me I would be making the biggest mistake of my life, but I thought she was just being evil, resentful that I wouldn't take her with me. She said I abandoned her. Said Chase forced me to do it. I didn't know how to care for what she had, and where she lives is nicer than a country club. Chase was dashing, a real go-getter. He seemed to know how to treat a lady, at least in the beginning. Mother said he had the face of a grifter and even predicted how long we would be together, that he would run off with some floozie and would meet an untimely death for his treachery. I went back to see her this morning after I read your name in the paper again. I didn't tell her about Chase. Her mind had already checked out on him. I showed her your picture and let her read the article. Want to know what she said?"

Pap gave a soft nod. He couldn't keep his eyes of Vilma. For the first time in years he felt safe, like her walls and her presence would protect him from all the evils gunning for him.

"Anyone who can tame the beast to sing is a man with the heart of an angel. She looked at your face and smiled, said you were lonely, said you had never fallen in love, said your only purpose in life had been to survive, to protect your friends."

Pap clung onto every one of her words, and his eyes started to drift. He had failed the friend that mattered most. Buster couldn't have made it alive. He took his head and lowered it into his cupped palm and then started weeping in silence for what amounted to less than an entire second.

"I come from important people, so obtaining the necessary release order was no trouble. Being the sole heir to a wealthy congressman with friends in the state judiciary has its privileges. How do you like your eggs, or would you rather some fettuccini Alfredo?" Vilma got up and went to the fridge for some vittles and a bottle of chilled Pinot Grigio. Pap kept his back to her. A sudden crash like a bullet through glass made him wince in imagined pain, but it was only the bottle that had slipped from Vilma's hand and shattered on the floor. She was quick to excuse herself, her jumpy nerves and fragile grip, to apologize for startling Pap. He stood up and moved quickly to help. Soon they were both kneeling over the spill until it was no more. Vilma had never seen a man submit himself for her sake. If Pap didn't want her to develop any positive feelings for him, he was doing a poor job. But Pap had other things on his mind.

"You've put yourself in danger, and I can't stay here any longer."

"Is it true? The part about the singing chimp."

Pap's eyes moved away just long enough to give Vilma her answer. "Can I use your phone?"

"Of course," Vilma said, hiding the disappointment in her voice. She promised no matter how hard her days had been, no matter what crazy advice her mother gave, she would not act desperate. What was she saying? She had just bailed out the owner of a notorious speakeasy and alleged underground kingpin without once having met him before. Pap stood up and dialed out. Vilma scribbled her phone number on a piece of paper. Desperate or not, something drew her to him just like Mrs. Worthton and her battered mind claimed. When Pap hung up, she handed him the note.

"I can do a lot for you and your musical animals."

Pap nodded, put the note in his pant pocket and started for the front door. Vilma followed behind. He opened the door and glanced outside. The only things keeping track were the trees. He turned to Vilma. "I'm in your debt," he said with an extended hand.

"You know the most important thing in this world. It's not money. It's loyalty," Vilma said as she clasped his hand with both of hers and stayed at the door watching Pap limp away until he was gone. At least she still had his mugshot inside the paper. The gentlest face she had ever seen on a criminal. She walked to the phone in the living room and dialed her father's old friend, Senator Angus Tolerante, a man she remembered as honest. Somehow she wasn't satisfied with what the papers had reported about Chase Griggs and Pazo Fanti.

- 77 -

The Savings and Loan Building was surrounded by lace-ups and pumps making prints on the pavement. This made Pap Fanti feel safe. As the cab met the curb, Pap's eyes were on high alert. He was deep within enemy territory, and Plagun's buttons could be anywhere. He paid the fare and felt another wave of quick-kick juice push him out the door, through the crowds and into the building. The burly security guard, Sam Stone, was missing. Bad sign. Pap hurried to the elevator. He should have taken the stairs to avoid a trap, but his legs wouldn't make it. He faced the front door to the law office. There were no guards on patrol. Another bad sign. Demur's nameplate was broken in two and lying on the floor. Pap twisted the door handle like he was dialing a safe and let himself in. Dead empty. Not even the new secretary who sat behind her desk. He hushed his steps to Basil's office, careful not to parade himself at the door. He was unarmed, and there would be little he could do should a gun be pointing at him from the other side. He curved his eye inside Basil's office. Plagun had beat him to it. Placards clung crooked on the wall; shattered glasses sprinkled around his minibar, shredded files decorated the floor. It was Demur's eleventh-hour effort to destroy any evidence of the clubs. And on the desk, with his face down in a puddle of blood-signed writs, Basil Demur. Lou gave up the whole crew, but Buddy knew Basil's connection to

Pap long before Pap would ever know that Basil was both the defense and the prosecution's chief informant. The phone rang like it was for him. Pap skinned the window blinds. Within the crowd of nobodies, clusters of men that didn't seem to have any design but to track him down. They were bunched up in threes. One group huddled around a car right in front of the building. Three more at each corner and one exiting a phone booth, surely after having made the call. Pap picked up the phone without saying a word.

"Like a dog returning to its vomit. Your lawyer can't help you now," the voice said through the receiver. Pap recognized Buddy Plagun. "You're gonna walk outside and get in the car without a fuss. There's no way out of that building except through us. If you're not out in thirty seconds, we come in." The phone went dead.

Pap looked out the window again. What thirty seconds? The goons didn't even give him to the count of five. His brain shot into a sprint. He rolled Basil from his desk and checked the top for some sort of weapon. He slid the letter opener in his pocket, then yanked at drawers. There was nothing in the middle box but pens, paper clips and one ink stamp. He opened the three on the right. The last one gave him a glimmer. A revolver on top of an envelope with the word "Calloway" scratched out and "Fishtail" scribbled next to it. He popped the chamber. Six bullets, six kills, and here Pap had never fired one. He barely recalled Lou giving him a couple pointers on the farm, but that was years ago. Pump-hard adrenaline would be his mentor now. He stuffed the envelope in his pant pocket and trotted out to the hall with the gun ready. If he had to use it, this time he would. The hall was clear. He rushed to the elevator and pressed the top of two buttons. The doors slid apart, and Pap got into the empty cart. He thumbed ROOF, and the doors closed. He kept his elbow cocked at ninety degrees with the gun annexed to his hand.

The elevator eased to a stop, and the doors glided open. Pap led, gun first, up a short flight of stairs to the access door. It was stuck. Pap shoved his shoulder into it and was on the roof. He hurried to the eastern ledge. The next building was a bird's flight away. Then he tried the west. No better. He peered down on the cars, the crowds, the triggermen. The rear of the building overlooked an alley. The fire escape would be his last shot. He carried a leg over the ledge and took his first step on the well. Shots rang out and dusted the ledge inches from him. Before Pap could get a visual, he returned fire, discharging two rounds that hit nothing. He had four left. He hunkered into the well until his body was secure behind the building wall. He poked the tops of his eyes and the bottom of his gun barrel over the ledge and spotted two killers racing for him. Their bullets took a head start and pulverized chunks of cement off the wall's edge. Pap pulled his trigger and made contact with the breastbone of one before delivering another lead dart into the groin of the other. That bought him some time. He didn't consider waiting for another wave and started down the stairwell like there was nothing wrong with either leg. The alley appeared clear. Too clear. He had two rounds left, and surely one of them would summon the law. When he got to ground level, he hugged the wall with his back like a magnet, eyes penetrating, turning his head left to right at the openings on each end. Buddy had the whole building surrounded, not a cop within blocks. When he reached the wall's bend, he twisted his eyeball to the sidewalk. Another cluster of buttons sewn up by a car. They were smoking bacos like it was a day at the track. Their eyes happened upon a foursome of hot hips, and that suited Pap just fine. There was a cab sitting idle at the corner. It could have been another button man, but the time for second-guessing was over. Pap darted for the taxi, then threw himself in the back seat and folded at the waist. The hatchets turned and saw a headless rear window just as the cab veered off.

"Step on it," Pap said, his head pressed against a cloth seat that smelled like crayons. Better than smelling his own blood.

An hour later, Pap was at the garage on 5th and Industry, South Leaf. He took the key Basil had left inside the envelope and slid it into the padlock. It snapped open. Pap pulled the garage door up. His Dunfer's trucks. He hurried to the one in the middle. The door was open, and the key was in the ignition. On the driver's seat, a duffle bag with six bottles of scotch. Pap uncapped one. On an empty stomach, it hit him like a bolt of lightning. He flipped the ignition switch. The truck growled to life. He reversed out and began the drive back to Harper East. He took the long way, south into Breaks, a pit stop at a hot dog stand, then up through Jester and past Twenties Slip.

Once he got to the dock, he searched high and low, strained his eyes as far into the ocean as they could stretch. No sign of Buster. He looked to the auburn horizon, waning by the breath. He could only imagine the struggles Buster withstood, all on his own, for the first time in his life, no one to help him, no one to towel him dry or tuck him into bed, no one to enjoy dinners or share a joke after breakfast, no one to offer a comforting hand or an encouraging word, no one to applaud him as he brought fever to the luckiest audience alive. Regret swelled into a cascade of tears. Spared of the hand of human cruelty, he was abandoned to a merciless ocean. Pap begged the waters to give Buster back to him like they once had. He took the hot dog and broke it into pieces. Then he set a trail from the dock's edge and waited. Minutes passed. For the avian pirates making figure eights above, the sound of the wind was a dinner bell. They swooped in and plucked the wiener trail clean. Pap fought the gulls off, but there were too many, and he was too slow. He refused to leave, but as the day closed, Pap felt his chances slip away. If Buster had to suffer the elements, Pap would endure them with him. All through the night, Pap kept a close ear on the waters swishing against the pier. When his body fell weak with fatigue, he returned to his truck and hid away in the sticks.

- 78 -

The white walls screamed sterile. In the center of the room, an ironing board of frigid steel. This was the operating table where Department of Investigations and Special Science (D.I.S.S.) would determine whether there was anything to the postulations of supernatural behavior from the chimpanzee. A team of five scientists with gray masks, oversized goggles and tight caps wrestled with the chimp's arms and legs. One took hold of his head. They racked him on the table. Mr. Crooner's back arched at the touch of the freezing steel. The scientists strapped his wrists and ankles down, then buckled a rubber belt across his chest. But Mr. Crooner kept fighting to break loose with his skull. With hands that jumped in and out to avoid the fanning flame of the chimp's maw, they grabbed Mr. Crooner by the temples. The disciplined hand of Dr. Simple strapped his forehead down. Dr. Simple was tall for a man, and his head was longer than it was wide. He seemed to suffer from jaundice, but that was nothing more than overexposure to the constant white light in the lab. He did nothing but eat and breathe the obscurities of science and never left the premises, not even to visit his wife and kids, who he had buried after bringing home a petri dish with anthrax that had accidentally found its way into their dinner. Mr. Crooner was now stuck, and the only things to escape were his bloody shrieks. One thick piece of tape took care of that. He trembled like a beaten dog, but it swayed not one emotion in the stolid scientists. Dr. Simple considered putting him to sleep, but theorized that agitated blood may project a more accurate manifestation of any mutations. Another scientist with maddening eyes approached the chimp with a syringe the size of a milk bottle and a needle as long as finger. He introduced the point into the soft part of the chimp's arm. Mr. Crooner's eyes gave a half revolution down and then seemingly continued all the way around until they were staring at his own brain. He felt like death incarnate at the sight of six fat vials of Mr. Crooner blood. That was his first day under government observation.

"Touch the rubber duck and you get the banana," said Dr. Simple. He was much kinder on day two, but the battery of tests yielded nothing. Could he read, could he write? They threw books and crayons at him. He threw them back. Could he use or understand hand signals? They waved and pointed. He picked at his belly and nose. Ultimately, could he speak and sing as the newspapers shouted? He grunted and whined, but it was a far cry from singing. Not even worthy to be considered a routine simian. He didn't eat. Didn't drink. He certainly didn't talk, and it was damned if he was to sing. He exhibited no signs of cognition or memory. He was classified as hostile and extremely dangerous. Every time they would try to get close, he would attack with criminal intent. He would defecate in his hand and fling it at them. It was the only trick he knew.

He now found himself seated Indian-style behind a circle of glass, one foot thick all the way around. To his immediate right was a small plastic box with a rubber duck inside of it. He glanced at it once, but his attention returned to the men in long coats with their long yellow pads, collecting around him like buzzards. Dr. Simple had hypothesized that primates could hold many of the same talents that man possessed, and with the proper training, they would be doing circles around their evolved counterparts in no time. Mr. Crooner didn't give an inch; he didn't touch the duck or the box. He just sat there and soon broke his stare. Then he scratched his ass and sniffed his finger. When they teased him with a piece of stale fruit slid in through a shaft that connected to the enclosure, he would sneer and flip the plate over like he did at Crystal Plats. Dr. Simple concluded shock was responsible for the chimp's resistance, so he decided to induce more out of him.

Every twenty minutes around the clock, they would flash rays of white light into his pupils. "Don't let him bat an eye." Maybe in a state of bewildered fury, the chimp would blurt out some famous human curse. But he gave nothing but grunts and squeals, sometimes even sleeping through the wake up calls no matter that they poked at him with sticks.

Days later, the blood came back clean. No glimpses into the mystery that was Mr. Crooner. But he refused to eat and was growing weak. His brain was prodded and sparked, spinal cord tapped, fluids drained from every organ, even biopsied. Soon, D.I.S.S. started to question Dr. Simple and his team. Taxpayers listening to weekly news programs and reading about the dumb chimp who couldn't toot a song complained for its release. It was concluded in Dr. Simple's final report that the mystery chimpanzee was no mystery at all. In fact, some started to speculate whether they had caught the right one to begin with. There were no others aboard that ship. But before they closed the books on the case, they wanted to monitor him a few more days, give him a couple of weeks to get used to his new digs, and perhaps after he assimilated to his environment and started eating again, he might preview some of whatever talents others claimed he had.

As the days wore on, the chimp gave nothing special. He eventually started eating their bland protein slime. He drank lukewarm water and slept as much as he could. He had even stopped flinging clods at the scientists. The game had run its course, and the tests, like the white coats had become his new routine. He was lonely and miserable, but at least he could get used to it again. No moonlit skies to sing the night away, no chirping crickets, no Pap, no Cats 6, no secret clubs, powder baths and tuxes. Most importantly, no Buster.

- 79 -

Buster kept the tip of his nose, and nothing else, above the surface. His paws treaded water with borrowed energy. Land must have been within sight. Then he noticed the first glimmer of light. It was coming from the direction he had been swimming all night. Rows of pastels started to blend as the light gained strength. If he knew nothing else of his instincts it was that he was headed east and the shore was west. His paws hung in the water like they had nothing more to do. His breaths were quick and powerless. He rotated until he was once again on his back and attempted to float, taking in giant breaths of air. There was no hiding from the impending light that soon swallowed up the entire expanse above the water in streaks of gold and teal. It was warm in the most disheartening of ways. Buster turned back on his belly and had his first look at his surroundings. Water in every direction, as far as the eye could see. He thought to call out to Pap in defeat, anyone, but there was no around. A bleat wouldn't help him here. He cuffed for air and made chuffing noises in an effort to propel himself forward. He remembered leisurely swims in brisk waters, Pap watching safely from a finger pier, just the two of them in a private paradise, always within eyeshot of each other. What happened to the land? What happened to his family? He had little time to think but all the time in the world. Buster thought about Mr. Crooner's many tantrums and how they somehow set him at ease to know there were others who feared the same things only more. Now all he had was fear, the desperation of being lost in a world of water.

A pod of silver wetskins swam fifty yards away. They took turns tasting the air with springs and twirls. Morning calisthenics. Buster had never seen such creatures (dolphins), but they seemed to be at one with their fluid domain. It tired Buster even more to see the grace with which they commanded their element. He returned to his back and continued to float aimlessly. The currents swished him from one quadrant of ocean to another.

The air was cold, but the midday sun cooked the surface of the sea into a canvas of wrinkled light. Buster recoiled under the touch of a thousand solar fingertips. He submerged with held breaths, up to thirty seconds a pop to keep from boiling. His hunger pangs soon subsided; so did his resolve to make it to the night. He called out to Pap anyway. "Pap! Are you out there?"

The hours moved the dogged sun from one end of the sky to the other, and soon cooler airs prevailed. Night number two was upon Buster. It promised to be longer than the first. As the sun was snuffed out on the horizon, Buster caught his last glimpse of his new home. Clouds rolled in and blotted out the stars and the moon, making visibility of the black waters nil. He was too worn to even float on his back and kept sinking feet into the water before catapulting himself up. Waves swelled and Buster took a gulp when he least expected it. He choked and coughed and with each exertion, found himself going under to take in more. It was a losing fight. Buster stayed under for several minutes and fainted.

Something circled around him and skimmed his side, then nudged him with its snout, then tapped him with a flipper. It was one of those silver bananas, and it seemed to have heard Buster's distress call. The dolphin bumped Buster to the surface and held him there for minutes at a time. Buster had no clue what was happening, and without realizing it, he had spit up all the water that was sinking him. One after the other, small breaths of oxygen returned to his lungs. He wasn't dead, and if whatever was holding him up continued, he might just make it through the night. The dolphin stayed with Buster until the waves died down and, without saying goodbye, swam off.

The night continued, and Buster continued to cry out, "Pap! Where are you?" He had very little left in his lungs except what was needed to breathe. Just as soon as he started to expel his emotions, he held them back. His thoughts traveled to Mr. Crooner. Where was he? He hadn't seen him in the water. Was he alive? Now was not the time to surrender. Suddenly, and from nowhere visible, Buster found the strength to paddle himself upright, steady and slow and with his snout held over the water's surface. He would not give in that night.

Buster's second morning at sea was better than his first only in that he knew what to expect. But perhaps delusions were starting to kick in. He hadn't eaten in two days. "When the rest of your world is falling apart, never underestimate the power of a good meal." Buster now knew what Pap had meant. He had forgotten what it was like to feel dry, the snug fit of a tuxedo or the soothing voices of his pals. What he would give to have Mr. Crooner yell at him just once right now. The scenery was no different than yesterday. Buster rotated to his back like he was on a spit and, out of the corner of his eye, noticed something in the water with him. He considered it to be one of those friendly fish like the day before, but this object moved with less speed and more calculation. Buster turned his head to what appeared to be the tip of a steak knife slicing through the water at its groggy morning pace. It was another thing he had never seen before, but something about this one made Buster uneasy. The tip pulled below the surface, and Buster thought that to be the end until he felt a striking blow against his bottom. More than a neighborly nudge, this thing meant harm. He sunk his head underwater to try to get a look. From his blurry eye, he counted a six-pack of ten-foot submarines with teeth. They all seemed bent on bear cutlets. Buster, acting on blind impulse, tried to measure the first attacker's approach. The shark's jaws split agape like an accordion fan. Buster pawed into the water with everything he had left in the tank. A perfect whop across the shark's snout sent it back to its corner. Buster went up for air and braced himself for another assault. He hadn't realized he was now spilling blood from his rump. The other killers joined in on the tribal dance. Buster was to be their sacrifice. He considered his next move carefully and wondered whether the dolphin would make a guest appearance and whisk him away from certain death. Without a bad bone in his body, Buster ducked in and curled up tight while the sharks darted at him from all angles. He swung wild paws, kicked and clawed with an untamed spirit, pegging sharks as they brushed by, poking at eyes, filleting flesh. He hated to cause harm to those creatures, but the way things stood, it was either him or the leviathans. One came in with undeniable intentions, and Buster opened his mouth and bit back, crunching the shark over the head with his eyeteeth. It stained the water cherry and sent the other predators into a state of heightened aggression. Buster came up for air. Another defensive maneuver like the last he simply didn't have in him. He could feel the verve of death encircling him from beneath the surface. Without warning, and not a moment too soon, a squall lorded over the sea and tore the water from itself. Buster was lifted up on a wave too great to measure and rushed away from the blood zone. And just as soon as it came, it went, and soon the water was free of sharks and blood minus the rivulets of red that continued to eject from Buster's backside. He was wounded and quickly losing his will to survive. Guilt over what he had just done overwhelmed him. What would the others think had they seen Buster, the perpetrator of such violence?

"The trumpet is a brass instrument, in the family of winds. It was invented as early as 1500 B.C. The kind that I play is the

Elmer Special C. If I change my embouchure, I can derive any pitch, but I can never force it. It has to come as naturally as the springtime flower. Chapter 8, Mastering the Trumpet by Fromp." In his delirium, Buster whispered chapters from the books he had ask of Pap. The words came to him like they were written on his tongue. For hours he recited verses from those many fine works and remembered his finer friend who had the heart to impart such a wise suggestion. If only he could see Mr. Crooner again to say thank you, he would surely not pass on the opportunity.

Around four that afternoon, Buster noticed another object floating on the surface of the chipped waters. It didn't seem to have a life of its own or any purpose other than to bob in and out of sight. Buster tried to float over to the object and soon discovered a piece or driftwood from their ship, just long enough to support him. He reached out and tried to get his entire frame over it, but he kept slipping off. Either his front paws or his rear would find refuge. He let his end dangle in the water, but at least he had some support. He fell asleep, the first time in days. Bouncing to the caprices of the sea, Buster slept till the sun clocked out once more. A million stars awoke him with tingling precision. "What do I do now?" Buster asked the air. A skipping wave smacked him across the face.

The next day preceded a couple more of the same. Buster had tried to take a voluntary gulp of water only to find that it stung his insides to the point of death. He could barely keep his maw open wide enough to let his tongue wag away the heat he'd sorely miss when the sun turned out again. Nothing he did brought him relief. His body convulsed in pain. He saw visions in the stars, the twinkling of flashing lights in the Calloway basement, diamond necklaces on the pretty women, shiny rings on the gents, sparkles from ice cubes falling over each other in glasses, tall and short. The gold handle on Pap's cane. He closed his eyes and this time considered leaving them that way.

When Buster awoke the next morning, it wasn't amongst the stars like he had wished, but rather against a sandbar. His flotation device long adrift, he was stuck in the mud with no desire to move. His eyes cracked open. Land. He dug himself out and let the water wash him onto the beach. The waves slapped him like he had insulted them, and he took it. His pulpy paws were easily cut by the sediment, so he dropped all his weight onto one side. No more exertion. He heard voices from afar growing louder. He didn't recognize them, and this brought one of Pap's most important lessons into focus. "Never approach a voice you don't know."

Nothing could be worse than the last few days, but Buster slid back into the waves and to the sandbar where he could hide from the men who were surveying the beach. They planted themselves at the shoreline and cast their lines out. They looked boorish. Long, wrinkled coats under stained dungarees. They laced the air with profanity. They carried a large steel pale and a tackle box. They were fishermen looking to catch breakfast. Buster had never stolen a thing in his life. He would gladly give up his own meal for another, but his thoughts deceived him, and he knew that if he didn't get something into his stomach, he would perish. With a careful eye on the lines in the water, Buster waited, new instincts born, until one of the lines went taut and trembled. The fisherman jerked his rod and started reeling in the catch. Buster submerged. The line was snapped, and the fisherman fell back on his haunches, empty handed and foul-mouthed. Buster took the fish between his teeth and swallowed it whole. Raw and icky. Nothing like what Lou used to make, but it left a nourishing impression. Buster's insides begged for more. The second fisherman's line stiffened, and Buster took his cue. The men stood bewildered with their snapped lines and decided to find a luckier stretch of beach. Soon they were gone, and Buster had two whole pouches of fishy fuel in his stomach. He returned to the beach and rested a few minutes before heading back out in search of more familiar settings.

Hugging the shoreline, Buster shifted with the currents, keeping his bearings on the land. The copper beach was soon cut by rivers of rocks and trees. Baby hills rose from the water and led to Buster's first glimpse of human involvement, what looked like crumbling houses pasted, one on top of the other. He passed on and, after another mile of drifting, observed a train yard, lime-stained cars dormant on the tracks. The water went slick with oil and brought instant discomfort. Buster attempted refuge on a buoy, but when he came within yards, he noticed he wasn't the only one trying to avoid the tainted waters. Dogs, brazen with bronchitis. Dogs with flippers and soapy skin, they barked like they were part of their own band, but this was no music. Hacking, mindless ferment, it was offensive. They weren't the type to share their tiny island either and kept snapping at Buster's heels to shove him off. He remembered staring at the water dogs with bleak eyes before washing away.

The landscape went empty for what seemed miles of gravel, pewter and dead until he came across something that jogged his most intense memories. Finger piers, docks, factories hidden within a cove. A rush of energy shook his blood. Pulling through the water, he arrived at his old stomping grounds, Twenties Slip and Calloway. The thought of Pisto Leroy didn't cross his mind. Arteries of oil stretched all around and pasted his fur. He swam around the finger piers, now caked in petroleum. He tried to climb on board but kept slipping. If only he was clothed again in soft fabrics instead of this waxy film. He disapproved of his current nakedness. All the insecurities that Mr. Crooner had preached about him, how true they were. He had to find his way back into the club. Surely, his pals would be there in hiding with a pitcher of chocolate milk and a bowl of spaghetti. Maybe even put on a show. He wanted to play with all his heart, as soon as tonight, if only he could keep from tripping over his own sludgy feet.

Buster cased the boiler room and pressed onward to the main building. He glanced in all directions just as Pap had taught him, then dashed across the yard and to the entrance. It was easy to open. No locks, bars, posts, no Trunks, no Turnip, no Gophers manning the bridge high above.

For the first time in many days he felt at home. He raced down the pitch-black hall, by rote, and swung the door, leading to the basement, wide open. A soft light peekabooed from below. He hustled down. A flickering lamp gave just enough of itself to reveal the markers, the yellow tape ribboned around the basement. It read: "POLICE." Everything he had once enjoyed was gone. He rushed past the spot that was once the bandstand, now a load of sawdust, and up the back flight of stairs.

Ink Tambo's sleeping bag was still rolled on the floor. Buster knocked on the washroom door, but when he received no answer, he barged in. The bare mattress, the empty tub, also in belts of yellow tape. He checked the stalls. Vacant. Buster fell into a ball and started sobbing. If there was any hope before, now there was none. His pals were gone, and he was the only one left. He heard a sound coming from outside, and his head perked up. Voices unfamiliar to him spoke of a chimp and all the gnarly experiments conducted at a place called D.I.S.S.; how he'd end up on some display case as the world's first unsung phony. They were talking about Mr. Crooner. *He needed a drink to get over singing in front of a new crowd! Didn't they know this? He was alive!* But Buster quelled his enthusiasm, sensing instead the threat. Ruthless experiments meant they would do the same to him. He made his way towards the side exit. He had never needed to use it until now, but Pap and Lou had trained him well. After a short stretch, it would lead into a tunnel. When he surfaced, he'd be clear of the compound and at an open shore. He helped the side door yawn and threw an eye out. There were now two police cars with coppers surveying the scene, but the manhole was within reach. Buster lunged into a sprint as a ringed net swooped down over his head. It was connected to a long, metallic handle that connected to the commanding grip of a policeman.

"What are you doing here?" the cop said as he twisted the handle and upended Buster.

He struggled to wiggle out, but with each tug, the net constricted in the cop's steel grip. With an unprecedented flash of bone-crunching fangs, Buster twisted his neck and chomped down on the handle. The copper bawled for backup. Buster swiped the handle clean from his fists and took off, the rim of the net yoked round his neck, the steel handle clattering against the pavement. Buster made a beeline to the dock's edge and tobogganed head first into the water. The cops crowded the dock and aimed their firearms at the surface.

"That was that bear they were talking about," a cop said.

"Probably looking for his buddy," another said. They remained until the bear decided to resurface, but that became a long wait. After several minutes of staring at a blank slate, the cops gave each other a crazy eye. "Probably just a white seal," said one, "or maybe a hairy mermaid," said another. They dispersed and returned to their mindless duties of assuming important poses.

Buster resurfaced a hundred yards out and kept a lookout on what had now become terra incognita. He was lucky to be in the clear. What's more, Mr. Crooner was alive, and with whatever strength he had left, whatever days his life would grant, he would apply his all to ensure that he found his friend and brought him to safety. But such optimism was fleeting for Buster knew he could never return to the place he once called home. There was no more family, no more living to show. Now it was living to live. How could he save Mr. Crooner, if he couldn't even save himself? His only priorities were to keep from being nabbed and to eat. He made good use of another piece of driftwood. When it was time to sleep, he would float out into the harbor. When it was time to eat, he took to the beach. Fish had washed up from the oil slick. They were cloaked in flies and harvesting maggots. He returned his catch to the water, rinsed the top layer clean and stuffed the rotten fish down his throat.

Day after day, the same watered-down ritual, and soon Buster got used to his new way of life. He started his mornings before the sun cracked a smile with another rotting fish, then it was off to the driftwood and sea. He was a loiterer by fate. Now as thin as Mr. Crooner. He thought of the privilege of holding his Elmer, even his old hunting horn. Buster started to wonder how many more days like this he had left. Each passing sun, he ate less, hoped less, slept more. He started to refuse fish carcasses and considered them less essential to his survival. A life without a purpose was death, and one morning Buster decided to stop fighting. He took his log out to the water and decided he would just float out as far as the current took him. And when the log was tired of floating and sunk, Buster would sink with it. He had given everything he had with a grace that was not to be found in this world, and it was time to experience the peace found around the bend of eternity.

When Buster awoke, he was still floating atop his log and nowhere near that better place. Maybe just one more round. The shore cut the sky. Off his side he paid heed to a harmless looking sailor in a rowboat with a fishing line in the water. He streamed over and had a closer look at the man, thin and disheveled, an immature beard smothered his cheeks and neck, his clothes tattered. It caused Buster moral anguish to attempt the theft from someone who appeared to need it more, but not enough to fully dissuade him. He went under as he approached the line and hoped to see a clean, fat catch sentenced to the hook.

The man felt his line jerk and pulled back so hard he nearly went overboard. He tugged and reeled with all his might. He reached for a small net and realized it would be insufficient for such a catch. Buster's head surfaced with the fish halfway in his mouth. He was too famished, too spent to care if he was made out by the eyes of a stranger. The man dropped his fishing rod and net and rose to his feet like a tree from firm soil.

"Buster," the man said. Buster looked up to the man and noticed that this deficient wretch was Pap. He threw himself into the water, swam to Buster and swallowed him with his arms. "I can't believe I found you! You're alive!" Pap whooped. Such relief as this Buster had never known, so he blacked out.

- 80 -

Pap split eyes between the road and Buster who did nothing but sleep. He pulled up to Vilma's country estate. The front gate was opened. He didn't know whether this was a good or bad thing, but he drove through anyway and jolted the Dunfer's truck to a halt at her front steps. Vilma appeared at the door at the same time Pap rushed around the grill to Buster's side.

"Mr. Fanti?"

"I need your help," Pap said. He scooped Buster out. Vilma noted that whatever was wrapped in his old coat wasn't human. She met Pap halfway down the steps.

"Oh dear, look at you. You look terrible," Vilma said as she put a hand on his arm. They entered the house, and Pap set Buster to rest atop the long seat in the foyer.

Vilma couldn't take her eyes of the frail bear. "Is that?"

"This is Buster Horn. He's the most harmless creature you'll ever meet, only I'm afraid he may appear a bit more harmless than usual."

Buster panted softly, his eyes snipped open. Vilma helped carry Buster to one of the guest rooms on the first floor. They rested him on the bed, and he bloomed an eye to Vilma. It was then that she realized something different about him.

"You are beautiful," Buster said to Vilma in a depleted voice. It shot a wave of surprise through her eyes.

"Did he just?" she asked, not even able to finish the thought.

"He'd give you a hug, too, and play you a song, but he needs to rest," Pap said. He was trying to keep things light but knew that Buster's fate was still hanging in the balance. Buster swallowed like a baby.

"He's the sweetest of things," Vilma said.

"You keep telling him that, he won't ever stop pestering you," Pap joked.

"What can we do?"

"What do you need, little buddy? Just say it and it's yours."

Buster grinned without a word and dozed off again. Pap cast a sad eye to Vilma.

An hour later, Buster's shark bite was disinfected and dressed, and Pap was showered and in his new clothes that Merlin had brought. He didn't shave, but he felt clean. Vilma was happy to have him and his furry companion. They sat at the breakfast table to coffee and muffins. Pap shared his story with her, how he came to find Buster and Mr. Crooner and all the wonders they had brought him.

"I feel guilty," Vilma said.

"Why ever for?"

"For not going in that first night at your clothing factory," she said. "He's going to make it, you know. You both will stay here with me. I won't take no for an answer."

"I can't repay you for your kindness," Pap said. But without realizing it, he had already started.

Vilma felt inspired to live once more. Her lonely days were gone, even more so her days spent in company that made her wish she was alone. The last few months of their marriage, Chase had such a hard time coexisting with Vilma. The very sound of her voice made his skin crawl. He would say such ugly things to her after a few drinks that she swore she had married an enemy. "Half your life bleeding, the other half dried up makes for a lifetime of bitching." How she hemorrhaged when Chase threw tongues at her.

For an entire month, she mothered Buster like he was her child. Breakfasts in bed, walks around the estate. They frolicked in the woods and felt safe. Each day, Pap fell deeper for Vilma and needed to show her just how much he was starting to care for her. He asked Merlin if he could find him an old hunting horn, nothing expensive, something he could cover with a bottle of scotch. Merlin obliged and was happy to take the bottle. In fact, he would not drink it alone and convinced Pap that the only way he would get his hunting horn was to enjoy the drink with him and Vilma every night around the dinner table. Pap agreed.

"Buster, guess what we brought you," Pap said with his hand behind his back. Vilma couldn't contain herself as she took her front-row seat next to Merlin. It was like being at a birthday party. She had fallen for Pap's pure heart just as her mother had predicted. Pap revealed what was in his hand. Buster's eyes grew bright at the sight of the hunting horn. He even asked if it was the same one he once played. "What say you show Ms. Vilma what you can do."

Buster scooted up from his bed into a ninety degree angle. He connected the horn to his snout like it was the first time. He closed his eyes and concentrated a narrow breath of air through the mouthpiece. It came out crackled and not in Buster's style. His lungs were damaged from the days on the sea, but he didn't let that stop him from blowing. Merlin and Vilma stood with their lower jaws hanging off the rest of their face. For them it was a glorious first. Didn't matter that Buster was missing notes, that they came out through a gravel bed, there was something masterful in the way he pawed the horn. He blew for five minutes and then set the horn to rest at his side. Vilma and Merlin rushed their hands together and cheered as loudly as Buster could remember. In an instant, all those smoky nights under the lights came surging into frame. Pap stood by Vilma with tears in his eyes. Buster dipped to a bow. He blew another couple of tunes. When he finished his last, his demeanor had changed.

"What's the matter, Bus?" Pap asked.

Buster was hesitant in response, but the more he waited, the more it propelled him to action. "I have to find Mr. Crooner," he said. His voice was unwavering. His eyes did not shift away from Pap.

For the first time, Pap had to lower his head in an effort to regain his thoughts. He feared this day would come. "Could we be left alone for a minute?" Pap asked Vilma.

She nodded and led Merlin out of the room, but before she crossed the threshold, she turned back and said, "That was magnificent, Buster. Thank you."

"Oh no, thank you, Ms. Vilma. You are a most lovely lady and a most gracious host," Buster responded.

Vilma blushed as she closed the door. But she remained within earshot and could hear the entire discussion. It didn't take long for it to escalate into something more.

"I can't let you do it," Pap said.

"I have to."

"You know I thought I'd never see you again. If you go this time, I know I won't. You're all I have left."

"The first time I saw someone in pain it was you at the farm. I really didn't know what it meant at the time, but I knew it was bad. I didn't know what things like death were until I saw Pisto Leroy. And then I saw the Fishtail and Lou. Poor Lou. It broke my heart. Now that I know these things are real, that real dangers exist, just like you said, Pap, just like you protected me from for all these years, I can't let that happen to Mr. Crooner. I can't be at peace knowing he's out there suffering. You waited for me, you searched for me, you never lost hope. I can't either," Buster said.

Pap's face clung to frustration. Buster was talking beautiful, uninterrupted truths, but to him it was all hooey, and he had to talk him out of it by any means necessary. "How could you even consider something like this after everything he did to you? You think he would go looking for you?"

"Doesn't matter."

"He never liked you. Told me himself. Said you were the worst thing that ever happened to him. Said you made him feel like a monster. Called you an enemy. An enemy! And you want to go out there and get yourself killed for that? I need you to quit all this nonsense. Remember who stuck his neck out for you since the start."

"I love you with all my heart, but there's nothing you can say that will stop me. I'm sorry, Pap. I have to find him." Buster had never been plucky, but here he was in Pap's face set to forge his own destiny.

"Why?"

"Because he's my friend, and nothing will ever change that."

Suddenly, thoughts of Lou resurfaced in Pap's mind. He had been there from the start, given of himself everything he had, even things that weren't his, like his grandmother's farm. And he stuck around till his end. Pap couldn't blame Lou for the cross. Most would have done it long before if they had any sense in them. Pap wouldn't dare tell Buster to consider Lou's death and how the bear had something to do with it. In fact, were it not for the bear, had the shipment come up clean as intended, perhaps no one would be dead now. Pap had to change his brain's direction before he started to look on that creature before him with contempt. After all, Buster was something that had brought with him, aside from the immeasurable joy, some of Pap's most painful experiences. So instead of reminding Buster of Lou's slaying, instead of recalling to his memory that Pisto Leroy was killed to protect him, Pap surprised him with the demise of another.

"Mr. Crooner is dead."

"Don't say that! That's not true!" Buster's voice cracked as he fought the sadness he felt with fleeting sounds of strength.

He burst from the room and brushed past Vilma in a blind despair.

"Buster! Come back! Don't do this to me!" Pap's words came out with a tremble. He clutched his chest like something had kicked his heart in. Vilma entered and saw Pap hunched over the bed struggling to catch his wind.

"Pap!" Vilma sustained him by the shoulders and eased him down on the pillow. "Please, Pap. Breathe. Everything's going to be alright. Just breathe."

"I'm okay," slipped past Pap's teeth just before the lights went dim and he passed out.

"Merlin!" Vilma screamed. "Call the doctor!"

Sylvester Cobard was the Worthton family physician. He was chief of internal medicine at Good Leaf General and had made the late congressman's final moments as comfortable as a man dying of arsenic-laced booze could have. Cobard's bald head was large as a bowling ball and enjoyed a daily shine. He grew a straightedge mustache, and when he diagnosed a patient with those emerald eyes, they knew it was serious. A cloudy three-piece suit was his traditional cover.

Cobard arrived at the Jester Estate thirty minutes after the call, just as Pap was coming to. The doctor gave him a thorough examination and advised him to check into the hospital. Pap refused. He wanted Cobard gone and told him so in no uncertain terms. He couldn't have a man of science lay eyes on Buster.

"You've suffered a mild heart attack. I'm a bit of a revolutionary when it comes to treating this sort of thing. I don't like my patients to recover on their own, but if you insist on staying here, I'll leave you with these. Take one if you feel any chest pain and call me if things get worse." Cobard left him a handful of Trintrin tabs. Then he pulled Vilma aside and said, "Keep a close eye on him. The man is as stubborn as your father."

Vilma followed Cobard to his car and forced him to take triple his standard house call fee. He refused, like the good doctor he was, but there was no arguing with Vilma about money.

She then returned to Pap's bedside and took a seat. "How are you feeling, and don't lie to me."

"I'm okay. Honest. I just got a little light-headed, but I'll be alright. Where's Buster?" Pap asked.

"Out back. I was just about to check on him."

"Talk to him for me. Tell him he can't leave."

"You just rest, will you? Unless you're thinking of leaving too."

"Nix and never."

"Then sleep." Vilma kissed Pap's forehead and went to see Buster.

He was outside behind the house, sitting among the trees and picking at shiftless blades of grass. Vilma kept an eye on him from her kitchen window while mixing him a chocolate milk. The weight of his thoughts was making his head hang low. She headed out back. "I thought you could use one of these." She handed Buster the drink.

"Thank you, Ms. Vilma." Buster took it with both paws and brought it to his mouth for a sip.

"You're Pap's going to be just fine."

"I know. Nothing bad can happen to him while you're around," Buster said with his head drooping low.

It shook Vilma to hear Buster paying her compliments while he suffered such agonies. "I know what it's like to be down in the dumps. If you want to talk about anything, I'm here."

"Mr. Crooner isn't dead. I don't know why Pap would ever lie to me." Buster knew Pap had bore false witness because he would never accept that his friend was gone. For the first time, he felt a bitter heart beating in his chest towards the only man he considered a father.

"He doesn't know how else to keep you safe. When you care for someone as much, sometimes you're willing to do anything, even lie to make sure nothing bad happens to them. That's how much he cares for you," Vilma said.

"Then he should care about Mr. Crooner."

"Who is Mr. Crooner?"

"Oh, you'd love him to pieces. He can be a bit of a drag, but I know deep down he's 18 karat. He helped me in ways I could have never known. Taught me to take things seriously. We made crazy tunes together." Buster shifted his eyes until they were firm on Vilma's. "He's the only other one I know, and I'll find him if it's the last thing I do." He then submitted his head in defeat. He knew he wouldn't get far without human help.

"Pap doesn't want you to go. He thinks it's too dangerous."

"He's right, but that won't stop me. Ms. Vilma, I have to find him. I don't want to get anyone else involved. I can do it all by myself." But Buster didn't believe a word he said.

"What if I were to say I'll help you?" Vilma asked. Buster's head propped up. His eyes longed for a miracle of their own.

"I would never impose."

"This last month with you and Pap has been the happiest of my life. I love your Pap, but I can't keep you from doing what you have to do. I know you have a more important mission here, and if it's to save your friend, then I'll do whatever you ask."

"What about Pap? I don't want to make him sore at me. He's all the good I've known."

"You're all the good he's known, but he'll understand. If you go, you should go tonight. I know someone who can help."

- 81 -

Of all the people to set foot in DC Stiles' office, Vilma Griggs walked in with Buster Horn. It was the middle of the night. Merlin provided another layer of cover between Buster and any outsiders. At this hour, they came across none. Stiles waited to hear what they had to say before uttering a word. He feared that Vilma was there to shake him down for Chase's death. He would swear he was in the dark about it. As far as Stiles knew, Chase had no connection to Pap Fanti, other than being a rich asshole who frolicked at his club and picked up one of his dancers. Mixed emotions kept Stiles' face empty. He had read of Pap's downfall and presumed the worst for Buster. But there was the magical bear, clad in a turtleneck, stocky plaid overcoat, gloves and corduroy pants that fit his thick legs loose and covered his paws. His paperboy was a large bag that smothered his eyes and ears, but the snout was still a dead giveaway. He looked confident. Stiles wanted to shake his hand and give him a hug. He loved listening to the bear blow his trumpet. What was he doing with Vilma? And why had they chosen such an hour to make an entrance? He never pinned either Vilma or Buster as a life taker. And Merlin simply looked too old to fire a gun. He couldn't put clues together fast enough. He should have taken his eleven grand and shut the office, but tonight he was still rubbing the sleep from his eyes and was lucky to remember to put on a robe before answering the door.

"Mr. Stiles is the best detective on the Leaf. If he can't find Mr. Crooner, no one can," were the first words out of Vilma's mouth. They were directed to Buster right in front of Stiles. "Hello, Mr. Stiles. Hope we didn't wake you, but we have an emergency." Vilma's tone was calm but assertive.

"Pap calls DC Stiles the clue catcher," Buster said, glancing at all the lobby cards on his wall. He paid special attention to *Bullets Don't Blink*, Lala Terre's last picture. The image reflected a creepy man with a gun to a horrified woman's head. Buster wasn't sure what to make of it. He knew nothing from movies.

"How you doing, Busboy? That's the famous Lala Terre." Stiles said.

"She looks like she's in trouble," Buster said.

"It's all make-believe, you know, for show."

"You know each other? You know Pap Fanti?" Vilma asked Stiles. It was at that moment that Stiles exhaled his first real breath. She hadn't connected him to Pap, and he was cleared of any wrongdoing, including, in his mind, the six G's he blackmailed from Chase just before he kicked the bucket. But there was another matter that had him by the collar.

Stiles looked to Vilma and her chauffeur. "Buster, he's quite the class act." Then he returned to Buster. "What are you doing with Mrs. Griggs?" Stiles didn't seem to be as put together with Buster standing before him. He was two seconds from being discovered a fake, not worthy of a silver dollar when the suspects he was paid to find hung out at the same places he ordered drinks. Pinning Chase Griggs with Holly Fountain was a cake walk compared to Lala Terre's son.

"I'm here to pay you $10,000 to find Mr. Crooner, the singing chimpanzee, and bring him back safely," Vilma said. What else was there to do when money did everything for you if not give in to such impulses? All in all, $21,000 Stiles stood to make from her and her stiff ex. Vilma Worthton, FKA Griggs, had the bees.

"And here I thought you wanted some dish on your husband's drop. Not that I would know anything more than what I read in the papers. Sorry about that by the way," Stiles said. He spoke very nonchalant, like Chase Griggs had suffered a fender bender and not a death.

"Spare me the sympathy, Mr. Stiles. I didn't come to speak trifles. I've already got people piecing the angles. I'm certain Pap Fanti was in the clear, despite the smears," Vilma said as she plucked a cigarette from her case and lighted it. She took in a puff of smoke and recycled it through her miniscule nose tunnels.

"Ten large. That's a lot of scratch to find a chimp. No offense," Stiles directed to Buster. "I'll want payment in advance."

Vilma took out her checkbook and used Stiles' cluttered office desk to write a check made payable to DC Stiles. "I expect all terms to be met," she said.

"Of course you do," Stiles said. "The kid stays with me for the job. That's my other term."

"Doesn't work that way. He'll be fingered a mile out," Vilma said.

"No, no, Ms. Vilma. He's right. If anyone stands a chance when we find him, it'll be me. I have to tag along," Buster injected.

"Listen to the bear. I'm not talking to that chimp alone. I'm not even putting a hand on him, assuming he's even alive. I've heard the stories. You sure you want to put your neck out for him, Buster?"

"He's alive, and I'd put out a hundred necks if I had them," Buster said. There was a small flame in his eyes that Stiles cared not to douse.

Stiles looked to Vilma and then Merlin. They seemed to relay the same fire. "Okay," he said with resignation. He lit a smoke and took a seat. "We'll start in the morning. I gotta couch you can crash on, kid. Where's Pap?"

"He's staying with me," Vilma said. "He's okay."

"He's staying with you?" Stiles asked. Funny how things worked out, he thought.

"Funny how things work out," Vilma said as she jotted down her Jester address and phone number on blank sheet of paper. "You have my number and my trust, Mr. Stiles. If you let anything happen to Buster, I'll never forgive you." She knelt down to Buster, removed his hat and knighted him with a kiss on the head. Buster reached out to her with a hug that melted her heart. She whispered into Buster's ear, "I'll take care of your Pap. You just take care of yourself."

Buster swung his snout up and down and looked to Vilma with encouraged eyes. She shifted between Buster and Stiles and then finally to Merlin before they left.

Sitting in the back seat of the car, Vilma wiped the tear from her cheek. She had known the blessing of motherhood for one splendid month. And in the 45-minute car ride to Stiles' office, she had taught Buster all of life's cruel lessons. "When you hail a cab, put a hand in the air like this." And she'd show him. "Make sure you always have your gloves on. When you order at a deli, keep your head inside your menu. Don't ever show your face, no matter that I think it's the most precious face in the world." She had given him a hundred bucks in emergency money. He tried to give it back, admitting that he never had a use for that brand of lettuce. But Vilma wouldn't let him go without taking it, so he slid the bills in his pocket and gave her another hug. "If you need me, I'm always here. It was my greatest privilege to have met you. Pap is right. You are an angel."

It was 6 am the next morning when Pap awoke to sounds of heartache, but it had nothing to do with his pumper. He folded out of bed and knew that Buster was gone again. And he knew that Vilma had taken him wherever he needed to go. She was sitting in the kitchen peering out the window at the spot Buster occupied the prior afternoon. The same trees reminisced about his memory. She tasted a cup of Joe and felt a draft of air, disappointed but not hostile, breeze in.

"Where did you take him?" Pap asked.

"DC Stiles, your friend."

Pap's neck went limp, and his head wilted like he had just been invited to Buster's funeral. "Stiles is a good detective, a good man," he said unconvincingly. Stiles had uncovered the truth behind Chase and Holly against Pap's every wish and sent Holly into limbo and perhaps Chase to his grave, but he still had to be a good man. Buster was under his care now.

"I trust him to get the job done and bring them both back safe and sound," said Vilma, but her words did little to raise Pap's head. "I'm sorry, Pap, but I couldn't stand to see him like that. He looked like he could conquer the world again when I left him."

Pap shook the melancholy off his chin. "I've always credited chance with my existence, until Buster came into it. Even though he needed me to watch over him, I always felt it was him watching over me."

"He promised me he'd come back and play his horn again."

"He's a goner. Those streets will eat him alive."

"I think he's more resourceful than you give him credit for."

"You don't know Buster." Come to think of it, neither did Pap anymore. Stay encouraged, stay wise, bend, don't break, compromise, no hard lines and easygoing wins the race. All words Pap lived by. He could have prevented this had he been a man who spoke with his gun instead of his heart. He had lost his faith in science, claims of man coming from monkeys and bears. They guessed right, only in the wrong direction. Neither was there God, his devil, no here nor there, no fidelity that couldn't be bartered. The entire universe: a sensational swindle. There was only chance and blind, unabashed competition, who could claim the greatest prize while keeping his neck off the cutting board. One bond connected all mankind, and at no time before had it convicted Pap more than now. The misconception, more than anything else, that of all the things he thought he controlled, his fate might be one. They were just lies he told himself to keep it together. Pap spent the rest of the day in the darkness of the guest room with Buster's hunting horn in his hands and a bruised soul under his feet. "Goodbye, kid. You were my greatest honor."

- 82 -

Captain Sert Johnson had called Buddy Plagun the same afternoon Pap was "killed." He felt it the smarter thing to do. Buddy would find out on his own and then Johnson would look like he was in on it, and Johnson would have to take Buddy and who knows how many other hoods down to avoid his own assassination. So Buddy knew right after he had left Fanti in the trick room that he flew like a bird. It took nearly thirty days, however, to get a sit down with the captain. Buddy was a pit bull on gun powder, demanded blood and restitution, threatened to blow up the precinct, talking all sorts of rubbish. He needed to cool down, and Captain Johnson was quickly developing a sour taste in his mouth over Buddy's disrespect, no matter how much money he had collected. Plus a meeting with Buddy so early after a botched hit on a caged rat would have required an army in security. He wouldn't take his calls. When Buddy tried him at the precinct, a muscle-bound sergeant threatened arrest if he didn't leave. The brush-off raised Buddy's suspicions. But Johnson finally agreed to a meeting to settle all business. Out in the open where Buddy wouldn't pull a fast one.

It took place at the Kernel Deli, downtown, during a breakfast rush. Buddy agreed. That the public saw them together was not cause for concern for either. Throngs of commuters minded their hash browns and sunny side ups. Johnson had undercover badges peppered throughout the deli, including the booths and tables surrounding them as another sound insulator. Buddy didn't know that. Lieutenant Quick Coogan parked conveniently in front of the large window where Johnson and Plagun were to take their booth. Buddy had buttons scattered along the dining counter. Jesse Under parked conveniently across the street from Quick Coogan. Johnson didn't know this. It was supposed to be a friendly breakfast, explanations given, hatchets buried. More than anything it was supposed to remain calm, no yelling, no finger pointing. Johnson was in his usual bull dress, a brown coat and slacks. His sunglasses blocked any lies, his cap a parasol over his brow. He kept one hand over his mouth and the other over a dark folder. Plagun donned his standard gray pinstripe, no sunglasses, no hat, his hair preened into luminous clay. A flower of smoke grew from his cigarette. Neither ordered breakfast. Just coffee.

"How was the vacation?" Buddy said.

"Cut the bullshit. That court order was official. The sergeant who signed his release was doing his job, and I didn't find out till two hours later. These ain't the Fist days. You make a move on a cop, you fry."

"Here I thought you were gonna tell me it was a resurrection. Those men were under your watch. You know I coulda finished it myself. You said no. There'd be too much heat. You said it would be taken care of. I walked out of that dog pound and not half an hour later, he's on the streets like he just left the theater. As for icing a badge, don't wet your bed. I'da done it long ago," Buddy said.

Johnson was visibly disturbed, both at the way Buddy addressed him like he was some delivery boy and something of even graver concern. For the first time in his illustrious career, Captain Sert Johnson had his own fish to fry. He slid the folder across the table like he was out of time and ready to cut the meeting short. Buddy opened it and read names like Vilma Worthton, the G.A.V. probe into the Good Leaf police department, Captain Sert Johnson, Lieutenant Quick Coogan, their connections to Bill and Buddy Plagun, Jesse Under, Commodore Cabra, the Ziggie Fist hit, the take down of The Fistail and a dozen other slayings, a grand jury indictment and charges of corruption, conspiracy and murder.

"I don't remember much about my old man, but this lesson stands out more than any other. He used to punch my hand every time I'd put it in my mouth. Said one day I'd bite it off. I was just a little runt, maybe two, three. The last time he punched it so hard, it broke. I never put my hand in my mouth again."

"Lessons are for wicked people," Buddy rebutted.

"You want to know how something like this happens? Favors. Something you know all about. The judge was dialed in to her old man and didn't turn her or her money down. He also happens to be on the anti-corruption committee that's responsible for this," Johnson said.

"Who's this?"

"The name Chase Griggs get a rise out of you?" Johnson asked. "That was her husband."

"You know how much I've paid you." Buddy's voice had forgotten there were gossips all over the place.

Johnson put a finger to his mouth. His voice remained monotone. "Glue yourself back together, and dig this: We're through. No more phone calls, no more meetings. You try anything, you blow away like dust. Show up within a mile of the precinct, I make you the first man on the moon. I told you to focus on the important things. You're lucky I don't have you snuffed out right here. Look around. A dozen bulls with itchy fingers just waiting to tar and feather you."

Buddy checked an eye on all his backup at the dining counter. They could finish it right here, he thought. Make the OK Corral look like the boy scouts.

"As for all your…political contributions," Johnson said as he wrote a large number, a "1" followed by six "0s," on a napkin and slid it across the sticky table. "That's on my desk first thing tomorrow."

Buddy contorted the expression of a man who had just been given twenty-four hours to live.

Johnson kept on the offensive. "That's right. You're gonna bankroll my way out of this jam, and then you're gonna peter out like the last drop of water in the desert. I don't get it, I send in the cavalry to break up shop and nail you to a cross. Then you can talk resurrections all you want." Johnson stood up and left.

Buddy Plagun's face flushed with evil blood. He'd kill them all, Johnson, Coogan, all the undercover pigs buried in booths waiting to watch him head to his car and blow, anyone who stood in his way. There would be no payoffs. He'd string a battalion around Crystal Plats and secure all his routes. If they tried to get inside the Dirty Spoon, they'd get cut to pieces at the door. This was war.

Johnson got in the car with Coogan and batted an eye to Buddy. Buddy pulled out his gun and fired through the window, killing both the captain and his lieutenant. The bulls and hoods joined in and turned the deli into a bloodbath, but it was all just Buddy's twisted fantasy. Either way, it was time for the captain to retire. Buddy left a couple of bucks on the table and took off. Bill Plagun had always told him to keep his temper to himself. A calm man was a feared man. Buddy had failed to use that calm when he tried to hit Fanti. Some guardian angel that coward must have had to dodge two point-blank hits. He got to the front door of his car and made eye contact with Jesse Under. Then with a slide of his head, Buddy got in and took a deep breath. He glanced to his passenger seat and the newspaper article. It was circled in pen. "Mystery chimp, all monkey, no music. To be auctioned at Good Leaf Livestock Market." There were only so many chimps floating around the Leaf and as far as Buddy reckoned, they were all picking their asses at Crystal Plats. He had a good idea what would have made any chimp sing too. It was to be found inside his warehouses. With the rest of his world caving in, Buddy was curious to know what the papers had originally publicized, no matter that they now sang a different tune. For all he knew, a change in racket might be right around the corner. Besides, no one stole from him or the memory of his father and got away with it.

- 83 -

Washed-up farmers formed a single file beside their malnourished livestock. Cattle, horses, sheep, the standard fare. They were lucky to get pennies on the dollar from bidding industrialists. Glue manufacturers with trailers waiting in the parking lot to load up the horses. Makers of soaps and shampoos picked out cows and sheep. The pigs went to cosmetics. The auction even brought out the innovation of some too poor to shop at the local grocer. Here they could get an anorexic cow on the cheap and boil the nutrients out, down the bone. A family of five could live an entire month on one of these five-buck steers. The air under the open-roof arena was dusty and filled with the stink of failure.

Greedy bidders formed two lines on each side of the auction row, including an old man in navy skin, a red-wine turban and a gray beard with streaks the shape of lightning that tickled his navel. He rubbed the garrote with his fingers like a rosary. He had come here for one thing only. He wasn't interested in another source of food or converting the living to the dead for a fast buck. There was a chimp that sat, droopy and spent, inside a caged cart. It was Mr. Crooner, and he was being pulled by a lever to the auction stage. The old man kept a watchful eye on him. He wouldn't be outbid. It was the chance he had always dreamed of. Mr. Crooner's cage was rolled into the auction box. Bidders scratched their heads in ire and set their sights on the sexy heifer that was next on deck. If there was one thing these Leaftons wouldn't dare, it was to eat something that could have passed for an uncle at the dinner table.

The auctioneer was a portly man with plump lips that flapped when he dribbled his thick tongue into the mic. He opened the bidding at one dollar on a news report that the chimp wasn't even worthy to be a bath rug. Mr. Crooner now looked old. In only a few weeks the gray on his whiskers had outclassed the black. The face of an animal that wouldn't listen to command, who would want it? But that was the procedure given to Mr. Crooner. The point was just to get rid of him, so the law could wash their hands. They had to wash their hands of a chimp in the public's eye while the blood of slain men washed Good Leaf streets exempt of recrimination. Such was the morality of the Leaf. The old man raised a speared finger at the auctioneer.

Buddy Plagun lifted an eye to the old man and said, "Two."

The auctioneer raised it to $3 and then $5. The old man and Buddy boxed each other until the high bid was a C note. Buddy dropped out of the race. It was obvious the old man was nothing more than some crusty sorcerer who was looking for the thrill of owning a washed-up simian. Besides, Buddy had other ways of finding out what was what. The old man gloated over his victory and snuck through the crowd like a ghost to claim his prize.

Buddy followed him all the way to the parking lot and approached like they were old friends. "Hey, chum. I see you won that chimp. To the victor the spoils."

"What do you want? I'm busy," the old man said as he approached the closed-box truck. The rear was open. A he-man, nearly twice as large as Mank Mill, with bug eyes pushed Mr. Crooner into the cargo hold. He was carted, sedated and shackled. The he-man then threw the doors closed like they were made of paper mache and took a stand next to the old man. Buddy backed down from no one, but this goliath tilted his confidence.

"You see, I own chimps. I have a zoo. Maybe you heard of it. Crystal Plats in Breaks. Used to be my father's. It's nice for the kiddies, you know, keeps them off the streets."

"Do you have any idea who I am?" the old man asked.

"I'd recognize a look as refined as yours."

"Now you'll remember the name. Tragico Hosiah. Get out of my face, piss ant, before you take a beating at the hands of a fossil twice your age," Hosiah said. His brassy smile was born of a sneer and when he sneered, gold vampire teeth ended most arguments, and if that didn't work he'd throw his he-man at them. He was too old—some said 80, others 90, some topped him out at over a 100—to mince words, but his wiry frame was strong. He had a mind to whip Buddy across the face with his garrote. Buddy thought the old man to be a hoot, considered the little this geezer could know about using that death contraption, but Buddy couldn't help but feel his bones crumple under the grips of that monolith next to him. It would take at least three high-caliber rounds to put him down.

"Sure thing, old man. Don't get excited. I'll let you and your giant go. I'm sure we'll see each other around. Again, kudos on your prize," Buddy said. He was calm. It didn't get him anywhere. But he wasn't about to tangle with an old fool in a clown suit over a chimp that looked like he couldn't pick his ass without a map, at least not around Anvil Temblor, part body guard, part attraction, a brute turned "hero." The size of Anvil alone put him in Gerard's Records Book for largest Leaf walker. He topped out at 7'10" and 600 lbs. Hosiah found him at three years of age, wandering a Bigup street alone. He later learned that the kid had just killed both his parents with an open palm because they kept trying to force food down his gullet. There was no murder trial. After all the kid was only three. The point of contention was what made his parents think that Anvil would start eating three years after his birth? Anvil Temblor, known as the Wind Quaker, was the only man known to have never ingested a calorie. He didn't eat. It made him sick. All foods, didn't matter whether it was animal or not. No water, ever. He derived an excess of nutrients and moisture from the air alone. Freak shit, but that was what Hosiah excelled in. He named his adopted son Anvil. They were all his sons and daughters if they were cast from the mainstream of existence. This was Hosiah's revenge on God. Whatever twisted form the Creator could derive in his mind and develop from the sands of revilement, Hosiah would embrace as pure and good. Hosiah was a man who created heroes from hell, a place he also credited to the Creator. The roof of the truck directly over Anvil's driver seat was cut out like the lid of a can. He wouldn't fit otherwise.

It was another dark drive for Mr. Crooner. The sedative did little to keep him out long. He could see nothing in that black space. He felt at the cuff around his neck and slid his hand down the iron vertebrae linking wrists to ankles. He tried to stand but the chain went taut before he could upright his head. So he dropped on his side to help absorb the shock against the road. It was a bumpy ride. The smell of vinegar and black powder enveloped him. He remembered this chilling night long ago when he was sentenced to Crystal Plats.

The men exited the truck. The old man couldn't stop yakking in celebration. "Behold! The greatest curse God has ever sent me! And I will share him with the world!"

Anvil swung the door and shined his lamp in Mr. Crooner's eyes. Hosiah appeared in all his splendor and smiled, that great, vampiric smile.

"He's awake. How was the trip over? Not too unpleasant I hope," Hosiah said.

Mr. Crooner cornered himself into a knot. The sight of those men dissolved any remaining courage. Anvil pulled the cage out and set it on a rolling dolly.

"Let him roam free. This is his home now, and I want him to feel comfortable," Hosiah told Anvil.

Anvil opened the cage. Mr. Crooner saw his chance and, in full chains, bolted across the empty field. Sea drizzled the air. For a moment, Mr. Crooner thought he might see his old crew. Neither Hosiah nor Anvil seemed too worried. When the chimp got about a hundred yards, he dropped out of sight.

"Some just can't appreciate their freedom," Hosiah said.

Anvil drove down to the ha-ha wall. The chimp was dug into the trench, tangled in iron and drenched in mud.

Two hours and another injection of downers later, Mr. Crooner's head pounded with miserable assurance. He grunted in the blind cavern. A snarl responded. Mr. Crooner wasn't alone. He inched a hand out and felt cool steel bars squaring him up. Then something wet licked his fingertip. Mr. Crooner snapped his hand back and tried to step clear, but he was chained to the bars.

"Buster? That you?" Mr. Crooner whispered. Another snarl responded. A door was heard opening. The approaching steps sounded like the devil himself. A flickering light grew as the steps got closer. Two hostile hyenas whimpered under Hosiah's torch and the fresh cow leg resting over his shoulder. It dripped blood behind each step. Hosiah dropped it to his pets, and they threw their mouths at the limb like it could possibly escape. Then Hosiah circled around the chimp like he was shopping for a car. The flame on the end of his torch cut sharp shadows into Hosiah's face and made his eyes look like smoldering briquettes. The tip of his cigar was hell-red. He smiled more than a fella of his manifestation should have. He wore thick mascara and raccoon eyes. Every piece of cartilage on his face was pierced with golden hoops to look like sutures. They shimmered by the flame. The lightning streaks of hair almost made him look normal in comparison.

"Good morning, my friend. We don't sleep much around here. The sleeper doesn't possess the advantage of conscious judgment," Hosiah said with a singsong voice. It wasn't a song Mr. Crooner wanted to learn, but he could never again excise it from his memory. It was the voice of a man who had dined with death and stiffed the tab. "I know this place may not be up to your standards. I promise I'll make it better for you, but first you must make it better for me. I know. I know all about it. All I ask is that you don't hold back. Be who God intended you to be, and your heart's every desire I will convey to you. So tell me what kind of song lives in your heart?"

The chimp acted clueless to what the man said. None of the kindness found in Pap Fanti's eyes was seen in his. The chimp sucked into a corner. This worked on Hosiah's nerves.

"Then again, we can always do it my way." Hosiah let himself in, making sure to lock the cage door behind him. It was a snug fit. Hosiah offered the flaming tip. "Do you like the light? Go on, touch it. It won't burn you unless I allow it to." He jabbed the firebrand at the chimp's head.

Mr. Crooner recoiled against the bars, but there was no wiggle room. He hooked at the torch in an effort to push it away, but the old man was too quick, predicting his every play. The chimp's resistance sent a rush through Hosiah's blood. It was the only thing he feared when acquiring the ape. Could he temper his sadistic flares? He would have to consult his only advisor, the Colonel. It was a wooden figurine no larger than a girl's doll. It was dressed like a full-bird, even had the colonel's hat. Paint marks measured its war-torn facial features, red drips for eyes and a scab for a mouth. It had no nose. It was a dread-inspiring figurine, and when "alive"—Hosiah never left batteries inside his doll while unattended—the Colonel was known to speak from a mind provoked of free thought. Only Hosiah had any knowledge of the Colonel. He would seek an audience with him during times of distress, such as he had faced with the chimp. The Colonel had made the recommendation to secure his services; even more, said it was of paramount importance that Hosiah not fail the mission lest he be "court martialed." The Colonel demanded the chimp. This same chimp that now hissed barbarically at the encroaching flames. One jumped the torch and made contact with more skin than hair; his coat was only starting to regenerate. Mr. Crooner screeched and beat a hand over his scorching fur. The incense of overcooked flesh seduced Hosiah's olfactory canals.

For two days and two nights, Hosiah blistered Mr. Crooner's skin within the confines of the underground shelter. It's where he'd discipline all his acts when they needed correction. But this was Hosiah's greatest challenge. Never had a hero resisted to the point of death. So Hosiah went to the garrote for alternate persuasion. The torch burning on its post cast a demonic light. He hooped the garrote around the chimp's neck and pulled his arms apart until the chimp's head was locked and his only remaining communications were aimless but punctual karate kicks.

"There, there. All I want is to hear you sing. It's not a wicked request. Sing, and all the suffering is over," Hosiah whispered into the chimp's ear.

Mr. Crooner had no air, no room in his windpipe to take any in. Hosiah gave one more tug just to feel the power running through him and then released all tension. Mr. Crooner gasped for mercy. Hosiah blew a giant plume of smoke into his face instead and watched the chimp cough a lung. He loved animals in this way. He could do what his mind dictated, and they could never squeal to the law.

He left the cage and sat in a chair, legs sprawled out, sucking and puffing. "At least tell me your name. You must have a name. Right?"

The chimp murmured his grievances against the bars in bestial hums. Hosiah uncorked a bottle of gin and took a slug. The smell attracted the chimp's pleasure center. He made prayerful eyes at the bottle like it was holy water.

Hosiah molded his lips into a half melon and uncaped his golden fangs. "This?" he raised the bottle to the chimp. "You want a drink?" Hosiah dumped the water from his dish and replaced it with gin.

The chimp crawled over and sniffed at the gin before taking a sip, then another. He kept his lips on the dish and let the liquid burn his throat. The chimp slowed his breath and remembered Buster. Then he sat up and gave Hosiah his affected eyes.

"You have something you want to tell me," Hosiah said.

After a few minutes of exchanging glances, the chimp delivered a cheerless chuckle. "Mr. Crooner," he droned monotone. "My name's Mr. Crooner."

Hosiah nearly fainted. "Dear God, the almighty creator of what I have just heard. You have revealed yourself to me, and I am supremely grateful. I knew it. You hold the power of the tongue. Tell me more. From where do you hail? What is your gift? Is it from the netherworld or from heaven? Have you seen the face of God? Have you shared a word with him? Are you God? Perhaps his emissary? What message have you for your humble servant? Are there more like you? Tell me you have friends that no eye has seen."

Mr. Crooner's mind turned to Buster. He would first die than give this freak wizard dirt on the bear, assuming his friend had survived. Then it hit Mr. Crooner hard. Buster was a friend.

"Oh sweet, innocent being, there's no sense in treating each other like this. Such poor taste. I do apologize for acting like a barbarian. I assure you I am a civilized man. Now that you have spoken, you must sing, sing of the things that inspire you most. Sing for me. You can speak; you must be able to sing. Please don't keep your endowment from me any longer." Hosiah rushed back to the cage and refilled the dish with gin.

Mr. Crooner drained the saucer dry until all his regrets were drowned. As his agonies faded, his personality was unearthed, and soon he was singing.

Tears of joy bled down Hosiah's face. He pronked and cavorted around the cage, crying out incantations. "This is going to just kill me on the inside! Sing! Mr. Crooner sings!"

- 84 -

The cucumber big top at Hosiah's House of Heroes sat a gaggle of a thousand, and tonight every seat was filled in anticipation of what Hosiah deemed the "converter of all faiths." A web of rainbow lights shaped as stars and hearts swung across the four-mast ceiling and rimmed the cupola. Children, both young and old, cheered and chattered through an air of popcorn and euphoria. An exhibition of sparkling women on winged horses trotted to the sounds of the twenty-piece big band nestled within a pit at the southern end of the tent. They were virtually out of sight, but their music blared throughout the stands. Spotlights, wide as small moons, made circles around the center ring. The horses started for the artist tunnel, each one in unison, including the one Holly Fountain was riding. She was last in line, and the scab of her smile told of a gal who wished to be a million other places than here if nowhere at all.

Hendrick Fountain never let her live her relationship with Chase Griggs down, especially after he read that he had been shot to pieces. "Gangsters and pimps, the biggies you run with. You make me proud to call you sis." He didn't accept her listless apology and didn't give her the job. She called him a heartless bastard to his face. In his mercy, Hendrick gave her another month's supply of B-drine, no charge, for the "bad days to come." Holly turned tramp and wound up at Hookville in West Leaf, taking to garbage dumps for sustenance before she took a trip to Strobile Island, "Where Dreams Become Reality." Hosiah offered her a gig as a bally broad if she made his dreams a reality for one night. She would have to wash up again like her days with Chase Griggs for this time she was explicitly rancid. She gave in and was now lucky to have steady work. At least here, everything was out in the open. Tonight, she was as curious about Hosiah's new barn burner as the audience. She had only known two acts that could best anything Hosiah had to offer. Buster and Mr. Crooner. She dismounted her horse and stood at the lip of the tunnel.

Hosiah's cantillating voice caromed through the speakers. "The probability of experiencing a congregation of giant killer crocs bathing in the Leaf's sewer is world's greater than what you are about to witness. Drum roll, please!"

Rataplan went the drum. The ground under the center ring started to slide open in two. A slowly rotating stage grew from the crater, bringing with it a tall box wrapped in polka-dotted gift wrap.

A spotlight followed Hosiah from the northern tunnel. He wore a long silver thawb, a tight tuxedo jacket of burgundy and top hat to match. "Now introducing our newest and greatest hero, I give you the world's only singing simian! Mr. Crooner!" he proclaimed as he pulled the ribbon off the box.

The band joined in with a competent tune, one that had been rehearsed throughout a whole week of gin, gramophone and knout. Tonight marked the first night Mr. Crooner would get a gander at his new band. The box opened on all four walls. Mr. Crooner was shelled in a yellow double-breasted zoot suit. He wore the mask of a human caricature and wrestled to get his voice into the mic. The crowd joined eyes on the thing in the canary colors. Mr. Crooner's left pant leg was a few inches longer than the right to cover the shackle on a short chain.

"Remove the mask!" Hosiah commanded.

Mr. Crooner yanked his chin and tossed the mask to the ground. He accosted his mic. From the collective throats of doubt sprang forth praise. There were no tricks, no lip syncing to a human voice. Mr. Crooner's arms, like his lips, moved as if the music was his trademark and the lyric his prayer. Hosiah hid in a dark corner of the tent and turned into an avid fan. He knelt down and worshipped the crooning ape, raising his hands to the skies in an act of capitulation. Anyone who needed to use the restroom, held it. Anyone who was about to meet with a heart attack, postponed the appointment. Under the hum of equine excrement, a miracle unfolded, and then things got ugly.

Mr. Crooner swiveled his head to his left and acknowledged a new set of faces in the band. These weren't the Cats 6. They were pale as skeletons and played just about as stiff. So he did what he did best. He tuned out the music and opened the swing band between his ears. Two different songs played at once; Mr. Crooner jiggled his lips into a full scat. The band tried to adjust, but it was useless. Mr. Crooner was just too quick on the bars. Hosiah let it continue until the chimp deviated from the program a few more degrees. He stopped mid-syllable and smiled ninety-proof eyes at the droves in the stands. The band maintained its melody on Hosiah's callous signal.

Against all former direction, Mr. Crooner began to ridicule the mic. "I knew a funny man once. Went by the name Ham Wails. He's probably sleeping with the fishes now. They lit that ship into a bonfire. We used to do shows around town, real secret shit." He turned to the band and yelled, "Are you giggers or gangsters? I swear I've heard more tuneful gunfire!" Then he continued to mess with the audience. "I tell you, this place ain't got squat on my last digs. It's like I went from the cesspool back up the rectum. Hey, I need a refill over here to drown out those sugar cones in the pit!"

The stage started descending into the ground as Mr. Crooner fluttered one last scatting tongue. The band played until the hole was once again nothing but dirt and Hosiah was center stage with the mic in his hand.

"How about that ladies and gentlemen? Mr. Crooner!" A tidal wave of cheers washed over Hosiah.

That night, Mr. Crooner slept his bender off inside his blind cage. Hosiah wanted to congratulate him and offer his review of the first of what would become a nightly ritual. He set his torch in the post and twisted from side to side, cracking his vertebrae like he was shuffling a deck of cards. Hosiah entered the cage, but Mr. Crooner made no movement, he slept through it all, including Hosiah's stomping foot on his head and face. He ground it into the chimp until he came alive.

"Your derision of everything I stand for did not go unnoticed. We can all bask in the light of fools, but if I don't see a way of teaching you otherwise, then I can force my lessons into you," Hosiah said.

With each passing spree, each crippling flogging, the morning wake-up calls under the garrote, the nightly brandings of fire to extract the seed of mockery from his tongue, Hosiah's aim was to create an angel that sang of nothing but love and beauty. He had enough filth from his other creatures to deal with it from this chimp.

Hosiah continued, "From now on, virtue will be your only master. You will neither slander with your mouth nor defile with your body. You will be a temple of the purest form of holiness. You will prove that your gift was given to you by God, so help me."

By now, Mr. Crooner was in the worst shape of his life. He could barely get up to drink and could barely sleep without a binger. His many blood-flaked scars were obscured with clown makeup. His songs turned to dirges. This pleased Hosiah in the deepest part of his heart. Only through suffering was virtue won, and after two weeks of hell, Hosiah had driven out every malevolent strain from the chimp's circulation.

On day fifteen of his "heroes" tour, the stage was raised, and the box unwrapped to standing room only. Mr. Crooner was on his belly, seemingly dead. Hosiah repented only for acquiring a creature that couldn't adhere to his demands. But he did lay off the chimp some. There were no more torches to the skin, no more whippings. The garrote he kept in hand for those special occasions when Mr. Crooner started to fill into his old skin. But one thing remained clear: Mr. Crooner would perform come rain or shine or he would die a slow, miserable death.

When word spread that there was a true-to-life singing chimpanzee, it didn't take long for the movie and music people to take interest. Every picture studio in the Lobo, every music publisher in Flim Flam Alley sent their best pitchmen. Several more became fly-by-night producers, handing out fake cards, advertising "several major projects in development" and catalogs of musical works no one had ever heard of. Some even signed false checks in an effort to secure the rights to Mr. Crooner. But talk of stardom did little for Hosiah.

Mr. Troop Luck of the Lucky Pictures Studio, however, had never heard the word "no" in his life. He started as a daredevil in silent pictures. He was the only man in history to nosedive his plane into the ground from a mile up and walk away unmarked. He flaunted a petit handlebar under a wavy nose, with eyes that were accustomed to having things done one way: his. In only five years, he went from swimming through fire to owning the leading production house in the Lobo. His pictures were a cornucopia of the macabre. Audiences found their greatest inspiration from them, a true sign of the times. People got their strength from witnessing the sufferings of others. But with this singing chimp, Mr. Luck felt he could encourage the populace and still give them a happy ending.

"I am prepared to deposit into your account this afternoon the certified amount of $1,000,000 for a standard three picture deal. That's three zeroes more than I pay my best leading man for a month of slog. Humans come cheap. All filming on location. You maintain full control. You lose no rights to your property. All we want is for him to do what you have him do here every night. In fact, we can just as easily film during a live performance. You cannot lose. This will make you and your chimp stars all over the world. Think of all the bizarre things you can make with that kinda dough."

Hosiah mulled it over. That was a lot of cash. "You come from the Lobo, is that right?"

"That's correct," Mr. Luck said as he tapped a finger on his cigarette holder, missing the ashtray by an inch.

"Where they make larger-than-life images move in the skies?"

"The skies are actually cloth screens, but that's a swell way of putting it."

"You sell many tickets?"

"Never an empty seat," Mr. Luck answered.

"And you can project onto these cloth screens most anything you desire, correct?"

"The limits of the imagination only scratch the surface."

"But none of it is real, true?" Hosiah asked.

"There is a level of misrepresentation that goes into every picture. What's your point?"

"How do you say the word 'no' without being crass? Oh, I know. My answer to your munificent proposal: Take your million dollars and stitch them into a seersucker suit, and then when you've got it tailored to fit you like a glove, light yourself ablaze. Anvil, see this man to the door, and make sure he never takes this route home again."

For Mr. Luck, Hosiah's rejection was laced with cyanide. He cursed the grandmaster to his face and behind his back went to work, plotting how he would get the world's only singing chimpanzee on the silver screen so that millions would know that Mr. Troop Luck was the man behind the marvel.

Three weeks later, it was done, and the impact was instantaneous. Throngs of movie-goers, thirsting for the glorified mendacity that only the movies could bring, clamored into talkie houses around the country to catch a glimpse. "He Talks! He Sings! He's Simian! He's Mr. Crooner!" The ballyhoo caught the nation by storm, and others were soon to copy, steal the formula with abandon. Movies with singing monsters of all shapes and sizes, crooning vampires and zombies, serenading spacemen, waltzing wolfmen, drippy denizens of the deep, each brought a different song to the screen. The trend was so catchy that clubs all over the Leaf started stuffing their lead singers into gorilla suits. It was known as the "scamp." Revelers would walk into nightspots all over town and ask, "Do you 'scamp' here?" But none of them were the real Mr. Crooner for there was only one, and Buster knew it.

DC Stiles knew it too. For weeks, they had scoured the Leaf and all surrounding boroughs. He tried Crystal Plats Zoo but was run off by a team of new security. Met Fanti was no longer employed there. Stiles asked the people at the auction for records of the sale but got nothing but red tape. D.I.S.S. said he was wasting his time. Stiles admitted that he wasn't the dick everyone claimed. He was a phony, befitted to nothing more than the title of the man who first pick-axed a mountain and struck gold. He had no peeper skills. His expertise was solely in being lucky, but Buster didn't buy any of it. He kept his faith in DC Stiles and knew that he would deliver like he said.

Driving back to his office one gloomy day, Stiles picked up the words on a marquee off Sebastian Street. "Mr. Crooner! The Singing Simian! Now Playing!" He purchased two tickets for the matinee and rushed back to his office to pick up Buster. The whole drive to the theater was a surprise, but Buster knew that Stiles was ready to burst with news of something.

When they arrived at the movie palace, Buster read the marquee and nearly shot out of the car. Stiles had to tell him that Mr. Crooner wasn't actually there. Then he back-stepped and said, "I'm not saying this will lead us to him. You know they make movies in the Lobo. That's like a million miles away. But maybe we can sniff out a clue. You ready to see your friend on the silver screen?"

"They won't be pointing guns at his head, right?" Buster asked.

"Remember, it's all make-believe. Loads of fun. Who knows, you may not even recognize him anymore. Those stars out in the Lobo grow fat heads overnight."

"Like Lala Terre?"

"She just grew a fat ass."

Stiles and Buster passed the concession stand. The smell of popcorn livened Buster's appetite. For days, he had been fasting, taking only the bare minimum to function. He vowed to enjoy that first big meal again with Mr. Crooner. They took their seats in the front row. Met Fanti kept an eye on both. He was seated three rows back and to the right. Pirouettes of smoke blossomed from his cig.

Buster couldn't understand what they might see on a giant blank wall until the lights dimmed and the screen glowed bright. He had never seen a movie before, didn't even know what one was. The titles appeared as though from the heavens. "The one and only...Mr. Crooner!" Buster held his breath at what was to materialize before him. Sweet patooties of chic design, money men in the snazziest threads reminded him of Pap. Fancy cars and exotic locales, beaches of sugar, deep-rooted umbrellas filled with coconuts, the air looked clean, no smoke like in their theater, like in their lives. They must have really pampered these picture stars, Buster thought. But when "Mr. Crooner" first appeared on the screen, Buster cringed. Something was terribly awry. He sunk his head and refused to watch the rest of the picture. Stiles observed his change in behavior. So did Met.

After the show, Stiles walked with an arm of consolation around Buster's head. Mr. Crooner had changed alright. So much that it wasn't even him. It had never been him. Imposters from the outset. The magic of the movies once again won the day and the box office for the next two months straight until they released *Mr. Crooner's Mistress!*

"You're right. It was all make-believe," Buster said.

"I know," Stiles admitted. He couldn't figure out how they imputed Mr. Crooner, of all titles, onto any form of singing chimp, whether human or not, without knowing something about the original. As they approached the car, Met slipped around the corner.

"I've seen better pictures in a Caille Happy Home Peep Show. That shit was for the birds," Met said.

"Yeah," Stiles responded like he didn't want to continue to chitchat.

"Ever since they found the real one, you know, Mr. Crooner, they just can't stop putting out that schlock. But I guess as long as the people open their mouths, they're gonna keep serving it down their throats. Do enough reefer and anything looks good on the screen, am I right?"

Buster spun his head to Met. Stiles froze and said, "Can I help you, mister?" Then to Buster he said, "Get in the car, kid."

Buster did exactly that. He swore he had recognized Met's voice if he even heard it once in his life.

"I said you're looking for the real Mr. Crooner, you and your friend." Met crept one eye into the passenger seat. He wanted to see what was bundled in all those many layers of facial wraps and made to look like a troll in a cheap suit.

"Who are you?" Stiles asked.

"I know where he is," Met said.

Stiles looked beyond Met to see if he had company. Then he looked behind his shoulder to ensure that no one brandishing a tire iron. Stiles felt the need to get in his car and race back to his office with Buster, but Buster was having none of that. With an ear on Met, he got back out of the car and joined the circle.

"You know where the real Mr. Crooner is?" Buster asked.

Met froze at the sound of the voice. He couldn't see a face under the hat and many scarves, but the voice came from a snout.

"Buster, what are you doing? I told you to wait in the car," Stiles said.

Buster didn't hear a word Stiles said, just the part about the stranger knowing where Mr. Crooner was. "Tell me where he is, please," Buster said.

"Who are you?" Met asked Buster.

"I asked you first!" Then Stiles looked to Buster and said, "Don't say a thing to this man, and get back in the car. We're leaving now." Stiles returned his attention to the stranger. "I don't want to know anything about you. Why don't you shove along." This outsider was about to make trouble, and Buster was about to be discovered just like his friend. Stiles might have been in it for the big score, but Buster had worn on him in a way that made him consider things outside of money's price range.

"It's alright," Met said with his eyes on Buster. He could tell Stiles was jumpy. "No trouble. I'll be on my way. Simple as that. You'll never see me again. But as soon as you get in your car, I run to a phone. That's not human," Met said pointing at Buster. "Are you the bear?"

"You're sloppy full," Stiles said. He put an arm around Buster, trying to force him back to the car. Buster wouldn't budge.

"Pap Fanti," Buster said.

"What about Pap Fanti?" The hairs on Met's neck went rigid.

"You were there that night on the dock. I remember your voice," Buster said.

A strange silence overtook the conversation. Stiles pulled a gun on Met and fanned him down. He was unarmed. "Get in the driver seat," Stiles ordered.

Met got in. Stiles looked to Buster and shook the worry from his head. Then he put Buster in the passenger seat and slid into the rear, the gun pointed at the small of Met's back.

"Drive where I say, or I poke you full of peepholes."

Met took them onto the street like they were headed for a Sunday picnic. In fact, it was a Sunday. Met kept glancing over at Buster and the funny way he fidgeted around.

"I was there that night," Met said.

"No yappin' till we get indoors," Stiles commanded. He was finally acting like he had a clue what he was doing. He kept an eye out for any law that might have happened upon his stickup.

Inside Stiles office, Buster took off his hat and unwrapped the scarves. The head of a bear, the body of a bear but nothing more. Met didn't have the words to say. There was more silence.

"So now you know. Where's the chimp?" Stiles asked. He kept his gun pointed at Met the entire time.

Met couldn't break his stare from Buster. He couldn't register another stimulant, not even Stiles' hardnosed questions. "Do you sing too?" Met asked.

"Mr. Crooner is the real talent. Me, I just play a golden toilet, I mean trumpet," Buster responded. Stiles knew there was little he could do to prevent this encounter. "Where is Mr. Crooner? Can you help us find him?"

"I can't believe it," Met said. "I used to see all kinds of weird shit when I was loaded. None of it was kind to the eyes. Now I'm clean. Been on the wagon for over a month, finally past the DTs, but this is some kinda new phase. What are you?"

"I'm Mr. Crooner's friend. Can you help us find him?" Buster asked again.

Met snapped out of his trance and perceived the gun in Stiles's hand. "I can't think straight when your heater's screamin' at me."

Stiles lowered his pistol.

"I can help you find your friend. What do I get out of it?" Met asked.

Buster forehanded a look to Stiles. Stiles backhanded it back to Buster.

"How about ten large?" Stiles said.

"I'm not interested in money."

"What then?" Stiles asked.

"Something more. Something that's gonna last," Met said. "I want this gatemouth to play the misery pipe for me. I want you to play for me. Would you do that? Just one song."

"I'd be happy to," Buster said. "But I don't have a trumpet anymore."

Stiles and Met left Buster in the office and drove to the nearest hockshop in search of a horn. They found a coronet that would have to do. When they brought it to Buster, he figured it to be awkward, hard to fit in his paws, but he made it work just the same, crunching his fingers as tight as he could to fit on the push valves. He blew a choppy melody that left Met in a drunken paradise. Met had even spoken the word "paradise" when Buster was done playing, a place where there was no suffering, a place he'd never seen before but knew existed because Buster had said so in his song. Buster couldn't help but wonder if it was the same paradise spoken by Mr. Crooner.

When he finished a twenty minute set, Stiles wanted answers. He wanted to know who this guy was and where he got his information. Pap never mentioned having a brother. Of all the places to hide a singing chimp, Hosiah's House of Heroes seemed the most illogical unless he was putting him out on display in front of thousands and the word was now out in the public. Stiles still couldn't make the connection to the movies, but it didn't matter. The ball was already rolling, Stiles would get his usual credit, and the plan was set in Buster's mind. They would go to Hosiah's to see Mr. Crooner and determine if he had found that place, the paradise he so wanted.

"You don't get it, kid," Stiles said. "Listen to what the man just said. It's a prison for freaks. Once you go in, you never come out."

"What's a freak?" Buster asked. He asked in the most honest way imaginable. Buster had never heard such a word spoken before. Pap never used it; neither did any of his friends, not even Mr. Crooner had seemed to know it.

"That's not what I meant," Stiles pulled back. Again the notion of having Buster at his side made him question his own definition of reality.

Met could tell that Stiles was reeling for an explanation. "Hosiah loves things that are…different…like you. You go in there, you'll find your friend. Hosiah will make sure. He'll sing, and you'll play your horn in front of thousand of people. I've seen it. Hosiah's not a kind man. He'll beat you, slap a yoke around your neck and call you mud," Met said. "The people love him; they just don't know him."

"If that's where Mr. Crooner is, then that's where I'm going," Buster said.

"Buster, did you get the wax out of your ears?" Stiles asked.

"I heard every word he said, DC. And you've been kind, a helpful man with a good heart, just like Met. I wish Pap had mentioned he had a brother a long time ago. We might have enjoyed more moments like these together. I'm going to find Mr. Crooner. I need to see if he's happy. If he's not, I'm going to get him out and bring him home to Pap. I understand if no one wants to come with me, but I don't have a choice in the matter." Buster started for the door. He opened it and took a step out. Nothing was going to stop him from getting to Strobile Island except everything that was waiting to stop him.

"Buster, wait," Stiles said. Buster paused. "Please, just close the door. Look at you. You're not even dressed. They see you like that, you won't get down the block."

Buster recognized this to be the case and returned, shutting the door behind him and putting on his duds. Stiles looked to Met. "We can't just stroll in and say we'll have him back by breakfast."

"No you can't. Hosiah's got triggers up the wazoo. I've been casing that joint for weeks. I know all the ins and outs, know how to make it happen."

"What's it to you?" Stiles asked.

Buster continued to dress but his attention was on Stiles and Met's conversation. What Met wasn't disclosing was that it was a heist. Mr. Crooner had a different destination, and it had nothing to do with Buster. If the bear could help streamline the job, maybe even pull a midseason trade, the bear for the chimp, or even better, two-for-one, then maybe.

"Don't worry about it. You interested or not because if you are, you better be prepared to lay it all on the line. We ain't going in there for cotton candy, but you may come out soaked in the same color," Met said.

Stiles watched Buster struggling to get his jacket on. He simply didn't have the arms to do it alone. He'd be slaughtered, and not only would Vilma never forgive him; he'd never forgive himself.

"We'll take you, kid," Stiles said. "But don't say I didn't warn you."

- 85 -

Holly Fountain brooded at the edge of an old, squeaky bed. It stunk like an unbathed groin. A rubber tent was what she now called home, and an aging candle was all the illumination she would rely on. She was loaded on B's from Heal Fast Pharmacy. It was the last of it, and she wouldn't be refilling any "prescriptions." It did nothing to improve her outlook. Some lonely nights were just lonelier than others. She was cold, but that was better than to wrap up in the used mule blanket trampled under her feet and straw. She glanced to a small box of splintered drawers and an even smaller mirror where she now made her face happy before each show. The bracelet that Chase had given her was on the top of the drawers. Claudette had called it. A queer. She couldn't even hock it for a wrinkled ace note. The tracks of her tears had carved a winding road down her cheeks, and she couldn't bear the sight of herself any longer. In her right hand was the answer. A slick-looking switchblade invited her to dance. Just one slice at her wrist to let the pain drain away at the pace of a pulse. What would anyone care? She had crapped out one too many times and was now lower than the vermin that found permanent dwelling within the many tents in the back yard, including hers. She noticed one of the rats. It was a foot long and slid along the canvas wall like it held no regard for Holly or her mission. She took her fake bracelet and threw it with all her might at the rodent just as it slipped out of sight. She would have liked to have Chase Griggs there so he could be party to her end. But she was certain he was in his own private...anything but hell. Not even for the impostor and the cheat, not forever, her brainless heart whimpered. If only she could discard one more tear, she might hold onto it for another time. If only she could spend another few minutes with Buster, she might forget herself again and wake up the next morning. Mr. Crooner. What a tragedy, she thought. But he got his just desserts. She remembered how he used to treat the innocent bear. The world had a funny knack for returning to sender whatever sender put in the mail. Sorrow filled her heart for the poor creature. No matter how much he might have deserved it, she knew what Hosiah was capable of. He had proven it the night he slipped her a Mickey and sodomized her with her own bloody tampon. She could taste her vomit each time she remembered. But beggars couldn't be choosers any longer. Maybe she could see Mr. Crooner one last time, confess to him the evil thoughts she carried in her heart; even give him one more spoonful of his own medicine before she filleted her wrist. She slid the knife inside her coat and twinkle-toed from her tent just like the rat.

The network of tunnels under the carnival grounds was made to confuse most any intruder, and they all had one aim. If for any reason, Hosiah got the order from the Colonel to evacuate with his most prized possessions, these would offer the escape routes. Of more common use was the transportation of acts like Mr. Crooner to the center ring under the big top. It was too risky to bring him in through the artist tunnel or any other surface entrance. Even Anvil himself couldn't take on a troop of a hundred at once. For Holly, the tunnels represented nothing more than a memory of her former life. She had traveled many a secret passageway in her days with Pap Fanti, and moving like the worms of the earth brought her no shame. She even knew where one of the secret entrances above ground was: Hosiah's single-wide trailer, where he went to rest. And the wonderful thing about Hosiah was that when he actually did sleep, not even the shattering earth could wake him. Holly hoped the bastard was numbed out, and if he wasn't she might just go for his throat with her jackknife.

She pulled open the screen door. It squealed for lubricant. She considered heading back. Surely the noise tipped Hosiah off. But the lights remained dead, and she didn't hear anything more than the motor in the back of his throat. She let herself in and shadow-stepped to the hatch under the living room rug. She grabbed the torch on the table and the lighter. The tip still smelled of kerosene. She slid the rug aside and dropped into the tunnel. She'd be out and back before Hosiah would feel his midnight bone.

Holly snapped the torch head into a fiery fit, and she started down the burrow until the smell of animals caught her attention. She came into Mr. Crooner's hidden den. The hyenas greeted her with a snarl. She greeted back with her fire stick. The sniggering beasts submitted under Holly's hand and then retreated back to their corners. Mr. Crooner appeared to be reaching down to his toes, hoping to stretch the pain away, loosen up like Buster tried to teach him, but the tips of his fingers touched the floor without effort, and the pain only intensified deep within his buzzing skull as all that blood he spoke of pooled towards his ears. He shot up, fearing it would spill out and rolled an eye of contrition to Holly. She aimed the light at Mr. Crooner to get a better look.

"You used to dance with the High Legs," Mr. Crooner said.

"I'm Holly Fountain."

"Have you seen Buster?" he asked. "Maybe you could get a word to him for me."

"I don't know where he is. I'm stuck here with you."

"Maybe you can take this." Mr. Crooner handed Holly an empty bottle of gin. It now carried clumps of his hair.

"What is it?"

"I know I'll never leave this place, but if you send that adrift, part of me will find its way back to Buster and the gang. So they know I'll be alright. So they know I had it good with them."

"Okay," Holly said as she slipped the bottle inside her coat pocket. It was a side of Mr. Crooner she had never seen, and it broke her heart. She wasn't ready to check out just yet. She had a job to do for Mr. Crooner. As long as they were to share the same abode, they might as well become friends.

"If you see Buster again, tell him no one gets off scot-free, and I deserved whatever happened to me. He was a good kid, best I've ever known," Mr. Crooner said. "You better go now. If the grandmaster catches you down here..."

"What do you think I would do?" Hosiah asked.

Holly and Mr. Crooner prayed for their eyes to disappear along with their bodies.

Hosiah continued, "Where would I be without the Colonel? You know this area is forbidden. Now fill me in on all the juicy details."

"I tried to kill myself tonight and thought Mr. Crooner might talk me out of it."

"Did he succeed?" Hosiah asked.

"Only if you let me go without punishment and promise to not take it out on him," Holly said.

"Who is Buster?"

Holly remembered all the great liars in her life. They had a talent for pulling wool over her eyes, and now it was time for her to pull one over on Hosiah. "Buster?" she said.

Mr. Crooner squeezed his nerves. No way would Holly give up the kid like that.

"A dangerous killer. He's probably looking for his lost chimp as we speak. I wouldn't want to be around when he finds him."

"Ah, yes. A charming gent. We've already met. Well, you needn't worry about that." Hosiah reached out his claw. "The torch."

Holly stretched the stick out without any sudden speed. Hosiah snatched it away and approached her head-on, blocking her egress. Putting his mouth close to Holly's ear, he let his breath out and then took Holly in through his nose. She thought about the knife in her pocket. Would she be fast enough to pull it and stick it in that bastard's throat? Instead, she held her ground and her breath until Hosiah said, "You're free. It would be a tragedy to lose you."

Holly brushed past him and headed back through the black tunnel. Hosiah stayed with Mr. Crooner.

"What did she tell you? Are you planning your escape together? You know you can tell me anything. I'm your friend." Hosiah waved his torch side to side like a toy.

"She wanted me to sing her a song," Mr. Crooner said.

"I don't give away my talent for free. If she wants that, then she will have to pay for it," Hosiah said as he left Mr. Crooner in his cage and the eventual darkness that engulfed the room. Pay for it is exactly what Holly did. Hosiah slithered into her tent and disarmed her of the knife and her honor once again. She asked for a mercy drink before he got to it. She was tearless, and by the time he was done, she had passed out. Hosiah took the knife and incised another knick under Holly's opposite eye to match the original scar. She didn't flinch. Then he lit a match and inserted it inside Mr. Crooner's bottle of hair, taking in the fumes like vitamins for his soul.

- 86 -

A briefcase with $50,000 and a handwritten note asking for more time was waiting on the desk of Captain Sert Johnson. It was from Buddy Plagun. Johnson never got it. It was all over the papers the morning after the delivery. "G.A.V. COOLS THE OVEN! CAPTAIN SERT JOHNSON ARRESTED ON CHARGES OF CORRUPTION AND MURDER! Also indicted: Lieutenant Quick Coogan and a ring of fuzz from the East 1st Precinct." Crystal Plats was raided, but Buddy beat the law to it and relocated his dwindling inventory. All the feds found were starved animals. Were they gonna bust him for animal abuse? But with Johnson and Coogan out, a new breed of cop was taking over the Oven. Like Ziggie Fist, the new captain didn't take snacks. The probe infiltrated City Hall. The clean up was swift. The mayor was impeached, all highbinders, including the police commissioner who had been on vacation for the last year, indicted. East 1st merged with East 2nd and 3rd. Buddy Plagun was now marked in bright red everywhere he went. One slip-up would be all it took. His warnings to Junior Plagun fell on deaf ears. "I've got plans for you that will keep you out of the rackets for good, keep you safe, keep the dough rolling in, the girls, the life, just like you always wanted."

"A singing monkey you saw in a picture show?"

"Fuck you! I seen him every night. I'm telling you he ain't no ringer, and he came out of our zoo, yours too because everything he left, he left for both of us. If you came down with me to Strobile just once you'd know I wasn't blowing hot air. Look, don't ask me about the why or the how. I'm just interested in the what, and 'the what' is that there's a real life singing chimp. Sings like Sinclair Frank, only better, and he's at Hosiah's waiting for us to bring him home and cash in."

"Maybe after that we can make a wish on a star and fly to Foreverland," Junior said.

"You've always had a bad bone for me. To this day I can't get why."

"Maybe I just never belonged. You went away, I found my own thing. The air was easier to breathe. Ever since you've been back, I've been choking on smoke. You know how many times I've had to pad a bull busting my balls for that Mank Mill hit?"

"I don't buy it for a second. The entire 1st backed us," Buddy said.

"You got the rest of Metro, West 2nd, State, Coast Watch? What about G.A.V.? Coming in here, giving me the business about Fanti like he was your lover. You think this is the Wild West where you can dust your jacket after a shootout and pull up to the bar for free whiskey. I don't give a fuck what you buy. Now I gotta buy some bullshit about a singing monkey? That Fanti idea really went to your head."

Buddy let Junior bitch all he wanted. "I haven't forgotten about Fanti, but we gotta figure our out. How we can both stay breathing without turning into stickup men. God knows you wouldn't last a day with a rod up your tight ass. Just once if you would treat me with the same respect I've given you."

"You mean slapping me around in public like I was half a punk."

"You ever think about our parents?"

"Go to hell."

"How hard they had it? I used to talk to the old man about you."

"I said cut."

"How much we had to protect you. You were special."

"I'm fuckin' warning you."

"You'd be spared of all this. You'd be the last one standing. Even beat me out. Isn't that what you always wanted?"

"You're a fuckin' cancer. You can shut me up with a dozen holes, but that don't change a thing."

"That's fine, but if you don't do what I tell you this time, G-Men are gonna sift through the ashes of this joint to dig you out. And here I thought you wanted to keep gettin' your pecker wet."

"I got my own plans to keep my pecker wet," Junior said. If only Buddy would stay out of his life for good. "I don't need yours." His plans included liquidating the Dirty Spoon and becoming a mouthpiece like Basil Demur. He had grown tired of all the fooling around, the trips to the doctor for diseases they hadn't discovered yet. He was through with the club business. If only he had lived to crack his torts book. The Dirty Spoon was raided the next evening and Junior Plagun was sentenced to one year of the minimum ten in exchange for dirt on Buddy. Rumor has it he never spilled the beans. Another rumor tells of Junior squealing his pig lungs when a pack of ex-Cabra goons cornered him in the washroom and took turns poking him in the keyster before a guard broke up the gangbang. A month in the infirmary on a diet of penicillin and antivenom and an altered gait where his right seemed to outrun his left, but Junior Plagun, like his father predicted, would survive.

From then on, Buddy Plagun kept his belly to the ground. He couldn't trust Junior or what beans he might have spilled, so he entertained other adventures, like sightseeing at Hosiah's House of Heroes. He'd been attending every night since watching "Mr. Crooner" on the silver screen. He was planning a major move, one that would bring the chimp into his custody without a contract. It was the heist of the century. Somehow it seemed a safer, more legit bet than dealing booze and killing rivals. There were no laws against selling tickets to a singing monkey. Sure, he'd find a way to keep the liquor flowing too—fuck the law and its mother—but Mr. Crooner was the key to his new success. If only Bill and Minnie Plagun were around to see this. So many times Bill took Minnie to the House of Heroes to see things unfit for Earth, to catch a little escape. If only they had stuck around to see the chimp opening its pipes, to know that it came from their menagerie, to know that it was put there to bring Minnie cheer. Buddy would do it for his folks. They would be raised from the dead through Mr. Crooner's voice. But to pull this off, he needed time to plan, take inventory of every exit, tally up security and how large a crew he'd need for the extraction. He couldn't simply go in blazing while the chimp did a number, or maybe he could. Hosiah had him chained by the ankles and had guards, mostly freaks with guns stationed throughout the exits. No one was laying a hand on Mr. Crooner except Hosiah. This time, just like with Ziggie Fist, Met Fanti would be tabbed for the job if he sought to cheat his own death.

Met had done everything Buddy Plagun had told him to do, including a long trip on the wagon. He was sober, but Sue Sandloer was out of his life for good, and soon he'd be blotted out of the history books as well. Buddy knew the stunt he pulled at Crystal Plats, how he betrayed his trust and sold Mr. Crooner to Pap Fanti. For weeks, Buddy took Met to the big top attraction. Buddy Plagun saw with his own eyes what was stolen from his zoo. In light of all his efforts to be a good solider over the years, no one could stay loyal in everything, so Buddy used his father's powers of mercy and reason and gave him one more pass. It came with a final condition. Now Met found himself on the same path Pap Fanti had taken. Only he didn't have two nickels to rub together. Fleeing the Leaf was futile. He'd sooner die in the sticks as he would to a Plagun bullet. He had no choice but to go along with Mr. Crooner's "prison break."

Buddy Plagun had plans for the chimp. He'd set him up at a Bigup dive for starters and leg his hooch in from the North. When the law stopped taking bribes, he'd sell him to some Lobo studio for enough money to disappear. And if none of that worked, he'd skin the chimp alive and make a scarf and earmuffs.

"You're gonna bump off the ringmaster. I'm gonna be in the stands watching the whole thing. Jesse Under will lead a crew to take care of security. The crowd will panic, trample over each other like a stampede. Expect casualties. You'll make fast for the chimp, cut his chains and put him to sleep. Jesse will blaze your trail. Stick to him like a shit streak. Then you get in the truck and zoom back to Plats. I'll see you there. You make good, we're gonna form something new together, something bigger than you can imagine. Since you discovered him, I'll give you first dibs, you know, run things for me, set you up nice. I took your entire record into account when offering you this chance, but it's your last. After all, we're all gonna end up killing each other sooner or later." Buddy dangled the carrot— he always knew the right things to say—and Met turned back into a bunny. He was desperate enough to want to believe every word again.

The black tuxedo fit Met like he was born to wear it. It was the first he had ever worn, and he wished for any occasion but tonight to sport it. He carried the scent of a new man, clean shave, plenty of Brazor and a slicked top. Sue Sandloer would never see him like this, and that would be her misfortune. When he looked in the mirror, he couldn't help but see Pap Fanti, and that was his misfortune. For the first time he started to think of defenses for his brother. Pap's judgment was harsher than the crime, and even if it matched, what did it matter? The judge was no less guilty. Then Met realized all he was doing was offering up a defense for what he was about to do. He carried his trombone case and came up the rear as the big band started to filter into the big top. A few gave him inquisitive looks. They didn't recognize Met and neither did the bandleader.

"You got a sick boner. He's all fucked up. Ask Hosiah. Brought me on last second. Hey, I was set up pretty at the Spoon, so if you got someone else to fill the gap, I'll draw my wages and walk. I don't need this shit gig," Met said.

True the trombonist was sick, only it was from an incurable disease. He was stuffed inside a cart of hay inside the horse barn, lungs filled with lead and straw. Another Jesse Under special. In fact, with a hit squad of four toughs, they gunpoked the rest of Hosiah's security into a permanent pause.

The bandleader sized up his new "trombonist," then let it slide with cautious consent. Met looked like he was up for the job. He took a seat inside the pit, the back row and the last chair on the left. He grinned like an idiot to his band mates and opened up his trombone case. It was larger than most gig bags because it had to hold two slush pumps. He removed his tram and faked some warm-up. Then he pushed his chair back a couple of feet to clear some space. The other musicians didn't notice or care. They were too busy caking their bows, draining spit valves and tuning their axes. The show got underway.

Stuffed elbow to elbow in the peanut gallery were the Gutter Gophers with Sister Second. Her faded habit drew the barbs of some girls of more liberal constitutions. They pointed at her, called her "Sister Sow" and "Holy Cow," but she ignored all the slurs. It was her headdress and her manly aroma that was causing the greatest concern. A man and his wife sat directly behind her, but her cornette blocked the stunted wife's view. The man kindly asked Sister Second to remove it. The sister kindly asked the man to switch seats with his shorter half. The coif stayed on her head, the habit on her body. Neither were rightfully hers. She called the theft a necessary sin, but when the church kicked her out decades ago, she refused to give up monastic life or her church uniform. Now she had to deal with pagan reprobates and their foolish requests. She wanted to cancel the outing. It was an act of mercy, not merit, that they were all there in the first place. In the sister's estimation, the louts had suffered enough, even if none had fully atoned. Burger Brasa had just turned 17. He had a fourth-grade education and was on his way out. Hustling the streets was on his mind and so were women. A couple months back, Burger had knocked up a girl in a high-school john. The chick cried rape. The sister mortgaged the house to pay her off and get her uterus cleaned out. Apparently, killing the unborn wasn't as bad when the perps were just kids themselves. Burger was once again spared. This kind of reckless attitude Sister Second credited solely to the influence of Pap Fanti.

Moony Butter was a nervous wreck after the Fishtail raid. He whispered to begin with. Now he could barely hold a thought. He spent most of his hours hidden beneath the sheets. Not knowing what had happened to Buster or Pap had sent him spiraling into a mental valley.

Anthony Mound, Mack Loyter and Dradle Prestij were picked up for armed robbery only days after being released. All three were sentenced to a chain gang—the youngest to date— clearing roads for forty days in South Breaks for the GLB (Good Leaf/Breaks) expressway.

Bobby Pin ran away three times, but he could never track Pap or any of the old crew and would be forced to find his way back. At least with the sister, they all had a roof over their head and breakfast for however long that was to last.

When they had learned that Mr. Crooner was headlining on Strobile in front of a thousand people, they organized a trip, told the sister to put up the fare or they'd walk. She gave in. Her convictions about the occult and the divine were grounded. She staked claim to having seen the appearance of the Holy Lady one night in the clouds, shortly after being dismissed from the order, even alleges to have spoken to her, received the message that she was to commit to chastity and homeless children. As such she did not completely discount the existence of mysteries too exotic for science to explain. Anything with the power of human song that was not of human origin had to relate to either spiritual extreme. She banked on this particular thing belonging to the occult, especially if it came from a man like Hosiah. Something about a singing ape reminded her of demon-led swine. She would put the matter to rest with her own eyes. The boys thought she was just a nutty old bitch with a blistering hand. When she wanted to instill the fear of God in them, it didn't take but one wallop, and these boys, bad as they were, weren't the kind to slap a dame. They had learned this from Pap Fanti. Tonight, however, there was little tension in their demeanors. They were jolly, like regular kids, jostling the air with dirty jokes. The sister let them be. For a couple of hours she wouldn't pester them.

"Can you believe Mr. Crooner's puttin' it on here?" Anthony Mound asked. He buried his hand in a box of popcorn. Mack Loyter snatched it from him and trickled a fist of kernels into his mouth.

"A fin says it's a queer," Burger Brasa said.

"Double or nothing says you're wrong," Dradle Prestij followed up.

"It's a bad bet," Bobby Pin said. "Mr. Crooner's dead with Pap Fanti."

"What did I tell you about bringing up that name?" Sister Second interrupted.

"Yeah, pull the dick out of your throat. They ain't dead, none of 'em," Dradle said.

"Dradle, what kind of language is that!" Sister Second exclaimed.

"What? Dick ain't no curse."

"Are you fuckin' stupid?" Mack said.

"Boys! That's enough!" Sister Second was starting to come apart. It was apparent that when the Gophers got together in public, they were hard to restrain.

"Chill the tongues, or the virgin's gonna shit her undies," Burger whispered to Mack and Dradle. Sister Second heard every word, but she had heard it all before.

"You think they take us all for suckers and put on a fake? Name him Mr. Crooner? Fat chance, Cheese," Dradle said.

"No one got the real Mr. Crooner. He's on the lam with Buster. They ain't ever gonna get pinched. Pap won't let it happen," Moony Butter said.

The sister didn't reprimand Moony for mentioning Pap. They were some of the first words he had said in a long time. He seemed excited to be in the stands with his pals, just like the old days. They were all in their caps and tweeds, smacking gum and sucking hard candy. No smokes in front of the sister. No drinking either, but that was on the up and up. If there was one thing Pap Fanti didn't teach them it was to drink. He always admonished them to be like him in that regard. "Of all the vices you see here, this one will kill you the fastest," the boys could remember Pap saying.

"Hey, Bread Loaf, were you on the Fishtail? Didn't you see it blow like the devil's asshole?" Bobby asked.

"Don't matter. Moony's right. Buster's too smart for them shit dicks," Dradle said.

"That's it! We're leaving," Sister Second ordered.

"Okay! I won't say dicks anymore. Promise. Shit."

"What if it is the real Mr. Crooner? I'm sure he'll wanna know we busted out," Anthony said.

"A million clams he's livin' it up with Buster somewhere past the Pony Currents," Moony said.

"Singin', blowin' for a house of stars. In your dreams, doughboys. They made furs out of both," Burger said.

"Shut your fuckin' pizza face, cyclops!" Moony yelled.

"Hey, you little shit, cut the bad talk. We got girls in the audience," a random man in an office uniform protested. He had a pointy six-year-old girl next to him with pigtails pulling hard at the sides of her head, making her face into the same snarky expression as Daddy.

The Gophers banded and joined one eye towards the complainer.

"What are you half-hoods lookin' at?" the man continued.

Sister Second put an arm around Moony. She could feel tensions rising, and jammed in between dozens of packed seats, there was no telling what style of riot her boys could provide.

"Sir, I apologize. They're with me," Sister Second said.

"Then wash their mouths out with ammonia, sister. You could try a little of the detergent yourself. Maybe a new dress."

Sister Second was shocked into silence. If she raised her voice, she'd make crumbs of the man, but then she'd join her boys in the clink. It was a standoff. The Gophers weren't backing down from a double asshole, no matter that they were at least a single. The crowd around them was taking notice too and started pointing eyes of scorn their way.

"Show some class, fellas. Like Pap would," Anthony said. "We'll miss the show, remember?"

"That's the best idea I've heard. You will all be able to see with your own eyes what you're looking for," Sister Second said.

Another few seconds and one-by-one, the Gophers settled their eyes on the stage. The man returned his focus to his girl. Sister Second controlled her breathing and tried to speed up the clock. They were safe when they were home.

"I'm still taking the bet," Burger reminded.

"I ain't no welch," Dradle said. "Make it a cool twenty since you're feelin' strong."

"Hey, Moony," Burger said. When he had Moony's attention again, he inserted the base of his right forefinger through the loop made by the thumb and first digit on the left. Then they shared a smirk. For the next twenty minutes, they slapped at each other's heads and bragged about how well they knew Buster and Mr. Crooner, how they were in with the toughest crew in the Oven, running speakos like they were underground gods, and when it was done, they'd go back home with that old bitch to determine what the future held all over again. But they did it all with class.

An hour later, Mr. Crooner was center stage under a scorching shine. The Gutter Gophers hooted and hollered, pointed their paws. "We ran with him!" They boasted to strangers in the stands, the man and his tiny wife, the loose girls who were curious to know more. It was the real Mr. Crooner! Buster couldn't have been far off. They were inseparable when they came together. At least that's the way the boys saw it. It was good to know that Mr. Crooner had gotten out alive and appeared to be in good shape. If he was singing for such large audiences in a tuxedo made of sun rays, he had to be doing okay. Sister Second closed her eyes at the first glimpse and started praying. Whether she thought he was divine or demonic, she would never say. One thing remained certain: Her faith had just been rattled like Grandmaster Hosiah had guaranteed.

- 87 -

The master plan, according to DC Stiles, was to buy a couple of tickets, as close to the stage as possible, so that Buster wouldn't face anyone but Mr. Crooner, so that no one could plant a clear eye on the bear. They would wait for the show to end, for Mr. Crooner to be taken back underground like Met described. They would remain in their seats until everyone had filtered out and then sneak over to the orchestra pit and meet Met. There was a small gig room behind the pit where they could hide once the rest of the band had cleared out. Then when the eye of every witness had vanished, they would move to the center ring and figure a quick way to open the ground and dip in. It would lead them to Mr. Crooner. The plan was foolproof. Both Stiles and Met would pull the stickup even if Buster was against it. He frowned on the idea of a rescue tainted with guns and considered their chances hindered as a result.

"That's never going to work," Buster said. "We won't need the guns. I don't want any guns. No one gets hurt."

"It's the only time you'll see him away from the crowd. He only comes in and out through that hole in the ground. It's a beehive of bouncers when he's on the outside, but I bet you anything once he's on the inside, he's locked in solitary. We won't need the guns, but we take them just in case someone wants to stand in our way. We won't shoot them, we'll just show them. Neither of us are killers. In fact, I've never shot a round in my entire life. It's the only way it'll work," Met argued. His lies were too quick to be incredulous.

"How do we open the ground?"

"There's a control room where Hosiah stands. He can open it from there, and so will we."

"Okay," Buster said, but when he took his first glance at Mr. Crooner, all the meticulous planning flew out the window. Part of him wanted so much for Mr. Crooner to be in that place where all suffering ended, where his song would match the days and his lyrics the night. He would let him go if Mr. Crooner had found such a place in Hosiah's. Instead, Buster was convinced to the contrary when witnessing the poisons that watered Mr. Crooner's eyes, the same ones he used to ingest at Calloway. Only now, the venoms did little to lift Mr. Crooner's spirits. He was all alone in the center of the ring, surrounded by a thousand judges, under a merciless light like an ant under a magnifying glass. He was out on display not as the Mr. Crooner he had come to love but as a puppet, and the steel strings were attached to his ankles. More than ever before, he needed to be saved from this place.

Buster leaped from his seat before Stiles could wrangle him back and raced across the rings like a shooting star in an empty sky. One spotlight caught him from high above and carried him to the center ring. Hosiah had his way of dealing with unruly fans that needed to touch Mr. Crooner, but the security he had banked on didn't appear. In full garb, the crowd couldn't determine exactly what he was even though the snout was out in the open and sucking wind.

Mr. Crooner caught sight of the one thing he could never question. "Buster," he said in the middle of his song. What a perfect time to break up his set. Maybe this time Buster would lay into him for being off cue. What a welcome sight that would be, but this had to be an apparition. Buster couldn't just run across Hosiah's big top like that.

"Mr. Crooner!" Buster yelled as his hat flew clean off his head, revealing to the audience another living wonder. It had to be part of the act, said their 'oohs' and 'ahs.'

"It's a talking bear!" "Another troubadour!" "This is the bee's knees!" were just a few of the exclamations from the crowd. Only the Gutter Gophers felt their instincts kick in, like they were working the lookout all over again. This wasn't a happy reunion. This was a break. They bumped through the aisle, knocking knees, before Sister Second could detect what was up. She grabbed Moony at the last minute like a boa. "Boys, get back here!" she screamed. Moony bit her arm—she screamed again—and escaped. Buster needed his help too.

"Buster! Not him!" Holly exclaimed in her heart. She mounted her horse and galloped into the ring at the sight of Hosiah blitzing with garrote in hand. His image in the public eye was that of altruist to the deformities of life. He couldn't allow himself to be seen as inhumane, but this new creature, sprinting on all fours, was set to tamper with his greatest prize, perhaps even commune with it. Hosiah's hunch was dead on. Mr. Crooner did have friends! He would catch the one they called Buster; subdue it without causing a ruckus. The show must go on! Soon it would showcase the two most famous acts known to man! Mr. Crooner and the talking bear!

Seated high in the crowd, Buddy Plagun turned his binoculars from Buster to Met in the orchestra pit. The time to fire was seconds ago! They would take the chimp and his pal as a bonus! Buddy thought almost out loud. It was the last idea that lit up his brain. A star of crystal shattered into Buddy's eye, followed by the rifle round that uncorked the back of his skull. Human wine sprayed all over horrified spectators. The crowds wriggled like wildebeests escaping a river with teeth and, just as foreseen, stampeded from the stands. Pandemonium. The Gutter Gophers were swept up in a human undertow.

The band went mute and turned back to Met. He pointed his sniper rifle at anyone who wouldn't clear his path. They shuffled out of his way like a zipper being opened, shielding themselves with their instruments. Met turned his scope on Hosiah and fired. He missed and hit Holly's horse instead. It crashed down on Hosiah and left him squirming over voided legs and screaming for breath and Anvil. His Goliath was unavailable, bludgeoned against the ha-ha by the weight of his own truck.

Holly took a second glance at Hosiah and relished in his suffering. She thought to finish him, but let him enjoy his pain and turned instead to Buster with tense anticipation. She wanted to reach out and hold him tight, but Buster was busy gnawing and slashing at the iron rings. He couldn't sever them.

"Buster, you can't break through those chains!"

"I have to!" Buster yelled.

Mr. Crooner stood still in wonder of his fearless friend. This couldn't be the same Buster he had met before. Met and Stiles converged on the scene.

"Get out of the way, Buster," Met yelled.

He cocked his rifle and fired. The chain link snapped like a bone. The final race was on. Mr. Crooner was too plastered to admit that this was nothing more than the dream he had lived each night in his cage. But this time instead of waking up to the sound of his own screams, he hightailed alongside Buster and into the chirping crowds that parted from the loaded hands of both Met and Stiles. They kept their guns at assault level and shouted. Anyone in their way would get shot was their simple warning.

Outside the tent, carnival goers scuttled and ducked as dusk welcomed its first fireworks. Met and Stiles led the charge. Holly ran fleet of foot alongside Mr. Crooner. Buster supported the rear. The main exit was within their sights.

The Gophers were spit out of the current. They spotted Jesse Under waving his machine gun from front to back in deadly stride. Locking arms, they formed a blockade. Jesse swung the butt of his Tommy at Burger Brasa first, knocking him cold on his ass. The remaining Gophers disbanded. Dradle Prestij and Anthony Mound thought to tackle Jesse by the legs until he pointed his lead pump at their faces. They scurried for cover. Moony Butter turned and shouted at the top of his lungs: "Run, Buster!"

The air popped a half-dozen times, much closer than the canon blasts from the aerial shells high above. It was immediately followed by a yielding bleat. Mr. Crooner turned back and saw Jesse Under unloading his machine gun like he was running heavy, and then his eyes took him away from the bullet bursts. Buster had come up lame and slowed to a halt, disoriented, defunct. Mr. Crooner summoned titanic strength and hoisted Buster over his shoulder. He bucketed for the exit amidst the crackling air. Stiles made an abrupt turn and fired to buy them precious seconds. He made contact with Jesse's heart instead.

Stiles' car was parked on the other side of the boardwalk. They made the last push past straggling pedestrians and dove in. Stiles cranked the engine. Met assumed the passenger side. Holly, Mr. Crooner and Buster flung themselves into the back seat.

When the gun smoke cleared, the body count included Buddy Plagun, Jesse Under, one trombonist, seven security guards, Anvil Temblor and a pointy six-year-old, accidentally trampled to death by her father and a wave of strong-willed spectators. Met leaned his clammy head against the window and moaned. He was bleeding from his right shoulder. Mr. Crooner, Stiles and Holly were unscathed. Buster's stainless fur was now a paintbrush of scarlet.

- 88 -

Pap Fanti and Vilma Worthton had each other now. They were as painless as healing wounds would allow. After discovering the fate of the Fishtail and his remaining crew, Pap was ashamed to have survived. That was a lot of blood to wash over two hands. At least the Gophers made it out, but he refused to read the paper anymore. He asked Vilma to do the same. To see Buster's picture on the front page would be unbearable. She agreed. If the news didn't come directly from Stiles, it wouldn't be good. Instead, they focused on each other. This was good. Each morning, Vilma would greet Pap at the breakfast table with coffee and toast. His favorite marmalade came in a raspberry. They would take walks around the house, explore the woods around them. Pap had even once picked out a Marigold for her. She felt like she was falling in love for the first time. Pap Fanti was all the gentleman she had dreamed of and more. He had no money, no family, and yet he was everything she could have wanted in a man. For Pap, love couldn't have come at a better time. He clung to Vilma those days like he once clung to Buster, and she was receptive. He was shy. It was difficult for him to give her a hug. Vilma thought he was cute. One evening she made the first move and gave him a kiss on the forehead. He grabbed her with loving hands and brought her into his chest. Then they kissed, and life started over. But Pap could never keep his mind off Buster. Neither could Vilma.

In the wee hours, the call came in. Both Pap and Vilma were up and ready to beat the sun to the horizon on what promised to be another day of discovery. But the call changed all that. They were words Pap never wanted to hear. He kept pushing it out of his mind until it was impossible to ignore. The phone had a nasty way of ringing when there was bad news on the other line. Vilma picked up and listened intently. With each passing word, her eyes lost the color of life.

"They shot Buster," Vilma said as the tears welled up. Pap remained silent. There was nothing in him except the desperate cries of a man too embarrassed to open up in front of her. "He's still alive. They don't know how long he has left."

"Let's go," Pap insisted. They got in the Dunfer's truck and peeled out of the driveway. Pap gave the pedal a heavy foot. He ran a couple of red lights and was lucky to avoid both law and accident, the two things that had plagued him all his life. Pap kept seeing the same images run through his thoughts. Buster with his eyes closed, blood escaping his body, looking as peaceful as when he was in full rhythm. He didn't ask Vilma any questions. He knew she didn't have the answers.

Stiles was no detective, and he was no surgeon either. He had no one else to call. A doctor would have summoned the law. So he did his best throughout the night to keep Buster from fading. Towels and sheets, even his own coat. They were all soaked in blood.

Mr. Crooner stood by his side, forgetting the pains of an imminent hangover. He held Buster's paw in his own hand and repeated, "Everything's gonna be silk. Whatever you do, don't check out."

Buster didn't yell or groan like Met, who sat in Stiles' chair. Holly had been tabbed to play nurse. Just like DC Stiles, she could do little to excise the lug in his shoulder. She applied steady pressure to the wound and kept him talking when all he wanted to do was sleep. Met was in better shape than Buster, but that didn't mean either would make it much further. And Buster seemed to be content with that.

He mumbled things that made no sense, repeated phrases, said them backwards. Mr. Crooner even swore he started speaking in tongues. "Pour that plum juice on the horn. Singing water. Cold as fire. Triple C's can't run off the page. Mr. Crooner, Mr. Crooner."

"Call me John. John Henry," Mr. Crooner said.

"I like that. John Henry Crooner. There's a tree on your head. Flowers playing guitar. I can see it now. That place. John Henry, that place. It's a paradise. Mutton with vanilla ice cream. I'm talkin' the coolest. A real ring-a-ding-ding. Hand me that skin. I think I'm gonna catch some shuteye. Naps are good for growing angels. We're not angels, are we? Maybe angels on the lam? Sing for me, Johnny. Take me to that place one more time."

"Buster Horn! You snap out of it this instant!" Mr. Crooner said clutching tight to his paw, begging him to pull through. "You ain't checking out! Don't make me smack you out of it!"

"I can't leave you, Johnny. Who would you bother if I wasn't there anymore?" Buster snickered under his breath.

"Attaboy! That's the spirit. You may find someone who makes you happier, but you'll never find the level of misery I've given you. You want a mint or a chocolate milk?" Mr. Crooner said as he sensed the presence that came through the door.

Pap Fanti was holding onto Vilma's hand. His eyes were yanked at the sight of Buster, fur stippled red, lying helpless on the couch under a bed of bloody towels.

"Buster," Pap's lips let trickle. He flew over and took a knee. Mr. Crooner gave them their space.

"Pap," Buster said through the side of his mouth. "How you doin', Pap?"

"Oh, Buster, look at you. How do you feel?" Pap held Buster's paw like he had a thousand times before. And each time, he would practice the art of missing his friend in anticipation of the day when it would become a reality. He still wasn't prepared.

Buster swallowed the air in his throat and gazed into Pap's eyes with all the love in the world. "Quack, quack, goose, right, Mr. Crooner?"

"Ducky, kid. You're ducky," Mr. Crooner answered immediately.

"You're gonna be okay. We'll get you patched up and back on your horn in no time," Pap said.

"Remember our good times?" Buster asked.

"And how. We gotta million more."

"You can say that again. Hey, Pap."

"Yeah, Bus."

Buster gazed intently into Pap's eyes. "You always made me smile."

"It's okay, little buddy."

Then Buster let his eyelids meet, and he faded into peace.

Pap fought to keep the floodgates closed, but it was no use. He let his head fall on Buster's chest and sobbed, soundless surrender.

Mr. Crooner looked to both Pap and Buster. They appeared to blend into one being for a moment of time. Vilma stayed by the door with a handkerchief dabbing her runny nose.

"I tried calling throughout the night, but the lines were all jammed," Stiles said.

Pap didn't remove his head from Buster's chest. Then he heard Met's voice.

"I'm sorry, Pap."

Pap shot to his feet and spun around to Met with a killer's drive. Holly kept clear of his stare. She had never seen the fires of hell in Pap's eyes, not even when he was bringing the rip down over Pisto Leroy.

"I didn't do this," Met's words leaked out.

Pap rushed Met, yanked his limp carcass off the seat by his lapels. He had not yet noticed that the jacket was soaked in blood too. Met gave a quiet yell. The skin on his face turned damp with fresh pain and fear as Pap shook him out of shock.

"The hell you didn't!"

"I'm hurt, man! Oh, God!" Met exclaimed.

"That's what happens when you break the rules!"

"What fuckin' rules? Yours?"

"The rules, damn it!"

"Let me go," Met whimpered silently. He couldn't keep his eyes from trembling and wanted to pass out.

Pap let him go. He knew he was just as guilty of turning his back on Met, of turning him into that desperate wolf that would prey on its own young to avoid starvation. Now was his time to let Met pass his judgment, but instead Met held his tongue and plopped back into the chair, trying to control his breath. So much he needed to unload, a multitude of agonies emaciating his mind and stamina, but none came out. The thoughts were pounding loud. Thoughts about lies, the way Pap deceived him, treated him like he was nothing, not even the pittance he flicked at him for Mr. Crooner. Just tests upon tests to make sure Met was on the level, but Pap couldn't realize that everyone had to earn a living. It was a bad hand, only Met didn't fold. He played it through to the end, no chips, no markers, just stinking, fucking poverty. Met was its natural born heir, and he was sick of it. Sick of it! The thoughts were draining all remaining strength. Such ideologies kept the sober mind seeking a switch, but Met wasn't going there anymore. He had to fight through this. Absorb the pain! Stay awake! Stay alive! He shook his head clear to avoid falling into an instant sleep and found in his eye the image of Mr. Crooner, his head prostrated over Buster. Look at him standing right there. Look at him! They were just thoughts. Not even a thank you where it counted. Pap made Met disappear. How he wished to force his self-approving brother to say it one time with his own dirty lips. Every man deserved a destiny, not just Pap, but Met too, and that chimp with magical powers came from Met!

As though Pap had listened to every one of Met's inner sayings, he admitted: "I lost the one thing that was pure because of everything you did."

"It was Met who got us out," Stiles said.

"Butt out," Pap growled to Stiles. "You're no better. You shacking up with her now?" Pap looked to Holly. Everyone in the room was fair game. "Is that why you wouldn't drop the case?"

"It's not like that at all, Pap," Holly said.

Vilma recognized Holly. There was displeasure tapered by the irony that, through the adulteress, Vilma had been led to someone better.

Pap kept his eye on Stiles. "I asked you for a favor. This is what I get." Pap looked to Vilma. She had a tear hanging on her lower eyelid. She didn't like to see Pap filled with such hatred, but she couldn't deny relating to it. It saddened her to think that Pap had failed to realize what else was standing there before him. This is what he got, just like he said. A chance at true love from a woman who needed it all the more. How Pap wished to swallow his words.

"Look what I got. This shit. My life. All for bringing you in, for trusting you. You ever think about that? You ever think that maybe I deserved a chance too?"

"You blaming me for something?"

Met recycled one final dose of anger through his veins and rose to his feet. "You robbed me! Admit it! I was nothing to you! Never have been! But you're no better. Just another swindler, you and whoever helped you. And when they didn't help you anymore, you were done with them too, just like Lou Licks. He came to me to make the deal. You tell me I'm wrong, and I'll call you a liar again."

Pap let the remnants of his hatred fly off his fist and into the soft part of Met's jaw. The punch sent him twisting over the chair and onto the floor. Vilma rushed over to Pap, hoping to restrain his rage with a woman's touch, and then out of nowhere a voice cried out.

"Pazo Fanti. You son of a bitch. He can feel it," he said referring to Buster. "It's not helping him."

"He's dead because of you! You did this!" Pap fired just before rushing the chimp.

Mr. Crooner felt his tongue moving in his mouth, only someone else was doing the moving. He howled, words no man had heard before, a language he couldn't even translate if he tried. It was the hollering of madmen, the chanting of saints, the confusion of hell, the ecstasy of paradise. It stopped Pap dead in his tracks, sent a shiver up his spine. No one in the room could move. Mr. Crooner was calling the shots and then in a breath, he collapsed. Silence. Pap stared at his dormant body, the wheezing of air in and out of his mouth. Everyone kept their eyes on the chimp, wondering what was next. Seconds told them nothing. The chimp was fast asleep.

"Plagun's dead," said Met.

"What did you say?"

"I killed him."

Pap couldn't believe it. He turned an eye to Stiles for confirmation and found it in the composed nod of his chin.

"No more lamming."

Pap looked down on his brother, weak and running low on life. He fell to a seat next to him and slapped his head in his hand. He reached out to Met, closing him in. Met winced but wouldn't dare break away from a gesture he hadn't known in decades.

Days came. Days went. Met recovered. Buster didn't. This time it was Pap who had asked Vilma to summon Dr. Cobard, and without fail, he was there. Again, Cobard fought to get Met to the hospital, but after Pap informed him of their designation as wanted men, the doctor did the best he could on the spot. Mr. Crooner hid in Stiles' back room while Cobard knocked Met out with a couple CCs of artificial sleep and removed the lead that was lodged against his scapula. Then he sewed and slinged him and left him napping. But before Cobard could walk out the door, Pap removed the sheet over Buster and introduced the doctor to Kid Cool. Dr. Cobard disclaimed that he was only versed in human parts, but Vilma convinced him to put his powers to work on Buster. Cobard checked for vitals and entry wounds. He found neither. Other than the dried blood stains and his breathless slumber, there was no sign that Buster had ever been harmed. Cobard found the case most peculiar along with the serene countenance of the bear. An ordinary animal Buster was not. The doctor once again apologized for not being of better use and excused himself, this time refusing to accept a dime from Vilma.

Pap wouldn't move from Buster's side, but each passing hour took another hour of hope away. All signs pointed to a farewell, but Mr. Crooner wasn't ready to say goodbye. Instead, he sang, sang for Buster. Vilma caroled alongside. They formed the prettiest duet Pap could remember hearing. And still in all their highs, their sorrow could not be replicated, not even if one were to burst open the very heart and allow the entirety of its contents to spill onto the floor.

By the end of the third day, Buster remained still as a word, and the heat he once radiated was gone. He gave off no foul odors. Pap kept himself awake, pacing three steps one way, three the other, glancing at him with bloodshot eyes on every about-face. He hadn't winked a moment's rest, and the flavorless skies made sure to remind him of it. Vilma put a bowl of hot chocolate up to Buster's snout, hoping the aroma might speak to him subconsciously. The chocolate went tepid after twenty minutes, just around the same time beans of rain wrapped the windowpane.

Mr. Crooner stared at his friend. He neared his face to Buster's snout, hoping to catch a whiff of a fleeing breath. Then he placed a hand on his chest. "There's so much I wanted to say. So much I never said. All those times I was a shitheel. All those times I treated you like you would last forever. I didn't know it then, but you were that place I spoke of. That song I sang. The one you asked me about that night. It was for you. It was all for you. I didn't want to admit it because I was scared. I was stupid. Paradise came with your song and with your heart. No one had ever spared their life for me, you know. And I know that you didn't either 'cause you're still here. You ain't gone nowhere 'cause I won't let you, you dig me? You can't leave me like this. We gotta a lot of business to take care of, jam sessions galore, you know, tell-the-sun-to-come-back-in-another-hour-we're-still-busy and all that jazz, only this time it will be everything you wanted. I know you can hear me. Buster, you are my friend. Just like Pap. You're all my pals. The only ones I've ever known. Now kick this dead act to the curb and get up!"

"He's gone," Pap said. Mr. Crooner threw his head up at Pap hoping he would say something different on a second pass.

"I know," Mr. Crooner said. "I know."

"We'll bury him out at sea. It's where he came from. He always loved the water."

Mr. Crooner sang through his tears. *"We're gonna march or we can promenade, however you say, just you and me, we're going all the way, and every time you feel them shoes getting heavy, I'll carry you, I'll carry you."*

Pap placed an arm around Mr. Crooner. It wasn't shrugged off but absorbed like water through soil. Pap knew that Mr. Crooner would now look to him like Buster once did. Pap needed to be there for him from now on. It's a promise he would make to Buster. "Keep singing."

- 89 -

Vilma and Holly got to know each other like first-time acquaintances usually do after a short afternoon at Sipi's Department Store. They both liked what they learned. Holly was a stupid girl who believed what people told her. But she had a heart, evidently like most, maybe just a little more. She had no clue about Vilma, and she was honest when she confessed it. She wasn't in on the scheme like other floozies working an extortion job. She couldn't stop asking Vilma to forgive her. It made shopping for strollers rather embarrassing. But the thing that stuck out in Vilma's mind the most was when Holly admitted that they were both better off knowing the truth, even if it cost Chase his life. Vilma didn't bother to ask. Holly didn't strike her as the trigger type. Sources revealed the murder was connected to the men that were after Pap Fanti. Unwinding the plot any further became irrelevant. Pap had proven to be a decent man, someone Vilma could attach to, just like Holly was doing with Vilma. Probably out of shame, lack of family, but Holly saw a mother figure, someone who wouldn't lie to her. In every couple, only one was the true liar. The other lied in defense. It wasn't Holly's fault she fell for the lie. It wasn't Vilma's fault Chase Griggs was filth. So they brushed away any rancor they might have felt for the other and returned to the reason for their shopping trip.

Vilma picked out a few articles of clothing, suitable for seafaring, raincoats and hats. Holly was embarrassed that Vilma was buying her clothes, but she accepted them with gratitude. Then they moved to the baby section. It smelled like babies. Baby lotions, talcs, even sweet milk from lactating mothers with stretched bellies, distended with future chapters of some unwritten history. They sifted through racks of doll clothes. Pink tutus and blue skivvies, the dress of future world leaders. Never did Vilma dream she would be buying another baby carriage and using it as a hearse, but it was the only way to get Buster and Mr. Crooner out of the building safely since Stiles' discovery. He had finally graduated into a full-fledged dick.

"Coppers doing rounds every fifteen minutes. These don't look venal. You walk Mr. Crooner out in the open, it's curtains for him and you," Stiles said. He had taken a stroll down the street just to get a feel for what the papers had been reporting. "$1,000,000 BOUNTY!" for anyone who could help track Mr. Crooner and his talking bear friend, "ALIVE!"

Hosiah was possessed with hunting them down, now from the confines of his wheelchair. He had dumped thousands into the "new and improved" police force, bought them all new office furnishings, paid vacations, even a fleet of new RMPs. He was, after all, a good citizen and expected his patriotism to be rewarded with aggressive service. He had even hired a private force of a hundred trackers and set them out all over the Leaf. His net was wide, but once the lammists got outside of it, he knew it would be over.

Pap had left first, around 10:00 pm. The night was sweating the way they did those final days in May. He had found a pigeonhole to park the Dunfer's truck. Now it was just a matter of filing away the minutes and hoping that Oleg Mercury would perform his end of the bargain. Earlier that morning he had paid a visit to Oleg on the wharf. It was the first time they had met in over three years.

"You come to pay me the balance?" were the first words out of Oleg's mouth.

"I come to offer you a job. You still have your dragger?"

"How else do you think I scrape by?"

Pap removed a thousand dollars from his coat pocket, a gift from Vilma, and presented them to Oleg. "$200 covers the tab. The other $800 is for the job. No guns, no running. Just a trip."

"$800 for just a trip?"

"That's all it is. I swear it."

"Where?" Oleg asked.

"Virgil Island," Pap said. "A hundred miles past the Ponies."

"Why?"

"You'll see when we get out there," Pap said.

"I don't run anymore," Oleg said. "If that's what you're dragging me out for, you can forget it."

"It's clean. No running, no chasers. The old farmhouse in Jester's Bosom. We'll meet you there at midnight. Can you do it?"

Oleg wanted to say no, but he couldn't refuse Pap Fanti. He could never refuse him. It's what led him to running the row with them years ago, and the same thing that got him burned. Some people just had that influence. And others were too weak to resist it. Pap hated to lie to Oleg, but it was the only way to get him to go along.

Virgil Island was a quiet place with few residents and plenty of clams. It was its own commonwealth, had its own government, and the best part was that no one there knew of Pap Fanti or things like Mr. Crooner, so they claimed. They could start over. This time it would be different. It was all Vilma's idea. She had her sights set on the island ever since her split with Chase. Pap thought it was too risky. He didn't have the money for the trip and didn't know what they would do on arrival. Pioneering had run its course in Pap's life. If it was up to him, he would have moved back into Dunfer's for the rest of his days, just him and Mr. Crooner. Vilma reminded him who she was again, more over, what hung from her purse strings. "What's mine is yours if you want it," she said. "I want you," Pap said. "I don't care about any of the rest." They would start their own family, far from the Good Leaf police, far from Hosiah's bounty hunters. Everything they could want would be within reach thanks to Vilma. They would bring Met and Holly along. They both needed a family. Vilma would send for Merlin after they settled in. He needed a home too. Mr. Crooner would be reared as their adopted son. He could sing when he wanted. They could put on nightly shows, just for them. They would make sure they had plenty of land, so Mr. Crooner could move about freely. They just had to get there.

11 pm. Vilma and Holly strolled out for a leisurely walk with their baby buggies. Vilma thought taking her "baby" for a walk at this hour to be as normal as boiling waffles, but in relocations, no one argued with Pap. Stiles had given the "all-clear" signal just after refusing Vilma's $10,000 check. He said he was officially retired and was going to settle out West, maybe go into show business.

Met kept twenty paces behind Holly and Vilma, his pistol limp in his left hand, his right in a sling. Whether he would ever have full use of his right arm he didn't consider, but he swore to not hold up the caravan any longer on account of his pain. He also refused any dope to numb it. He wanted the reminder fresh to keep him sharp. The sidewalk offered a strange silence. The stroller wheels were blaring in their ears. Each bump in the walk sounded like a gunshot. Turning the corner, headlights blinded them in flashes. But none seemed interested in pulling them over. They continued down a couple of blocks, Holly and Vilma, side by side, on a late-night stroll with their "babies," Met ambling behind them. The rush of passing cars insulated the pounding in their hearts. Then they slipped into the blind alley. Pap blinked his lights once. He was parked, rear first. He swung his door open and helped Vilma push the stroller to the back of the truck. There was a lamp and one open crate, a foot deeper than the 3X3 Pap had fished out. It would be a snug fit for Buster and John Henry, but they'd make do. Pap rolled the stroller up the ramp and into the truck. He then turned on the lamp and closed back the umbrella top. Wrapped in fresh linens was Buster. He reached under his bear and cradled him out. Then Pap rested him in the crate with all the sweet sorrow in his hands. John Henry hopped out of his carriage, crawled into the crate and took a seat. He placed an arm around Buster and made a circle with his forefinger and thumb for Pap, letting him know everything was going to be jakeloo. Pap closed the lid and hammered nails along the seams to make it secure. Tiny cracks between the planks allowed sufficient air. He pushed the stroller into the alley, closed the rear door and skipped as well as a gimpy leg could to his driver seat. This would be the last move, and Buster wouldn't have wanted him to mope on the job.

Holly and Vilma were sandwiched in the cab. Met crowded the right window. Pap got in and started the truck. They pulled out of the alley thinking the worst behind them and waited to swing a left at the first clearing.

"Stop the truck!" shot out from a loudspeaker. Off to their right, on the other side of the street, two radio cars flamed their headlights. Pap punched the truck into oncoming traffic, clipping the rear bumper and nearly sending them into a spin. Met turned to his right and, with his left hand, fired. He hit three tires with four shots and crippled the immediate pursuit. The cops fired back. Six rounds were pumped into the trailer wall. One ricocheted off the rear, right rim and sent shards of lead into the rubber. The slow but stable leak wouldn't be enough to stop them.

"I thought you said the coast was clear!" Pap said.

"It was! Those things popped up from the ground, I'm tellin' you!" Met said.

"Alright, just keep calm. Check for a tail."

Met snuck his head out the window. "We're clear. Make tracks."

Holly and Vilma simply hung on for the ride. The night couldn't end well. They headed straight for a familiar hideout: Dunfer's. Once on the grounds, Pap limped the truck into one of the garages and closed them in. He patched up the flat with some Pegaseal they found in the glove, but no matter how much glue he shoved in the rip, the tire would find a way to whistle. Then he rummaged through a pile of tools until he found a tire pump. Timing would be key if they intended to make it to Jester's Bosom. That meant refilling the busted rubber seconds before attempting another trip, hoping it would get them off the Leaf before blowing apart and praying that the law dogs would be picking at another bone wherever they were headed.

They waited over three hours before getting back on the road. Pap had taken a seat next to the crate in the trailer and talked to Buster and John Henry for a whole hour. Pap did all the talking. His voice must have had that lullaby effect, too, because John Henry slept through it. Soon after, Pap had nodded off just the same. Vilma and Holly snoozed in the truck cab. Met had taken up Salty Well's old post and was pulling recon, but as the hour pushed into 3 am, he knew that they would have to blend into the night and vanish immediately or else.

Met hurried back and woke Pap up. Never in all his many moves had he fallen asleep on the job, but like he once told Basil Demur: He was out of gas. Met helped Pap fill up the tire and pump another shot of Pegaseal into the rip. Then they got moving, slow and steady and on the whims of a bad hoof. As luck would have it, the roads into Jester were patrol-free. Not even the Breaks Bridge was policed. Pap's fear was that they wouldn't see Oleg at the dock either. But he was there, asleep on his trawler, just as promised. He should have known better. The midnight hour turned into the next, and now it was a quarter to five. There had to be a reason to leave under cover of night. But something about holding $800 for a job undone made him nervous, especially with a man like Pap Fanti.

"You said no running," Oleg said amongst a dozen other expletives. His eye was locked on the crate in between Pap, Met and Vilma.

"It's not what you think," Pap said. "Can you give us a hand?"

Oleg scooted in between Met and Vilma and put his hands under the crate as an automatic response to Pap's voice. "What's in here then?"

"Remember that night? Remember the little thing you wanted me to throw back over? It's him."

"What are you talking about?" Oleg had no clue what Pap was saying. This whole trip. $800, not counting the balance of $200, couldn't be for the little creature they fished out. It made no sense to Oleg, but now wasn't the time for discovery.

"We're taking him back home," Pap said.

Dawn was upon them with damning signposts. Every third mile or so, through cuts in the fog, Pap could make out squads of police, on banks, over bridges—no wonder there were none on the Breaks, they were all out here—some manning heavy artillery. Who were they after, Al Capone? Either that or Oleg had picked the only winding channel he knew that would be teeming with law. But it wasn't so. Pap simply failed to realize that every port, every inlet was now a checkpoint, and no ship left without a thorough inspection. There was no other way out. Coming around the bend another mile ahead was theirs. Pap, now down to a sweaty shirt, opened halfway down his chest and his slacks, took a spot next Oleg on the trawler's bridge.

"That's a police boat," Oleg said. "You sure you're not running?"

"It's over," Pap said to himself. He could do no more to escape what was coming. Turning the ship around would do no worse to seal their fate. If it was going to happen, better now under the morning sun. It shined like a contented sun, without all the savagery it normally displayed when it wanted to make a point. Then again it was only 6:05 am.

Pap returned to the deck and told the others to remain calm. There would be no fighting. He asked for Met's piece, said he would surrender it at first request. Met tossed it into the harbor instead.

"You know they're gonna take me down for Plagun," Met said.

"Just keep your shirt on. No one's going nowhere unless I go too," Pap responded, ready to give himself up in Met's stead. He also promised Oleg that if there was any trouble, he would front the cost for his defense via another of Vilma's favors. If this was the price to pay for the life they led, it was better to pay it in full, not leave any debt. Buster was already gone, and there was nothing more he could do for Mr. Crooner but pray.

The police boat waved a red flag in the air and brought its siren to a howl. That meant stop. Oleg trolled his ship to a crawl and then to a standstill. The waters remained quiet as though they contained no life.

"We're inspecting all ships leaving this port. Are you carrying any weapons?" the cop in the plastic uniform asked.

Oleg threw his rope to the police, and they returned with their planks. "No," he answered.

Five armed gold-hearts boarded and scoured the Cruison from top to bottom. When they entered the hull, they switched on their lanterns. Pap, Vilma and Holly were standing beside the crate. They all wanted to see with their own eyes what the police would do to Mr. Crooner, perhaps beg them to go easy on the poor soul. It wasn't his fault that he had been blessed with a human curse.

Met sat in a dark corner, monitoring shallow lungs. It was his last-ditch attempt to remain unknown. A cop lit up his face with his flash stick. The light felt hot to Met's skin but not hot enough to make him move his eyes away from the cop. What was the use in hiding anymore?

"Light yourself, and touch the sky," the badge with speaking power ordered. He melted a hand around the butt of his revolver.

"I ain't packin'," Met responded. He raised his left hand, palm open and took unthreatening steps towards the others. Pap was ready for anything. He had seen how cops operated. They would have to take him out too if they tried anything against Met.

"Both hands!" the power badge urged.

"I can't raise this arm. It's lame."

"Fan him. Make sure to check inside the sling," the badge ordered his duplicates.

A second cop spun Met around and frisked him.

"I told you I ain't packin'," Met said.

"Shut up," the second cop said. Then he dug into Met's sling and played a game of arm wrestling.

Met yelled at the top of his lungs, "God damn you! My fuckin' arm!" Then he crumbled to the floor.

Pap separated himself from the crate and marched to Met's defense. "Leave him alone. Take me."

"Freeze! Stay where you are!" the badge commanded. "Fan 'em all."

The cops seized Pap by the arms and gave him a rough search before pushing him to a seat next to Met. Then they felt Vilma, Holly and Oleg only to confirm that no cop was in danger.

"We don't want any of you," the badge said to Pap. He kept giving Met dirty looks until he looked at him no more. Just like that, Met was off the hook. Even if the cops had suspected him as Plagun's killer—and they might have—that's not who they were after. Word behind closed doors at police precincts and City Hall was that the man who offed Buddy Plagun was a hero, and that's all they'd have to say about it. The papers once again reported his slaying, and Jesse Under's, as gang related and closed the books. "Open the crate," the badge then ordered his fellow flattie.

"What are you looking for?" Pap asked. He was filled with pre-fight fluid and didn't know how else to stall. He could launch an offensive, rush the nearest cop, but the other two would shoot him through the chest, and they'd still open the crate and take Mr. Crooner and Buster away. It didn't matter that Buster was no longer with them. He couldn't dare think that even in death, they would desecrate his gentle spirit by pumping his cavity with formaldehyde.

"Stowaways," the badge replied out of duty.

"You ain't gonna find any here. We're fishermen," Pap said.

"Yeah right."

The lawman wedged the crowbar and cranked it back. The lid splintered and popped open, slapping the hull. A light was thrown inside. Pap's eyes went into rigor mortis. It was empty. No Mr. Crooner. No Buster. They were gone. Not even a note. The crate was sealed just like the time Buster was found. It was too much to bear. The anguish cut into Pap's neck and made him fall onto his face.

Met, Vilma and Holly were too stupefied to move. How in the world? Where in the world?

"Nothing here," the badge pronounced with a dry indifference. After one last cast of the eye in Met's direction, they got off the ship and let Oleg about his business. "On your way."

The rest of the day, they cruised to Virgil Island on Vilma's advice. She even offered Oleg another $500 for his trouble. Soon Oleg was kissing her ass. She had just made his next six months.

Pap sat at the stern staring out to an anonymous ocean with unseeing eyes. Several times he considered telling Oleg to return to the truck to see if perchance they were still inside the trailer. Maybe they snuck out before boarding the boat. Met kept a watchful eye on Pap. He had never seen him so low. It was clear what Buster meant to him. But a thought had been itching his brain for the better part of the morning. He didn't know where it came from, but something in his heart told him to get it out before he scratched his brain to pieces. He approached Pap.

"How's the shoulder?"

"Fuck that copper. I'll be alright." Truth be told, Met was in terrible pain. "You okay?" he asked.

Pap twitched his chin. He kept his eyes on the sea.

"I can't believe the blue balls let me off the hook just like that."

"We've been lucky."

"Yeah, that's kinda what I've been mulling over. A crazy idea really. Just occurred to me. I don't even know where it came from. It's probably a foul ball, but I just can't keep this locked away."

Pap stood there without plans to shut Met up.

"Alright, here it is. Just try to follow with me. I'm no one to blab about these things, like I'm no Joe college, but it's dying to come out. Maybe it's the shoulder talking."

"Spit it already," Pap said.

"Okay. Here goes nothin'. Let's start at the beginning, alright? The Big Man. He's real, right?" Met said.

"Come on, mac. Enough with the doubletalk."

"Just hear me out."

Pap's face gave a subtle change, like one that would allow a few more seconds for the pitch.

"He made the angels. Am I warm?"

Pap didn't respond, but he didn't close an ear either.

"He made gees and dames like that book says," Met continued.

"If you say so," Pap said.

"I'm thinking maybe this same maker doled out one angel to each bird. Who knows, maybe some needed more than one. Maybe some got a raw deal, gypped to none. Everyone could use a guardian angel, am I right? I know I could always use a gang of 'em. Just keep up with me. The angel's gig was to watch after their person, kinda like a P.O., keep 'em outta jams, that sort of squash. The trouble was that some angels weren't up to snuff. You know, maybe they weren't down with the rules. Mr. Boss busted those up good. For the worst of the lot, I'm bettin' gone forever. For misdemeanors, maybe just a roundtrip. I don't know, maybe down here, anywhere that wasn't, you know, up there. And maybe, just maybe, while they were touring the dirt, they needed someone to keep an eye over them. I mean why not. Can't a guardian angel need a guardian somethin'?"

"You're not talking English again, man," Pap said.

"Buster and the Crooner. Maybe they came in twos."

"You're saying Buster was a hooligan with a harp in the clouds? He doesn't know how to get out of line. Wouldn't try it if you gave him a swimming pool of chocolate milk."

"I don't know, Pap. Was just a thought. All that tea stuck in my brain makes me think wacky things sometimes."

When night touched down, Pap and Vilma stood on the bow, hand in hand, peering out to an endless canopy with more questions than answers. Where did they go? There was a hole in Pap's heart the size of the ocean. Why did you disappear like that Buster? Mr. Crooner, John Henry, there was so much more for you to do. You could have been happy, too, just like Buster was those precious years running around with fugitives. The best years of Pap's life. They couldn't last forever. The smartest man Pap had ever known had told him that, and just as the court cat, Basil Demur, preached, it was time to get out. And he was out and still breathing. His enemies were dead. His history was buried forever in that deep ocean, the same place Buster was supposed to be. Pap couldn't stand still. He smoked one paper after the other. A proper burial. The little respect he could have paid, and now things stayed unfinished.

Met stood to Pap's right, thinking so many things to keep his mind off his wing. He had never seen his older brother with a dame, didn't know he had it in him. His mind drifted to Holly. He needed to thank her for watching after him at Stiles' office but didn't know the right words. If Sue had taught him one thing, it was that he wasn't fit to talk to a woman. Met filled his lungs with brackish air.

Out of the furthest corner of the heavens, a star smaller than all the others erupted like an aqua shell and drew a line from east to west. A tear drop fell on Pap's cheek, but it didn't come from his eye. Then another. It was rain. The firmament was as transparent as a baby's soul, and the water appeared out of nowhere. It was refreshing to the touch. No one tried to sidestep it. They remained baffled. The rap of a thousand drum rolls to remind Pap of the glory days. He closed his eyes and let the rain wash over him. The sounds were unambiguous; he even swore he heard the faintest Elmer trumpet coming from the ocean. It played just for him, just like the first time. He would open his eyes, and the tune would fade away forever. As it intensified, more acute, like it wasn't going anywhere, like it would leap onto the boat, he had to experience it with his own eyes. Pap looked to Vilma to see if she heard the same thing. She didn't. He glanced to Met. He was struggling to light a smoke, each flicker of fire met with spit from the sky.

Holly felt the need to get inside, away from the rain that gave her a sudden sense of nausea, never mind that the real culprit was the last remnant of Chase Griggs, growing, feeding from within Holly's womb. She didn't even know it yet, but a bastard was coming.

www.ingramcontent.com/pod-product-compliance
Lightning Source LLC
Chambersburg PA
CBHW032254020726
47495CB00001B/108